THE COLOUR OF MYSTERY

A gripping crime thriller full of twists

JOY ELLIS

Ellie McEwan Mysteries Book 2

Joffe Books, London
www.joffebooks.com

First published in Great Britain in 2024

Cover art by Nick Castle

ISBN: 978-1-83526-345-7

AUTHOR'S NOTE

Those of you who have read *An Aura of Mystery* will know that it was my first book, and very much an apprentice piece. Because there was interest shown in it, I immediately embarked on a sequel: this book, *The Colour of Mystery*. I felt a real empathy with the characters and had it in mind that there should be a series. Sadly, it came to nothing, and both books were relegated to a cupboard, and then finally to the attic, where they were to sit for two decades. At that point, I knew I had to make a decision about my writing. I was not going to give up, but I knew that I needed to choose one specific genre: crime or the paranormal? By this time, we had moved to the misty fens, and the location was perfect for both, but considering I had an in-house police procedural advisor on tap, I soon realised that it should be a life of crime!

And here we are now, with three series of crime novels running . . . but I am *thrilled* that Joffe Books have offered to publish these two precious vintage books. They are exactly as they were, so please understand if they are not perfect in every way . . . They were my first cautious steps into my apprenticeship as a writer. So I hope that you enjoy something a little different . . . from Joy Ellis.

CAMEO ONE: LILY FRAMPTON

An uncomfortable chill trickled its way down Lily's spine. The long dimly lit D-corridor seemed endless, and at this time of night she always imagined nameless horrors lurking down the side passages and in the darkened storerooms and clinics. The soles of her soft shoes on the hospital floor made a high-pitched squeak, and she felt an irrational desire to take them off and tiptoe the remaining yards to the foyer with the lifts.

Lily did not mind working nights. As a staff nurse it was a matter of course. It was just that awful walk from the staff car park to main reception. It seemed a different place in the daylight – a bustling, noisy highway carrying patients and staff to and from the wards, the accident department, and the outpatient block.

'Nearly there.' Her voice came out as an echoing whisper and she startled herself. It had not been her intention to speak out loud. She drew her navy fleece tighter round her ample body, grasped her old handbag closer, and practically ran the final lap to the bright oasis that beckoned to her.

Just as she was about to exhale with relief and berate herself for her foolishness, she froze in her tracks as she felt a bony hand clasp her arm.

Stifling a scream, she turned slowly . . . to gaze down into the vacant, cadaverous face of Edith Higgins.

'Edie! You frightened the life out of me, pet! Oh, look at you! Where are your slippers? And you're in that silly little nightie again!'

She slipped off her warm jacket and placed it around the old lady's shoulders, where it hung like an army greatcoat on the stick-thin woman.

The corridor lost its terror, as Lily's compassion for her elderly patient flooded the area with its warmth. 'Come on, sweetheart, let's get you back to the ward and make you a nice cup of tea. I'll bet Sister Marsh is turning the whole hospital upside down looking for you.'

Lily Frampton knew she would not get an answer. Edie probably didn't even know what century it was, yet alone why she wandered off with nothing on her ice-cold feet.

'Poor darling,' thought Lily, as she commandeered an abandoned ENT Clinic wheelchair for the old lady. 'There but by the grace of God . . .'

CHAPTER ONE

Ellie McEwan sat in the pleasant warmth of the summer house, and gazed at the elegant script on the cream envelope that lay in her lap. When the post arrived that morning, she had instantly recognised the handwriting. She had put it to one side until she had disposed of the junk mail, and swiftly scanned through the ever-present bills. Some things were worth waiting for.

She smiled as she made a mug of coffee, and decided that she had earned a few minutes break and would take Dr Alice Cross's letter out to her garden sanctuary to read it in peace.

Snug Cottage, normally renowned for its air of tranquillity, other than the odd barking dog, was undergoing one of Mrs Scrubbs's quarterly bouts of intensive spring cleaning. Curtains had been stripped from windows, and the vacuum cleaner seemed to have been screaming its way around the lovely old property since dawn.

Outside, the air was fresh, and still held the leftover chill from a hard winter. Daffodils, golden yellow, white and orange, gathered in great clusters all around the lawn that stretched out from the octagonal shaped summer house. The garden held an ever-changing beauty throughout the seasons:

a tribute to the elderly Scrubbs, who regarded this Surrey acre as his own special bit of heaven, to tend and nurture.

Ellie was eternally grateful that the old gardener felt that way. It was almost two years since she had inherited the lodge, and in that time, she had come to deeply appreciate the Scrubbs' constant care of house and garden.

Her hand wandered to the half-moon shaped scar on her forehead, and her mind fell back to those dreadful happenings of the not-too-distant past. It had been a time of death and destruction, but also, of unimaginable new beginnings. The carefully styled fringe of fair hair fell back to conceal the old injury, and Ellie sighed, as her eyes fell on the water feature to the right of the garden room.

A pumped watercourse meandered over flowering, alpine terraces. It formed oxbows around unusual pieces of statuary and specimen conifers, then fell in a cascade, like a mountain stream, over plant-covered rocks to a deep, dark-green pool at its base. It was a complicated design that managed to look entirely natural. It had been the brainchild of her dear friend Carole Cavendish-Meyer, who sadly never saw its beauty, other than on her artist's sketch pad.

Carole had been a casualty of a bloody awful year, one that had seen Surrey terrorised by a sadistic murderer.

A blur of tears smeared trees, shrubs, flowers and grass into a hazy confusion of colour. The vast fortune of the Meyer estate had fallen into her lap and that of Professor Michael Seale, another close friend of Carole's, who had worked beside them to outwit a killer.

Ellie brushed away the tears and thought, not for the first time, that both she and Michael would give up every penny to have their caustic and irascible friend back here where she belonged, in the kitchen of Snug Cottage, surrounded by her beloved dogs.

Ellie smiled and reached down with her hand. Before it travelled far it encountered a silky, warm, furry head. The cold nose sniffed her fingers, then gently licked the whole hand. Little Digger never left her side. His pack leader was gone forever, so he attached himself to Ellie like a canine limpet! There had been five dogs altogether, and it had been Michael and Ellie's willingness to take them all on, and not split them up, that had ensured them their inheritance.

In private moments together, they still marvelled that they'd had no idea of the extent of Carole's wealth.

In her mind, she pictured Carole standing in the doorway, her muddy Wellington boots leaving large wet marks on the wooden floor. She saw the grizzly grey hair that managed to appear windblown, no matter what the weather. She visualised the old corduroy trousers, elderly hand-knitted jumper under a torn Barbour . . . and that indecipherable, half smile that left you totally perplexed as to what she was thinking. There had been no clue to her wealth, either in her dress, or her mode of living. Even her car, Ellie grinned broadly at the thought, gave no suggestion of money. It was a Morris Minor station wagon, complete with orange indicator arms and wood-framed rear windows. It was a marvel that it continued to serve Scrubbs, and obviously functioned very successfully on a wing and a prayer.

That Carole, together with her partner Vera, who predeceased her, had amassed a fortune between them, had been a massive shock to everyone. Ellie felt a profound sadness that she and Michael had been so close to Carole and Vera in so many ways, yet they had known next to nothing about their lives.

Neither she nor Michael had really come to terms with the inheritance. Both were adamant that they must use the money in ways that would please their lost friend; and there was an enormous weight of responsibility on them both to do the right thing.

Ellie had finally sold her little house in Weybridge, and moved into Snug Cottage in Compton, partially because she loved it, but mainly so that Carole's dogs would not be further distressed by a move.

As her professor friend was a healer, and Ellie herself was in possession of a powerful gift, they decided to realise a collective dream, and open a healing centre as a memorial to Carole.

They had searched for the right property for a long while. It was very important that it felt right for them both. Just as Ellie was beginning to think they would never find somewhere, Michael discovered the perfect place: a manor house in ten acres of grounds on the outskirts of Ripley. One look had been enough, and after six months of conversion and decoration, the Cavendish-Meyer Healing Centre was up and running.

Michael, as the director, lived in, but kept his tiny Bloomsbury flat in the capital.

To his delight, Janet Cooper, his assistant from his London clinic, decided to join them in the new venture. Having recently lost her elderly mother to a long illness, she decided that a fresh start in the country might be just what was needed.

The clinic was impressive, and whenever Ellie drove up to the ornate front doors, she was overwhelmed by the enormity of it all. It was theirs, somewhere where they could offer help, healing and comfort, to whoever needed it. They had introduced a sliding scale of charges; patients were assessed and they paid what they could afford. It ensured they never had to turn anyone in need of help away. The Centre was still in its infancy, but already incredibly well attended.

She sighed and gazed out across the garden, seeing Scrubbs hard at work in the herbaceous border, the spade rising and falling rhythmically as he prepared the bed for its usual display of summer colour.

Her own strange gift, a legacy of a different kind, was in an odd way bringing the whole healing centre together.

As the result of a car crash, she had woken from a coma with the ability to see auras around people and all living things. She saw life forces as rainbows of colour. At first it had been a living hell; her whole life had been turned upside down, but with Carole and Michael caring for her, helping her, and teaching her how to manage her frightening new ability, she finally succeeded in taming the beast. Now she was using it as an instrument to diagnose illness and disease. With ease, she could observe a healthy, or an unhealthy, aura.

She reflected on her role at the clinic. She was the coordinator, so every client or patient saw her first. She would focus on the lights that surrounded them, and then make suggestions for helpful treatments or management. Sometimes a diagnosis was enough, a worrying mystery solved. At that point, they discussed whether it was something that should be dealt with by taking a medical route, or whether one of their complementary treatments might be helpful. And then, every patient who had received treatment saw her before they left, when she would assess their improvement.

Ellie felt that the Centre, under the loving care of her professor friend, would continue to grow. To date they employed a homeopathic doctor, a reflex zone therapist, an aromatherapist, a reiki healer, a chiropractic, a hypnotist and a dietician. Many other therapists, all people with a gift to offer, came in and used 'open' treatment rooms on a self-employed basis.

There were spas, saunas and steam rooms to facilitate treatments such as thalassotherapy and massage, along with a library and a quiet room for meditation and visualisation.

Ellie's favourite place was the old orangery. She could not take credit for the incredible structure as it had been beautifully restored by the mansion's previous owners. A huge domed Victorian glass roof covered the area, and the whole place was stocked with climbing plants and indoor trees. It had a wonderfully tropical feel to it, and was heated, both to support the incredible collection of plants and to enable it to be used all year round. The great conservatory-like structure was also the favourite of some of the visiting healers who took classes, or gave their services free of charge. Michael, a colour healer, actively encouraged local therapists to use the facilities rather than make rivals – an idea that seemed to be paying off and was giving the clinic a generally favourable reputation.

Still turning the unopened letter over in her hand, Ellie contemplated Stage Two of the Centre's development. Plans had been drawn up and agreed for the building of a pool complex that would house a state-of-the-art hydrotherapy unit. Work was due to start any day now, and the designated spot would be far enough away from the main house so as not to disturb the day-to-day running of the clinic. Luckily there was back access to the property, so the construction workers would use that and, hopefully, not cause too much disruption.

She finished her coffee, and directed her full attention to Alice's letter.

She had procrastinated long enough and tore open the envelope.

Alice was in Ireland running some tests on a patient suspected of suffering from the syndrome that was her special field of medical research. It was ironic that she was staying in County Tyrone, where Ellie's great grandparents were born. She had never made the trip herself, and had been sorely tempted to accompany Alice, and do a little bit of genealogical ferreting.

Her new commitment to the healing centre had won the toss, and warning bells rang loudly in her ears. Her last relationship had broken down because work always came first. Ellie certainly did not want history to repeat itself, but Dr Alice Cross was a very different proposition.

Before she met Ellie, Alice had been totally obsessed by her research. She lived and breathed the Azimah Syndrome. If Ellie had not been one of her patients, and managed to overcome the dreadful optical manifestations without a prescribed drugs regime, she would never have known Ellie existed. Ellie was a professional enigma to Alice, and it was not until Ellie's life was in danger that the doctor finally acknowledged her true feelings. She had sworn to find a balance that would allow them a chance to be happy together.

Ellie loved Alice's old-fashioned love of letter writing, as opposed to lengthy telephone conversations. True, they spoke frequently, but when it came to matters close to the heart, Alice always picked up her pen.

Today's epistle expressed her sadness at the distance between them but positively waxed lyrical about the beauty of the countryside where she was staying.

It's on a salmon river, darling, and at night I can hear the sound of the water rushing over the weir. Oh, I so wish you had come with me! You would just adore this place. As soon as your clinic does not need you so much, I will bring you here with me for a break. We needn't fly, we could get the ferry and drive across in the Range Rover, then we could bring the dogs, they'd love it! We could go walking, breathe some truly fresh air, and get legless on gallons of Guinness!

Her enthusiasm and tenderness flooded from the rich cream stationery and curled itself comfortably around Ellie's heart. Then an inner voice reminded her not to take this relationship for granted. It was one that would always take hard work. The fact that they loved each other deeply was not enough. People who had another burning passion in their lives found compromise difficult, and it was so easy to give that other area just a little too much space.

Ellie sat up straighter in her chair and told herself she would never let that happen — Alice would come first. That tiny inner voice piped up again, this time saying if that was the case, then why was Alice alone in Ireland?

Staring down at the little cocker spaniel peacefully snoozing across her feet, she regretfully admitted that their path was not going to be an easy one.

The last pages of the letter were a progress report about her case study, making Ellie feel a little less guilty about being a workaholic herself. The young man she had been asked to see was indeed suffering from Azimah Syndrome, and not handling it very well. Alice explained that he had suffered a serious head injury after being thrown from a horse. His mother owned a stud farm, where her son often helped with exercising the horses when he was staying with her. Jake Kennedy was a 'likeable, baby-faced, rich kid' as Alice put it.

He apparently had his own flat in Docklands, but also spent some time with his father at the family home in Haslemere. Which brought Alice to her final request. As soon as Jake was well enough to fly home, she wondered whether Ellie would allow her to treat the young man at the Centre. She realised it was a bit unorthodox; after all, her brand of medicine was strictly allopathic, a far cry from complementary and holistic healing. She used hard drugs to help her patients combat the symptoms of Azimah. Apart from the redoubtable Miss Ellie McEwan, so far, no one had managed to drag themselves back into even a partially normal life again without complex medication. Jake would need hospital care on his arrival, and Alice thought it would be several weeks before he was discharged.

> *To be honest, darling, I am hoping that you will be able to spend some time with him. He is in a bad way, psychologically that is. You know what he is suffering, and I have no doubt that if anyone could give him some hope it would be you. I've told him that he is not the only one to suffer this condition, and how brilliantly you have coped, but it is not enough. I am willing to admit that his depression is cause for concern. Think about it, Ellie, I am always prepared to hope that someone else may be taught to handle it like you did, and avoid having to take chemicals for the rest of their lives. I'll be home on Friday, and as soon as I have reported into my hospital, I'll drive down to Snug Cottage for the weekend. I can't wait! I miss you. Very much!*

Alice signed off in her usual affectionate manner, and Ellie rose from her chair, brushed a few stray dog hairs from her indigo denim jeans, and stretched her aching back.

She had been sitting in the summer house for over half an hour. She opened the French windows and Digger, refreshed after his nap, scampered out to find the rest of his pack. The sounds of laughter and barking were coming from the adjoining orchard, and Ellie realised that her neighbour, the local doctor's wife, Marie Littlewood, had called in and taken the other dogs out for their daily game of ball under the old apple trees.

Ellie looked at her watch; there was another hour before she had to leave. She had taken the morning off to catch up on her personal paperwork, but she would see two new patients that afternoon, and had promised Michael she would join him for lunch at one o'clock. She carefully folded her letter, pushed it into her back pocket, and went to join Marie.

The orchard was reached through an archway from the courtyard that backed on to Snug Cottage. As she ducked under a swathe of early clematis shoots, Ellie was delighted to see that her friend Marie was not alone with her four-legged charges. Her neighbour was happily engaged in a strange version of piggy in the middle, throwing a bright yellow frisbee across the bouncing heads of four canine 'piggies' to her son, Daniel.

Ellie had not seen Daniel for weeks and automatically tuned in to the man's aura. For a moment she caught and held him, his hand raised in greeting, a silhouette surrounded by a muted and many-hued light force. The colours and their growing strength surprised her. Daniel had suffered a nervous breakdown during the previous year and there were times when his family had doubted his ability to pull through. Hardly surprising considering what the poor guy had gone through. Ellie recalled that one of his two children had died tragically, and his wife, wrongly blaming him for the accident, had run off with his young son. He had lost his home, his family and his job in a few short weeks.

Her spirit soared, however, as she perceived the radical difference in him.

'Ellie! We've got some wonderful news!' Marie and her son hurried towards her.

'Daniel . . . tell her!'

The man could barely contain his excitement, and soon a broad grin spread across his face.

'It's Della, my wife. She's had a change of heart.' He shook his head almost in disbelief. 'I don't know what has brought this on, but she says I can see my son again. I can have him to stay here with us! Isn't that wonderful!'

Daniel glowed like a pink-and-green beacon and showered Ellie with such brilliance that she had to make a conscious effort to 'turn him down' and bring the radiance under control.

Ellie hugged them both, and noticed that years seemed to have fallen from Marie. Her face was less lined and her shoulders had lost the familiar droop that had mirrored the awful sadness she had felt for her son. Marie's silver-streaked hair had regained its former lustre, and her soft green eyes were alive again. There had been times when Michael, Carole and Ellie had feared as much for this courageous woman's sanity, as they had her beleaguered son.

Ellie felt an exhilarating rush of amazement that things could change so dramatically in a comparatively short space of time, while a more suspicious side of her privately prayed Della was not playing some horrible game to hurt Daniel. He would never cope a second time — of that she was certain.

She stayed chatting with them a little longer and then excused herself to go and get changed for work. She glanced back at the couple and saw the man give his mother an affectionate hug before running off in hot pursuit of Benji, who had stolen the frisbee and was heading for the woods with his trophy.

She stood for a moment, framed in the archway, recalling the silent, empty-eyed young man with no colour in his skin or his life. There was no comparison with the laughing ball of energy that was wrestling the toy from her dog's mouth, and she knew which one she would prefer to see.

She did not even notice that her fingers were crossed until she lifted the latch on the kitchen door.

CHAPTER TWO

There was something most evocative about the heavy tropical perfume that greeted you as you entered the orangery. It sent Michael Seale back to a childhood visit to the hot houses at the Royal Botanic Gardens at Kew. As a rotund and bespectacled schoolboy, he was unaware that one day in the distant future, the strange heady fragrance that assailed his nostrils would send a rotund and bespectacled professor into a paroxysm of nostalgia.

The stone pool here did not hold one of the famous Victoria amazonica water lilies, but if he half closed his eyes, he could still see the great flat leaves with their upturned edges stretching across the surface of the water. The nasal tones of his natural history teacher intoned that this variety of Nymphaeaceae could grow to twenty feet across and were buoyant enough to take the weight of a small boy. His eyes had wandered across to the young Michael, and he added, 'With the possible exception of Seale, here.'

Michael smiled wanly, and glanced down to his still corpulent paunch, where he fully expected to see the tight waistband of his short, worsted school trousers.

He sat on the wide stone ledge that surrounded the pond and tried, for the thousandth time, to assimilate the fact that this joy of a property was his and Ellie's dream come true. He dipped a finger into the warm water and watched the reflection of the round, bearded smiling face melt and alter like the changing of the patterns in a child's kaleidoscope. After a moment or two, the benign face swirled back into focus and continued to grin back at its owner.

His reverie was interrupted by the doors opening and a small group of people entering for their yoga class. There was a square wooden floor space at the far end of the great conservatory that Michael supposed was a dance floor in a previous life. He could certainly imagine a Palm Court orchestra playing as elegant young things enjoyed a tea dance. Will Ryan, the yoga teacher, lifted a graceful hand to Michael and enquired if they would be disturbing him. The professor shook his head and told them to proceed; he had only called in for a moment on his way to lunch with Ellie.

Shutting the doors gently behind him, he still heard the echoes of small boys giggling at the thought of Seale sinking the great water lily.

His office was on the first floor, and as he paused to look out of the long casement window on the landing, he saw Ellie's car pull into her space outside the front entrance. For some time after her accident, he had feared that she would not drive again. No one would have blamed her, having been cut out of her wrecked VW, more dead than alive. Then there was the boy she had killed. Certainly not her fault. She could not have been expected to know that a teenager, high on Ecstasy, would vault a crash barrier and land under her wheels. Michael knew they had Alice Cross to thank for helping Ellie come to terms with the awful guilt that had threatened to destroy her.

Seeing her now, as she made her way up to the front door, he could hardly believe the transformation. Ellie McEwan was poised and confident; there was barely a hint of a limp and her head was held high. He knew that the leg still troubled her if she over-exercised, but that was hardly surprising considering there was probably more metal supporting her than bone! Carole had described the X-rays of the multiple fractures, and Michael still felt quite queasy when he thought about them. He could not help but admire Ellie's determination; as soon as her injuries had healed and she had got control over her auric sight, she made herself get in the car every day. Some days she only drove up and down the lane at Snug Cottage; other times, when she felt more confident, she would drive right through Compton, up to the roundabout on the A3 and back again. He was thankful that, to date, she had had no flashbacks to the crash, and now she drove as naturally as she had before. Her limp was more pronounced as she climbed the stairs to meet him. There was a lift, but she preferred to keep the leg moving and gave it little by the way of special treatment.

'Hello, my friend . . . got the lunch in?'

'Ready and waiting in my office. Did you have a successful morning?'

Michael opened the door for his younger business partner and ushered her inside.

His office was a grander version of his tiny Bloomsbury clinic. The only one who could ever find anything in the glorious confusion was his faithful Janet, who seemed to find her way around by telepathy!

Books lined the walls and formed wobbly towers around the room. He still had his two battered old leather armchairs and had refused to be parted from his ancient and dilapidated desk. The same pictures and wall charts stared down at him. The only difference was that when you gazed out of the window your vista was that of a landscaped garden, rather than a grey wall and steep stone steps up to the grimy London pavements. That, and the fact that you could get more than two people in the room at the same time!

They sat in the old chairs either side of a large ornate fireplace, now housing a rather elaborate Georgian style electric, coal-effect fire. Being a traditionalist, Michael hated it, but was forced to admit it was effective and threw out enormous quantities of heat at the touch of a switch.

Together they enjoyed a simple lunch from the Centre's coffee shop and discussed some of the latest developments at the clinic. Michael was more than happy for Alice to use the Centre whenever she wanted. He had a lot of time for the young doctor, and quietly respected her formal request for permission, rather than taking it for granted that she could use the facility because of her relationship with Ellie.

'What do you think about inpatients, Ellie? I sometimes wonder if some healing and recovery would be quicker if we employed specialised nursing staff, and offered in-house care.'

'Well, we certainly have the space and the funds.' For several minutes they both sat silently contemplating the extent of those funds.

Carole Cavendish-Meyer had owned properties, large and small, both in and out of the country. It had taken Michael and Ellie two weeks to visit the UK ones alone, and decide what to do with them.

He could remember the two of them huddled in the corner of the saloon bar of The Green Man pub at Kirton Fen in Lincolnshire. The wind across the flat misty landscape had chilled them to the bone, and they had taken refuge next to the roaring fire in the local. They had both nursed double scotches and tried to make some kind of sense of the pile of documents pertaining to all the properties they had seen. By last orders they had decided to sell all but Snug Cottage in Compton; the Cornish miner's cottage in Trewellard; and a lodge house on Rutland Water. The proceeds from the sale of the hundreds of acres of fen farming land, the Maltings, and the big house in Lincolnshire, had allowed for the purchase of the healing centre.

The remaining profits were invested with the financial fortune that had been the other part of their inheritance, until such time as they knew exactly what they wanted to do with the money.

Apart from the Centre, the only other thing they had agreed to set up immediately was a trust fund for Alice's research. Her deep commitment and zeal had been undeniable, but Ellie and Michael knew she operated on a shoestring budget and found the restrictions of having limited finances horribly frustrating.

Michael drank the last of his tea and stared intently at his cup. 'I suppose we'll have to buckle down to some decision making soon. I don't know about you, but my mind is still in turmoil. Whatever, we can't just sit on that money; it needs to be doing some good somewhere, don't you agree?'

'Totally. I think I have finally come up with some ideas. How about you come down to Compton this weekend? Alice will be there, and we can throw a few thoughts around.'

'Sounds good to me. Could I cadge a lift with you when we finish on Friday?'

'No problem. I will be glad of the company.'

The clock chimed two, and Ellie left to go and welcome the first new patient of the afternoon.

Michael sat a little while longer and wondered why Ellie seemed to be handling the life-changing inheritance so much better than he. They had both lost a dear friend and, on top of that, the girl had survived the physical trauma of the accident; the mental trauma of finding herself in possession of the almost supernatural gift of auric sight; and finally found herself the intended victim of a sadistic murderer. He really did wonder about her incredible ability to cope.

'Ah, well.' He stood, dusted a few crumbs from his jacket and muttered to himself, 'At least the horrors of the past are over now and she can get on with her life.'

Walking to the door, he wondered why a part of him felt uncomfortable with that last statement.

CHAPTER THREE

Friday night saw the professor sinking comfortably down onto his favourite sofa in front of the roaring log fire. The smell, the spitting apple wood, and the warmth made him pledge to get rid of the awful electric thing in his office as soon as possible.

Snug Cottage had been his second home for nearly a year, while he helped Ellie to understand her new talent, and he felt as happy there as he did anywhere. Sadly, he kept expecting Carole to stride in from the kitchen, with a tray of tea and some of her wonderful homemade cakes or biscuits. The fact that her beloved dogs were still here, and they had never been far from their mistress's heel, made the expectations seem quite real.

Just one dog, the biggest, oldest Springer, Orlando, had not coped with the passing of Carole. Although Michael had read of animals pining for a dead master or mistress, he had never witnessed it, until he watched the spirit go out of the lovely spaniel. One month to the day after Carole's death he had let the five dogs out into the orchard to play, but only four came back. He found Orlando lying under the only tree in the orchard that had wind chimes tied to the branches. Ellie told him later that Carole's dear friend Vera had hung them there years ago to mark the spot where her own dog, Monty, had been buried. Too heavy to carry alone, Michael had run indoors to get a blanket to wrap him in, and to call Scrubbs to come and assist him getting Orlando back to the house.

On returning to the orchard, he had been shocked to see two spaniels chasing happily through the trees, tails wagging and tongues lolling from their soft jowls in puppy-like excitement.

For a moment he'd felt foolish. He had to have made a mistake; perhaps the big dog had only collapsed, or run into a tree and stunned itself. He glanced back into the courtyard where Scrubbs was hastily making his way towards him. Michael was just about to call out that it was a false alarm, when he looked again to the orchard . . . and saw the sad, unmoving shape of Orlando lying under Vera's tree. There were no other dogs around, and after much soul searching, Michael decided that Monty had come to take his friend home. Stranger things had happened here.

He slowly swirled the glistening malt whisky around in his glass. He could hear Ellie and Alice laughing in the kitchen, and remembered the times when there was no laughter, just fear and sadness.

Removing his half glasses, he rubbed his sore eyes and decided he could do with a bit of his own healing! He was really feeling the responsibility of Carole's money lying heavily on his shoulders.

He recalled that initially there had been a sort of euphoria, with visions of shopping in Savile Row, Harrods, Fortnum and Mason. Of having wardrobes full of stylish suits and fashionable jackets, having his shirts tailored for him. Oh bliss! And a healing centre, which had always been just a distant dream, but with Ellie's incredible gift he knew they could really make a difference. That was one of his few sensible ideas, and one that they both agreed should go ahead without delay, but he still indulged in wild fantasies. He would have a live-in chauffeur with a fleet of cars, and a cook and a butler! Oh yes! Someone to lay out his expensive suits for him, to select the matching shirt and tie.

Then the guilt had set in. This really was not right. He had never been particularly well off, and an old childhood adage that you had to sow for that which you reap, kept haunting him. He should use it wisely, maybe give most of it to charity?

Luckily, Ellie had sensed his confusion, and insisted that apart from the Cavendish-Meyer Centre and the Azimah Trust Fund, they should do nothing for at least six months, maybe even a year. Give themselves time to adjust and avoid making silly mistakes through knee-jerk reactions.

She had been absolutely right, and although he was by no means clear in his mind what exactly he should do, at least he had got over the sublime and the ridiculous notions.

Now, staring at the fire, he was intrigued by what Ellie might come up with at their discussion over dinner.

* * *

Supper finished, Alice poured Michael another single malt, and a snifter each for herself and Ellie. Then, surrounded by spaniels, she and Ellie flopped unceremoniously onto the matching sofa on the opposite side of the fire to the professor.

Alice took Ellie's hand in hers. 'Would you guys like me to leave, as you want to discuss business? I have been burning the midnight oil over the last week, and to be honest, an early night would not exactly go amiss.'

Ellie squeezed the hand affectionately.

'Michael and I have no secrets from you, Alice, you know that, but I have to say you look shattered! Why don't you go on up. I'll join you later.'

'I have to admit, I'm out on my feet.' The young doctor pushed at the sweeping blonde lock of hair that constantly fell over her right eye, then leaned over and kissed Ellie lightly on the lips. 'I'll take my nightcap with me, as if I need it! See you up there. Night, Michael, good to see you again. Sleep well.'

Alice left, and Ellie put another couple of logs on the fire. For a while neither of them spoke. They just watched the tiny flames lick around the crisp bark of the wood, then flicker and grow until the logs were engulfed in a yellow and orange inferno.

'Well, let's have it, young woman. Put me out of my misery! You're not going to let me buy that pink Rolls Royce and matching Lear jet, are you?'

Ellie laughed. 'If that's what your heart desires, I'll log on to the internet and order you one right now!' Still smiling, she looked long and hard at her friend. 'It's not been easy, has it? Apart from all the terrible things that happened to us, I think it's the shock of losing Carole, and then finding out that she was unbelievably, stinking rich! She could handle it so easily because a lot of it was old family money, it had always been there. It was nothing special or unusual to her. When she had Vera, they used to enjoy life to the full, well, as much as they could with poor Vera's failing health, but they did have a good life. They travelled and they enjoyed the best of everything. Then Vera died, and the light went out of Carole's life. Until my accident, when she took me in, and I became a sort of mission for her, I think she was at a very low ebb indeed. She really couldn't give a shit about the money, or the properties. Let's face it, Michael, she never ever gave either of us a clue about her history, did she?'

'Never. I knew she was comfortably off – I mean no debts or anything, and you could tell she came from money, but how many upper-class families have landed in the brown and sticky stuff over the years, thanks to bad investments, escalating bills on old money pits of properties, gambling, overindulgence. Maybe just trying to hold on to a something you can no longer afford; the list goes on. I honestly never had a clue! The problem is, now I feel a terrible onus to respect this money that has been ignored for decades, and do the right thing with it, not fritter it or waste it, but really use it well.'

'So, no pink Rolls?'

'Probably not . . . although?'

They both laughed.

'Who would have thought that this money would have given us such a problem. Do you think lottery winners feel the same?'

'I don't know,' mused Ellie. 'Maybe. We all think we know what we would do if we won a fortune, but how many people really are so level-headed to be unchanged by money. Not many, I'll bet.'

She placed her glass on the small table beside the couch and leaned forward towards Michael. 'Look, I know your share of all this is yours to do whatever you like with, but I've been thinking . . .' She gave him a hopeful grin. 'The Healing Centre is our dream, our real commitment. You have the annexe to live in, and I know you love it.'

'You're not wrong there!' replied Michael. His apartment had been purpose-built by the previous owner: an American company director and his family, to house visiting guests in comfort. Although it could be accessed through the main house, it was completely self-contained, and had a conservatory with French windows which opened out into a small private walled garden. He could fit his whole London flat into the open plan kitchen/breakfast room! Yes, Ellie had understated what he thought of his new abode, plus he was in full agreement about the Centre.

'And I have here,' she continued, 'and it's perfect for me and Carole's boys.' She tickled the ever-present Digger under the ear as she spoke. 'In fact, with Marie to help exercise them, Scrubbs to tend the grounds, Mrs Scrubbs to look after the house, I have all the time in the world to devote to the healing, and to my relationship with Alice. Michael, I really don't want more than that, so regarding my share . . .' She paused and took a deep breath. 'I would like to plough a large proportion into the upkeep and extension of the Centre. Invest enough to keep Snug Cottage, and the other properties we agreed to hold on to, running smoothly . . . you know, a sort of estate fund to pay for continued upkeep, repair, and the like, then calculate a healthy monthly wage, and give the rest away. Plough it into supporting charities that need financial help.' She sat back resolutely, picked up her glass and drained it.

Michael thought for a while, got up to pour them both a top-up, then finally spoke. 'It's strange, isn't it? It all comes down to being happy and content in what you're doing. I've been so obsessed with all the things the money could provide that I forgot to ask myself what I really want out of life. You're right. If there are sound investments that will cover the maintenance and care of the properties, for as long as we should choose to keep them, and enough of a personal allowance to cover a comfortable lifestyle, in other words an income for life, then I, too, am very happy to put a large part of the inheritance into the Centre. I suspect there will still be a considerable amount left in the slush fund, and I am already warming to the thought of being the mysterious anonymous benefactor to various good causes. Frankly, I don't think I'm really suited to the Lear jet set, do you?'

Ellie grinned. 'Nah . . . I've got you down as more of a Robin Reliant man, myself!'

Michael glared over his half glasses in mock anger. 'Charming! You could have at least admitted to me looking good in the Rolls Royce!'

They laughed easily together, both feeling a weight had been lifted from them.

'God, but it's good to make decisions!' Michael beamed at Ellie. 'We can concentrate on the clinic in earnest now. We should contact our advisors first thing Monday with our proposals, and as soon as they come back with some figures, well, you can start throwing your money around like a woman possessed!'

Ellie was already bursting with ideas and showered Michael with her thoughts about gifts for her friends. A new car for Gill, and a cash injection for her brother Phil's business. Then there was that Victorian-style conservatory that Marie had always coveted. A cheque each for her staff at the flower shop, who had remained loyal right through the time of her accident. Maybe some specialised medical equipment for the Royal Surrey Hospital. The list went on and on, until he interrupted her by asking for her opinion on the inpatient idea.

'Ah, yes. Why not? That should be our first venture. It could be a really good use for all those wasted rooms on the second floor.'

Michael considered her suggestion. The whole of the second floor was empty. Although originally servants' quarters and storerooms, the American had decided to make a massive conversion and use the space for a nanny flat for his children's governess, a huge playroom, a billiards room, and a separate games room. Even after his major renovation had been completed, he was still left with several rooms with pretty dormer windows that he simply decorated and left without a particular purpose. With a bit of added plumbing, showers, loos, basins, and so on, they would serve as perfect rooms for inpatients. The nanny flat would provide excellent accommodation for a night nurse or house warden, and the playroom would easily make a comfortable visitors' lounge. The games room could stay as it was. There was even a huge unused Victorian-style bathroom. Very few changes would have to be made to enable the new facility to go ahead. 'What a perfect solution! I can't wait!'

Ellie looked on with unconcealed delight, as Michael leapt from idea to idea. It was some time since she had seen him so animated.

He knew she had been witnessing some of his internal struggles of late, and it had been a difficult time, knowing that such a wonderful bequest was causing him such concerns.

Sometimes he could hear Carole berate them from afar. 'For God's sake, you stupid pair! It's only money! If I'd known you were going to fanny around like this, I'd have left it to the bloody dog's home!'

They talked on for nearly another hour before their yawns were becoming more frequent, and Michael heard his gorgeous marshmallow bed in the guest room calling him.

'Oh yes, before I say goodnight, when is your good doctor's Azimah patient going to be joining us?'

'Well, Alice said he was being flown home today. He's going directly to one of the London hospitals, I forget which, probably her hospital at UCH. Then, once he is discharged, Alice will take over his care. I suppose he will stay at his family home to begin with. He won't be able to look after himself for a while.'

Michael looked thoughtful. 'Perhaps he could be our first resident? It wouldn't really matter if we've not had time to recruit a suitable night nurse. I will be on the premises anyway.'

'Good idea. Suggest it to Alice tomorrow. She knows more about the lad's condition than I do. It would be great from my point of view, as Alice wants me to spend some time with him, having him right at the Centre would be perfect.'

Ellie went to let the dogs out for their late-night run and Michael made his way up to the familiar room overlooking the orchard. Pulling the curtains, he felt a pang of sadness as he saw Ellie, with Carole's old Barbour draped around her shoulders, waiting for her four boys to complete their business and get back into the warmth of the kitchen.

It was a sight he had seen so many times before . . . but with a different woman wearing that jacket.

A slight mist drifted between the trees and blurred the definition of his view. As they ran into the light, he clearly saw the two smaller spaniels scamper through the archway and across the courtyard. He smiled at their purposeful trot. Their business was over and a cosy bed was waiting for them.

Benji sat at Ellie's side and waited patiently for Tug, the other Springer, to finish sniffing his way around the perimeter of his domain. Michael could not see the last dog from the window, but he could hear Ellie calling his name.

A moment later, and the animal raced back to join his brother and his new mistress. Ellie ushered them back towards the light from the kitchen door, and noticing Michael's silhouette at his window, waved goodnight, before shooing her boys inside.

Michael stood a little longer, taking in the beauty of the hazy moonlit scene, when he saw another dog framed in the archway. The halogen security lights had come on. Ellie must have activated them when she locked up for the night, and the animal was thrown into stark relief.

Confusion swept over Michael. He had counted each dog indoors, and yet here was a big brown-and-white spaniel gazing hard at the kitchen door of Snug Cottage. Then a movement towards the far end of the orchard caught his attention, and this was closely followed by a whistle. The whistle he had heard so many times before. Powerful, commanding, and the dog turned tail and ran through the trees.

He could see nothing substantial, but the mist seemed to have a soft green, then a soft blue hue to it. Then nothing. No dog. No coloured mist. Nothing.

An icy finger drew its frozen nail slowly down his spine. If he had not known better, he would have blamed the last whisky.

He drew the curtains, changed into his pyjamas, and sought the comforting warmth of his duvet.

As he drifted away into sleep, he remembered the dog at the gate. The dog with one pure white ear. He then saw Scrubbs and himself, gently wrapping Orlando in the thick tartan blanket to bury him. His last vision before Morpheus claimed him was the old gardener tenderly tucking an escaped snowy ear under the soft material and muttering 'God bless.'

* * *

The smell of bacon frying, and the sound of a coffee grinder in action dragged Michael from his slumbers. For a few minutes he lay, cocooned in the warm duvet, and relished the thought of having Sunday breakfast cooked for him. He had to admit that Ellie could vie with her predecessor when it came to the full English breakfast.

His thought of Carole brought back the odd vision from the night before. He was not scared; it was an accepted fact that Carole and Vera had been clairvoyant, and many strange, inexplicable things had happened at Snug Cottage. Both ladies had died there, Carole in the summer house, and Vera in the orchard. He was very sensitive, and the fact that he had probably tuned into something did not surprise him. He decided that all he could do was keep an open mind, and try not to get disturbed by what he saw.

He wondered if Ellie had had the same experiences in the orchard, and made a mental note to ask her when they were alone together.

He sat up and swung his legs over the side of the old bed. Time to show himself, he thought, putting on his slippers and dressing gown. Before he got to the top of the stairs, he heard his name being called.

The kitchen was warm and inviting. The dogs ran over to greet him, and Ellie motioned to him, with a bright floral tea towel, to take his seat at the big old pine table.

Alice was already seated, also garbed in a dressing gown and a pair of scruffy trainers with no socks. She looked up from her task of pouring coffee from a cafetiere, and gave Michael a broad grin. 'Good here, isn't it? A girl could get used to this, you know.'

'In your dreams, sunshine!' Ellie laughed, and deftly flipped an egg over in the pan. 'It's your turn next weekend, and I like my egg yolks runny, but with the white firm, okay?'

'Oh,' said Alice, looking crestfallen, 'I'm afraid my cooking isn't quite of this calibre. Even my toast usually turns out as cinders, or totally uncooked.' She looked up at Ellie appealingly. 'Do you think you could cope with a bowl of cereal? Not too much can go wrong with that.'

Ellie gave her a withering look and placed her plate in front of her. 'Enjoy it, Doctor. It's cornflakes from now on!'

The dogs settled in their huge bed next to the Aga, and the threesome tucked into their leisurely breakfast.

Adding a little more sugar to her coffee, Alice suddenly put her spoon down and turned to Michael.

'Honestly! Where are my manners! Michael, I'm so sorry, I completely forgot to thank you for allowing me to see Jake Kennedy at the Centre.'

Michael helped himself to more toast and smiled affably at Alice. 'No problem there. In fact, I'm not sure if Ellie's mentioned this already, but we were wondering if you might like him to stay with us at the C-M Centre.'

'I left that for you to discuss,' said Ellie, as she collected empty plates. 'I did tell Alice that we were hoping to take in residents and make use of the second floor.'

'Great idea, on both counts.' Alice looked excited. 'Young Jake is not looking forward to spending too much time under his father's roof. Sadly though, he knows he is not yet ready to fend for himself. This could be the perfect solution; out from under Daddy's feet, but knowing he has someone there if he needs them. Are you sure you're happy with that, Michael? It will restrict your movements a bit until you find someone to do nights for you.'

The professor sat back and gently dabbed at his lips with a napkin. 'I think there will be plenty to keep me occupied, Alice. I have made no plans for the next couple of months, and if we want to make this inpatient idea work, then I will probably be eating and sleeping business. I might be glad of the company!'

Alice looked thoughtful. 'He is not the happiest bunny at the moment. I had hoped he would be discharged before I began the full drugs regime, but it looks like I may have to start it much earlier than I would like.'

Concern flashed across Ellie's face. 'Isn't that dangerous?'

'Frankly, yes. But I have to weigh up his mental state. You know the suicide rate with Azimah patients. It's a double-edged sword, Ellie. If I administer the drugs too soon, I could kill him, or reduce him to vegetable status, depending on his particular brain damage. Or I wait until the prescribed moment, and find that he's topped himself the night before!'

'Is he really that low?' Michael rubbed at his beard in an unconscious manner.

'Hard to say. He's doing his best, I know that, but . . .' Alice sighed and reached for the coffee pot. 'Oh, Ellie, you know better than anyone the terrible suffering that Azimah causes. Without dark glasses you're blinded by the light forces that surround everything. You cannot even make out a familiar face unless the room is practically blacked out. Your normal sight is reduced to a firework and laser show whenever there is anything around you with a life force. This lad has enjoyed everything a rich daddy and mummy could provide. He's twenty-six, an aerial photographer, a helicopter pilot' — she grimaced — 'and he can't see. He is devastated. You had a different kind of attitude, darling, something I had never seen before or since. You were so unbelievably determined to master it without drugs, and of course, you had Michael here, and Carole. I was hoping that you could do the same for Jake, although, well, he's no Ellie McEwan, that's for sure.'

Ellie sat staring out of the window. For a moment she allowed the full force of the rainbow auras surrounding every tree, shrub, flower and blade of grass to impact itself on her retina. Yes, she could remember exactly what the young man was suffering. She, too, had sunk to an all-time low, had cried herself to sleep night after night, and she had been lucky enough to have friends beside her to help and encourage her. Now it was part of her life, a wonderful gift, but there were days back in the hospital when she would never have believed that possible. Days when she wished it had all finished with the car crash.

She shuddered at the thought, and tuned out the shining lights. 'We'll do all we can, Alice.'

She spoke softly and both Alice and Michael knew where she had been for the past few minutes.

Alice covered Ellie's hand with hers, and squeezed it gently. 'Thank you. I know you will. He's a nice kid, it would be terrible if . . .' Her voice trailed away, no more needing to be said.

Ellie broke the ensuing silence. 'Hey, let's put all the dogs into the Range Rover and take them down to the coast.

The beaches are open as it's still off-season. We can have a glorious walk along the seashore, blow all the cobwebs away, and have a pub lunch somewhere before we come back.'

'Great!'

'Brilliant!'

'Decided! Let's get this lot into the dishwasher and head south!'

CAMEO TWO: RODERICK BLACK

Roderick Black stared around the empty classroom and absent-mindedly brushed some white chalk dust from his dark-green chinos.

The first day of the new term was over. New kids, different names and weirder than ever haircuts.

Rod gathered up his notes, plans and books, pushed them all into a scuffed and battered leather attaché case, and reached for his jacket.

He was just smiling to himself and wondering how every term some bright little sod managed to find yet another innovative way to wear the school uniform, when a small voice pierced the silence.

'Sir?'

'Hello. Evans, isn't it? Jason Evans?' It was not easy trying to remember names after only one class, but that was one of his fortes — a near photographic memory.

'Yes, sir. Could I talk to you for a moment?'

The boy looked uncomfortable and, Rod quickly noticed, very troubled.

'How about walking down to the staff room with me? We can chat on the way.'

The corridors were empty, apart from a few stragglers looking for lost football kit, or missing lunch boxes.

The boy, small for his eight years, had lank, mousy hair, and a badly fitting blazer. The teacher knew before the child opened his mouth that his story would be of bullying. A vague discolouration showed below the dirty shirt cuff, and Rod's keen gaze had noticed a healing cut over his left eyebrow.

It was remarkable that the boy had seen fit to put his trust in a school master after only one session, and Rod decided that he must have been desperate.

At the entrance to the staff room was a small waiting area with a few chairs, a shabby coffee table and a large dying plant. It was quite a private place, but there were no closed doors. Rod hoped the boy would feel protected, but not intimidated.

Rod listened attentively to the expected tale. He had heard it a dozen times before, but every time he felt a wrenching pain in his chest when he realised the agonies that these pint-sized victims went through. As the child finished his story, a knot had formed in Rod's stomach, and he found his knuckles were white and his hand painful where his nails had dug into the palms. How anyone could treat a kid like this was beyond him. He thought of his own child: protected, loved and happy. Then he looked at Jason Evans and his heart went out to him.

By the time the boy left, Rod Black was, once again, formulating a plan of action that would ensure a child a happier and safer future.

CHAPTER FOUR

Cruel lights hurt his eyes. His head throbbed with pain. Jake could not even make out the clock face clearly enough to know when he would get more drugs to ease the constant agony behind his eyes.

Big boys don't cry.

A tear made its way unheeded down the side of the strong aquiline nose. Bollocks to those particular big boys! They obviously did not feel as shitty as he did.

He started the mantra again. 'If she can do it, so can I. If she can do it, so can I. If she . . .'

He had never even met Ellie McEwan, but he hung all his hopes on her. She was all he had left to cling on to. Dr Cross had spent hour after hour with him, trying to explain what had happened. He understood the basics. On very rare occasions when a head trauma occurred, a chemical called Azimah was released into the brain at impact. It produced a variety of symptoms – the worst being a severe ocular disturbance that left the sufferer with the ability to see auras, life forces around all living things. If you were unfortunate enough to get the complete syndrome, you could also experience strange smells and 'see' what Alice Cross referred to as phantoms: odd shapes or coloured masses that were not observed by normally sighted people.

He suspected he was the lucky winner who had scooped the whole thing — the full works.

Several times, on the night before he was flown home, he had called the nurse because he could smell burning. Nothing was discovered, and no one else could smell anything remotely like smoke. Then there were the times when he distinctly saw hazy shapes in the room with him, but he was later assured that he had been completely alone.

He desperately wanted to speak to this Ellie woman. He was aware that it should be several weeks before he could safely start Dr Cross's drug regime, but he did not know if he could hang on that long. There was a dreadful panic in him that surged to the surface, and he was unsure for how much longer he would be able to subdue it. He just knew the feeling was dangerous, and it was becoming more and more difficult to fight.

Perhaps Ellie could help him hold on. 'If she can do it, so can I. If she can do it, so can I. If she can . . .'

'If *who* can do *what*?' asked a soft voice.

With his eyes tightly closed, he had not realised that a nurse had come into his room.

'Oh, nothing. Is it time for more painkillers? Please, nurse, I really need something, now.'

'All right, Jake. It is a bit early, but I can see that you're suffering. I'll get you something.'

A gentle hand lingered for a minute on his forehead.

Squinting through his dark glasses, he saw a brilliant fizzy mass of pink and lilac and blue move towards the door. He did not know her name but he recognised her colours. She had helped him settle in when he arrived from Ireland, and was a warm, kind person. He knew nothing about auras, but the rays she gave off made him feel good. A bit like being given a motherly cuddle.

Some of the others, one in particular, a nurse they called Mel, made him feel very uncomfortable. She gave off a strong orange glow, especially from one specific part of her anatomy, and to his horror he found that this fiery radiance seemed to have a rather dramatic effect on a similar part of his own body.

His little guardian angel bustled back in and pushed two chalky tablets into his hand. He heard her pouring water into a glass and then he felt the cold tumbler passed to him. He murmured his thanks and gratefully swallowed the pills.

She fluffed up his pillows and he sank back, knowing it would take a good half an hour until he started to feel any relief.

'Would you like the radio on, or maybe listen to a CD?'

He appreciated her thoughtfulness, but said he couldn't concentrate until the pain had eased. She left with the promise of bringing him back a cup of tea when she had finished her round.

Alone in the room, he pulled on the thick black eye-shade that the doctor had left him, and allowed the pain to drag him into an agonising half sleep where, once again, he flew his helicopter over England's green and pleasant land.

* * *

As Professor Michael Seale replaced the telephone receiver on its rest, he felt the tiniest thrill of excitement chase through him. They were releasing Jake Kennedy into his care the day after tomorrow. It was earlier than he had expected, but the hospital administrator seemed to think the young man would be better off in a more therapeutic atmosphere.

'He has no stimulus here; he needs to have things going on around him that he can interact with. If you are ready for him, Professor, I will arrange his discharge.'

Michael had assured the woman that if Dr Cross was happy with the arrangements, he had everything organised at the Cavendish-Meyer.

He glanced down at his leather-bound diary, and read through his report of two days ago.

First stage completed. Three individual rooms ready for occupation. All clean and fully kitted out with beds, new bedlinen, and furnishings, etc. Plumbing already installed and checked. Each room has en-suite loo, hand basin and walk-in shower.

Night nurse's flatlet cleaned and aired and communal lounge furnished and comfortable.

N.B. Lounge TV aerial needs adjusting. Remember to tell delivery man tomorrow when he brings the TVs and radios for the patients' rooms.

Large, shared bathroom may benefit from heated towel rails. (?)

The work had been finished in record time, due to a local plumber finding himself out of a job when a builder he was contracted to went broke. Michael wouldn't wish ill on anyone, but quietly thanked his lucky stars for the fortuitous timing.

He looked at his entry for today and saw that he and Ellie were interviewing all afternoon for the live-in nurse.

Slowly turning over the pile of letters and CVs, he whistled softly at the number of answers they had had to their advertisements. He was mightily surprised at the distances people were prepared to travel for an interview.

His hand fell on one that had intrigued him earlier. The faintest hint of perfume issued from the crisp white paper and the writer, a senior nursing officer with a wish to 'take a new direction', was motoring down from North Yorkshire in the hopes of winning the post.

He had the sneaky suspicion that it was not going to be an easy task. Ellie was always calling him an indecisive Libra — the scales always tipping back and forth as he weighed pros and cons with serious deliberation. He hoped that her Arian directness would influence their final decision.

Checking his watch, he noted that Ellie would be finishing with a patient who had completed a course of treatment and was having her final re-assessment. He was impatient to tell her about Jake's impending arrival, so placed all the interviewing correspondence in his briefcase, and left his office.

Ellie's suite was on the ground floor and was comprised of a single large room with a small separate office that housed her computer, fax and answerphone. She had been insistent that her main room had very little by way of electrical equipment in it. She found it disturbing, and wanted her clients to feel as relaxed and tranquil as possible for their appraisals.

Every time Michael entered the lovely room, he swore that his blood pressure dropped a few degrees. This time it was no different.

'Sit down, my friend. I'm just finishing with my last patient's report and I will be with you.'

Her voice echoed from the back office, and for a minute he wondered how she had known it was him, until he remembered a carefully placed mirror that allowed her to see into the main room.

The room had a high white ceiling with a very ornate coving. The walls had been subtly marbled giving them a warm golden glow and their only adornment were three large poster prints from the Metropolitan Museum of Art. Each print, simply framed with a plain black edging, was of a Louis Comfort Tiffany stained-glass window.

Michael marvelled at the colours and, as always when he sat back on the deep, soft sofa, found himself staring at the pictures, one after the other, with almost total absorption.

The first picture was one of his famous landscape scenes. From blue mountains in the background, a meandering stream found its way between silver birches and blossom trees to fall in a cascade to a pool afloat with water lilies and surrounded by purple and blue iris.

Michael could feel the damp green moss on the banks of the stream; he could smell the fresh spring blossom and he could hear the trickling water as it fell into the emerald pool.

Michael had to tear his eyes from the peaceful scene in order to enjoy the next one. The second bore the humble title of *An angel in profile*. He knew nothing about this stained-glass window, except that it was strangely beautiful. An angel knelt, gathering an armful of lilies, its celestial countenance and folded wings made curiously human by this simple mortal task. Again, it was difficult to move your gaze from the earthy tones of the angel's garb. You were drawn into the folds and creases of the material. Michael believed it to be the finest, lightest, warmest wool, and he thought if he just reached out and touched the surface of the glass, he would feel the soft fibres.

He sighed and moved on to the last picture. Another landscape, but as the first had been clad in the raiment of dawn, its hues of green and blue, this last window glowed with the gold of the sunset on autumn leaves. A lake reflecting the setting sun was flame and blood red. Leaves, both on the trees and heaped beneath on grassy banks, were russet and copper. The glass had captured that rapturous moment, a glorious final burst of light before the twilight falls.

'Oh Lord! He's in the windows again! I thought you were quiet!'

Ellie's laugh brought the professor firmly back to terra firma where he was forced to smile at himself. 'They get me every time, don't they?'

His friend gave him a lopsided grin. 'Well, that's what they're meant to do, although they are really there to calm the patients, not the director!'

She looked around her room, pleased with the finished effect. She had done next to nothing to it, except have the wood around the fireplace restored to its original beauty, after someone had painted the splendid oak a nasty shade of Swamp Fever green. That, and hang her pictures, and add some wonderful Tiffany-style lamps and two soft, expensive sofas and a huge, low, glass-topped table.

Her clients were much happier talking in this sort of atmosphere, and she found the whole room most suitable for exploring their auras. The light from the floor to ceiling bay window was diffused by festoons of clematis and wisteria. At certain seasons it looked much like a living version of one of Louis Comfort Tiffany's exquisite designs. As the natural light deserted her, she would pull the heavy drapes and use the softer glow of lamplight.

'How about we see the new prospects in here, rather than the boardroom, Michael? It is a bit impersonal and cold, not everybody responds well to formal interview procedures, do they?'

Michael agreed. He had arranged for them to wait in the orangery with a welcoming cup of coffee. Then, at their designated time, Janet would bring them through and make the introductions.

'When is the first one due?'

'In about half an hour, I think. Time for a quick snack and we'll see what turns up. It's quite exciting, isn't it?' Ellie smiled at him. 'I've hired and fired for years, owning my own florist business, and I hated the same old question and answer game. But now I have my gift to help me, it will be very different.' Her expression became serious. 'Although, the final decision should come from you. This person will be living in very close proximity to your annexe, it's essential that you both get on.'

When she expressed this thought to Michael, an alarmed look flashed across his face. 'Oh dear, I was really rather counting on you to be the positive one, you know what I'm like!'

'Don't worry, I have the distinct feeling that we'll know when we've found the right person for the job. Trust your own judgement, Michael, that's what you would tell me! Now, let's grab a coffee ourselves. They will be arriving soon.'

'Mm, you're right . . . and I still have to tell you about Jake Kennedy.'

* * *

Although Michael had doubted his ability to choose wisely, at the end of the afternoon, they were left with two clear candidates.

The nursing officer from Yorkshire, Maureen Shaw, shone above the other women applicants, and a very personable nurse, Callum Church, from West Horsley, was streets ahead of his male competitors.

Janet was duly asked to notify the unsuccessful candidates, thank them for coming, and give them a cheque for out-of-pocket expenses. She should then take the remaining two to the coffee bar for some refreshments.

After a few minutes' deliberation, Ellie broke the silence. 'I don't know how you feel about this, Mr Director, but what if we offer this post to our north country lass, and find another one for the local lad? I liked them both enormously, and if the Centre continues to expand, we could certainly use them both.'

Michael rubbed at his beard. 'The second position would not have accommodation, of course, but if the salary was attractive enough, he could commute or get digs. Horsley is not that far from here. Yes, I agree, subject to checking their references.'

They spent a little more time discussing formalities, and Ellie made a call to the Leeds Infirmary, where Mrs Shaw had spent many years. The glowing recommendation the Chief Administrator gave was enough for both Michael and herself, and the decision was made.

Callum had provided excellent letters of recommendation, one from a consultant well known to Michael, and another from Médecins Sans Frontières, with whom he had just completed a year as a volunteer in Bosnia.

They decided to walk down to the cafe and put their two prospective employees out of their misery. Michael nudged Ellie as they approached the couple, who were seated at one of the coffee shop tables, and from their gestures and the tone of their voices, were getting on extremely well.

'That is a promising start, don't you think?'

Ellie allowed the two auras to flood into her vision, and she liked what she saw.

Callum had sharp multicolours, flaring and radiating several feet from his body. He was animated and sincere — she had no doubt of that.

Maureen's colours were less intense, but nevertheless, pure, clear tones glowed in a more regular pattern around her. She was older, more in control, but just as sincere, and in Ellie's opinion, an honest person.

'Very promising indeed,' she replied softly. 'Let's go and make their day!'

They joined Maureen and Callum, and the two expectant and nervous faces were all too much for Michael. After a quick, imploring glance at Ellie, he beamed across the Formica table, and declaring that he hoped the decision would please them both, launched into the proposal.

Ellie, who had never considered herself particularly tactile, was astounded to see the two candidates jump up and hug each other! There was no doubt in her mind that these two could work together. They could have been mother and son at that moment, locked in a delighted embrace of pure joy.

To Michael, this was a totally natural reaction, and Ellie decided that he was having trouble remembering his position, and not joining in with a group hug.

However, he compensated with the giving of one of his famous double-handed handshakes, the recipient's hand firmly encased in two warm, bear paws, and shaken emphatically up and down.

Ellie remained a little aloof, but still grinned from ear to ear, and thoroughly enjoyed the spectacle. She never remembered it being like this at her florist shop. But that was another life.

Their new night supervisor was whisked away by Michael on a conducted tour of her second-floor apartment, while Ellie remained with Callum to discuss details of his hastily evolved position. She ordered more coffee and they sat for another twenty minutes talking about the C-M Centre, about Michael, and Callum's previous work.

'This is going to seem a bit tame, I'm afraid . . . it's not exactly a war zone,' said Ellie.

The young man looked thoughtful. 'I need a break. I think I've existed on adrenaline and black coffee for the last three years of my life. There is nothing to say that I won't return to that kind of fieldwork later, but not for a good while yet.' He looked his new employer directly in the eyes and said, 'My mother does not have the best of health, and I owe her. I shall not be venturing overseas to work, at least not in her lifetime.'

The man had a way of making you listen to him, making you want to tell him your deepest secrets, making you believe that his opinions were important. Ellie appraised him with interest. He had black, wavy, slightly dishevelled hair, and the darkest eyes she could remember seeing. He had a gypsy-like quality that made her think of a photograph she had once seen of her paternal grandfather as a young man.

'Have you any Irish blood, Callum?' she enquired.

He smiled impishly. 'Hard to say. I'm adopted. Makes tracing the old family tree a bit difficult.'

'I'm sorry.'

'No need for that. I was chosen as a son by the sweetest, most loving couple you could imagine. There is not a day goes by that I do not give thanks for my good luck. See what I mean about owing. I would not dream of asking my mum about my natural parents, although that's not to say I'm not curious, of course.' He looked at Ellie conspiratorially. 'I *know* that Mum knows all about my real family. There are times she lets things slip out, she is unbelievably naive, in the most lovable way.' He looked more serious. 'I just want her to realise that she is so special, I do not need another mother.'

They talked a little longer about the Centre, and then they set off on a walkabout. As they strolled through the orangery, Callum asked her about her particular form of healing. For a while she hesitated, unsure of how much, or what to tell him. In the end she told him everything. The accident, her involvement with the Surrey serial killer, about Carole, and finally about her extraordinary gift. He listened intently and showed no signs of amazement or amusement.

'Miss McEwan, I've seen a lot working abroad. I have been shoulder to shoulder with death. I've come across strange things, things I do not begin to understand. That is one reason I wanted to come here. It's the other end of the spectrum, isn't it? I want peace for myself, and I want to help other people achieve it, too.' He paused for a moment, gently stroking a giant, glossy green leaf. 'I think you may have been right about my original parentage. Dad says I'm fey, if you know what that means? I sort of *know* things. Not real clairvoyance or anything heavy, I just sometimes get feelings about things before they happen, and I sense atmospheres. I used to think it was a kind of heightened sensitivity, until I spent six months working in Rwanda. I can tell you, in that time, I saw poverty and death, and some of the weirdest shit on this earth. Sorry, Miss McEwan, I didn't mean to swear, but I would never laugh at things I can't explain.'

They continued the trip in near silence. Ellie was certain they had made a good choice with this unusual young man. She had seen an old suffering in his young eyes when he spoke of the poverty in Africa. He possessed compassion in abundance, and she was sure he would be an asset to the clinic.

He was free to start immediately, and happy to commute until the end of his three-month trial period. He had a motorcycle and assured her that, if the weather was awful, he could always use his father's car. They shook hands and arranged for him to start the following Monday. As he walked through the front door, Ellie felt a strange presentiment of something very bewildering.

She looked around her. The entrance hall was empty. She could hear sounds coming from the other rooms, music, voices, a peel of laughter, but all coming from a distance. As Callum left, she had sensed the hall was full of people. She could not see them, but she had felt them all around her. The whole atmosphere felt disturbed, as if a breeze were blowing through the deserted hall, and moving the very air around her.

By the time she had become fully aware of it, it had disappeared, and Michael was chaperoning his new neighbour down the staircase.

It was obvious, without asking, that he was more than happy with their selection. He escorted Mrs Shaw to the front door; then they went to Ellie's office to finish up.

Tidying the last of their paperwork away, she tentatively enquired if Michael had ever had any odd feelings while in the entrance hall.

His answer was negative, and she brushed away his obvious concern with a comment about a bit of draught.

By the time they had made plans for Jake Kennedy's arrival the next day, and she had closed her computer down, she had forgotten all about it.

* * *

Things had not exactly gone to plan after Jake's arrival at Ripley, and Michael called a hasty meeting with Ellie and Alice.

'I'm sorry, Alice.' The furrows deepened on the professor's forehead. 'I don't think my preparations were sufficient for your patient. His sight is far worse than I'd anticipated, and his mental state, well . . .' Michael left the sentence unfinished. 'I have temporarily moved into the room next to his on the residents' floor. There is no way he can be alone at night. Maureen Shaw starts in a few days' time, but I think even with her there, I could have to stay in situ so to speak.'

Ellie gave Alice a long, serious look.

'I fear some of this is my doing.' She gave a deep sigh, and tugged absent-mindedly at a skin tag beside her fingernail. 'I'm not getting through to him. It's as simple as that. I've tried everything that Carole did for me. I have altered my approach to try to suit him specifically. Alice, he cannot relax, he cannot meditate, he just can't take charge of his own thought patterns. It's not that he's not trying, that's the bloody shame, he is trying so hard, maybe too hard, I don't know. Bottom line is, that he put his faith in me, and we are getting nowhere. I know how I managed to overcome Azimah, but I'm afraid it is not going to work for Jake.' She paused and dejectedly asked, 'How long before the drugs really kick in?'

Alice ran her fingers anxiously through her blonde fringe, pushing it back over her head, and repeating the procedure every time it flopped disobediently back into her eyes. 'His neurological signs are not good. He didn't just hit his head when he fell. The horse kicked him. It's a wonder he's not dead, or wired up to a machine somewhere with a brain about as active as a wet sponge. The swelling, the bruising, the healing in general, is taking longer than I had hoped. As you know, I started the low doses before he left the hospital, long before I wanted to. I've been slowly building them up, and assessing their efficiency. He needs the full dose now, but the risks are so great, I'm just not sure.'

Ellie bit the inside of her cheek.

Michael shifted uncomfortably on his seat. 'So, what now?'

Silence lay like a heavy fall of snow, but after a while Alice took a deep breath, then exhaled noisily. 'I'll go and talk to him. Explain the risks again. The final decision will have to be his, but if we're all in agreement that his condition is serious cause for concern, then we have to accept the fact that I may have to go ahead with the maximum dose, very soon.'

'What about his family? Should we be talking to them as well? And the hospital, what about his neurologist?' Michael's concern for the young man was even more apparent now that they were considering accelerating such life-threatening treatment.

'He's twenty-six, Michael. I will advise he talks to his mother and father, but unless we decide that he is bad enough to be sectioned, then the outcome of this is still in his court. As for the hospital, his consultant is fully aware of the situation. I have his blessing to treat Jake as I see fit, there is nothing he can do for the lad, so he has left the judgement call to me. Naturally, I'll inform him before I proceed.'

The doctor stood, and while admitting that she was not relishing her forthcoming task, said she should go and do the deed.

‘He should be in the Quiet Room with Callum. I don’t leave him unattended at present, and he seems to get on with our new nurse.’

‘Right. Give me a while with him, then I’ll report back. We’ll take it from there, okay?’

Ellie and Michael nodded. There seemed to be little else to do.

CAMEO ONE: LILY FRAMPTON — PART TWO

'Sister! I can't find Edie again!'

Sister Laura Marsh threw down her protective gloves and cursed yet again that the powers that be saw fit to mix her elderly medical patients with those with psychiatric problems. Edie, and others like her, needed specialist nursing care — they should not be thrown onto general wards. It was not fair on them or the other poor souls with sound minds and bodily illnesses. 'Or us!' she muttered, as she strode down the ward looking in cubicles and cupboards.

'Who saw her last?' she called out to anybody who was listening.

'Sorry, Sister, I've been bathing Florrie. She hasn't been near the bathrooms or the sluice, or I'd have noticed her.'

'Okay, have you seen Lily? She seems to have the golden touch in finding our missing Alzheimer's patients.'

An auxiliary called out from the nurses' station that the staff nurse was late back from coffee.

'That's unlike Lily,' said the sister softly. She generally had to beg the woman to take a break. 'I hope she's all right. She looked pale and tired when she came on shift, even though she said she was fine.' She paused, then called to one of the other staff nurses. 'David! Give security a call will you, ask them to find Edie and to get her back here ASAP, she is definitely not on the ward!'

A bell rang and she could hear somebody shouting at the other end of the ward. She strode off to check on the caller thinking that this had all the hallmarks of the night shift from hell!

* * *

Harry Burton's radio crackled into life and his boss demanded to know his whereabouts. 'I'm outside the path lab, sir. Some kids were seen mucking around here earlier, but no sign of them now.'

'Forget the kids, Harry. Old Edie has gone walkabout again. Pearson is checking physio and occupational therapy. Will you have a nose around outpatients, and if you find her, get her back to Cavell Ward on the double? Sister Marsh is climbing the walls.'

Not for the first time, thought Harry as he acknowledged the call and made his way through the back of the X-ray Department to the deserted clinic areas.

The lights were down except in the few places where the cleaners were working, and Harry moved methodically, checking changing rooms and examination areas. He had played the hunt for Edie game many times and remembered that once she had managed to get as far as the staff car park before she was missed. He silently hoped she was not out there in the night — it was not as cold as it had been, but it was raining heavens hard, and from experience Harry knew that Edie would not be dressed for anything other than bed.

Thinking about her last Great Escape, he decided to check the D-corridor that led down to the rear exit. Harry was used to roaming the rambling old hospital, mainly at night, and felt quite at home pacing through its deserted halls and clinics.

Except for the D-corridor.

He had worked this unsociable shift since his wife had died three years ago, and never once had he walked that particular corridor without feeling strangely uncomfortable. He had never seen anything to frighten him, in fact he rarely saw anyone on that long, silent, dimly lit avenue. He just knew he would rather be anywhere else in the building than there.

To his dismay, tonight was no different. As he left the brightly illuminated area by the lifts and headed into the shadows, his purposeful step faltered and an uncontrollable feeling of dread came over him. He slowed to a halt and unclipped his radio.

'This is ridiculous!' His voice came out louder than he had anticipated, and he jumped as his words echoed down the deserted hallway. Silence returned and he stepped uncertainly forward. He glanced back to the haven of light that suddenly seemed so far behind him, and realised he was not alone.

'Burton! Where are you? We've got a member of staff gone walkabout now! See if you can see Staff Nurse Lily Frampton, will you?' The radio spat and crackled loudly. 'Oh, for God's sake, Harry, will you answer the bloody radio!'

It wasn't that he did not want to answer the call. He stared hard at the black radio clasped in his left hand, but somehow his mind would not make the connection that would allow him to use it.

His eyes wandered back to the tableau before him and, again, his brain could not manage to send the right signals to his paralysed body.

That was how Pearson found him five minutes later, standing motionless, staring at the two blood-soaked figures in front of him.

Staff Nurse Lily Frampton sat in a grim parody of the lotus position, her back to the store cupboard door and a scalpel clasped in her hand. A little further into the cupboard, huddled in a pile of blankets that she had dragged from a shelf as she fell, was Edith Higgins. Her eyes, as usual, blank and staring, but this time there would be no more lucid moments when she encouraged her fellow patients to sing along, her little piping voice remembering the old songs of her youth. There would be no more wandering off, alone and cold.

Her favourite nurse and a sharp knife had made sure of that.

CHAPTER FIVE

A chill wind whistled and cried around the eaves of Snug Cottage. It tried to prise its cold fingers under the roof tiles, and being unsuccessful, settled for rattling the old sash window in Ellie's bedroom.

Digger growled softly in annoyance that his sleep was being disturbed, and snuggled deeper into the duvet at Ellie's feet.

She too was awake, but it was not the bad weather or the restless dog that troubled her. Jake Kennedy troubled her or, more to the point, it was her complete inability to help him that gave her sleepless nights.

It was two weeks since they had debated on their best course of action. Jake had finally taken the decision away from them, by begging Alice to give him the complete medication. His family had fully supported him, and his mother made an impassioned telephone call to Dr Cross imploring her to go ahead with his treatment. Her cry was from the heart. Her father had taken his own life, and the thought of her only son following a macabre family tradition was too much for her.

Alice had commenced the total regime the next day, and although there were no guarantees to its full effectiveness,

Kennedy was, at least, showing no disastrous side effects from the lethal cocktail.

After three days, he had noticed a slight change in his vision. He had declared that the lights were a little less blinding, and his headaches were subsiding somewhat. He had, from that point onwards, continued to progress, albeit very slowly, until yesterday, when Alice decided he was no longer a threat to himself.

Ellie turned on her side and listened to the wind howling through the orchard.

She hated the fact that it had taken a massive concoction of chemicals to ease Jake's suffering. She felt an irrational anger towards him because he had not been able to fight his problem without the drugs.

She turned again, drawing the warm duvet tighter around her, and admitted to herself that it was her own failure she hated most.

It wasn't Jake's fault. For the hundredth time she questioned why she should be the only one of Alice's patients to resist the frightening effects of the syndrome, without artificial help. And, for the hundredth time, she had no answers. She berated herself for not simply being thankful that he was getting some relief, no matter how he came by it. How could she be annoyed at him, when she, more than anyone, knew exactly what he was suffering? Hardly the thoughts of the compassionate healer, were they?

Somewhere outside there was the sound of a branch snapping in the gale. She sat up and looked at the green digital display on her clock radio. Two fifteen, and no sign of sleep. She considered reading for a while, but glancing at the paperback that lay on the bedside table, she decided its convoluted tale of deception and anguish was not exactly what was called for tonight.

'Something really light, that's what I need, Digger.'

The little dog lifted an eyebrow, decided that he really wasn't too fussed about his mistress's choice of reading material, and went back to sleep.

Ellie found her old towelling slippers, pulled on her dressing gown and padded down to the kitchen. The other dogs had formed a 'huddle of spaniel' in their giant bed, and barely moved as she entered. Benji made the effort to give a feeble wag of his tail, but getting up for a full greeting was not an option tonight. She made a hot drink and poked unenthusiastically through the magazine rack for something to read. Finding nothing that she had not already seen, or that took her attention, she went into the library, hoping for inspiration there.

As she opened the door, the coldness hit her like a slap in the face. She flicked the switch for the wall lights and the room was bathed in a soft glow. Across the room, she saw the drapes at the French windows blowing around in an angry flurry of brocade.

She drew back the heavy curtains and found one of the side windows fully open to the elements. She pulled it shut and cursed herself for not checking the house properly before she went to bed. Her old friend DCI Bob Foreman of the Surrey Police would give her hell if he knew she was alone in an old country house at night with the windows wide open! She had better have a quiet word with Mrs Scrubbs, as well. The old lady had obviously been airing the room and had forgotten to close it before she went home.

Remembering why she had come to the library in the first place, she gazed along the shelves for a suitable book. Nothing took her fancy, and she was just about to give up, when she noticed a small pile of volumes sitting unceremoniously on the hearth.

Puzzled, she bent down and picked them up. She was fastidious when it came to the books. Before Carole had died, they had spent hour after hour categorising them, and putting them into strict alphabetical order.

Mrs Scrubbs never touched the shelves, so why this strange collection should be there was a mystery. She noted the titles — there were five altogether — and her puzzlement increased.

There was an old dictionary; a book called *Women's Letters in Wartime*; a book on tarot reading; an ancient Haynes manual of the Morris Minor; and a large volume on water garden design.

She stared down at them, and a slight shiver coursed its way across her shoulders and down her backbone.

Her theory that she may have pulled them out en bloc to dust the shelves faded into oblivion. These books came from totally different shelves and positions in the room. The thing that was so disconcerting was that they were all specifically Carole's.

Okay, she thought, most of the books in here had originally belonged to Carole, but . . . she cast her mind back to the time just after her friend's death. The dictionary lived beside Carole's bed. If she could not sleep, she would do the *Times* crossword. Ellie had found it there when she cleared her things out after the funeral.

Scrubbs had returned the motor manual to her at about the same time. She recalled him trying to fix something rather than take the car to the garage.

Carole read the tarot, probably better than the author of the book, but she had used it to illustrate some point or other to Ellie. She vividly remembered Carole's finger stabbing at a page and saying, 'See! It's here as clear as daylight, even the old fool who wrote this has got it right!'

Practical Water Garden Design spoke for itself.

Then there was the book of letters. Carole had been delighted to find, when leafing through it in a Guildford bookshop, that it contained a series of letters from an old ATS friend of hers. She had insisted that Ellie read them, to, as Carole put it, '*Make you aware of the damn fine role that women played in wartime!*'

Ellie rubbed her eyes wearily. She was tired and this little conundrum was all too much for her. She decided to leave the books on her desk and ask Michael if he could throw any light on the subject. He always spent hours in the library when he was at Snug Cottage. Perhaps there was a simple explanation. Picking up the book of wartime letters, she took her now cooling drink, and returned to bed.

Moving the little dog, who had taken full advantage of Ellie's absence, she knocked Carole's book to the floor. As she retrieved it, a slip of paper fell out. Thinking it to be a makeshift bookmark, she tucked it back between the pages and proceeded to reclaim her part of the bed from a grumbling Digger.

She finished her mug of tea and started to read. After a while the tome had the desired effect, and although the writing was by no means boring, she felt her eyes closing. Her fingers deftly searched for Carole's marker, pulled it from between the thin pages and placed it at the end of her last completed chapter.

As she closed the book, her sleepy eyes took in the sheet of paper, and snapped open with the speed of an activated mousetrap.

The four words were in capital letters, and in writing she recognised instantly. Her hands shook slightly as she stared down at . . .

ELLIE. HE NEEDS YOU.

Her mind whirled, and for a moment her auric vision spun out of control. The little dog blazed with light, dazzling her unprotected eyes. She quickly brought it back to an acceptable level and breathed deeply to calm herself.

She looked again at the paper and wondered how long it had been in the book. She had never seen it before and it looked clean and fresh, certainly not old or faded. There was no doubt at all that it was Carole's writing.

With her head still spinning, she placed note and book on her bedside table and huddled down into the warm bed.

'Oh, Michael. I wish you were staying over tonight.'

She slipped into an unsettled sleep, and awoke in the morning with her light still on, and feeling awful.

* * *

Michael's night had been about as restful as Ellie's. He had been relieved to be able to return to his own apartment, and had passed a pleasant evening doing what he referred to as 'me' things. He had soaked in the bath, topping-up the hot water until he threatened to turn into 'Prune Man', Ripley's own Superhero! That over, he had trimmed his nails and snipped at his neat beard. The evening had been peaceful and relaxing. He had enjoyed a good hour in the company of the London Philharmonic, and a large home-poured Islay.

When he had finally laid his pampered body down for the night . . . sleep had suddenly deserted him.

His concerns over young Kennedy, and tiredness from his self-imposed night watches, drained every ounce of tranquillity from him, and when he did slip into a troubled sleep, it was wracked with dreams.

He struggled up at seven o'clock, and lumbered to the kitchen for a reviving cup of tea. Instead of having the correct effect, the water tasted of chlorine and the milk was off. He sat at his breakfast bar and wished he had some bottled water. Settling for a glass of fresh orange juice, he lethargically made himself some toast and took it out to his conservatory, where he usually ate his breakfast.

Dawn was casting a candle glow over the red brick wall that surrounded his garden, and he sat and watched the metamorphosis of dark shadowy forms into plants and trees with shape and colour. As a hunched and deformed goblin became a stone trough full of pansies and trailing ivies, he remembered his dream, or part of it.

He had been sitting with Carole and Vera in the old Morris Minor. Carole had been driving and there had been a desperate feeling of being too late for something. It was night, and they were flying along a wide straight road. There was no other traffic, but his heart pounded because he knew that no matter how hard they tried they would never be in time. Vera urged Carole to go faster, and Carole cursed the engine to produce more speed. Over and over, he heard her say, 'Why won't she bloody listen to us. Good people will die. It's not what they think! It's not how it seems!'

Sitting on the colourfully upholstered cane chair, and biting into his crispy toast, Michael could still feel the dreadful frustration and tension from his dream. What with grim dreams and no early morning cup of tea, he decided it probably was not going to be the best of days.

CHAPTER SIX

In the staff lounge, Callum Church was busy stuffing big, padded, lime-green-and-black riding gauntlets into his motorcycle helmet. He greeted Michael with a mischievous smile.

'Beat my record today, boss. Must have had the wind behind me!'

Michael watched as he peeled off the black leather suit with the vivid green insets, revealing snug fitting jeans and a charcoal grey T-shirt with a Médecins Sans Frontières logo on the back. Hellfire, thought the professor, and said out loud, 'You must have frozen on that bike, lad! It's not summer yet.'

'I don't like the heat. Every day that I served in Africa, I swore that, when I got home, I would savour the chilly English climate. I really don't feel the cold much, never have.'

'Want some tea?' asked Michael, busy stirring the dark leaves in the green Denby pot.

'Love some. Strong, please, no sugar.'

Michael passed him a steaming mug and commented that he was glad to get him on his own for a few minutes. They sat opposite each other across the table and Callum looked enquiringly at his employer. 'Is it about Jake, sir?'

'Partly, but first, I want to tell you that Ellie, eh, Miss McEwan, that is, and I, are more than pleased with the way you are getting on here. We realise this is a very different kind of work to what you are used to, but, well, we hope you are enjoying yourself at the C-M?'

'That is exactly what I am doing, Professor. I am enjoying working with all the different professional people that you have here. I have time to spend with the patients, and I'm learning something new every day. The surroundings are lovely too, a far cry from Bosnia, I must say.'

'Do you miss risking life and limb helping people on the front line?'

Callum stared at the tabletop and slowly drew his finger through a drop of amber tea that had splashed onto the shiny lacquered pine. 'I think . . . if I am honest, even if my mother's health had been good, I would have had to come home for a while. Eastern Europe was bad, but Rwanda . . .' His voice softened almost to a whisper. 'Rwanda affected me in a way that I just can't explain. A million Rwandans died, Michael. Mass inter-ethnic killing. We were there to try to help reconstruct some sort of health system, and to cope with emergencies, but can you imagine . . . ?' He shook his head in disbelief at what he had witnessed.

'No,' said Michael simply. 'I cannot begin to imagine.'

'It is very easy to burn out. You don't always see it coming until it's too late. I'm lucky, this is the kind of work I need right now. As I offer help to others, it is affording me some healing of my own.'

Michael felt an admiration for the man. It is not always easy to heed warning signs in time. Callum had been aware of how he was dealing with things, or maybe not dealing with them, and he had done something about it. Probably saved his sanity, thought Michael. It would be very easy to blunder on, caught up in the terrible vortex of suffering and death. He glanced at his watch; Callum would be wanting to start work. 'I'm really pleased you are happy, but if anything should bother you, do come and have a chat, either with me or with Ellie.' He paused for a second. 'Now . . . about Jake Kennedy. He has passed the danger period regarding his drugs and his head injury. We are no longer overly worried about the regime reacting badly. His symptoms are declining and it appears he is responding quite well. What I would like you to do, Callum, is give me a report on his mental state over this coming week. I want your observations. I am still concerned about him. Not to the point of considering him a danger to himself, but nevertheless, I am not totally happy with his progress. I won't go into details, I do not want to influence you in any way, and I may just be being fanciful. However, I want you to go with him, as you did last week, on his outpatient appointment up to London, and generally spend some time with him, okay?'

'Fine by me, sir. He's an interesting guy. Clever, too, it's not easy to fly a chopper. I spent some time with the army helicopter chaps; they reckoned no matter how good a fixed-wing pilot you were, nothing could prepare you for your first spin in a helicopter. Poor bloke, it must be really rotten to know he may never be able to fly again.'

'Exactly. So, get him talking to you. Get him to open up if you can, and we'll reassess next week.'

The door opened and two of the resident therapists came in, chatting amicably.

'Ah, Professor Seale! Mrs Shaw is looking for you. She's with Janet in your office.'

Candice Mason smiled at them both and went to put her bag in her locker. She was the resident aromatherapist and masseuse. Her willowy form and long dark hair made her look more suited to life as a folk singer, but she was remarkably good at her job. Michael had strained his back a few weeks ago and had been mightily impressed by the treatment that she gave him. He had confided to Ellie that he was not sure where she hid her muscles, but he felt like he'd been gone over by half the London Irish by the time she'd finished with him.

As he walked up the stairs to his office, Michael was aware of a ripple of apprehension between his shoulder blades. He had a feeling he was not going to like what Maureen Shaw was going to say.

From the faces of the two women who stood by the window gazing out over the gardens, he knew he had not been wrong.

Janet greeted him and said she would bring in his appointments after he had spoken to Maureen. His assistant left closing the door softly behind her.

Michael indicated an armchair and asked Maureen what was troubling her.

'Jake is having nightmares, Michael. You asked me to let you know if he was showing any signs of stress, and I think this comes into that category. Lucky really that he is the only one on the residents' floor, except for me. I had to go to him twice last night. He was screaming and sweating profusely. This morning he remembers nothing, not even my sitting with him. Dr Cross is due here tomorrow to see him. I did not know whether I should contact her today about the bad dreams, or leave it until she arrives in the morning.'

'I need to speak with Dr Cross myself, Maureen. I'll tell her for you, then she can decide whether she wants to come down earlier. How does Jake seem now?'

Maureen Shaw grimaced. 'It's hard to tell, Michael. He keeps his feelings quite close to his chest, doesn't he? It is so difficult with a head injury case. You have no idea of their prior behaviour or ways of reacting to things. We would all show a very different side, I'm sure, if we suffered such a severe accident, and were then told we could have permanent visual problems, maybe never be able to drive, or in Jake's case, fly again.'

Michael wholeheartedly agreed. 'And yesterday he had his flatmate with him for an hour or so. Jake told me he liked company when he stayed in London, and he didn't like leaving his flat empty when he was working away, or when he was with his father, or in Ireland with his mother. A friend of his from university, I think his name is Ben Lomax, was happy to be a live-in caretaker and keep an eye on the place. Jake only asked that he chip in with the bills, and for that he got to live in a very classy Docklands apartment.'

Maureen shrugged and looked at Michael with an expression of displeasure. 'I could be wrong, but I had a good look at that young man yesterday, and I think he's taking our Jake for a ride. He's not a bit like the Kennedy boy. He's flash, if you know what I mean. Oozes money and fake charm. He arrived wearing a World War Two flying jacket, complete with long white silk scarf, then he flung himself down on the sofa in the visitors' lounge, and stuck his shiny boots up on the arm of it!' She frowned and shook her head. 'No breeding whatsoever! That, or a complete disregard for other people's property. Anyway, after he left, Jake was in a very odd mood, and finished up going to his room until supper time. Visitors normally cheer you up, don't they? And they seemed to be getting on well while the other boy was still with him. It was when he left that Jake changed.'

The professor tried to get her to describe the odd mood, but all she could tell him was that Jake had seemed very distant and almost aggressive in his manner, which Michael agreed was most uncharacteristic.

'Would you like me to stay in one of the residents' rooms again tonight, Maureen?' he offered.

'Oh, I'm sure there is no call for that. After all, I am on duty all night, that is what I'm there for. I would naturally call you if there was anything seriously wrong.'

Mrs Shaw left to get some sleep. She was working from eight till eight, and, as she only had one charge to watch over, her shifts had mainly consisted of reading and watching late-night television, until now.

As soon as his door closed, it opened again and Janet came in with the diary, a list of client details, and another mug of tea. They swiftly sorted out the day's work and his assistant left to type some letters and liaise with the local newspaper who wanted to do an editorial on the Centre.

Michael picked up the telephone and put through a call to Alice. He sighed and tapped his pen on the desktop as he listened to the engaged tone. Dr Alice Cross may not consider Mr Kennedy a cause for concern, but he had warning bells ringing all over the place where that young man was concerned.

CHAPTER SEVEN

Her journey to work had been dreadful, nothing like Callum's record-breaking trip. Her bad night had left her tired and ratty, and the absence of hot water for her shower had done nothing to improve her frame of mind. She suffered the shortest cold-water ablution in the world, grabbed something to eat, rushed the dogs out into the orchard, then rushed them back indoors again, in order to make time to call in on Scrubbs on her way out. The old man had immediately offered take a look at it for her, and either fix it or call out the plumber; whichever way, he would deal with it.

She had been just a little later than normal as she drove out of the lane and down to the junction with the road through Compton. Reaching the bottom of the road, she had found a tractor with an antiquated trailer stopped, right across both lanes. The driver had been nowhere to be seen, and although Ellie was not a great one for using the horn, she had sounded it long and hard, and to absolutely no avail. There had been no way around it. There was a ditch on one side and a large hawthorn on the other. It had been some fifteen minutes before she had seen a motley crew of assorted farm workers arrive to unhitch the trailer from the immobile tractor.

After several more, albeit less dramatic hold-ups, she arrived at the Cavendish-Meyer, very late and ready to tear the heads off little old ladies and disembowel kittens!

She skipped her usual trip to the staff room and went straight to her office. She just couldn't face the friendly pleasantries that normally started the day. Janet had booted up her computer ready for work, and Ellie sat heavily on the swivel chair and stared at the screen saver.

Photographs of blazing sunsets, crystal waterfalls, dreamy, deserted palm-fringed beaches and other natural wonders took their turn on the screen. She sat for several minutes completely immersed in the glorious pictures.

By the time she had accessed her personal calendar and taken stock of her appointments and duties for the day, she decided that she would, once again, be safe around other human beings and small furry animals. She took an armful of patient studies and went out to the main room to look at them.

All the therapists who were employed by the clinic reported directly to her on their findings, their successes and, occasionally, their failures. Sometimes one kind of complementary treatment did not suit a patient, and it was Ellie's job to find one that did.

She sat engrossed in her work and hardly heard the soft tap on her door. Calling out for whoever it was to enter, she found herself confronted by the enormous form of Edmund Hargreaves. Edmund and his wife, Sylvie, ran the coffee bar and provided a kitchen service for staff. Although she had seen on the computer's diary that she had a meeting with him at ten, she had totally lost track of time. She offered him a seat and, excusing herself for a moment, went into the back office for some figures that she wanted to talk over with him.

Glancing in the mirror, she could not help but be amazed that such a colossus of a man could be so very quietly spoken and light on his feet. He epitomised the term, gentle giant.

He sat admiring her Tiffany prints, his hands relaxed in his lap and an almost reverent smile on his big face.

'Ed. I'm sorry not to be prepared. I got intrigued by some of my patient records and forgot the time. I am sorry.'

Edmund smiled and shook his head. 'Please! It is a treat to get away from the cafe for a while. We are unbelievably busy. Far busier than I imagined, I have to say.'

'That's what I want to talk to you about.' Ellie leafed through her paperwork and produced a batch of figure-covered printouts. 'I know this was all a bit of an experiment really. Having a coffee shop in the Centre seemed like a good idea, but you never really know whether it will work or not. Well, it has worked, to a point where I'm thinking we should extend what we can provide.' She paused, giving Edmund a knowing smile. 'Michael and I were wondering if you and Sylvie would like to take it on as a business venture, something of your own. We would provide financial support until you were up and running, then it would be all yours.'

Edmund sat with his mouth slightly open.

As words were obviously not an option at that moment, Ellie continued. 'We will be needing you to stay open in the evenings as we are soon to be having regular inpatients. You will need more staff and probably more kitchen equipment but, as I said, the Centre will sort the finances out for that.'

Although the expression was changing slightly, Ed was still having trouble enunciating his words, so Ellie ploughed on with her speech. 'I have printed you out a complete set of figures for the time the coffee shop has been operating. Compare it with our original projection, here' — she waved another piece of paper in front of him — 'and prepare to be pleasantly surprised! Anyway, talk to Sylvie, look over the calculations and, well, let me know, I guess . . .' Her voice trailed off and she could feel a laugh well-up in her throat. 'For heaven's sake, Ed! Say something!'

He beamed his reply. 'This is brilliant, absolutely brilliant. Oh, Sylvie will be so delighted when I tell her. I just don't know what to say.' He leaned across and grasped Ellie's hand in his. 'Thank you. This is just what we need right now.'

The offer had not been made lightly or to offload the responsibility from Ellie's shoulders. She had been very aware that the couple needed something to boost their morale. Ed had been made redundant at the age of forty. He had given up a good, solid job after being headhunted and promised the world. He had been with the new company for less than a year when they went to the wall. If some of their investments had not been in Sylvie's name, they would have lost everything. Later that year, their daughter died. The couple were devastated, but thankfully they did not tear each other apart in their grief, as her friend Marie's son and his wife had done. Ed tried several jobs, but could not settle. Sylvie then saw the ad in the local press, and they had joined the Cavendish-Meyer as co-managers for the new food and drink facility.

Michael and Ellie had decided that this was the way their legacy should go, and as she sat and smiled at the leviathan with a tear in his eye, she was utterly convinced they were right.

Edmund left with a pile of rustling papers in his shaking fingers, and Ellie went in search of refreshment herself. Not the coffee shop, she would let them enjoy Ed's good news alone. There was a water dispenser in the orangery so she would get a glass before her next appointment. She could do with cutting down on the caffeine anyway.

She paused, holding the cool plastic beaker in her hand, and listened to the melodious voice of the Tai Chi Ch'aun master taking his pupils through Holding the Circle, and into The Stork Cools its Wings.

As she stood beneath a ten-foot ficus benjamina tree, and breathed in the semi-tropical air, the peace in that great glass house completed the evaporation process on the tension that had earlier threatened the safety of those close by.

She sat for a while, in the place where she so often found Michael, on the stone ledge beside the pool, and considered her morning tantrum. Yes, she had been tired and unrested. She still had the strange mystery of the books in the library to sort out, but even the broken-down tractor would not normally have caused her such angst. She wondered if there were some other agenda that she was psychologically blocking, and it was coming out sideways, as the stress counsellor would have said.

Well, if she was blocking something, she was doing a really good job. There was nothing obvious, that was for sure. The day before had gone well. Very well, in fact. They had had a breakthrough with a patient who had been attending regularly with a severe back problem. Construction was well under way for the hydrotherapy pool, and generally all was well with the world. Even Michael's apprehension over Jake Kennedy was only a professional concern, nothing worrying enough to give her sleepless nights and foul tempers. She thought perhaps Michael was fretting somewhat unnecessarily over Alice's patient. Apart from coming to terms psychologically with his new lot in life, Jake had sustained a severe head trauma, and his body was trying to deal with a massive daily dose of chemicals. No wonder he was not exactly Mr Cool, Mr Calm or Mr Collected. She had spent some time with him the day before, and was very interested to compare how he now perceived auras compared to herself.

Initially the lights had presented themselves in an identical fashion, but the further Jake got into the course of medication, it became clear that his 'sight' was changing radically. He was no longer blinded by them although they were still very bright. The strange smells had disappeared completely, but he confessed that he still occasionally noticed some of the odd, blurry shapes floating around.

All things considered, Ellie thought the young man was doing well. She hoped that Michael's fears were unfounded, but she knew the professor too well, and respected him too much, to dismiss his concerns out of hand.

She dragged her hand through the water and splashed glassy droplets onto an emerald leaf that was hanging over the side of the pool. She would chat to Michael later. Then perhaps, when Alice came to assess Jake, they could involve Maureen and Callum, and hear their observations as well. An overview might help to put things into perspective.

She shook her wet hand and wiped it on her trouser leg. Her contemplations of the last five minutes had done nothing to provide an answer to her weird state of mind, and watching the easy flow of movement from the Tai Chi class, Ellie thought perhaps she was making too much of a few unbalanced bio-rhythms. Maybe she should spend some time on her own Yin and Yang.

She glanced at her watch and hoped she could catch Michael between clients. The leaf in the pool had reminded her of Carole's water garden, and that in turn had led her mind to the pile of books in the library.

Dropping the water beaker into the bin beside the dispenser, she dashed off to try to find the answer to her mystery.

* * *

Michael Seale's telephone conversation with Alice Cross did nothing to assuage his worry about Jake Kennedy, although it should have done. Alice had spent a great deal of time explaining to Michael about the delicate balance of the drugs Jake was taking. She was certain they were responsible for both his nightmares and any sort of mood swing he may be experiencing. She asked the professor to keep a careful eye on the young man, and that she would be there, crack of dawn the next day, to assess the medication.

Michael had assured Alice that they already had Jake under close observation, but he would still feel happier when the doctor had checked him over.

Just before saying his goodbyes, Alice's voice had taken on a slightly more animated tone. 'I have something to show you, Michael. I will bring it with me tomorrow. Perhaps you can see if Ellie will be free to join us. I think it will be of great interest to her, and maybe give you an idea of what young Kennedy has been going through.'

If she had been going to reveal any more, she wasn't able to as her bleeper went and she left Michael with a hurried, 'Gotta go!'

The professor replaced the handset and decided to go and check on his patient himself.

He found Jake sitting in a quiet corner of the orangery, in deep conversation with Callum Church. Before approaching the two men, Michael stood for a while unnoticed, watching the young pilot's body language.

He still wore dark glasses, but Michael guessed that being surrounded by the trees and plants in the conservatory, the energy lights they gave off would be quite strong. He was obviously telling the nurse a story. His arms waved vigorously, then flapped up and down like a small boy pretending to be an aeroplane. After a few seconds both men laughed. Michael considered that Jake's guffaw was a little too loud to be natural, but he was certainly showing no signs of being withdrawn, as Maureen had described him.

He decided not to interrupt and quietly left the two to their conversation. Walking back to his office, he saw Ellie waving to him from the door of her room.

'Have you got a moment, Michael? I need to talk to you.'

He nodded. *Oh, yes,* he thought, *I have plenty of time on my hands today. My appointments are finished, my telephone calls all made, and no diversions left. In fact, far too much time to dwell on the vague and the tenuous.*

He placed his well-upholstered derriere on Ellie's equally comfortable couch, and stared thoughtfully at her. 'Why haven't I seen you today, my friend? Where have you been hiding yourself?'

Ellie looked distracted and began rearranging cushions. She lifted them, placed them on the sofa, then repeated the procedure after giving the unfortunate articles a thorough thumping. 'Sorry, Michael. I got in a bit late. I was in a foul mood after a rotten night and an awful journey, then before I could get to say hello, the day took off without me.' The cushions finally in an acceptable position, she sat down and leaned heavily on them. 'I gave the figures and the news to Ed, by the way. He was delighted.'

'Good, good. I hope it helps them. Maybe give them a bit of focus for a future. Now . . . why did my favourite person have a rotten night? Or shouldn't I ask?'

The whole thing flooded out. How as soon as she had tried to sleep, her frustrations about her inability to help young Jake had taken over her mind. Then there was the open window, the pile of books on the hearth, and finally, the note.

She went to the outer office and returned with the scrap of paper.

'Here. Recognise the writing?'

Michael took the note that Ellie offered him, and his solar plexus contracted as if he had been poleaxed.

'Hmm, same reaction as me,' murmured Ellie, then sat back and stared hard at him.

It was some time before he spoke, and his voice was low, and uncharacteristically serious. 'Have you seen anything at Snug Cottage recently? Any lights, or maybe you've heard voices or something?'

The woman's gaze fell to her feet and in a soft voice she replied, 'If you mean, have I seen Carole or Vera? Then no, Michael, I haven't. I have not seen either of them, since . . . since the . . .' She faltered, her breathing coming in short, rapid gasps.

Before Michael could stop her, the sentence was complete.

'Since the day the killer tried to make me his sixth victim.'

That awful truth being spoken out loud seemed to enable her to continue in a calmer manner. 'Fact is, I used to see Vera all the time — a wonderful amethyst light floating in my peripheral vision. Carole was Aegean blue, I can remember that pure, clear colour now. But no more. I sometimes think they are around me. I sense their love, but I can't see them, and I can't tell you how much I miss them.' She looked sadly at him. 'Have you seen anything, Michael?'

He slowly nodded. 'I've seen Orlando, and the coloured auras of Carole and Vera in the orchard. Now, I'm dreaming about them.' He shivered slightly. 'Ah, and I heard Carole whistle the dog. I'd know that whistle anywhere. You could hear it a mile away. I hope nothing is, well . . . wrong, if you know what I mean?'

'I'd hoped you would be able to put my mind at rest, Michael,' said Ellie glumly. 'Sadly, I feel really worried now! I suppose the mystery of the books in the library is not about to be revealed either?'

Michael shrugged, lifting his palms upwards. 'No idea. And as for the note, well, that is Carole's writing, no doubt at all. Sorry, Ellie, but I think they are trying to tell you something.'

'They?'

'Carole and Vera. You don't seem to be able to see them anymore, so they are doing their best to attract you in whatever way they can. Open windows, piles of books, notes . . .'

Ellie's expression said that she wished she were somewhere else.

'Come on, Michael. Perhaps Carole had been going to leave me a note about something. *Before* she died. Perhaps she thought about something when she was in bed, started to write it down, then changed her mind. She simply left the scrap of paper in her book as a bookmark.'

'Look at it, Ellie. The letters are centralised. This was the whole message, not part of a sentence. It says, *"Ellie. He needs you"* full stop. Sorry, old girl, but the only mystery I can see, is who is "he"?'

Her slender shoulders slumped down dispiritedly. 'I think I knew this all along. I just didn't want to admit it. Everything has been so wonderfully normal, recently. After everything that happened a couple of years back, words like normal, routine, natural, humdrum, even boring, sound good to me!'

Michael left his seat and sank down next to his friend. He put a reassuring arm around her, and beamed his moon-faced smile. 'They always said they would be there for us. If ever anything went wrong, we should ask them for help. Let's assume that something, somewhere *is* wrong. They know about it, and they don't want us to be caught napping, so to speak. I think by accepting this, we will be taking a giant step.' He gave Ellie a hug. 'It's reassuring to know we have the good guys on our side, don't you think?'

She smiled ruefully at him. 'If it's all the same, I'd rather we did not need the good guys at all!'

Michael looked at his friend and considered all she had endured. He smiled at her, his heart full of compassion, but the smile hid a grave apprehension that Ellie McEwan was not yet through with danger, and nor, for that matter, was he.

CAMEO TWO: RODERICK BLACK — PART TWO

Neville Wilson gently placed the telephone receiver back in its cradle, and noticed a feeling of nausea that was cramping his stomach. It had begun an hour ago when his deputy head told him that 2B were late returning from their field trip to the old quarry.

The distressed teacher had rung their accompanying master's mobile phone, and had been dismayed to find his ringing tone unanswered.

Already anxious parents were waiting in the playground.

The headmaster was grateful that the local police had taken his request for help seriously, and as he looked out from his window, he saw a police vehicle speeding along School Road and make a sharp turn through the open gates.

He left his deputy to man the telephone and went down to meet the officers.

It only took a few minutes for PC Millett to assess the situation and report back to the station. Quickly checking his notebook, he assured the headmaster that a search would be underway just as soon as they could get their men to the area. 'Let me just clarify this one more time, sir. You have five pupils, all boys, out with one master, and a prefect. They were on a field trip to the woods around Hobhole Quarry.

You say that they were not going into the quarry itself, is that right?'

'Absolutely. It was a biology study. The particular flora in that environ is quite unusual. It was the surrounding woodland and meadows they were visiting. Mr Black would not take the children anywhere near the quarry itself. He knows the terrain and its dangers. That is why he had such a small group with him, so he could keep a close eye on them.'

'Is Mr Black one of your regular teachers. Do you know him well?'

'He's the best, Officer. You would not find a more dedicated teacher if you searched every school in Britain. He has been here for four years now, and is probably our most popular member of staff.'

'What about the prefect?'

The headmaster rubbed his temple distractedly. 'Johnny Baker. Fine pupil, good scholar, got all the makings of a teacher himself one day. He likes Mr Black, and often helps him with the younger children on outings, or suchlike.'

'You have rung Black's mobile and got no reply. Is there a chance that the prefect, Johnny, has one? Most kids do these days.'

'He does, but sadly the battery must need charging or he's forgotten to switch it on.'

The constable muttered a soft oath under his breath, and said something about being hard to get a youngster off his mobile, so this one had to be the exception to the rule. 'Right, sir. Well, we are . . .' He broke off as his radio spat into life. 'Yes, Sarge. Right . . . okay . . . I'll pass that on to Mr Wilson. Message received and understood.' He switched off and turned back to the waiting headmaster. 'We have located the school mini-van, parked where you said, sir. Our main party of officers are following the exact route that you reckon Mr Black always takes. We have another group of men searching from the far side of the quarry, just in case they've got lost or disoriented.'

'Roderick Black would not get lost, Officer. He knows every blade of grass around that quarry, believe me.'

'I don't doubt you, sir, but any number of things could have happened. We'll find them, sir. There is another hour before dusk, they can't have gone far.'

The headmaster wished he felt as confident as the policeman looked, but he had a very bad feeling that something was very wrong at Hobhole Quarry.

* * *

A gloomy sky had replaced the late afternoon sun and WPC Paula English felt the first few spots of rain hit the rim of her black bowler. They had been searching for an hour and, as time passed, a niggling unease had replaced her earlier feeling that the children would soon be found and returned to their fraught parents.

The teacher's preplanned route had been covered once, and although there was evidence that a group had passed that way recently, there had been no sightings of the children or their master.

The search had been widened. A party of officers was examining the Hobhole Quarry itself, although from first examinations, the fences that surrounded it did not appear to have been breached at any point. Even the overgrown path around its perimeter had not been disturbed or trampled. So far, it did not seem likely that Mr Black had broken his own rule and taken his precious kids into a dangerous place.

Paula shivered as the rain trickled down between her collar and her neck. Her boots, a size too large, were making her feet sore. She stopped for a moment to wrench an uncomfortable sleeping sock from where it had gathered into a knot under her instep, when she heard a sound.

She was in a wooded copse. Clusters of trees gave way to small clearings where bright green moss and snaggly patches of bramble gathered in islands in the pale new growth of the bracken.

She called to the officers nearest to her to stop and to listen.

An eerie silence descended over the woodland.

Then there was a whisper in the air, and a pipistrelle bat dipped over her head causing her to gasp in surprise. As the tiny creature flew off, Paula English was suddenly aware of the approach of evening. Shadows were deepening and a feeling of dread seeped through her, like ink through blotting paper.

It was there again. The faintest of sounds, and it was ahead of her.

She moved silently through the next clump of trees, and into a small grassy space. Where she froze.

The children were scattered around the clearing, and the sounds she had heard had emanated from the torn throat of an older boy.

Their teacher, their hero, their rock and protector sat with his back against the rough bark of a tall and resplendent tree. In his hands he held two small branches, both smothered in a fresh spring growth of leaves. Beside him, carelessly dropped onto the mud-spattered blazer of a dead boy, was a blood-covered lump of wood. A heavy branch. A solid club.

Paula knew little about trees, but a useless bit of stored information in her grey cells identified it as oak.

She was on her radio before she had had time to take everything in.

Moments later fellow officers arrived at her side and stood for a second in a kind of pagan circle, trying to assimilate what they were seeing.

A tall, shaven-headed, young PC broke the ritualistic ring and moved towards the older boy. Paula gathered herself and slowly approached the man.

She stopped a few feet from him and heard a soft whisper.

The eyes were as dark as his name. They were focused entirely on the tender green shoots in his hands.

'Oak before ash . . .' The voice was hushed and had a sing-song quality.

'. . . we are in for a splash.'

He tapped first one branch, then the other, on the bloody chest of the dead child lying next to him.

Paula's throat was parched, and she swallowed hard as she gazed into the unseeing eyes.

'Ash before oak . . . come on, Johnny, tell them! Speak up, boy! You'll never make a teacher if you can't enunciate properly.'

There was a pause, then, 'We are in for a soak! There you are! Now it's your turn, Johnny. Johnny . . . ?'

* * *

'You have to be joking, Sergeant! He's root-toot! There is no way you'd get anything out of him, even if he were fit to interview. Believe me, he is so far away with the fairies, he'll never come back!'

Detective Sergeant Wendy Brown was beginning to wish she had not made the request to see the suspect in the first place.

Detective Chief Inspector Bob Foreman looked even bigger and greyer than he usually did. His deeply furrowed brow threatened to engulf his eyes if he frowned any harder. He ran a huge hand through his thick silver waves, took a deep breath, and then threw a battered copy of *Butterworth's Law* in the vague direction of his overflowing bookcase.

'I know this one is hard to take, Wendy. Dead children are the worst thing of all to cope with . . .'

He was pacing the office now, with giant's strides.

Wendy watched him. She felt as though she were at the zoo, watching a great grey bear lumbering backwards and forwards, backwards and forwards.

'. . . but at least we have him here, in a place of safety. He can't hurt any more poor little mites.'

She knew he had a family of his own. Three kids, all loved to bits. It was bad enough for her, and she didn't have any children; she couldn't guess what he was thinking right now.

She had been in court all afternoon and had just arrived back, as DI Jonathan Leatham, recently transferred in as a permanent member of staff, and a team of uniforms were bringing the murder suspect in.

The station was in a state of stunned disbelief at the carnage they had found in the woods, and the story had reached Wendy's ears in more pieces than a jigsaw puzzle.

She hoped that when he had finished wearing out the office carpet, he may tell her the whole story.

He finally flopped heavily into his chair. For a moment Wendy could not believe that the piece of furniture would stand such abuse, but after a second or two she was relieved to see her boss had avoided a severe spinal injury — this time, at least.

'We have gone the whole hog with this one, Wendy. Custody sergeant called the police surgeon. Surgeon called the medical social worker. She demanded the prisoner's GP, and they will finally get together and section him.' He gave a grunt. 'Weird! From all the evidence that's coming in, this guy is a regular saint. Loved by everyone. Has an adoring wife and child. Never put a foot wrong. His headmaster could not speak higher of him. So, how come he takes five of his little cherubs, and a loyal prefect, on a field trip to the Promised Land?'

'Are they all dead, sir?'

'The older lad is hanging on. He has a fair chance, they say. He's in ITU with head injuries and a severely lacerated neck. God, Wendy, he nearly tore the boy's throat out! One other child will probably make it as well. He regained consciousness in A&E, but he's being kept sedated for the time being. There is a special team coming down to deal with him, poor little sod. He's probably our main witness.'

Bob Foreman heaved himself out of his chair, stuck his head out of his office door and asked one of his constables to fetch them a couple of coffees.

'What could make a local hero turn into the Angel of Death?' Bob was speaking partly to himself and partly to Wendy.

Wendy leaned back and raised her eyebrows. 'Drugs? A mental breakdown? Maybe some sort of brainstorm, I don't know. Drugs would be favourite, I suppose, we know what people are capable of when they're freaked out on something heavy.'

Bob shook his head. 'I would be willing to bet that our schoolteacher would need an armlock to take a paracetamol. The MO reckons he's clean, and the hospital will check him out, but . . .' He paused. 'I don't know. This is a weird one, by no mistake.'

They drank their coffee in silence, and from the look on his face, Wendy thought that Bob was probably thinking of the grieving parents, and what on earth would he and his wife do if anything like that ever happened to their kids.

She herself was trying to understand how a gentle, loving man could become a cold-blooded killer, in the twinkling of a child's eye.

CHAPTER EIGHT

A dismal misty rain drifted across the long driveway up to the Centre. Alice's Range Rover crunched over the gravel and pulled into one of the empty parking bays. She was very early. It had paid to escape from the city before the traffic built up, but it found her in Ripley long before the C-M officially opened. She pulled on her rain jacket, locked the vehicle, and ran to the front door.

To her delight the main door was not only open, but when inside, she was greeted by the welcoming smell of freshly brewed coffee. She walked down the wide corridor and into the cafe area at the back of the house.

Surprisingly, several tables were already occupied. Ellie had mentioned that a few of the therapists had asked if it would be possible to start their clinics early, in order to accommodate businesspeople who could get a session in before going to work. It still amazed Alice that the little cafe should be so busy at seven o'clock in the morning.

She put her damp jacket over the back of a chair and went up to the counter. She was greeted by a bubbly, smiling Sylvie, and a gangly beanpole of a lad, who was new to her.

'Have you heard the good news, Dr Cross . . . about the cafe?' Sylvie didn't wait for her reply, but rushed headlong into her story. '. . . and then Miss McEwan tells my Ed that we can have it as our own, if we'd like it! Can you believe it? We're going to open in the evenings for the staff and inpatients . . . do a much wider menu, and . . .'

Alice took her coffee and a warm croissant from Sylvie, noting that so far, apart from ordering her breakfast, she had not been allowed to utter a single word. The woman was absolutely delighted with Michael and Ellie's generous gesture, and Alice knew exactly how she felt.

She went back to her table, sipped her drink, and remembered that evening at Snug Cottage when her two friends had told her about their plans for the Azimah Trust. She could remember sitting with her elbows resting on the old pine table, and gazing in disbelief at Ellie, as she explained their idea. Her speech had been interspersed by an excited Michael, adding snippets he thought relevant at the time. He had reminded Alice of an oversized schoolboy who was dying to tell a secret. Alice had arrived in Compton in her Nissan Micra, with an overdraft, a small mortgage on her two-up two-down in Balham, and a burning ambition to complete the unfinished work of Dr Azimah Siddiq into the connection between brain injury and the syndrome. She had little funding and was forced to work appalling hours at the hospital, in order to finance her research.

She broke the flaky, warm croissant and covered it with butter. She still found it hard to comprehend how her life had turned round.

She had left the cottage the next morning with a folder clasped tightly in her hand. Inside were papers for her to present to her solicitor. Papers that formed the basis for a fully financed research programme. One that would allow her access to all her patients, wherever they were in the world. One that gave her a sturdy vehicle to travel the length and breadth of the country in safety and comfort. One that removed her mortgage and presented her with a perfectly situated mews cottage, close to the hospital. And one that gave her enough money to realise her dream.

In a few short months she had completed her thesis on the Azimah Syndrome. It had been read with interest, and finally published in the *BMJ* and *The Lancet*. She had achieved more in six months than she had been able to do in six years. Thanks to Ellie and Michael.

She pushed the empty plate away, and went for a second cup of coffee. Back at the table she continued her thoughts. One of the best things was that the investment had made it possible for her to cut down her time at the hospital and spend it on research, and more importantly, on Ellie.

Alice could not help but smile when she thought of Ellie. Her warmth, her courage, her incredible willpower that had overcome the effects of the terrible accident and, above all, her ability to reach Alice, who had been cocooned in her all-consuming passion for knowledge.

She loved Ellie, and the thought of her made her whole body yearn to see her again.

She stared into the dark liquid, slowly moving the spoon to and fro, making spirals and waves in the cup. They had debated living together. They still were. It was just there always seemed to be something that had to be dealt with first, always something that took priority.

She had searched her soul and honestly believed they were not trying to avoid the issue; they were just trying to juggle too many other items.

Her mind still firmly with Ellie McEwan, she did not notice Jake until he was standing right beside her.

'Hello, Doc. Mind if I join you?'

'Hi, Jake. Of course. Sorry I was miles away. Can I get you something to drink? Have you had breakfast?'

'I'm fine. Mrs Shaw made me some toast earlier. I wouldn't mind a lemon tea, if it's not too much trouble.'

Sylvie, who was cleaning a table close by, signalled that she would fetch it.

'Big day today, Mr Kennedy. Medication review and assessment. Vision checks and . . .' She paused, smiling. 'I've got a new toy that you might be able to help me with.'

Jake tilted his head to one side enquiringly.

'It is something another AS sufferer has helped me put together. I just had an idea, and my friend, the genius, designed it for me. If you can wait until Ellie and the professor can join us, I'll reveal all!'

'Can't wait. I like surprises.'

Alice noticed a slight lethargy about her patient, and the tiniest slur to his speech. His hair was lank, and the doctor suspected that Jake had not showered that morning. There had been a hint of stale sweat as the man sat down. She looked into the hollow eyes, and decided that she could see why Michael was concerned.

'We are going to use Professor Seale's office for your assessment, Jake. Can you be there at nine?'

Jake nodded and Alice left to get her notes and drug sheets from the Range Rover. She also wanted to be sure that her new toy was all set up and ready for when the others arrived.

The rain had eased and a watery sun was endeavouring to make an appearance. She was fighting her way through the heavy entrance door when a friendly voice called out to her.

'Want a hand, Alice?'

'Michael! Great! Yes please. If you could take this briefcase and this box, I'll bring the computer and the printer. Thanks for the use of your office, by the way. The treatment rooms are a bit small for four of us, and all my stuff.'

'Apparently!' laughed Michael, as he puffed his way up the stairs. 'That reminds me, Ellie and I were thinking you might like a consulting room of your own. We had set one up for the new counsellor who was due to join us later this month, but it doesn't look as though he will be starting until late summer. If you would like his room, it has a telephone, a fax and a computer socket, all the usual office equipment. If you want it, we can always sort him out another one, nearer the time.' He pushed his own consulting room door open and held it for Alice. 'Remind me to show it to you before you leave. I must just pop down and see Janet. Will you be okay with all of this?'

Alice assured him that she would, thanked him for the offer of an office and got on with sorting out her computer equipment.

By the time Jake arrived, Alice was sitting behind a glowing computer screen and grinning like a Cheshire cat.

'Working like a dream! I'll just run a few checks on you before the others get here, and then I'll show you this little baby.'

The next fifteen minutes were taken up with blood tests, sugar levels, heart rate, and a brain frequency scan.

As the young man sat with a headset across his skull, Alice traced readings and graphs, scribbling notes quickly into a notepad, then when the passes over the brain were completed, rerunning them for comparison.

With every reading, Alice's bright smile faded a little more. It was clear even before the trial had finished that Jake Kennedy's medication regime was not right. Well, in essence, it was. According to every other patient that had been on the programme, the drugs were in perfect balance, but in Jake's case, the results were a mess.

A strange shiver of apprehension crept insidiously down Alice's back.

This wasn't right.

She removed the headset from the dull, lifeless hair, and told Jake to go and make himself comfortable in one of the armchairs, while she went over the figures.

She spent ten minutes checking and rechecking her findings. She even ran a ten pass check on herself, just to make sure the frequency scanner was not malfunctioning. The reading was normal, showing no abnormalities, other than a slight deficiency in one of the delta regions. Considering her poor sleep patterns, that was to be expected. So, it was not the machine.

Excusing herself for a moment, she stepped out of the office, moved a little way down the hallway, and rang Ellie's mobile.

She swiftly explained that she needed a bit more time alone with Jake, before she and Michael joined them. Ellie said she would find Michael, and they would give Alice another half an hour, if that would help.

She returned to the professor's room and sat down opposite her patient.

'Right. No point in beating about the bush, Jake. Your tests and scans don't make sense. And frankly, you look awful. I want you to tell me exactly how you feel, and what you've been doing in the two days since I saw you last. From the information that I have here, it looks like something is badly affecting the chemical balances. So, talk to me.'

'I don't feel good. But I can't really explain it, Doctor. The auric vision is much better. I can do without my dark glasses for nearly two hours at a time now. Things are a bit fuzzy around the edges, and of course, if I get very tired, or when it gets near to the time for my pills, the colours flare up and it gets a bit difficult for me. Other than that, the sight is incredibly improved. I should be feeling great, but I don't. I feel truly shitty. I get a weird headache, nothing like the one I had before. It makes me feel as though I am looking down a tunnel, and I can't think properly. I get very angry with myself, too. It passes after a while, but it leaves me very tired. Too tired to be bothered with anything really.'

'Like showering and washing your hair?' asked Alice gently.

Jake looked embarrassed. 'Exactly. I'm sorry, Dr Cross. I should have made the effort. Mrs Shaw dropped enough hints this morning, but I just could not drag myself into the shower.'

'Don't worry. We'll get you sorted out. Something is definitely messing up your medication. As soon as we find out what it is, we can get you back on an even keel again. You were fine for the first couple of weeks, so there is absolutely no reason why you won't be again. Now, let's see if we can get to the bottom of this.'

For the next twenty minutes, doctor and patient discounted a myriad of possibilities. Jake had taken no added medication, no painkillers or indigestion remedies. He had taken no alcohol. He had never smoked, so they disregarded that thought. He had not swallowed any vitamin pills or food supplements. He used only homeopathic toothpaste, and had adhered to a diet with very little added caffeine in it.

To all appearances, being very conscious of the fine balance needed with his medication, Jake had been the model patient. His activities had been minimal. There had been one trip to the London hospital for an appointment with the neurologist. He had been accompanied by Callum Church, and his only examination was an EEG and the usual blood pressure and eye tests. Other than that, he had been visited by his father, Ben, his flatmate, and an old friend from uni days, who lived in nearby Shere. None of them had taken him out, all stayed in the visitors' lounge or in his room with him. Other than a walk around the grounds, again accompanied by his nurse, he had only listened to music, watched a bit of television or partaken of some of the soothing therapies that the C-M Centre had to offer. Alice even checked the oils that were used for an aromatherapy massage.

When Ellie and Michael arrived half an hour later, Alice declared that they had drawn a blank. She would have to return to the medication itself; just maybe, there was a flaw in the complex cocktail. This seemed the only rational conclusion, but the question arose of why the lad had started so well, then suddenly taken a dive. True, the build-up programme had been accelerated due to his fragile state of mind, but a reaction to the increased drugs would have had a very different presentation to what they were seeing now. Azimah Siddiq had documented a case history in one of her medical papers, where the patient became a danger to himself in the very early stages of treatment. The medicines had been administered after an unsuccessful suicide attempt, but he suffered several minor bleeds, then a massive cerebral haemorrhage from which he did not recover. This was the far end of the scale, but the drugs could cause small vessels to burst, hence Alice's reticence to move too quickly. Jake's apathetic manner and mood swings did not follow any known pattern of symptoms.

Then there was the fact that his sight was improving. For the second time in the treatment of Mr Jake Kennedy, Alice considered a Catch-22 situation.

Change his drugs, and disturb his recovering vision.

Leave the drugs alone, and he suffers headaches, personality changes and a torpid disposition.

The little gathering in the professor's office were at a loss to know how to help Alice. With a sigh, she declared she would have to go back to the drawing board. To try and pinpoint the time when Jake had begun to have the side effects.

'I trust you, Doc.' Jake gave a weary smile. 'In the meantime, what is this famous new toy you have been telling us about?'

The decision made to look into the medication, Alice brightened somewhat when she thought about 'AZSEE'. 'Okay, gather round. Come and meet a new kind of computer game!'

They formed a semi-circle around the monitor. Alice sat Jake in front of it, and she started up the programme.

A rainbow slowly extended from one side of the screen to the other, then burst into a shower of coloured stars. As they fell gently to the bottom of the screen, they left behind the legend, 'Welcome to AZSEE. Share the gift of Auric Vision'.

Before she went on with the programme, Alice briefly filled them in on its history. 'I have been working for a while now with a patient of mine up in Scotland. He, like Ellie, did not contract the whole syndrome, just the visual disturbances. The drugs worked amazingly well, and I managed to bring him under control very quickly.' She looked at Jake. 'Sorry, Jake, I'm not meaning to rub your nose in it. That's just how it was with Gordon Lamont. Anyway, Gordon is a computer buff. Not just a nerd, a real expert. His area of expertise is virtual reality. This is a simple device to allow normally sighted people to experience what it's like to see auras. More to the point, it is for doctors to fully appreciate what a sufferer of the Azimah Syndrome is going through. I've brought this copy to show you, and to allow you to show me exactly what it is you are seeing. Gordon is at present building a full machine, complete with hand- and headsets that will allow you into a "virtual auric world". I've used the prototype, and it is mind- blowing. It could be a major breakthrough for the Azimah Research Programme. Even this is good. Very good, actually. Right, let's go! Jake. Move the cursor to that box marked "Show Me" and double click.'

A giant eye filled the monitor screen. The huge lid closed, opened again, and the iris was filled with a menu box. Above the eye were the words, 'What would you like to see?' The choices on the menu were People, Animals, Landscapes, Trees, Plants and Flowers, and Rocks and Minerals.

'Click on People.'

Jake obeyed and a sub-menu appeared. This time the choices were Female, followed by Bairn, Toddler, Tweenager, Adolescent, Young Adult, Adult, Early Wrinkly, Geriatric. There were the same headings for Male.

Alice grinned. 'Please note that this is Gordon's own particular way of identifying categories. When we are happy with the way the system works, we will make it politically correct.'

For some reason, Jake chose Female, Young Adult.

The screen changed and an additional sub-menu appeared. Select Mood. There were lists of different dispositions and frames of mind. Jake chose Euphoric.

'Oh boy!' muttered Alice. 'You sure know how to pick them!'

A black screen flashed up with the words, 'This is Anna. She is extremely happy. This is how you see her.'

A pretty young woman filled their vision. Her body language gave off sheer delight, and her face held an expression of ecstasy.

The screen blacked out again and a single sentence appeared. 'And this is how I see her.'

All of them, including Alice, jumped back from the monitor, each one gasping out his, or her, own words of exclamation.

Alice laughed. 'God, I never get used to that! Even though I know what's coming!'

The picture was hardly discernible as a woman. A vaguely human form was shown as a blinding white core, with an explosion of colours flying from it. It moved constantly, the lights flaring, dying, and being replaced by other equally brilliant hues. It hurt their eyes to look too long and very soon the picture faded and on a soft green screen was the legend, 'That's Azimah for you!'

Michael was the first to break the amazed silence. 'My God, Alice! That was incredible!'

Ellie exhaled, then looked back to the computer, where Jake Kennedy was selecting Flowers. Season? Summer. Variety? He looked helplessly at Ellie, who told him to click on Roses.

An exquisite blood-red bloom came into focus, being replaced by the eruption of a dazzling scarlet glare.

'Alice, this is phenomenal. That is exactly as it seemed when I first saw auras.' Ellie was shell-shocked. She left the young man who was glued to the machine, and went over to the sofa and flopped down.

Alice joined her and whispered, 'I'm sorry, darling. I really wanted you to see this first, but what with the problems with Jake . . .'

'It's fine. It's just taken my breath away, that's all.'

'You have only seen the bare bones of the programme. It is very sophisticated. I can set it at any stage of progression through the medication regime. It is set on "initial sight after trauma" at present, which is obviously the brightest. I can tone it down to whatever state the patient is in at that moment. But, listen to the best of all, Gordon is perfecting a headset that, when worn by a patient, will allow me to "see" exactly what they are "seeing". We simply connect you through the box, bit like a digital camera, and whatever you look at comes up on the monitor! With any luck, he could be finished by the weekend, and he is going to have it couriered down to the Centre straightaway. I've tried his first model and I thought that was perfect. Gordon, however, disagreed. "A few more weeks and it's all yours, lassie, ye'll just have to be patient!"'

Alice stretched and leaned back. 'The great thing about this is the fact that I can monitor the exact effect the medication is having on the auric vision. Even as it is now, I can set the brilliance at different levels until it matches what the patient is seeing. I can then ascertain how, and at what rate, the drugs are working.'

'Why didn't you tell me about all this? It is a positive miracle machine!'

'To be honest, I never really believed it would work. Not like this, at any rate. Then I never heard from Gordon for weeks on end. I thought he had lost interest or was having problems. Finally, I get a call to say would I care to pop up to Inverness for a test drive! When I get there, he presents me with a fait accompli, and he is three quarters of the way through engineering the virtual reality set-up. That's where I went on the weekend you were having a girlie break with Marie and Wendy.'

'You sneaky devil! And there was me feeling guilty that we were being pampered, while you were slaving over a hot operating theatre!'

'Well, it was supposed to be a surprise, but it all went a bit pear-shaped, didn't it?'

Ellie shook her head. 'I think it's incredible. Tell me more at dinner tonight. You are staying, aren't you?'

'If it's okay with you, I'll be here for a while. I can't wander too far from him at the moment, can I?'

They looked at Jake Kennedy, still tapping keys and moving the mouse determinedly. Hunched over the computer, he looked almost possessed by the programme.

'Perhaps we could use your AZSEE to run a little experiment, Alice? I'm sure Jake's auric sight varies at different times. It certainly is nothing like mine or Michael's, although Michael's visions of auras are slightly different to mine anyway.'

'It can't vary, Ellie. Unless he is mucking around with his prescribed doses.' Alice looked aghast.

'Honestly. I've spoken to him on several occasions and I'm certain it changes, and that's nothing to do with tiredness or time of taking medication. Plus, Mrs Shaw dishes out the pills, and she is utterly conscientious about them, so he can't be messing around with them.'

'We'll talk later. It's time for Mr Square Eyes to have a rest. And I need to start running these blasted drug checks.'

The others, except for Michael, left, and Alice set about closing down the programme.

'When you have done that, my friend,' said Michael, 'I'll introduce you to your new consulting suite! Hardly the Ritz, but it's a pleasant room, with a view over the back of the property. It's nice and quiet, and by the look of all that paperwork, I think it may suit you down to the ground!'

CHAPTER NINE

It was nearly midnight when Ellie heard the Range Rover pull up outside. She had stayed at the Centre with Alice until about nine o'clock, then driven back to Compton to get something together for them to eat. Alice had existed on cups of strong black coffee, refusing even a sandwich, until she had exhausted every avenue to find the suspected fault with the medication programme.

She looked drained and gaunt as she stepped through the door, and into Ellie's arms.

'No luck?' Ellia whispered.

Alice hugged her tightly, and sighed. 'Nothing. Nothing at all.'

A large tumbler of whisky and dry ginger stood waiting for her on the table, and Ellie saw Alice's eyes wander to it and a flicker of desperation pass across her face.

Ellie passed her the glass. 'Come on, you've earned it.'

'Problem is, I *need* it.' She drank deeply, closing her eyes for a second, then letting out another long sigh.

Ellie pulled a face. 'After today, I'm not surprised you need a drink, sweetheart. I'm damn sure I did. I came in, threw my bag on the floor, hung up my coat, hugged the boys, and tore open the drinks' cupboard door like a mad woman!'

She served up their late supper, and they sat together in the cosy kitchen and tried to make some sense of Jake Kennedy's problem. It was really too late to eat, but the comforting heat from the Aga and the warmth from the scotch relaxed them and they realised they were both famished. Ellie had made a pasta dish, and served it with hot ciabatta bread and a green salad. It was not long before they were staring at two empty bowls and a few stray crumbs, all that was left of the loaf. They pulled their chairs over to the big old cooker and sat either side, with the dogs at their feet, the picture of latter day, rural domestic bliss. Nursing the remains of their drinks, their thoughts returned to Jake.

'So, what now?' asked Ellie.

'Search me. Unless he has some underlying, and previously undetected, medical condition that is affecting him. But if that were the case, I'm sure it would have shown up in the tests. I really don't know where to go from here.'

'Michael said that Maureen had kept a sort of diary regarding his mood and diet and so on. Did she show you?' asked Ellie.

'Yes. I went through it with her, and I've asked her to continue with it in as much detail as possible, but up to now, it shows very little to help. Apparently, Michael has asked Callum to do a report on him as well. He has requested that he shadow him, spend all the time he can with him, then make copious notes and observations. Something might show up. Please God that it does.'

Ellie hated to see Alice so despondent. Sometimes she wished she were not such a loner where work was concerned. An assistant would be a great asset at a time like this. Another brain, someone else to bounce ideas off. 'Oh, Alice, I really feel for you. Everything else is going so well, especially AZSEE. Then you get a setback like this. I know you'll sort it out; you're not the type to do otherwise, but it's so very frustrating!' She paused for a moment, her voice changing its tone. 'Did you hear the late news on the car radio? Those murders? At least our problems are surmountable. Heaven knows what those poor parents are going through right now. It kind of puts things into perspective.'

Alice visibly stiffened, and Ellie suddenly realised she was thinking about what had happened to her during the last spate of murders. The mention of the word murder seemed to turn Alice's blood to ice.

'Er, no, I had a CD playing, sweetheart.'

Being very aware that Alice did not want to discuss it, Ellie simply said that some children had apparently been killed when their teacher had some kind of brainstorm and attacked them. She then went on to ask what time Alice wanted to get back to the Centre the next day.

The relief was obvious, and Ellie was left wondering why Alice was still so raw, when she believed that she herself had moved on from that horrendous time in the past.

Alice's presence next to her that night was wonderfully sleep inducing. She felt herself slipping gently into slumber with arms wrapped tightly around her. Her last thought was that sometime tomorrow she must phone Wendy. She had the awful feeling that those murders may have taken place on her patch. If she was having to deal with something as traumatic as that, the young police sergeant may just need an understanding friend to chat to.

* * *

A scream echoed through the deserted halls of the Cavendish-Meyer Clinic.

It was loud enough to awaken Michael, who was deeply ensconced in his 12.5 tog duvet in his apartment. For a moment he wondered if he had dreamed it, but he suddenly thought of their only resident, and hurriedly pulled on his dressing gown and slippers.

On the second-floor landing, he found Maureen Shaw, kneeling over the collapsed body of Jake Kennedy.

'He was sleepwalking, Professor. He had another night-mare. I heard him talking to himself, then he started to get very agitated and let out that awful scream; it turned my stomach to hear it! Next thing he ran out here and fell in a dead faint.' She gently held her hand to his forehead.

'He's coming round, but he's burning up. Can you help me get him back to bed?'

Half carrying, half dragging him, they got him back to his room and Maureen pulled the warm duvet over his shaking body.

'I don't know what to make of this. He's shivering like he's frozen, and dripping in perspiration at the same time. I had better give Dr Cross a ring. Would you stay with him while I go back to my room and call her?'

Michael went and got a flannel to sponge the young man's dripping face. He then sat quietly with him and 'tuned in' to his aura.

Michael's gift of seeing auras had been with him since birth — a natural gift. He always said, in a matter-of-fact way, that some people were born left-handed, some could naturally play musical instruments, or draw or paint. He could see auras, no big deal.

He gazed down at the sleeping form of Jake and was at a loss to know what he was looking at. Auras, when healthy, sprung out from the body in bright rainbow hues. They formed a corona of light around the human outline. There were often gaps in places where there was injury or disease. Sometimes illness or low spirits made the auras dull or depleted. He would simplify his way of healing by saying that it involved putting the colour back.

As he sat on the edge of Jake's bed, gently sponging his forehead, he decided that in all his fifty-five years, he had never seen an aura like this.

He had looked at the man dozens of times since he had come to the Centre and seen nothing he would not have expected to see in a patient with a severe head injury . . . but tonight, well, the professor was totally nonplussed, and sincerely hoped Ellie would accompany Alice Cross when she came to see her patient. He could badly use another pair of auric eyes on this one.

A healthy aura could project some three feet from the body; Jake's was more creeping than projecting. It oozed around his frame in a peculiar fluid fashion that was more liquid than light. There were certainly colours there, but instead of being clear and individual, they were all mixed together like an overused artist's palette.

The door opened and Maureen Shaw reappeared. 'The doctor's on her way. How is he?'

'Sleeping. The temperature is subsiding, I think, but he is one poorly lad. I am wondering if he should not be back in hospital.'

'To be honest, he's getting better care here than in a big facility. Let's face it, it's one to one, round-the-clock care at the moment. I don't think he would benefit from going elsewhere.'

Michael nodded in agreement. 'Of course, you are right. I just wish I knew what we were dealing with.'

'You and me both.'

* * *

'The cafe opens at six. Sylvie will be most surprised to find that her first customers are Miss McEwan, Professor Seale, Dr Cross and Mrs Shaw,' said Michael.

As they all walked together down the corridor, Ellie slipped her arm through Alice's. 'You look dreadful.'

'Thanks a bunch! You don't look quite your usual well-tailored self, either.'

The normally elegant, but casual Ellie, glanced down at her strange choice of garb, and decided it was casual all the way today! It had, after all, been a bit of a rush to get dressed and back to Ripley to see Alice's patient. Four in the morning, when she didn't get to bed until one thirty, was never her best time for carefully selecting a stylish outfit.

They converged upon the cafe tables and waited for Sylvie to finish her early morning preparations for breakfasts.

As one, they felt strangely elated, and completely baffled by the puzzling Mr Kennedy.

'I did see what you meant, Michael. Just for a fleeting moment when we arrived, his aura was so weird. Then, well, it was a bit like a neon strip-light. It flickered a few times and was back to how it normally is. It was very strange, indeed.'

'Yes, and the minute his aura recovered, his temperature dropped, his shaking subsided, and he fell into a deep, peaceful sleep.' Michael stared at his hands, placed palms up in his lap, and allowed a bemused expression to cross his face. 'I wish you had seen him earlier, Ellie. It had improved somewhat when you arrived, although as you say, it was still odd.'

Alice yawned and shook her head. 'I can't see auras, Michael, but from what you and Mrs Shaw tell me, he was in a pretty poor state. Then, when I check him over an hour later, he has a normal pulse rate and his blood pressure is one twenty over eighty. He is sleeping like a baby right now, with no recollection of a nightmare or sleepwalking, or anything. I really don't get it.' She looked up and exclaimed. 'Ah, here's Sylvie. Let's get some breakfast inside us. My little grey cells need all the help they can get!'

Maureen finished first, and went back to stay with Jake until Callum Church came on duty. She commented as she left that she was going to have quite a changeover report for the young man this morning.

* * *

Callum raced into the staff room, apologising profusely that he was a bit late.

Ellie, who was arranging a reiki appointment for a new patient, tried to hide a smile as the young man took in his boss's new look. She thought he hid his amusement rather well. It was not every day that he saw her clad in jeans and a huge baggy sweatshirt, covered in paw prints and emblazoned with the legend, 'My dog walks all over me!' She had completed the ensemble with a pair of lilac Converse boots and on seeing the young nurse's incredulous glance to her feet, she seriously considered going home to change.

'Blimey! Miss McEwan. I think it should have been you, not me, out there just now! I've been trying to catch a stray dog. Every time I got within grabbing distance, he ran away. That's why I'm late.'

'You don't start for another half an hour, Callum. You're hardly what I'd call late.'

'Yes, well, I like to be a bit ahead of the day, it has a nasty habit of overtaking you if you let it!'

'Did you catch the dog?'

'No.'

'Was it here in the grounds?'

'Yes, that's why I thought I should try to get hold of it. When I parked my bike, it was sitting right behind me. Then we played this game of tag, halfway round the perimeter! The dog won! It finished up jumping the fence at the bottom of the gardens and running down the lane to meet two old ladies. Must have belonged to them, one of the old girls whistled to it . . . hell of a whistle! And it was off like a shot. They smiled and waved to me and walked on with both dogs.'

'Both dogs?'

'Oh yes, they had another one of the same kind. It was trotting next to the thin woman's heel. Really well-behaved animal.'

Ellie's hand flew to her mouth. She felt as though she had stopped breathing. A distant conversation washed into her ears: 'I'd know that whistle anywhere.' Then another: 'My dad says I'm fey, if you know what that means?'

'Miss McEwan? Are you okay?'

'What did the dog look like, Callum?' Her hand was clenched in front of her mouth and her throat was dry.

'Eh, well, nice looking dog, friendly, biggish, brown and white. Some kind of spaniel, I think. Nice floppy ears and a smile, if you understand what I mean?'

'Its ears, Callum. Did you notice anything about its ears?'

'Apart from being floppy. Not really, apart from the fact that one was brown and the other one was white. Hey, are you all right? You look as if you've seen a ghost!'

'Not exactly.' Ellie took in a deep breath, held it, and exhaled slowly. 'It's not me that's seen the ghost.'

CHAPTER TEN

Spring was gently giving way to the longer, warmer days of summer. It had been over a month since Jake's sleepwalking nightmare, and from that day, he had improved. Alice was completely baffled. She had neither changed nor implemented his medication, yet his readings were now what she considered normal, all things considered.

Jake Kennedy had opted to stay on at the Centre, but went home, or to stay with either his mother or his father, at the weekends. His condition had unnerved him, and he liked the company at the C-M. Alice kept a regular check on him and was starting to relax a little, thinking that his strange episode must have been some kind of glitch due to starting the treatment sooner than she had wanted.

She was delighted to receive the headset from Gordon, and before using it on her patients, she spent long hours working with Ellie, to perfect her expertise with the uses and capabilities of AZSEE.

She had also been recognised by a particular group of neurologists, who until recently had considered her work a bit avant-garde. This, to the lay person, might not seem too important, but to Alice, it was one of the high spots of her career. This notable group of the higher echelon were considered to make or break young researchers and scientists. The fact that they had chosen to recognise her publicly, and that she had been asked to speak at a brain trauma conference was, more or less, her seal of approval for greater things.

Azimah Syndrome patients were being referred to her from all over the world, and from her first speech, there came requests to lecture and give talks in a dozen different locations.

Ellie had tentatively suggested she take on a partner, or at least another doctor with an interest in A.S. to help her. She was not sure about that at all. For some reason she was not ready to share her baby with someone else, and that was sad, because she did regret that her work was once again robbing her of time with Ellie.

Driving back from a symposium in Oxford, she felt so tired that she had to pull off the road and get herself a coffee in a service station. It was late and the big eating hall was all but empty. She watched a man slowly push a huge soft broom between the tables. He seemed to walk in a dream, turning the brush, this way and that, to collect discarded napkins and crisp packets.

She sipped the hot, tasteless liquid, and gazed around.

The cleaner had joined another man, a lorry driver by the look of him, and they both stared up at a big TV that sat on a wall-mounted shelf high above a planter of weary looking houseplants.

Together they shook their heads from side to side in joint disbelief at a late-night news bulletin.

Slowly, Alice stood up and walked to within earshot of the set.

'. . . said a police spokesman. We will bring you more of this as it comes in. This is Piers Harker for News Tonight, in London.' Before the screen changed, Alice saw a concerned looking, middle-aged reporter standing in a smart Central London street.

She returned to her seat and finished her coffee. Another disaster of some sort. She really did not want to know about it. Deep down, she always dreaded something else happening locally, and the police asking Ellie to help . . . as they had before.

She wished Ellie were with her now.

She walked slowly back to her 4x4, pulled on her jacket and gloomily began the last leg of her journey home. She wanted to go to Compton, she longed to climb into Ellie's soft, welcoming bed, but she had a meeting at the hospital early the next morning and she just did not have the energy to get up at the crack of dawn to get back to London.

Before she reached the outskirts of the city, she felt her eyes getting heavy again. She had seen too many crash victims in her line of work to risk an accident, so once more she pulled up, this time in a lay-by. All she wanted to do was get home, have a hot shower and go to bed. Not too much to ask, she thought.

'Shit! Shit! Shit!'

She got out of the vehicle and took big gulps of the cool night air. Reaching back into the cab, she located her case, and after fishing around in it for a moment or two, found a packet of fiery hot mints. She crunched a couple of them, stamped her feet in the dirty gutter and decided to try to make it home. Before she pulled away, she switched on the radio and turned the volume up high. For the first time she was beginning to think that Ellie may have a point about getting some help. This journey was a nightmare and she knew the more she was in demand, the worse it was going to get.

She managed to get to within a quarter of a mile of home before the late-night DJ butted in with the news bulletin. Alice reached for the OFF switch, but needed both hands to negotiate a roundabout . . . so, as she finally drew up to the cobbled mews, whether she wanted to or not, she found out why the cleaner and the truck driver were so incredulous.

She sighed audibly. Horrible as it was, at least it wouldn't involve Ellie.

* * *

The evening had been quiet and WDS Wendy Brown was taking full advantage of the unusually hushed room to catch up on some reports. Typing was not her forte and her mates would say that they could hear the keyboards shaking with terror when they knew she was heading for them. DCI Foreman and DI Leatham were deep in conversation in the Super's office, and apart from her pounding on the computer, the only sound was a murmur from the television in the mess room down the hall.

The last statement that she was transposing from her pocketbook was not going very well. She saved what she had done and stomped off to get herself a cup of tea. She needed a break from the bright monitor screen for a while. As she poured the boiling water onto her tea bag, she found herself drawn to the newsflash on the TV.

Three minutes later, she was knocking on Bob Foreman's door and feeling very worried indeed.

'I'm not sure I follow you, Wendy. I see the similarity, but how can there be a connection with a Surrey school teacher, and some do-gooder in a soup kitchen in the middle of London?'

'The thing is, sir, when we arrested Roderick Black for murdering those kids, I remembered another case that had been mentioned in the *Police Gazette*. It was a nurse, sir, a real live Florence Nightingale. Another saint, but this time she slashed a sweet, eighty-year-old woman to death with a scalpel. Now this thing tonight . . . a widow, who has spent every spare hour she has, not to mention every last penny she owned, trying to feed and find shelter for London's homeless. Suddenly, she smothers six of them in the beds that she provided! There has to be something, guv. Nice people don't kill the ones they love and care about.'

The two men looked at each other, then back to Wendy.

'It is odd, sir.' Jonathan Leatham bit his bottom lip. 'I must admit I haven't caught the details of this last one, but I read about the case of the nurse, umm, Lily someone. The thing is, I believe that she finished up a bit like our Mr Black.

He is sitting quietly in a padded cell repeating old country proverbs, over and over. She is also locked away somewhere, offering anyone who speaks to her a nice cup of tea. Nothing else, that is all she has said since the murder.'

'Do you know any more about tonight's deaths, sir?' Wendy enquired.

'Little more than you. The woman, Elizabeth Ryder, a widow, was found with a pillow in her hand, sitting on the bed of a dead girl. She had apparently turned her lounge into a shelter for the homeless. She had been providing dropouts with soup, sandwiches and a clean bed for the night for the last four or five years. Tonight, the routine was a bit different though. She had six Z-beds, you know, those beds that fold up and store away, in the room. All her "guests" came in at different times. As soon as each one settled down for the night, she smothered them. Simple as that. Then she turned them on their sides, pulled the duvets up high around their faces so they appeared to be asleep, and waited for the next one.'

'I see that old Craddock has got the case. Good bloke, used to be at Woking. Perhaps I'll give him a bell in the morning, see if there are any obvious similarities with our Mr Black's murderfest. But . . .' He glared at Wendy from under his heavy iron-grey brows. 'Don't hang by your eyelashes. This is too tenuous a link, and by the way, nice people do commit murder, especially if they are a sandwich short of a picnic. Have you finished my reports yet, Sergeant?'

'Almost, sir. I'm on the last one.'

'Tomorrow will do, as long as it's the crack of dawn. Now get yourself home, it's getting late.'

Wendy smiled at her boss. For all his growling and grumbling, she liked and respected him enormously.

'Thanks, boss. I was hoping to get home in time to give Ellie a bell. We are hoping to have a weekend away again next month. Her doctor's off at some conference in Norway, so we thought we'd rope in Marie Littlewood, and all bugger off somewhere swanky. Leave the men and the job behind for a few days!'

'Give her my best, Wendy. I don't see her very often, but I do think of her.'

'Me too,' added Jonathan. 'Oh, and can you ask her if the Cavendish-Meyer Centre has a resident hypnotherapist? If not, does she know one locally. A friend of mine has been advised to see one, and does not want to get some charlatan. He wants personal recommendation, and I don't blame him. I wouldn't want someone telling me to behave like a chicken every time someone said good morning to me.' Jonathan looked suspicious. 'To be honest, I don't think I'd like to be hypnotised at all.'

Wendy grinned. 'Me neither, but I'll ask her anyway. Night, sir. Night, Jon. See you tomorrow.'

* * *

As Alice was tied up with more commitments than Ellie believed she could handle on her own, she invited Michael down to Compton for the weekend. He jumped at the chance as he was no longer required to be on hand at the clinic. Maureen Shaw had got their new residents well organised, and Jake had gone back to his flat until Monday.

Friday evening had been quiet. Both friends were tired after a long week at the ever more popular Centre, so they had cheated and bought a take-away from the local Chinese. The next morning, they went shopping in Guildford, and called in at the supermarket on the way back to Snug Cottage. They had invited Marie, her son, Daniel, and Wendy Brown for supper. Just because her partner was too busy to join her, Ellie had decided she was not going to stagnate. She admired and respected Alice's work, and there was no doubt in her mind that she loved her very much. But there was no way she was going to put her own life on hold, while she waited for her to either come to her senses and employ some help . . . or burn out. She sincerely hoped it would not be the latter, but after their last conversation, she wasn't too sure which way it would go. She had assured her that the Trust would adequately fund another full-time wage, but still she prevaricated. It had come to a point where Ellie was loath to mention how exhausted Alice looked, or how little she saw of her now. She knew that she still loved her, and that made it worse. She really didn't want to make her feel even more guilty than she already did, but she was very aware that one day they would have to face some life-changing decisions. She was prepared to let things ride for a bit longer, and would just keep a careful eye on the situation, and not let events spiral out of control.

'Mind if I root around in the library?' Michael's voice filtered into the kitchen and dispelled her worrying thoughts.

'Be my guest. I'll join you as soon as I've finished out here.'

'Are you sure I can't help you, my little culinary gem?'

'All under control, thank you. You're the guest tonight, remember.' Ellie squeezed lemon juice over the avocado starters, covered them and put them in the fridge. She loved cooking and was saddened that the days of dinner parties seemed to have been relegated to the 1970s and '80s. Tonight was fun. She had prepared a real feast with a starter, a small fish course, a homemade sorbet, main course, dessert and a fancy cheeseboard. Initially she'd thought they should eat in the dining room, the least used room in the house, but on reflection she'd chosen to eat in the kitchen. Everyone who came to Snug Cottage loved to sit around the old pine table for their meals. It was the embodiment of the heart of the country home. The Aga not only cooked very well; it gave off constant warmth, and although summer was on its way, the evenings were still chilly.

Tonight, Ellie had opted for lighting the oil lamps and having flowers and candles on the table. Having spent most of her working life as a florist, the one thing she could provide was a beautifully arranged dining table.

Making sure everything was ready to go, and the things that were already prepared were well out of reach of a spaniel's nose or paw, she took off her apron and went to join Michael in the library.

'Is it too early for a small reviver, Professor?'

'Oh, I think the sun is well over the yardarm, my dear. Mine's a scotch.'

They laughed and Ellie went to mix some drinks.

'They'll be here in about half an hour.' She handed Michael his whisky and sipped her dry martini. 'I'm looking forward to seeing Wendy. We keep in touch regularly by phone, but it's nice to have an evening together with friends. I hope she's okay, Michael. It was her station that had to deal with that dreadful murder of all those kiddies. I keep meaning to ring Bob Foreman, it must have been terrible for him. If you remember, he and Rosie have three children, and for all his severe outward appearance, you know what he's like.'

'I'm sure they're fine, Ellie. It's their job, unfortunately. Police work covers a lot more than sorting out petty theft and traffic violations, doesn't it? Some of it is rather grim, I'm afraid. The bit we saw was enough to last me a lifetime.'

'Yes, I think that's why I'm a bit reticent about ringing the superintendent. I'm afraid he might want me to resume my post as the aura detective again. That team were a great bunch to work with but, if I had the choice, I'd give it a miss, if there were a next time.'

'I don't blame you.'

They both took a long swallow from their glasses to prevent being dragged away into their private recollections.

'Ellie?' Michael sounded pensive.

'I don't like the sound of this, Michael.'

'I was wondering if anything else had happened since Callum's incident with the runaway dog?'

'Nothing definite, but he was sure he saw one of the two women with the dogs sitting in the orangery. He excused himself from the patient he was with, but when he went to speak to her, she had gone. He described the woman as tall and thin, smartly dressed in a purple suit with a lavender-coloured blouse and a gentle smile. No prizes for guessing that one!'

'Vera?'

'Vera.'

'That boy is very sensitive, isn't he?'

'Unbelievably so. I get the weirdest feelings when I'm around him. Sometimes it's as if he is surrounded by spirit forms. The very air about him seems full of movement. Yet there is nothing to see, not even a disassociated aura, you know, the way I used to "see" Vera and Carole — a sort of misty coloured mass. I don't think he is aware just how extra-sensory he is. His dad jokes with him, says he is "fey" and he must have fairy blood in him.'

Michael looked seriously at her. 'You know, I don't like that word. People use it to mean elfin-like or, as you said, fairy-like. It can mean whimsical, or eccentric, or someone who is able to see into the future. All that is true, but it is really derived from the Old English word, *faege,* which has a far more sinister meaning. They say that those who are fey are . . .' Michael was cut short by the ringing of the doorbell.

'Tell me later, Michael. Go get the door for me, would you? I have to put the grill on.'

* * *

It was nearly ten o'clock by the time they came to the cheeseboard, and no one wanted to disturb it. It looked so pretty. Ellie had decorated the flat platter with several different cheeses of assorted colours and textures. They were laid in beds of leaves, and interspersed with clusters of green and black grapes. Brightly coloured nasturtium heads finished the picture, with their glorious red, orange and yellow faces complementing the rich cheeses.

'It's a work of art!' whispered Daniel reverently.

They all stared at the food, no one wanting to be the first to desecrate the arrangement.

To Michael, it was a stark reminder of Ellie's past and everything that she had left behind so she could use her incredible diagnostic gift, and create the Cavendish-Meyer Centre for Healing.

'For heaven's sake! It's only a cheeseboard!' Ellie plunged a curved knife into a piece of red Leicester, plucked a few grapes from the plate and helped herself to a water biscuit.

The others followed suit.

The conversation followed the usual pattern of general chitchat, and it was not until several bottles of wine had disappeared that any serious topics were broached.

They talked about Daniel's son, Christopher. His wife had been true to her word, and the little boy had been to stay with his father and his grandma and grandpa several times already. The man looked down at his plate and quietly stated that he did not dare even to think further than tomorrow as to the boy's future, and what part he would be allowed to play in it. Marie declared she believed he was doing the right thing by not hounding his neurotic ex-wife. She considered that the only way to deal with Della was 'softly, softly, catchee monkey'. Any sudden moves and she could take off like a rocket.

Ellie asked Daniel if he would like to bring his son to lunch next time he was staying; the little lad would probably enjoy playing with the dogs.

'He would love that. I've told him all about them. He knows all their names, and he's dying to see them. Thanks, Ellie, that would be great.'

Unconsciously, she checked into his aura. The colours were brighter than she had ever seen them. The man was healing, both physically and mentally. When she pulled herself away from Daniel's corona, she heard Marie asking Wendy whether she'd had any dealings with the 'Teacher in the Woods' murders. For a moment Ellie's attention was back with Daniel, concerned that having lost his own baby daughter, he could react badly to talk of death, especially the death of children. She was relieved to see that there was no response other than a normal one.

The papers and the media had covered the murder extensively, and obviously Wendy had seen no reason not to admit to her friends that she had been involved in a minor capacity. Ellie already knew. They had talked about it recently, the sergeant being aware that she was safe to do so, as having already worked alongside the police team in the past, Ellie would have signed the Official Secrets Act.

They discussed the horrors of life for a while. Then Michael asked if anyone had come up with a reason for the apparently 'perfect' teacher doing something that was totally alien to his nature.

Wendy placed her knife back on her plate. 'He's not the only one acting out of character. There are two other cases you may have read about in the papers over the last couple of months. One only a few days ago.'

'Oh, yes! The woman who killed those youngsters in the shelter! That was not exactly rational, was it?' Marie had seen it on television.

'You say there was another one, Wendy?' Michael peered over the rims of his glasses.

Daniel interrupted. 'I think I read about the other one. It was a hospital nurse, wasn't it?'

Wendy nodded. 'Another angel. Another inexplicable killing.'

The five friends spent the next fifteen minutes hunting for plausible reasons for simple, good folk turning into mass murderers. In the manner of people who had imbibed a little too much alcohol, their ideas became more and more fanciful. Wendy, the only teetotaller, sat back and listened with amusement to the wild suggestions, wondering what her boss would say if she put some of them forward.

'Well, I think they were members of a cult!' exclaimed Marie.

'Great cult, Mum. One that only recruits really nice, honest souls, convinces them to bump off the most important people in their lives, and then insists they go loony-tunes so that they spend the rest of their days in a nut house! Not convinced!'

'Okay, oh-brilliant-son-of-mine! What's your theory?'

Daniel thought for a minute. 'They have all ingested something. A drug? Not intentionally, of course.' He paused.

'No, someone has given them something. Bit like those nutters who went round putting powdered glass in baby food. I reckon someone has introduced some chemical into the food chain that changes personalities. So' — he twisted the imaginary ends of a Poirot-style moustache and continued — 'my friends, we are looking for a madman, or woman, sorry, a mad-person, who is actually responsible for the deaths of all the victims so far. Our nurse, our teacher, and our do-gooder are not to blame; they are also victims. We are looking for just one killer. I rest my case.'

Ellie watched Wendy's expression and knew exactly what she was thinking. For all the party game theorising on the murders most 'orrid, Daniel might well have a point. She determined to have a private word with her detective friend before she left.

The party broke up at eleven and Ellie asked Wendy if she would like to help her out to the orchard with the dogs. As the spaniels nosed around the trees looking for the perfect spot upon which to pee, the two women linked arms and discussed Dan Littlewood's hypothesis.

'Forget the food chain, do you think it's possible that someone else is to blame for what they did? That somehow they were influenced or drugged by someone? That would mean they didn't have to know each other, the only common denominator that linked them and their actions is Mr or Ms X, our unknown mad-person.'

'It's possible, Ellie, but how on earth could he, or she, have done it? Are there drugs that could make you kill?'

'I should think so. Shall I ask Alice when she calls?'

'Please. I don't want to get laughed off the Force if I submit this without having done some pretty substantial research. When will you speak to her?'

'She may call tonight. I told her to ring about midnight, if she was still awake. If not, I'll ring her tomorrow morning, then I'll phone you, okay?'

'Thanks, Ellie. I'll wait to hear from you, then I'll try to put some sort of report together to see what the DCI thinks.

He sends his best wishes, by the way, and Jon Leatham, too. Oh, he wants to know if you have a hypnotherapist at the Centre?'

'Yes, we do. A good one. Does Jon need help with something?'

'No. It's a friend of his who's been told to see one, no idea why, but he's frightened he might pick a bad one if he goes via the Yellow Pages!'

'Quite right! Do you know, almost anyone can set up as a hypnotherapist in this country? Our chap came from the Psychology Department of the Sheffield Hospital with an impressive training behind him. Get Jon or his friend to ring me at the Centre, and I'll get him fitted in with Dr Ambrose.'

'Will do. Thanks for a lovely evening, Ellie. We'll talk tomorrow, and we'll make definite plans for our weekend away.'

They herded up the dogs and Wendy left, waving out of the window of her old Escort.

As Ellie locked the door, she found Michael sitting alone at the table. 'What a very odd thing!'

'What's up, Michael?' Ellie felt a slight shiver of apprehension as she noted the look on her friend's face.

'Well, you all went out, so I loaded the dishwasher for you, put the pans away, and wrapped the leftover cheese in cling film. I wiped the table down and put the vase of flowers in the centre, just like you do.' He paused, his head tilted to one side. 'I went over to the windowsill to turn off the paraffin lamp, and when I went back to the table, I found this. It was propped up next to the flowers.'

Ellie stared down at the paperback book clasped in his hand, and noted the twenties style cover design. 'It's a Virginia Woolf, isn't it?'

The professor fixed his friend with a direct stare. '*Orlando*, to be precise.'

CHAPTER ELEVEN

The limey clusters of leaves on the trees around the courtyard were edged with silver droplets of morning dew. The sky was light and clear, although the sun had yet to materialise. The damp grass beneath her feet looked green and fresh with early summer growth. Ellie loved the peace of the garden at this hour.

Okay, it was Sunday, which normally necessitated a lie-in, but she had four dogs with bladders that only took them to six in the morning. Ten past six meant pathetic whimpers. Quarter past six gave you the sharp, intermittent bark. Anything over six twenty, and you were in for the full howl: a choral rendition for a quartet, to be sung fortissimo.

It really was not a problem. Ellie got to see the best of the day, and the boys, relieved, got a biscuit and returned to their snoozing for another couple of hours.

Before she realised it, the dogs had left the orchard and she was standing alone, breathing in the cool morning air.

Feeling a little foolish, and sincerely grateful that no neighbours overlooked the property to see her in her night-dress, she turned and made to follow her dogs. As she reached the archway, she heard the hollow, melodic sounds of Vera's wind chimes.

She stopped still. It wasn't windy.

She slowly turned to see the dull, silvery tubes thrashing around as if caught in a high wind, and beneath the tree she saw a swirling mist. A mist of soft lilac and Aegean blue.

The wind, which belonged to her garden alone, ruffled her hair and blew her nightdress in swirls around her legs. It increased in intensity and she heard indistinct words in its breathiness.

She stood, like a Greek statue, immobile except for the frail material that blossomed and danced around her. She strained her ears to hear, to make sense of the sounds.

'Ellie. He needs you.'

'Who needs me?' she cried out loud. 'Carole! Vera! Who needs me?'

The wind was dropping.

'Carole! Please!'

A whisper drifted through the orchard. 'So hard . . . to reach you. Too hard . . .'

The morning returned to bright stillness. Digger gently touched his mistress with his paw. Ellie jumped. The little dog wagged his tail, returned to the kitchen door and sat waiting for her.

It had been nice to know that his old mistresses had been out in the orchard again, but right now he needed a biscuit.

* * *

At breakfast Ellie told Michael what had happened that morning.

He listened thoughtfully. 'I had odd dreams again. Very disjointed, I can't remember much now. I do recall that Carole and Vera featured heavily. At some point I recall having that Virginia Woolf book thrust at me, and someone, Carole, I think, shouting at me.' He took a mouthful of cornflakes and chewed them slowly. 'It's a long while since I felt as confused as this. It is quite plain that they're desperate to tell us something. We have to fathom out who "He" is, and why he needs your help in particular. Have you got a sheet of paper?'

Ellie put her spoon down and went to the dresser.

'Write down all the men in your life at present. We'll look at each of them, and see if anyone stands out as being in some kind of trouble.'

Taking a deep breath, she listed everyone she could think of. 'That's about it, I think. Some of them are not particularly close but, who knows . . .'

'Read them out.'

'Well, there's you, of course.'

'Right. Do I need your help? Probably, with the Centre certainly, but there is nothing disastrous going on there, only run of the mill administration problems and small glitches. No, I do not think it's me. Go on.'

'Daniel.'

'Ah, now he could be a possibility. Put a star against him. He's had mega problems in the past. Maybe there's an agenda there that we don't know about.'

'He is so much better, Michael. I was watching him last night. His aura is almost healed. I don't actually think it is him, but I'll keep an open mind. Next is Scrubbs.'

Neither could come up with anything regarding the gardener or his wife.

'How about Callum? He is frighteningly clairvoyant and doesn't really know it. Maybe it has something to do with him, after all. He has seen both Carole and Vera, and Orlando, of course,' mused Michael.

'Another star there, you could be right. There's a lot going on around that lad. He is a definite possibility. And Jake Kennedy has been a major player in our lives recently.'

Michael nodded slowly. 'He was my first choice to be honest. He does have A.S. and you were trying to help him. Perhaps he needs you to help him in a way the drugs can't. Certainly worth pursuing. Anyone else?'

They spent the next few minutes listing some of the therapists she worked with regularly. None of them had any problems they knew of, and none of them had been acting in any way stressed or preoccupied.

Last on her list was Phil McEwan, her brother.

'Frankly, Michael, he's a possible, too. Carole liked him and she knew he had a lot of health problems. I will phone him later today and check on him. I haven't heard from him for about a fortnight, I should ring anyway.'

'Is that it?'

'Think so.' As Ellie laid the pen across the pad, a heavy cast iron pan crashed to the floor from its hook on the wall, shattering one of the quarry tiles, and practically giving Michael a heart attack.

'Good God!'

Ellie picked up the old skillet and stared up to the brass hook where it had hung in a row with several other saucepans and frying pans. The hook was still firmly attached to the wall. She turned the pan around in her hands; there was a hole through the iron handle — a solid metal ring. She looked helplessly at her friend, who was feverishly checking his pulse.

'Ellie,' he said firmly, 'I think you may have missed someone off your list!'

She hooked the pan back up on the wall. 'Well! They could try being a bit more subtle with their reminders!' She swept up the broken pieces of tile and made a mental note to ask Scrubbs to get it fixed.

Back at the table, she once again lifted the pen. 'Right. Okay. Now, I'm doing my best, so if I don't get it right first time, I would be glad of just a gentle nudge, not have the kitchen demolished!'

The professor made a pot of tea and they sat together, both waiting for the next flurry of culinary equipment if they could not find the right man.

Sipping from his mug, the steam misting his glasses, Michael slowly let out a long, 'Ahhh . . .'

It was definitely a 'bad news, ahhh', not a 'gosh, this tea's good, ahhh', so Ellie did not hurry to ask him what he had thought of.

Looking sheepishly over his half glasses at her, he finished his sentence. 'What would you say if I told you I think it may be Detective Chief Inspector Bob Foreman who needs you?'

'Shit, probably. But you're not going to say that, are you?'

'Yes, I am.'

'Shit.'

A warmth enveloped the kitchen. Everywhere was suffused in a golden glow, as if the room had been lit up with shafts of sunlight.

The professor blinked myopically. 'Well, that's infinitely better than the cookware missile, I must say. So, Ellie, I think your wish to give up your career as the aura detective might have to go on hold.'

'Oh hell! Just when I thought it was safe to go back into the police station!' She placed her mug on the table and slumped forward, head in hands. 'I think, if I'm honest, I could have arrived at this conclusion some time ago. I just didn't want to.'

'Well, no one in their right mind would blame you if you walked away from this. Your last dealings with the criminal fraternity were not exactly pleasant.'

For a while both friends sat in silence, their minds going over individual aspects of the dreadful Surrey murders of the previous year.

After a time, Ellie leaned back in her chair and stretched. 'Like it or not, I cannot ignore all these messages from Carole and Vera. Apart from genuinely respecting their wishes, I don't want to see Snug Cottage demolished around us!'

Michael smiled. 'Quite so. A smashed quarry tile is one thing, but heaven knows what they are capable of if you simply refuse to help!'

'I'll err on the side of caution and make some calls. Pour us another mug of tea, Michael, and I'll ring Alice as she never phoned last night, about personality influencing drugs, then Wendy to fill her in on what Alice says, and finally Bob Foreman . . . to offer my services, if he really, really needs me.'

She fetched a notepad and a pen, brought the telephone back to the table, and sitting down, stared long and hard at it before she reluctantly lifted the receiver.

All she could think about was what on earth Alice was going to say when she told her of her decision to get involved once again. As it happened, she was not about to find out. The call was not answered until the tenth ring and a sleepy voice mumbled back to her cheerful 'Good morning, sweetheart. How's my favourite doctor, today?'

'Oh, Ellie? God! What's the time? Oh no, I should have left by now! Damn and blast, I . . .'

'Alice! It's Sunday, darling . . .'

'I know, I know, but I have to get back to the hospital. There are some important test results coming in from abroad and I said I would be there when they arrived. Look, Ellie, I'm sorry, I'll ring you from work, as soon as I've got these reports through. I really must fly . . .'

'Okay, okay! Just one thing before you hang up. Wendy has asked me a medical question. Are there any drugs that could make someone act completely out of character? Make them do things that are totally against their normal beliefs or ideals?'

'Of course there are.' Alice sounded irritated, as if Ellie were wasting her precious time over something she should already know. 'You only have to look at all the weird things that used to happen back in the sixties with the hallucinogenic drugs. People were trying to fly off the tops of tall buildings and God knows what else. If someone has a predisposition to a certain medication it can precipitate a psychosis, no problem.'

Ellie could hear her opening drawers and obviously trying to pull clothes on while she spoke to her.

'They can spark off any number of major paranoid states. Ellie, I'm sorry but I really don't have time for this, I have to go. We'll speak later, I promise.' The old Alice crept back into her voice. 'I love you, and I'm really sorry to dash away like this. I'll make it up to you, honest.'

The line went dead, and left Ellie staring thoughtfully at the silent receiver. Burnout seemed to be creeping closer and closer, day by day, hour by hour. The thought crossed her mind that not too much more time would pass before she and her darling doctor would be having a very serious talk indeed.

'Anything wrong?' The professor peered at her over his half glasses.

'Oh, not really. She's just overslept and is late for some foreign tests being sent into the hospital this morning. She sounded exhausted, and short tempered as well, not like Alice. Well, not like the Alice we both know and love!'

Ellie's fingers unconsciously rubbed the long scoop scar on her forehead.

Michael smiled gently at her. 'I think we might have to find a way to slow your young woman down, before God does. If we don't listen to our bodies when they send us helpful, warning communiques, then they often get rather more unsubtle, if you know what I mean?'

'Yes. Rather like the medical version of the iron pan on the tiled floor!'

'Exactly, and we do not want that for our heroine, do we?'

'Oh Michael, I just don't know how to get through to her. I have tried, really I have. She just doesn't want to know.'

'Would you like me to have a word? I'm not sure I can do any better than you, but I'll give it a try if you would like?'

'Please, Michael. She may well listen to you. I'd appreciate your help, do talk to her, whenever you think the time is right, and you have my full permission to go for the jugular! Just make the idiot see some sense. I really preferred the starving young doctor with a burning ambition and little else to this stressed out and professionally sort after consultant! Well, I suppose worrying about her won't do any good, so I will proceed with my calls before our spirit friends get impatient with me and resume destroying the cottage.'

For a while they discussed the frightening effects that drugs can have on unsuspecting human beings. The more they talked, the more she realised that there was a strong possibility Daniel had come up with a very plausible idea.

'When I was little more than a teenager,' Ellie recalled, 'I was put on some pills that really depressed me. I felt as though I was not in charge of my own thoughts. I was unbelievably bad tempered and I did not like myself one bit. It was odd, I could hear myself saying things and all the time I was thinking "this isn't me, that's not how I feel at all". Thank heaven my mum had a word with the doctor and they took me off them. I really understood after that, how youngsters finished up as suicide cases, and that was proper prescribed medication which was supposed to be helping me!'

Michael nodded in agreement.

'My wife was once put on some hormone pills of some description. She must have felt much the same way as you did, but she was much older than you were and soon realised that they were the cause of her feeling so awful. I can remember her now, tipping them down the loo and wishing goodbye to bad rubbish! Drugs don't always have the effect that people think they will. You hear of so many kids having "bad trips" and even dying because of one little tablet!'

As soon as he'd spoken, he remembered the boy who'd died in Ellie's car accident had taken Ecstasy tablets.

Ellie smiled ruefully at him. 'It's all right, Michael. I can cope with thinking about him now. Alice really did make me see sense over that.'

'Good. I'm glad. Now, how about getting on with your calls, or maybe you'd like to see the rest of the Le Creuset hit the floor?'

Laughing, she reached again for the telephone. 'Point taken! I'm on the case!'

Wendy was at home and not on duty until later in the day. She admitted that Daniel's idea had kept her awake for most of the night. It really made sense that these apparently perfect members of society had been got at in some way. 'Chemicals seem to be the favourite option. I just cannot come up with anything else that could affect them and make them do the uncharacteristic things that they have done.'

'I agree,' said Ellie. 'I'm just sorry I didn't get any further with Alice. She might have given us a bit more information on what kind of drug we should be looking for. Anyway, she will ring me later and I'll keep on at her, try to narrow things down a bit. Are you going to present this to Bob?'

'Yes, it won't hurt that my hypothesis is a bit hazy. The main thing to do is try to get him to agree that these are not isolated incidents, that we are looking for one murderer. Someone who has used these other poor souls for some undetermined purpose, just doing his, or her, dirty work, and there is my big problem! Motive! Why? Why kill a harmless and befuddled old lady? Why kill a bunch of school kids? Why murder a handful of penniless, homeless dropouts? Whatever way you look at it, it does not make sense!'

'In a way it makes it all the more possible that it is the same person. All the victims are ordinary folk, a cross section of society today. The elderly, the young and the poverty stricken. No villains, no rich racketeers, no underworld gang bosses, just real people.'

'Hmm, I suppose so. It's a very vague connection, but it is a connection of sorts. Anyway, I'll speak to the guv'nor when I get in this afternoon.'

Ellie took a deep breath and tentatively asked her friend if she thought DCI Foreman might like her to call in on him and maybe offer any help she could. Before she could finish, Wendy was almost shouting down the phone that she was sure he would be delighted to talk it over with her.

'God! He'd be over the moon, Ellie! Give him a ring, he's always going on about you and your gift. Even if you can't help with the investigation, he'd love to see you again.'

They talked for a little longer; then Ellie finally found the courage to ring the police officer.

His response to her was exactly as WDS Wendy Brown had prophesied, and within a matter of minutes, arrangements had been made for Bob to call on her at the clinic the next morning.

She hung up with a feeling of elation, and a feeling of dread, vying for precedence in her mind.

CHAPTER TWELVE

Callum Church sat in the orangery and stared unseeingly through the dark glass into the black night beyond.

He should have left hours ago. He was clad in his motorcycle leathers, ready for the road. His sinister black helmet lay on the floor at his feet. Pictures of Africa played like a film in the ebony panes on the great window before him. He could hear screams and cries, shouts and whimpering. His memory brought about the smell of destruction, of burning, of excrement and of blood. The hateful metallic cloying smell of blood.

He shivered. The boy who never felt the cold shook like a willow in a high wind. He gripped the worn leather riding gloves that lay in his lap and willed his teeth to stop chattering. Slowly the freezing air warmed around him and the dreadful smells were replaced by something so different that his senses had trouble recognising it. Flowers?

A heady perfume filled the orangery. The horrors of Rwanda faded and disappeared, leaving in their wake the image of a little boy with his father in a garden. The child was sitting on a seat, a huge bunch of purple and white lilacs lying at his feet. The child looked crestfallen and stared down at the flowers.

'I picked them for Mummy. I thought she'd love them, they are so beautiful, but old Mrs Bailey, the lady next door, said they are unlucky and they must never cross the threshold into the house!'

The man put his arm around the child's shoulders. 'Mrs Bailey may not want lilacs in her house, Callum, but your mother worships every flower that God has given us. Don't you worry, son, she will love them, and you are right, they are so beautiful.'

Callum could still remember his relief as his mother reached out for the bouquet. He could see her standing there smiling at him. He could see the love in her eyes, and he believed her when she told him how special he was. He saw her reflection in the shadowy glass. His mother, his lovely mother, but was it her? She seemed older. She still smiled, there was still love in her eyes, but it wasn't his mother.

He turned swiftly, but he was alone, and when he looked back, a blank windowpane met his startled stare. A warm breeze wafted around him; the scent of the flowers was still strong. She may not have been his mother, but he knew who she was, and she had dispelled his demons for a while, and for that he was grateful. He sighed and picked up his helmet. He was safe to ride home now.

* * *

Jake looked around his living room. His eyes were not focusing too well. It was not the syndrome; the lights were not dazzling him. He supposed it was just tiredness. He hardly slept when he was back in London, and he felt awful. The room made him feel sick. He had always been house-proud, but now, well, he hardly lived up to his reputation of being domesticated to the point of anal retention.

Cups and glasses sat on every surface and some lay discarded on the floor. A dark stain billowed over the cream carpet from an overturned wine goblet. Jake had no idea how long it had been there but there was no liquid left in the bowl of the glass, just a deep red, powdery deposit. Part of him was horror-struck at the damage to his pure wool floor covering and wanted desperately to get a bowl of warm water, a scrubbing brush and some carpet cleaner. But as it was, the usual lethargy washed over him and he simply continued with his apathetic appraisal of his home. There were pizza boxes, half covered with abandoned copies of the *Times* and *Horse and Hound*. Old packaging that had at one time held sandwiches, clustered around the waste bin. There was an unpleasant smell about the place and, even in his debilitated state, Jake knew he had to do something about the devastation that had been his smart Docklands bachelor pad. If he had had the energy, he would have cursed Ben to the ends of the earth. His so-called 'caretaker' had been partying for days. Then when Jake had arrived home for the weekend, he'd buggered off with his current woman, leaving his friend with the wreckage.

Knowing full well that he was no match for the job, Jake found his copy of the Yellow Pages stuffed under the sofa, and searched through cleaning contractors until he came across a local company. Expecting an answering machine as it was Sunday, the young man was surprised to find his call answered by a very chirpy chappy, who promised to pop round that evening and give him an estimate for a thorough spring clean.

When a suspicious Jake asked if there would be a Sunday call-out charge, the fellow laughed and promised that there would be no charge at all for the estimate, and as he had just taken over the franchise from a friend, he wanted to get all the new custom he could. That, and the fact that his mother-in-law was visiting that evening and he was glad of the excuse to escape!

Two hours later, the Cockney man, who introduced himself as Kev Jones, surveyed the flat and let out a long, low whistle. 'Blimey! Someone's been enjoying themselves!'

Jake sank down onto a chair and followed the fellow's incredulous eyes around the place. 'Dreadful, isn't it? And it wasn't even me that had all the fun!'

He gave a brief excuse for the state of the apartment and, without argument, happily accepted the man's quote to clean it up. Although Kev was not aware of it, he could have charged double and Jake would still have paid it. His second surprise came when the eager Mr Jones volunteered to make a start early the following morning. Jake wasn't too sure if he could cope with dawn, and they settled for nine thirty — a time that Jake still thought was the middle of the night, and Kev Jones thought was nearly lunchtime!

The arrangement suited Jake Kennedy perfectly. He would stay until the work was done, then have a car pick him up and take him back to his friends at the Surrey clinic. He wanted to see the doctor again. This awful fatigue couldn't be right. For a while he had felt great, so this lethargy was a puzzle. With his sight so much improved, he was sure he should be bouncing around by now, not having to gear himself up mentally and physically to do the simplest of tasks, like bathing or feeding himself. Food? When had he eaten last? He wasn't sure. As he hauled himself to his feet and made for the kitchen, he was interrupted by the ringing of the telephone.

'Jake? Look old chap, I'm really sorry about the mess!'

'Ben! So you bloody should be! It's that bad I've had to get a contract cleaner in to sort out your crap!'

'Sorry, really, but I really couldn't ignore Angela's needs. She was really hot for it, and you sort of took the edge off things by turning up like that! You know how it is, old fellow, I couldn't let my end down, now could I?'

'I'm sure you have no trouble keeping your end up wherever you are, Ben,' replied Jake wearily. 'But we really have to talk about you looking after this place properly. I can't let you stay if you leave it like this. It's a bloody health hazard, and I'm not up to caring for myself, yet alone farting around after you. I'm serious, Ben, do you understand?'

'Totally. Won't happen again, old fruit, I promise. In fact, by way of an apology, I've left you a little present. It's in the carved wooden box in your bedroom, so don't let your skivvies find it, for God's sake! Enjoy!'

With a soft laugh, Ben hung up and left Jake biting hard on his bottom lip.

* * *

Bob Foreman left the warmth of his bed, and his beloved Rosie's body, and lumbered into the kitchen. He boiled the kettle and popped a teabag into a mug. Sleep had not been his friend since the schoolteacher had butchered his pupils. His mind constantly returned to the bizarre case, and then on to the other strange deaths that had occurred of late. It was his private opinion that this may be the tip of a bloody iceberg. He prayed that, if that was the case, then the next incidents would take place somewhere other than in his manor.

He sipped the hot tea and thought about his call from Ellie McEwan.

Drawing his big towelling dressing gown tighter around his huge frame, he wondered why she had offered, once again, to put herself in the firing line on a murder case. Not that he didn't appreciate her suggestion to talk about the case. He smiled grimly to himself. There was not a single officer in his section that did not admire Ellie and her peculiar gift. No one who had worked with her ever belittled her, especially not if their guv'nor was around to hear it! He was looking forward to seeing her again and he'd already decided that he was going to ask her to meet Rod Black, their child killing teacher. Then, well, maybe he could arrange a trip to see Lily Frampton, and the do-gooder.

He sighed. Perhaps he should take it one step at a time. He was not yet too sure if his aura detective was really up to another dice with death. He placed the mug gently down on a coaster that sported a picture of Bart Simpson. The drink had felt warm as he swallowed it, but it did nothing to dispel the dreadful coldness settling in his gut. He had felt that iciness before, many times, and it did not lift until someone evil had been safely locked away, or resided in a more permanent kind of prison.

* * *

For the two human occupants of Snug Cottage, the night had brought little in the way of rest. While the dogs snored, twitched and dreamed of chasing rabbits in their sleep, Michael and Ellie tossed and turned in their beds and prayed that they would at least grab a few hours of slumber before dawn. At four, Michael gave up, pulled on his satin dressing gown and slippers, and went to the library. An uncomfortable feeling had settled on him as soon as he realised Ellie was going to pitch in with the Surrey Police and, hellfire, he had been the instigator. Discovering it was the detective chief inspector who required Ellie's help had been like finishing the *Times* crossword puzzle. He had a sense of accomplishment, the last piece in the jigsaw puzzle. Then after the euphoria came the realisation of what it meant; that Ellie would very possibly be in danger. No, very probably be in danger. He could have kicked himself. He had become so involved in the hunt for the mysterious 'He' as in 'He who needs your help', that he had completely disregarded the consequences.

He sat by the fire, idly pushing at a half-burnt log with the poker. As he turned it over, he noticed the tiniest hint of orange. Last evening, they had walked the dogs for miles along the surrounding country lanes and returned home, quite chilled. Although the central heating was still on low, Ellie had lit the fire and they had sat, each with a glass of single malt, and talked until well after eleven o'clock.

'I hope I haven't done the wrong thing, encouraging her to contact Bob Foreman.' As he spoke his thoughts out loud, there was a popping sound from the warm ashes and the charred log burst into bright flame.

Michael jerked back in his seat and dropped the iron poker on the stone fireplace. 'Oh, my!' He stared at the flames and saw that the brilliant orange tongues of fire were surrounded by a violet haze. As he gazed deeper into the light, he saw a soft blue light join the amethyst glow. Without taking his eyes from the crackling flames, he felt, rather than saw, two figures approach his chair. A firm but gentle hand touched his right shoulder. A moment later, slender fingers caressed his left shoulder. A soft and distant voice whispered in his ear, causing a shiver to run the length of his spine.

'Dear friend, you have done no wrong, just be there for her. But you must know this, there is a black heart among you with a deadly disease. He brings harm to the good, to the innocents.'

'Who? I don't understand! Who are you talking about?'

'Michael! Whatever's the matter? Who are you talking to?'

Michael stared around the room, his eyes wide, hunting for his spirit friends. All he saw was a worried looking Ellie, with bare feet and Alice's over-large robe draped around her shoulders.

'Ellie! It was Vera and Carole! They were warning me about someone. Someone who means harm. I think they mean the person who is causing all the deaths.' Michael pulled at his beard in the most distressing manner. 'Oh dear, they said that this black-hearted person was among us. Do you think that means we know him?'

'Hold on, hold on . . . what exactly did you hear?'

Michael told her what had happened and repeated as best as he could, word for word, what had been said. His friend stood thoughtfully, staring at the dying ashes of the fire.

'I don't know, of course, but I think they mean "among us" to mean walking this earth. Not someone we share our coffee break with.'

She stared down at the agitated professor. 'Come on, Michael. Let's get you a cup of tea. You look dreadful.'

'I'm frightened, Ellie.'

She smiled wanly at her friend. 'Come on, wasn't it you who told me never to be afraid of Carole and Vera, that they were here for us, to protect and help us?'

'Oh, don't misunderstand me. I could never be frightened of them. I am, however, frightened of what they told me. Very frightened indeed.'

The professor's body language verified that he was not lying, and although they both returned to their rooms to lie and wait for the morning, even the lightest sleep had been lost to them. By breakfast time, neither felt fit to face the coming day, yet alone the new week, but it was their own business, their own baby, and as the buck stopped with them, they showered, dressed and dutifully set off for Ripley.

CHAPTER THIRTEEN

Bob pulled the car over at the top of the drive to the clinic, and paused to admire the great house and splendid gardens. He liked Ripley. He was never quite sure whether it was a village or a small town. He supposed it to be a village — it certainly had the atmosphere. A plethora of antique shops littered the High Street, or the old A3 as most people called it. The restaurants were very good, the pubs friendly, and it boasted all the amenities to keep you ticking over. Goodness, there was even a small police station! Not open twenty-four hours admittedly, but a station, none the less.

The Centre lay about a mile away from the shops in a very beautiful spot indeed. The grounds had been tastefully designed by the previous owner, and were flanked on one side by the River Wey Navigation, and on the other by rolling meadows. The day was clear and bright and he could see the lovely old remains of Newark Priory beside the Abbey stream. Bob looked around him at the pastoral scene and decided you would be hard pushed to find a more peaceful setting for a clinic.

He waited a little longer before completing his journey to watch a narrow boat make its unhurried way down to Papercourt Lock. The boat was a vivid block of scarlet on the watery green landscape. Its sides were decorated with ornate gold and black script that reminded him of the signs on the rides and the roundabout at the Steam Fair that came to Leg of Mutton Green every year. Its name, *The Annabel Lee* was surrounded by a carefully painted garland of colourful flowers, and it even boasted two brightly decorated buckets of plants.

He sat quietly, a part of him envying the slow, unrushed way of life that the rivers and canals afforded. Another side of him was unashamedly proud of the stressful and pressured job he did. A job that helped to keep others safe and protect them on these byways, highways and waterways of England's green and pleasant land.

He watched as the canal boat chugged out of sight and thought about Ellie and Michael. He was pleased for them and sincerely wished them well with their venture. They were good people, caring and compassionate. They deserved everything that Carole Cavendish-Meyer had left them. He remembered the cantankerous and bombastic woman well. He thought that probably everyone who ever met her would remember her. She was not the sort of character you forgot. Bombastic maybe, but hell, he had never met a braver lady. He wondered what she would make of this latest spate of killings.

The big grey man sighed. She would most likely have more of a handle on things than he did, that was for sure. He felt lost on this one. It didn't follow any of the usual patterns. He had listened patiently to WDS Brown and had agreed, in essence, with what she was saying, but still the same question arose. Why? Nothing connected either the dead victims, or the brain-dead ones who they were loosely calling the murder suspects. It was ridiculous. They had most certainly committed the crimes but were, if you took one look at them, victims themselves.

Arriving at the Centre, Bob Foreman made his way up the steps to the big entrance doors and, as he passed through, he could still hear his boss's voice booming down the phone before he left. 'Bob, if what you suspect is true, if these random deaths are in some way connected, well, eh, we might have another one. The details are being couriered down and will be on your desk later this morning. It's not on our patch, it's another one for the Met, but I've asked that you be kept informed.'

The Super had paused.

'I don't need to tell you, Bob, but it won't be long before some bright hack puts two and two together and comes up with a nationwide panic. Scaremongering is the easiest thing in the world and then every nutter in the land will crawl out of the woodwork. They'll be blaming the food chain, the water supplies, the government, germ warfare, Saddam Hussein, Bin Laden, Elvis Presley and aliens. We need an explanation, and fast! Now, I don't ever remember saying this before, but for once in your life as a copper, budget is not the main issue. I want some answers and I am not too worried how you come by them. Just bloody get them!'

'Bob!'

The policeman towered over the owner of the voice. 'Ellie! Good to see you! Hey, you look great!' She grimaced and he noticed the tired eyes.

'I obviously look better than I feel! I've not been sleeping too well.'

'Tell me about it! We are back on the merry-go-round again, and my sleep patterns are the first thing to go out of the window.'

'Come on, DCI, let me drag you into my chambers and ply you with fresh coffee and doughnuts!'

'Best offer I've had this month!'

They linked arms and with unconcealed camaraderie, walked down the corridor to Ellie's office.

The doughnuts were delicious and, as Bob sipped his second cup of coffee, he realised how good it was to talk to someone who was nothing to do with the Force. Ellie's opinions were coming from a very different angle to the official one. They were still constructive, but allowed for the unknown, the unexpected, and as such did not rely on the hard facts a policeman deals with. Before Bob could get around to asking her whether she was up to a trip to visit Rod Black, Ellie leaned back in the comfortable sofa, looked him straight in the eyes and asked if it would help if she met the suspects, to see if their auras showed anything unusual or interesting.

'Thank you.' It was all he could think of saying. 'Yes, I would appreciate that very much.' He arranged to pick her up early the next day, and if it could be organised at such short notice, they would see all three suspects. There was no time to lose, and it might prove easier for Ellie to compare their auras if she could see them in a short space of time.

Before he left, Ellie gave him a brief tour of the clinic and made him promise to come back as soon as the case was over, so both she and Michael could treat him and Rosie to a day of pampering and being totally spoilt. He had always rather thought the health farm treatments were for rich, overweight housewives, and bored executives, but a glance at the steam rooms and the peaceful orangery made him consider taking her up on their offer. He would not even have to ask Rosie. She was always sighing pathetically over the adverts in the glossy magazines that offered weekends in country clubs or health spas. She would have her bathing costume out of the cupboard, and the kids packed off to her sister's, before he could blink! He imagined her delight when he told her of Michael and Ellie's kind offer, and made a point not to forget. Rosie deserved a break, and what better place.

As he drove back to the station, a heavy cloud began to descend on him. He had felt almost elated meeting his old friend again, and was looking forward to any insight that her talent could give to his inquiry. But the closer he got to the nick, the less he wanted to know how the latest victim, or indeed victims, had met their Maker. The Super had told him nothing about the Met's new murder and he wondered what on earth he would find when he finally got back to his desk.

* * *

PRIVATE AND CONFIDENTIAL
For the attention of DCI R. Foreman.

Bob,

Nasty one this. Don't know if it fits your criteria for the 'Slaying of the Innocents', but your superintendent has asked that we send you info on anything that could be connected.

For the last few days, we have been trying to locate a missing child: a boy, name of Charlie Keene. He's twelve, comes from a good home, and apparently loving family. One younger brother and an older sister who is married and lives in Leytonstone. The two boys and their mother and father live in a terraced house just off the Mile End Road in the East End.

There has been particular concern for him as he has to take regular medication after a tumour was removed from his brain about a year ago.

He has no record of ever being in trouble. A perfect child. Glowing school reports. A 'brave little angel' according to the doctors and nurses who looked after him at the time of his operation, idolised by his doting family.

Bob did not like the way this was going, and a knot was slowly forming in his stomach.

At seven o'clock yesterday morning we had a 999 call from a church in Bethnal Green. The curate had found a body in the crypt under the old building. The body of the priest, Father Dominic. The curate also found Charlie Keene. The boy, splashed from head to toe with, by then, dried blood, was sitting bolt upright on an old carved chair, quietly singing hymns. At his feet was a heavy, old rusting thurible. It was dented, bloodstained and bore traces of the priest's hair and other organic tissue. The priest had been dead for about twelve hours, so the boy, it would seem, had also been sitting there for all that time. He was stiff and cold when the paramedics got to him, but they said it was the creepiest thing to hear the crackly little voice, still singing a croaky version of 'All things bright and beautiful'.

All the reports that we have available are attached, and we will send copies of the others as we get them.

Bit of a twist on your blameless kids getting topped, when it's the angelic child who does the topping, don't you think?

Ring me at the station on Ext. 443 if you need anything more.

Len Craddock

Bob skimmed through the accompanying paperwork. There was little doubt in his mind that this was a connected death. It was not so much the murder itself, but the report from where the boy was being cared for. It declared the child was in a 'trance-like state' and had not uttered a single word since his apprehension. He simply sat, with his hands folded neatly in his lap, and softly sang hymns, repeatedly.

The detective shivered involuntarily at the picture in his mind of that scene in the crypt. Further statements filled in gaps that Len's initial and brief communication had not covered. Charlie often helped Father Dominic with odd jobs; the priest had been a family friend for many years. It had been Father Dominic who the boy had asked for as he came round from his brain operation, and it was the good Father who ran alongside Charlie when he took part in a Charity Fun Run through the East End. They had been best friends, three decades apart, but best friends no less. The day before Charlie Keene went missing, the priest had flown over to Ireland to visit his family. He had not been expected back until the next weekend, but a Ryanair flight schedule showed that he had come home earlier, probably because he had heard the child was missing. Whatever his reasons, they had cost the man his life.

DCI Foreman slowly closed the folder and slipped it back in the brown manilla envelope. This was not for him. The Met should be setting up a Murder Squad to handle these deaths. The teacher at the Hobhole Quarry was the only case in his area, the rest were all in and around the Metropolitan territory. Rubbing his chin thoughtfully, he decided to take Ellie on her visiting round, see what came of that, then contact the Super about handing everything over to a task force who could deal with the whole nasty ballgame. He did not like the thought of pursuing some weird and fanciful idea. He liked a solid adversary, a Moriarty to his Holmes. If he had to catch murderers, he liked them to be flesh and bone. Full of hate or revenge maybe, but a real person with motives and reasons, not some tenuous wraith floating into good, honest people's lives and turning them into Grim Reapers.

Calling in WDS Brown, together they started gathering the permission required for Ellie McEwan and himself to see as many of the suspects as possible.

* * *

Michael was having a great deal of difficulty in concentrating on his work. He joined Ellie at lunch and could not help but notice her surreptitiously summing up his aura.

'I know, I know! My aura is depleted, and I look like poo!'

'Not quite my words, Professor. More a case of your aura looks *abysmal*, and *you* look like poo!'

'Thank you. Your professional diagnosis is succinct, as always.'

'Come on, have one of these fantastic doughnuts that Ed has provided. Bob had three!'

'How did your meeting go?'

'Pretty good. I have no qualms about helping out. Bob is going to let me see the suspects' auras. I do not even have to go in with them if I do not want to. I can just observe them through glass.'

'Well, I suppose that's a bit of a relief.'

'Maybe, but it seems they are all, without exception, totally uncommunicative. In a world of their own, apparently.'

'Not a world I'd like to venture into.'

'No,' Ellie agreed.

Michael bit into his sugary doughnut, then looked up at Ellie, as a sudden thought crossed his mind. 'Does Alice know you are about to set sail on a sea of sorrows, with the Surrey Police Force?'

The pause said it all.

'Not exactly, Michael. In fact, "no" might be a more honest answer.' Ellie exhaled. 'The problem is, I haven't seen Alice for two whole weeks now. If I didn't ring her, I doubt very much whether she would even find time to speak to me. She is run ragged, and frankly, if she threw a wobbly over me helping Bob again, I think I'd probably lose it with her and say things that I shouldn't, things I would regret. I decided I'd go with the DCI tomorrow, and ascertain if I could be of any help. If there is nothing I can do anyway, then nothing is lost. If I am really needed, well, she will have to know then, won't she? Damn it! I have no idea when I will even see her again!'

'Well, tomorrow actually, except that you will be interviewing murderers. Jake rang earlier, he's not well, and said that he badly needs to see Alice. So, your doctor is driving down here, early a.m.'

'Perfect! What great timing! Oh well, I shall have to ring her tonight and risk a fight. I don't want to lie to her about where I am when he arrives.'

'That could be difficult. She's in Paris today, flying home last flight tonight. I've no idea what time she'll get back to London. Look, why don't I say that you had a call out of some kind, that you said you'd talk to her first, but I told you that she was in France. She can't argue with that, can she? Let's face it, I only found out where she was because Jake has some kind of emergency number for her secretary at the hospital. It was she who made the arrangements with Alice and Jake. She knows we hold the Kennedy boy's room open for him, so she only called the clinic as a matter of courtesy.'

'It's a shame Dr Alice Cross can't employ a bit of the same courtesy, and let me know where the hell she is! Honestly, Michael! If you get a chance, do try to have that chat with her. If she doesn't slow down, I dread to think what's going to happen to her.'

'I had it in mind, Ellie. As soon as she's seen the boy, she will want to discuss her findings with me and with Maureen. I'll use that time to pin back her ears, all right?'

'Thank you. I miss her, Michael. I know I'm mad at her, but I really care about her and it hurts to see her behaving like this. She's an accident waiting to happen.' Ellie stared at one of the Tiffany pictures.

'With a little help she could achieve even more, and not kill herself in the process. She's just being so bloody stubborn!'

The professor stroked his short, neat beard, and gazed at the few specks of sugar on his plate. 'I suppose she spent so long on her own trying to complete Azimah's work. No one really had a lot of time for her then, or offered any help or finances. Perhaps she just feels her baby is not quite ready to be handed over to the childminder.'

'Her baby will be at uni before she is ready to let go of the reins!'

Michael laughed. 'Let's hope not. But try not to worry too much. I have my speech ready, perhaps it will be better if you are not here tomorrow when I talk to her. At least I will know that you will not walk in and interrupt our man to woman chat!'

'True. Well, you had better give her my love and tell her to call me. She never answers her mobile and not many of her answerphone messages either, so it's down to her now, okay?'

* * *

'Where did you get these Danish pastries, Ed? They are as good as I've ever tasted and, believe me, I've tasted some pastries in my time!' Callum ordered a pecan and maple syrup one, just to see if it were as good as the apple and cinnamon that he had previously devoured.

'They are rather good. In fact, everything we have been sent from the new bakery is excellent.' Ed beamed at Callum, and refilled his coffee cup. 'We've got two new suppliers this week that we are well-pleased with, and Sylvie is delighted at the way our extra staff have settled in. I'd say things are looking pretty good for the cafe.'

'Good luck to you, my man. You both deserve it.' Callum moved off to a table and was joined by the clinic's resident hypnotherapist.

'Hi. Mind if I join you? I've been rushed off my feet since I got in this morning. It would be great to talk to someone who is actually awake!'

'Well, I'm not too sure on that score, but you can give it a try and see if I'm any brighter than your patients!'

Dr Tony Ambrose grinned. 'The mere fact that you are not laden with psychosis or totally eaten up with phobias would do!'

The nurse's face darkened. 'Frankly, Tony, I'm not too sure about that either.'

The hypnotist sobered instantly. 'Hey! There was distinct concern in that statement. What's troubling you?'

'Sorry. Nothing. Honestly. I've just been getting rather a lot of flashbacks recently. You know I was in the war zones for a bit. Bit too long probably. I thought I would be over them by now, working in such a good environment. It's really peaceful here but, well, over the last week I have felt decidedly flaky!'

'That's really weird. Several of the other staff have been complaining of feeling uncharacteristically bad tempered or worried recently. I even heard the professor curse when he dropped some files the other day. I mean really curse! Not like him at all. It's strange. Perhaps we should check with Gilly, the metaphysician, maybe the moon is in a bad conjunction with some of the planets. I know it sounds ridiculous, but do you know the positions of the moon and the stars really affect people's emotions? I used to wonder why I got a lot more patients at certain times of the year. Gilly Tremaine soon put me wise on that. She worked me out a chart to highlight all the particularly difficult interplanetary alignments. I was staggered. I marked these "black" days on my calendar and sure enough, every psychological problem known to man showed up at that time.'

'Primitive races would go along with that theory,' agreed Callum. 'And they are usually spot on. I suspect my problem is a little closer to home, though. I know I'm sensitive, and I simply don't protect myself enough. I seem to soak up other people's problems like a sponge.'

'That is the most common of problems with therapists. You have to know how to seal yourself up, to stop taking on the world's worries. I can help you with that one, Callum. Drop into my room any time after four, and I'll give you a few exercises that will help. A bit of grounding and learning to cross-circle yourself should sort you out.'

'Thanks, Tony. I'll do that, if it's not too much trouble?'

'No problem.'

Callum left, waving to a smiling Sylvie as he went. It was time to prepare the orangery for an AbPhab yoga session. He admired the able-bodied helpers as much as he did the disabled kids in this particular group, and he enjoyed helping the teacher. He wished he had as much poise and serenity as Will Ryan. He had once made the young instructor laugh when he had suggested that Will must be short for 'Willow' as he had never seen a more graceful man.

As he got the mats out of the cupboard, he remembered that Maureen had left a Post-it on his locker door, telling him that Jake Kennedy would be back tomorrow, and could he reschedule some of his tasks to spend as much time as possible with the young man.

He would never admit it, but his heart sank when he read the note.

He was more than concerned for Jake. He had made copious notes and observations for Professor Seale on their patient. Every time there was something that gave cause for concern, it was never bad enough or clear enough to allow Dr Cross to do anything definite to help him. Jake remained an enigma. Callum was not at all surprised that he was unwell again, but for some reason he dreaded having to spend so much time with him. Perhaps it really was time to take up Dr Ambrose on his offer of some protective exercises.

CHAPTER FOURTEEN

Permission had been granted for the detective and Ellie to visit Rod Black, Lily Frampton and Elizabeth Ryder. The two women were both being held in the hospital wing of HMP Holloway. The governor had allowed them a short time with the suspects, but had made it plain that their condition was poor, and as an interview was out of the question, their visit would be very brief indeed. Rod Black was also hospitalised, but in High Down Prison in Surrey. It was doubtful they would be able to see young Charlie Keene. At twelve, he could not be detained, but because of his mental state, he had been admitted to a children's hospital with round-the-clock care. Ellie was mildly relieved, as she considered seeing three sick souls in one day might be about as much as she could face.

The police car made little of the journey to north London, and before they knew it, they were approaching the A503 Camden Road, and her first, and hopefully last, expedition into the famous women's prison.

'It will be the same as before, Ellie. A search, and leave all your belongings in a locker. We are, of course, seeing them in the hospital, but believe me, the security is just as tough.' The detective paused and gave her a sheepish smile. 'Sorry to put you through this, again.'

Ellie smiled. 'At least it won't come as such a shock this time. I will be expecting to have someone poke around in my ears and check the heels of my shoes! Maybe I could write a book? Perhaps *The Good Slammer Guide*, with a star rating, of course.'

Bob smiled at her attempts to cover her obvious nervousness. Ellie knew he was remembering their last prison visit, and how it had been less than pleasant for her.

The architecture was very different from before, but as Bob had warned, the security was the same. If anything, stricter.

Searches over, and the last set of doors slammed and locked behind them, they found themselves being chaperoned into a corridor with a string of small rooms on either side.

'Frampton is in here. But you won't get anything out of her. The other one, Ryder, she's the same, I'm afraid. She's further down on the right-hand side.' The prison officer unlocked the door to what may have been referred to as a private room in a normal hospital.

It was light and clean. The sun shone in through a high, frosted glass window, with a series of bars in front of it. The room housed a hospital style bed, a chair, a shelf with a plastic water jug on it, and a toilet and wash basin.

Lily sat on the bed. She was composed, and at first glance, Ellie thought she may have nodded off to sleep, the sunlight shining on her pale skin.

DCI Foreman spoke gently to her. Told her who they were and that they were there to talk to her, if that was all right with her.

'Don't worry, pet. As soon as I finish this, I'll get us a nice cup of tea.'

The voice was clear and made them both jump. She had not looked up and still sat staring forwards, a set smile on her face.

Ellie shook herself mentally, and did what she was there to do. Standing across the room from the unmoving woman, she tuned into the poor soul's aura.

For a moment she was completely confused. She then moved to the opposite side of the room and concentrated again on the energy field that surrounded Lily Frampton.

Well, she would have done if Lily Frampton had an energy field. They stayed for a few minutes more until she heard Bob asking if she'd seen enough.

She did not know what to reply. She had seen nothing, and that was not possible. For a dreadful moment Ellie thought her amazing gift had deserted her, but she only had to look at Bob, or the prison officer, to know she still possessed her uncanny talent. The uniformed woman had a rather dull aura, probably due to bad health, bad diet, and constant stress. But compared to poor Lily, the officer shone out like the aurora borealis!

She shook her head and indicated she was through.

Elizabeth Ryder did not recognise their existence either.

She sat, ramrod straight and shook an imaginary collecting box. 'Please give. The homeless need your support. If you have a roof over your head, please give something for those who haven't. Please give.'

The voice was cultured and very 'To the Manor Born'.

A giggle rose in Ellie's throat. She coughed to disguise the nervous laugh that was threatening to break free. God! This was too bizarre for words! This woman had no aura either! She looked helplessly at the policeman, and then back at Elizabeth Ryder.

The sun was not shining on this side of the building, and Ellie forced herself to 'see' something, some sort of life force or energy around the lady. After a while she made out a sluggish sort of light creeping and slithering around the woman's upright form. Light was too strong a word; it was a vague phosphorescence that clung to her outline, more like an oil than an energy force. It did not change, did not flare up and radiate out like a normal life light. It just seemed to adhere itself to her body and ooze around her.

Then it disappeared completely.

Ellie felt vaguely nauseous. She lightly touched Bob's sleeve, and he immediately indicated towards the door.

The officer let them out and turned the lock on the well-dressed woman with her illusory collection box.

* * *

The driver had threaded his way through the London traffic and was well on his way towards Epsom before Ellie felt up to trying to describe what she had seen.

Her face was grim, all traces of the hysteria that had nearly overcome her in the prison had gone. She spoke to Bob Foreman like a lecturer to her student.

'Everything that has life has an energy field around it. That is fact.' She punched a clenched fist into a cupped hand. 'Fact, a universal energy field surrounds all life. Human beings have a many-layered auric field around them. The fields all relate to different things: emotions, drives, relationships, experiences, divine will, spiritual ecstasy and serenity. I can see all these layers, Bob. I have learned what they mean, and I can easily see disease in human auras. You know this.'

Bob nodded earnestly, after all, he had seen her at work, first hand.

'Okay. So, auras can vary. A healthy aura can stretch out three feet away from the body. People who live in harmony with nature can have wonderfully healthy auras. There is a magical interface with human beings and nature. Imagine the charge your energy field gets from a mountain electrical storm, or a cascading waterfall. Most "civilised" townies laugh their socks off at the thought of hugging a tree, but the energy pulsation rate of some trees is almost identical to a human auric field. You can get a recharge just from sitting with your back to the trunk of a tree. Anyway, people who live in high density areas can have smaller auras. Sick people have damaged auras. Disease shows up as sludge colours. Drugs distort the aura colours. But the aura is still there, maybe damaged, maybe broken, maybe dull and lifeless, but damn it, it's still there! Bob, I've seen better auras on dead people!'

A silence clung to the interior of the speeding car.

Ellie faced her friend, and in a softer voice, said, 'I really mean that. Those who have just passed over retain some of their most spiritual lights. A dead body can look quite beautiful. So, whatever has happened to those two poor women? And what do you think we are going to find when we meet Roderick Black?'

* * *

Their trip through security was a nightmare. There had been some sort of incident prior to their arrival, and their access to the hospital wing took over two hours.

As they finally left the prison and made their way back to the police station, they discussed the meeting with the schoolteacher in hushed tones. Ellie was no longer the orator, expounding her views. The vision of Rod Black would probably never leave her.

He had been lying, full length, on his bed. His eyes were open and unblinking.

She and Bob had stood at the bottom of the bed, and it was soon apparent that he was totally unaware of their presence.

He spoke in a careful tone, not as cultured as Mrs Ryder, but he clearly enunciated his words for his pupil to understand. Because he was still speaking to his favourite scholar.

'Red sky at night, shepherd's delight. Red sky in the morning, shepherd's warning. You see, Johnny, sheep do not like rain, remember, they are prone to foot rot, unlike cows, of course. A red sky around dawn is a sure indication of rain.'

He had lapsed into silence at that point. Ellie had stared hard, but could find no trace of an energy field at all. She had shrugged helplessly at the detective, and they asked to be let out. As the door closed, Ellie could hear the educated voice intone, 'Now, the ten Archangels, Johnny. Remember? They are Raphael, Archangel of Mercury. His flower is the iris, his day is Wednesday. Michael, Archangel of the Sun. His flower is the marigold, his day is Sunday. Gabriel . . .'

As they drove through the security gates and into the station car park, Ellie let out a long sigh. 'I don't know what I thought I would see, Bob, or what I could do to help you, but I never imagined a day like this. It was awful, and I simply don't understand. I must talk to Michael as soon as I get back to the clinic. If your driver could get me back there, I'll ring you later.'

She hugged him tightly. 'I'm sorry. I think I've let you down. I expected more of myself.'

The bear of a man hugged her back. 'You wouldn't know how to let me down. Go on, get back to the clinic, get a hot drink, and talk to your professor. Perhaps he can shine some light on all this, and maybe we should forget about going to see the Keene boy. I think we both know what we would find, and the sight of a hymn-singing child with no life lights, as you call them, might be a bit much for you.'

The last statement held no chauvinistic undertones. Ellie knew Bob Foreman was simply concerned for her welfare, and knowing his own shortcomings where children were concerned, he had no wish to put either of them through an unnecessarily traumatic experience.

'If we have to go, naturally I will see him, Bob, but I think you're right about what we . . .'

Her sentence was left unfinished as the policeman's mobile burst into life. His face was serious as he thanked the caller for the message. 'Lily Frampton is dead.'

'Dead? But we only saw her a matter of hours ago!'

'I need to know more, Ellie. You get back to the clinic, speak to Michael, and I will ring you when I have had a chance to get hold of the prison governor. Higgins! Take Miss McEwan back to Ripley, and get back here on the double! Thanks again, Ellie, we'll speak later.'

Before she had settled herself back in the car, the huge detective was already through the main doors and thundering up the stairs towards his office.

* * *

The clinic was unusually quiet when Ellie got back. She was shocked to find it was five o'clock, and that discovery made her realise she was starving. Michael was ensconced with a patient, so she decided to go and eat. A few clients and members of staff were seated in the cafe area and Ellie made her way through them to order a meal.

As she sat down, she noticed on the far side of the hall, Callum Church and Tony Ambrose in deep conversation. After a while, Callum lightly touched Tony on the shoulder, and turned in her direction. He waved and she beckoned him over.

'Hey, you look done in, Miss McEwan! Maybe you could use some of these great exercises Tony has just given me. They help protect you from other people's negativity or bad attitudes.' Callum dropped into a chair opposite her.

'It's okay, I have a little regime that I practise before I start work every day. You need some extra help when you are working with illness and emotional problems all day long. This has just been a particularly draining day, and I missed lunch, and that's serious! Anyway, I'm glad to see Dr Ambrose is advising you how to protect yourself. For some reason I kind of thought you would know all about that.'

'I do, but only in a limited way, so Tony has filled me in with some really good information about shields and bubbles. I've done a bit of creative visualisation in the past, and it seems to be a similar process. I'm quite excited really. I fancy being encased from top to toe in a bubble of light!'

Ellie laughed. 'You are anyway! If you could see auras, you would know that is exactly what you are.'

'How do you see me, Miss McEwan?'

Ellie sat quietly for a moment and looked at the young man's form. 'It's the end of the day. You are a little less vibrant than I have seen you, but you have a lovely aura, Callum. You are surrounded by a rainbow of colours. You are predominantly a wonderful indigo, purple and dark blue, but all the other colours are there, too. And you have misty patches of brown that are quite unusual. Strangely that often comes from just what you have been talking about. Taking on the problems and bad emotions of others. Do you ever get a sort of mood come over you, for no apparent reason?'

'Absolutely! Quite often, in fact.'

'It's what's called a transported condition. You would do well to get yourself into a regular pattern of cleansing and protecting your energy fields. You will instinctively know what is right for you once you begin. Stick with Tony's exercises and talk to me if you need any more help. Did he show you how to ground yourself?'

'Yes, and how to cross-circle myself.'

'Good, you're off to a healthy start, but do ask if you are worried about anything, okay?'

Sylvie arrived with an omelette, French fries and a big, leafy fresh salad. Ellie thanked her and offered Callum something to eat. The nurse said that he had promised his mum he would go with her to some talk at the village hall that evening, so he had better get away on time.

'Jake is back. He looks dreadful. Dr Cross spent ages with him this morning. Have you seen him yet?'

'No. I have to see Professor Seale as soon as he is free, then I'll take a look at him.'

'Mrs Shaw asked me to dedicate as much time as I can to him, but he has slept ever since Dr Cross left him. I don't know what to make of him.'

'Sadly, I don't think you are alone with that statement.' She sighed then smiled across the table at the young nurse. 'Go and enjoy your Women's Institute meeting and I'll see you tomorrow!'

'Good grief! You don't think it's the Wims, do you?'

'I wouldn't be surprised! My mother did that to me once, but she forgot to tell me I was the guest speaker!'

'No shit! Oh, sorry, Miss McEwan.'

'Believe me, Callum, that was nothing compared with what I called my mother!'

'I'll bet. Well, if you see me come to work tomorrow with a very red face, you'll know that history has repeated itself! Bye, and Dr Church recommends an early night. If I could see auras, I think yours would have shrunk to three inches!'

With a grin and a wave, the young man headed off to the staff room.

Ellie finished her supper and arrived at Michael's room just in time to see the retreating figure of his last patient. As she sank into one of his comfortable chairs, she heard the sound of a stopper being removed from a bottle.

'Can I tempt you? Just a small one, maybe? I know you're driving.'

'I could kill one, Michael, but a strong coffee will have to suffice, until I get home that is . . . and then, drinks cupboard, here I come! Hell! What a day!'

'Before I forget.' Michael withdrew a cream envelope from his pocket. 'From Alice. She was insistent that I give it to you as soon as I saw you.'

'Thanks. I'll read it when I get home and providing she is still in this country, I'll give her a ring. How did she look, Michael?'

'Tired, worried, miserable. We had a long talk, Ellie, and she went away for about an hour, then came back with the letter, so . . . ?'

'Thank you, Michael. Whatever the letter says, I appreciate your efforts.'

'So how did your prison visits go?'

Ellie spent the next half an hour relating the happenings of the day. Michael made her a coffee, and then sat quietly as she talked. When she had finished, he still sat in silent contemplation on what she had said. Finally, and without looking up from his glass, he spoke. 'Do you think I may be allowed to see one of these people?'

Ellie was nonplussed. She had tried to convey her exact impression of what she had seen, and wondered what else her friend would be looking for. 'Well, I . . . I suppose so. I mean Bob would have to get permission from the governor, and as Lily Frampton has died, I suppose Rod Black would be the best one to see. Why, Michael? What do you think you might pick up that I didn't?'

Her friend drew in a long breath and looked at her intently. 'I don't remember a day without seeing auras. From a tiny child I have seen cascading lights issue from those around me. There is no way I am underestimating your gift, Ellie, and I am not putting down your incredible methods of diagnosing illness and disease. It's just that I have been watching and interpreting life energies for half a century, and there are some phenomena I'll have come across that you will not, that's all.'

Ellie regarded her friend and felt a little foolish. Her thoughts had been petty. Naturally Michael would know more than she. She was about to apologise when he continued.

'The thing is, I believe I have witnessed this before, many years ago. Before she died, my wife and I went on an extended holiday. We both knew she was very ill and probably would not see another summer, so while she still had the strength and could enjoy herself, we just took off for a month or two. We weekended in Paris, Florence, Naples and Vienna. We island-hopped around Greece, that was her favourite place, then we flew out to the Caribbean. Sounds very jet set, I know, but what was the use of our savings when my beloved Georgia wasn't going to be with me to enjoy them. Anyway, for a few days we stayed in a beach hut on a really remote island. It was heaven. We were lucky enough to miss the rains that can apparently wreck an idyllic holiday there, and we had a fantastic time, until the afternoon we were due to leave.' His face darkened. 'There was a native community on the other side of the island. They were paid by the hotel company who owned the beach villas to clean and cook for us. They were lovely people, but very simple and uncivilised. As we were packing to leave, we heard wailing and shouting. When we went to see what was wrong, we found Rosa, the woman who had been looking after us, running along the beach in hysterics.' Michael took a sip from his glass. 'We took her back to her home, a ramshackle dwelling near the harbour, and found some dreadful argument going on among her family. To cut a long story short, an uncle had been wrongly accused of something, and he had cursed Rosa's son. I mean put a curse on him. The poor boy was lying on the dirt floor, twitching and shaking, and saying some native rhyme, over and over. We sat him up and tried to calm him, but although the tremors ceased, he seemed to slip into some sort of trance. He continued to repeat the rhyme, and was still doing so hours later, when the boat came for us to leave the island. The thing was, I had chance to have a good look at the lad, and he appeared to have no aura. Like your suspects. After a while, the native islanders calmed down somewhat, and I managed to get some sense out of an old man, who seemed to be their sort of wise man, or doctor. He told me that the islanders believed the lad had had his spirit stolen. The uncle had taken the boy's "fire" and thrown it into the sea. I asked if that was why he had no lights around him. The wise man asked if I too was a doctor, as I could behold the human fire. He had never seen a Westerner with that power before. I asked what he could do to help the lad, but he said that, without his spirit, he was already dead. There was nothing he could do but wait, and bury him. Just before I left, the old man took me back to the child, and stood alongside me. I can see him now. He knelt, with crackling joints, and took my hand, bringing it to within inches of the boy's head. 'You said that he has no lights. He does. They are just very hard to see. What do you call these lights, man?' I told him we called the energy force an aura. 'Well, the boy has a black aura, put your hand over his forehead and you will see.' Ellie, it was the strangest thing I ever saw. Black is an absence of light, but when my hand got close to his eyes, I felt a coldness, like reaching into the freezer, and I could "see" this awful darkness between my skin and his. It was indescribable.'

Ellie sat clutching her coffee mug and trying to ignore the slithery snake of fear that was sliding down her spine.

'I think you should see Mr Black.'

'What a very unfortunate name that poor fellow has.'

'He'll be even more unfortunate if you're going to suggest that they'll all die!'

'I'm not saying that, but it does sound as if they may have black auras, doesn't it?'

'I wish I had known what to look for.'

'How could you? It's only your very thorough description that made me even think about the Caribbean boy, and I have only seen the black aura once in my entire life.'

'I may have seen it three times today, but not known it! Oh Lord! Michael! What about the little boy? Charlie Keene, you don't think . . . ?'

Michael's phone rang loudly, making Ellie gasp out loud.

'Ellie, it's the DCI. He has some news for you.'

She took the receiver and noted a slight tremor in her fingers. They spoke for a while, and towards the end of the conversation Ellie asked the detective if he could arrange for Michael to see the Keene boy.

She hung up and leaned back in the chair. All the energy seemed to have run out of her. 'He will get straight on to the hospital, but does not think he will get an answer until the morning. He'll do his best. He said that the prison have no idea why Lily Frampton died. One minute she was offering the prison doctor a cup of tea, the next she was gone. They have ordered a post-mortem. Bob also said that Johnny Baker, the prefect who was attacked by Roderick Black, has also died. It was most unexpected. The boy was thought to be doing well, but there must have been some kind of bleed in his brain. Michael, the death toll is rising by the hour. Whatever is going on?'

* * *

The road to Snug Cottage seemed darker than normal and even her fleece jacket did not stop Ellie shivering. Then she saw the porch light glowing warmly through the trees, and knew her precious dogs would be waiting with a welcome that would help to lift her spirits. To find the Range Rover parked outside was the last thing she had expected.

Fast asleep in the driver's seat was her exhausted doctor.

Ellie knocked gently on the side window until Alice awoke with a start and clambered out of the vehicle. Ellie unlocked the door and let her boys out into the garden.

Still standing in the porch, she pulled Alice close to her. 'Why on earth didn't you say you were coming tonight?'

Alice kissed her hair and clasped her tightly. 'Last minute decision. I was halfway back to London and I thought sod it! I need a hug! Badly!'

'I was beginning to think I'd never see you again, unless I booked an appointment with your secretary!' Ellie gently reproved.

'Oh Ellie, I'm so sorry, really I am.' She pushed her fingers through the recalcitrant blonde cow's lick that hung across her left eye, and pushed it roughly away from her face. As her hand moved away, it fell disobediently back across her forehead.

'Come on, Doctor. Let's get inside. Have you eaten? You look terrible! Go on into the kitchen and I'll bring you a drink. Oh, and I'm sorry, I've not read your letter yet. I was waiting until I got home.'

Ellie threw off her jacket and went to get some drinks. If ever she needed one, it was now. By the time she got back to Alice, she was sitting in one of the old pine chairs beside the Aga, with Digger on her lap, and her eyes closing again.

Ellie made sandwiches, as she had had a late lunch at the clinic and did not feel much like eating, and poured them both double whiskies.

She sat down next to Alice and, with the dogs at their feet, it felt just as it had before Alice became bogged down with work.

'Why, oh why, did I allow myself to be dragged away from this?' Alice sipped her drink and looked at Ellie. 'How could I? I must be mad!'

Ellie smiled at her and noticed the deep lines of tiredness under her eyes. 'Mad? Yes, well, maybe a little bit.' She wondered what on earth Michael had said.

Ellie knew there was a lot to say, but tonight was not the night. Her own traumatic day was catching up with her, and Alice was out on her feet. It was not even ten o'clock, but they fell into bed and held on to each other as though they were drowning. The warmth of Alice's body, together with that particular smell of hers, the tightness of her clasp around Ellie, and the regular sound of her breath as she slept, allowed Ellie to fall into the deepest, dreamless sleep that she had had for months.

When she awoke at six the next morning, she was alone.

Anger and sadness swirled together in her head. Then she heard the sound of the shower, and heaved a sigh of relief. Alice's side of the bed was still warm and Ellie rolled into it, burying her face in the pillow that had, until a few moments ago, supported another sleepy head. She breathed in the warmth and tried to decide what that wonderful smell was. It was just Alice. She stayed a little longer, luxuriating in the fact that she was no longer alone, then got up and went to make them some breakfast.

Over toast and coffee, the doctor, who looked considerably refreshed by eight hours sleep and a hot shower, uttered the words Ellie had been longing to hear.

'I've decided to take on a partner. In fact, if you think the Fund could stand it, my workload also needs a research assistant and a secretary. Doris is doing her best for me at the hospital, but I have to share her with two other doctors, and it isn't exactly perfect.'

Ellie's smile said it all. 'You've got it! Whatever you need, it's yours, as long as you stop trying to shoulder everything yourself!'

Alice looked down at her plate. 'I never told you, but I came off the road the other night. Fell asleep at the wheel. I am *so* careful, you know that, but, well, this time, I had no warning. Luckily, I was in the middle of nowhere and it was late at night. There was no damage to anything, other than a bit of hedging and a rotten gatepost, but it frightened me badly. I didn't dare tell you, because I knew what you would say.'

'You're not wrong there!'

'All the way home, the "what if" scenario kept playing. What if I had hit someone? What if I'd written off the Range Rover? What if you had been with me? What if I had badly injured myself and no one found me? By the time I got home, I'd more or less decided I was going to ask you for some help. Then when I saw Michael yesterday, he really let me have it with both barrels!'

'Good for Michael. I should have done it myself ages ago.'

'Honestly, Ellie. It was the accident that focused me. Up until that moment, I thought I could cope. If you'd nagged me, I'd probably have fought you all the way. Idiot that I am!'

Ellie decided not to take it further. Alice was clearly shaken by her very literal wake-up call. 'So, now that light has dawned, what are your plans?'

'Well, I've had a few ideas, but I really wanted to know that I wasn't overstretching the finances first. And there's something I'd like to ask of you and Michael.' She bit her lip and looked earnestly at Ellie.

'I would like to leave the hospital and, well, I wondered if I could set up a special Azimah clinic at the C-M? If you think there would be room, of course. We would only need a consulting room, an office, and a computer room for the AZSEE equipment. Oh, and some sort of waiting area, I suppose, although that's not particularly important.'

'You really *have* thought this through, haven't you?'

'It's all in my letter, and a bit more, but that is personal.'

It was Ellie's turn to apologise. 'Alice, we were so tired last night, I haven't even opened it yet! I'm sorry.'

'That's fine. I never thought I would be here telling you all this . . . that's why I wrote it down. I was planning on ringing you and asking you out for a posh meal, and apologise in person. But I just could not drive back to London and not see you.'

'I'm glad, and I'll put your thoughts to Michael as soon as I get to work this morning. It might not be suitable, but there is a small annexe in the grounds of the clinic. It used to be a sort of pavilion, right next to the tennis courts. It's a bit like a log cabin, there is one long room with a veranda, and a couple of smaller rooms off. One, I know, was a changing room, and I've no idea what the other was used for. Sports equipment probably. But there's a loo, and basins, and a shower as well. If Michael says it's okay, then we'll look at it and see what needs doing.'

She poured some more coffee for them both, and thought how much better things would be if Alice was based in Ripley with her. But right now she had a confession of her own, and it wasn't going to be easy.

'Alice, I know you've had problems talking to me about all this, and I'm afraid there is something I need to tell you, and I don't know quite how.'

The doctor looked concerned.

'Don't look so worried! It's nothing dreadful, it's just that I've been helping the DCI again.'

Alice's face took on a granite facade.

'Now before you get mad, it's nothing like last time, I promise. There is no danger. I have just been looking at some auras for him, that's all.'

'Whose aura, may I ask?'

She hesitated. 'Just some very sick people. One has died since I saw her.'

'And where did you have to go to see these sick people?'

'Alice, I don't need the third degree.'

'Where?'

'Okay. Holloway prison, if you must know.'

'So there is no danger! Oh fine! Ellie, what the hell do you think you're doing? You nearly died last time! Have you got a death wish or something?'

Alice got up and threw the remains of her coffee down the sink. She was shaking with rage and gripped the edge of the worktop to steady herself.

She was gazing out over the garden and Ellie wondered what on earth was going through her mind. She slipped her arms around Alice's waist, and felt the woman let out a long, painful sigh.

'You just don't get it, do you? I know I've been awful over the past weeks, but I love you, and it tears me up inside to even remember what happened before. God, I nearly lost you. Please, Ellie, don't put yourself in jeopardy again. I don't think I could take it. I am so worried about work, and about Jake, I think I will fall apart if I have to start fretting about you as well.'

Ellie closed her eyes and exhaled. 'Okay, okay, I'll talk to Bob. Tell him . . . oh I don't know, tell him something. Where will you be today, Alice? Where can I get in touch with you? We have to talk, about us, about Jake, and about the clinic.'

'I'm at the hospital all day, but I need to see Jake when I've finished. I'll be back at Ripley by five, if I'm lucky.'

Alice grasped her, and Ellie felt a desperation in the embrace.

'I'm sorry for my outburst,' sighed Alice. 'I think I never really got over what happened, or more to the point, what could have happened to you last year, but just recently, my nerves have been shot. Overwork, I suppose. Whatever, I'm sorry. Perhaps your detective could just use you as a consultant, you know, discuss things over the phone, or maybe call to see you, but not put you on the front line. What do you think?'

'I think that I'll talk to him.' Ellie was serious. 'I don't want to let him down, but I don't want to hurt you either. I promise I won't do anything without talking to you first, just as long as you tell me where you are! France, indeed, and not as much as a postcard!' She kissed Alice lightly on the cheek and she, at least, had the good grace to look abashed.

'That was unforgivable, I know. Time just ran out on me. For a week I did not seem to stop to draw breath.'

'Okay, let's make a pact to talk to each other from now on.'

'I promise.'

'Me too. Now, you get off before the traffic builds up, we'll talk later, and I'll see you at the clinic around five.'

They kissed, and then kissed again.

As the Range Rover pulled out onto the bumpy lane, Ellie was not sure what she was going to say to her policeman friend. It was difficult, but Alice had to come first and, after all, she was finally prepared to shed some of her workload. They would find a compromise, she was sure.

CHAPTER FIFTEEN

WPC Paula English turned the key in her locker door and heaved a sigh of relief. Three days off! She seemed to have been at work for the last month without a break. Now she could go home, have a long, hot bath, throw some things in a case, and bugger off to her brother's caravan on Romney Marsh. Not everyone's cup of tea maybe, but Paula was a bit of a loner and liked her own company. Her hobby was bird watching and she had, over the last few years when her shifts allowed, become a bit of a night naturalist.

She called a friendly goodbye to the rest of her departing colleagues and walked across the car park to her old Ford Escort. It only took about thirty minutes and she was turning into her numbered space outside her flat. She had a spacious one-bedroom flat that overlooked the cottage hospital grounds in Leatherhead. As she unlocked the door, she heard Melody sing a feline greeting, and in seconds the chunky tabby was winding its way around her legs.

'Hello, Poppet.' She put down her bag and picked up the heavyweight moggy. 'Just time to feed you, and then you are going to stay with Auntie Edna for a couple of days.' She tickled the old cat's ears and held its furry head to her face. 'You are going to get spoilt rotten, aren't you?'

She put the cat down and went to run a bath. While the water was running, she packed a bag for Melody. In it she carefully placed tinned food, dry food, cat crunchies, cat treats, two slightly mangled soft toys, a box of cat litter and an old tartan blanket. She placed the bag alongside a clean litter tray, a combined water and food bowl and a wonderful bed that looked like a plush, warm igloo. She smiled and remembered the days when she actually took the cat with her when she went off for a holiday. Melody had loved the car and was happy to walk on a cat lead. Now at seventeen, she preferred to lounge around in Paula's neighbour's flat until her wandering mistress returned.

She fed the cat and spent the next fifteen minutes luxuriating in ylang ylang bubbles. She lazed back and thought of what she would do over the next couple of days. The nightingales should be singing by now. Nowhere else in England had quite so many of these elusive songsters. She loved the big skies that dominated the bleak landscape. It was more like Lincolnshire than Kent, but it suited her. She would go down to the RSPB reserve at Dungeness; she should see some Sandwich terns at this time of the year, and the place would be alive with waders and other waterbirds. She had enjoyed a two-day break there back in March which had given her first sighting of a black redstart. As she dried herself off, she felt quite elated about seeing the swallows and the yellow wagtails again.

'Sad woman!' she said out loud, then laughed softly to herself. Some people, she reflected, were made for marriage, for deep relationships or long-term partnerships; she was not. She loved her independence. Loved her bachelor flat. She was content that if she wanted to leave the washing-up in the sink for three days, she could! Not that she would. The flat was neat and tidy, in a lived in and comfortable sort of way. She had only once embarked upon a live-in affair, and swore that it would be the last. She liked to iron shirts her way, and she soon found she was far too set in her ways to appreciate being told, 'Surely it would be easier if you did it this way?'

No thanks. She was her own person and liked it that way. Apart from anything else, it also suited her career. The cat could put up with grim shifts and unsociable hours, but it did not always make for harmony in the matrimonial home. She had seen that many coppers, male and female, divorce or split up. She shook her head thoughtfully and called the cat.

Edna happily received her boarder, and assured her young policewoman friend that she had her mobile number, and the vet's number on her pad, should the need arise.

As she placed her bags, hiker's rucksack and walking boots in the car, she looked up at Edna's window. The old lady held the cat close to her and gently waved one of Melody's paws at her. Paula waved back, not sure if she were actually waving to Edna, or her feline friend of seventeen years. Both, probably. She smiled, checked she had her maps and her binoculars, and climbed into the driver's seat. A ten-minute dash around Sainsbury's in the Swan Centre and she would be on her way.

* * *

At the same time as Paula English was pulling into the Swan Centre car park, Michael Seale was sitting alone in his conservatory, and on his second single malt of the evening.

It had been a strange day, awesome in its complexity.

It had started with Maureen ringing his emergency number saying that she could not wake Jake. Michael was at the point of trying to reach Dr Alice Cross, when the lad simply stretched, yawned, and arose from what a few minutes before had looked like a coma.

The professor had returned to his apartment to find a message on his answerphone telling him to ring DCI Foreman as soon as he picked up the message. On returning the call, Michael was told that a car was being dispatched to take him to the London Children's Hospital where Charlie Keene was being cared for. He would be accompanied by DI Jon Leatham and his visit had to be as brief as possible as the boy was considered to be very poorly.

After a scant five minutes with Charlie Keene, Michael decided that 'very poorly' was an understatement. Drawing near to the child, he had been transported back to a hot, sunny island, where a child repeated a terrible mantra while he shook and trembled on a dirt floor. The similarities had been frightening.

This boy's room was clean, and he lay on hygienic, white bed linen, but the strained young voice intoning, repeatedly, the easily recognisable hymn had made it equally as grotesque as the voodoo curse.

Michael had spoken softly and slowly placed his hand over the lad's eyes. The coldness was there, as was the hardly visible, black aura. He hadn't needed to see any more.

Jon Leatham had returned him to the Cavendish-Meyer, spent a few minutes arranging an appointment for his friend with Dr Ambrose, and had sped off again.

Michael had immediately rung the DCI, but had been somewhat unsure of what to tell him. He finished up by assuring the policeman that the boy was indeed in the same condition as the suspects Ellie had seen. He then added that, in his opinion, the child might not recover. Bob Foreman did not seem surprised at his candour, and after a moment's hesitation, informed the professor that Rod Black had also died in the night.

Michael had sat in his crowded and untidy office, and wondered who was stealing spirits, and why?

Ellie had then burst in with some request that Alice have the tennis pavilion for an Azimah clinic. She was elated the young doctor was finally going to get some assistance, but concerned that she had asked her not to work closely with Bob anymore. He had told her of his findings with the Keene child, and that the schoolteacher had died. Her mood had become very sombre indeed, and it was clear to him that Ellie was stuck between a rock and a hard place, torn between loyalties to both Alice and Bob.

As she had left his office, Callum Church arrived, worried he could hardly get two words out of Jake Kennedy and that the pilot had spent over an hour in Dr Cross's office, logged into the AZSEE programme. He was not sure if Jake had permission to use it without Dr Cross being present, and when he had questioned him about it, Jake had told him to piss off. On top of that, he had to prevent a near bout of fisticuffs between one of the therapists and the cleaner. He had no idea what had sparked the fight, but neither protagonist was prepared to back off, and it had been fortunate that Callum had been on hand to defuse the situation.

As he sat and sipped his scotch, too tired to even cook some supper, he reflected that the only good thing to come of this God-awful day was the sight of Ellie and Alice walking hand in hand from the tennis court area. From their smiles and dramatic gestures, he gathered that the pavilion was going to be a suitable venue for Dr Cross's new A.S. Clinic.

* * *

Bob stared wearily at the memo from the Super. The Met were indeed setting up a Murder Squad for what they had codenamed 'Operation Innocents'. That was good news. But they wanted him and a small select team to help run it. That was bad news.

The murder room would be in the Metropolitan area and it looked as if he and his team could kiss goodbye to home comforts for the duration of the investigation. They would be motoring up to the city every day.

He swore loudly, then tried to decide who would be most useful to him. It did not take long to pick Jon Leatham, Wendy Brown and two other officers who were well known for their stamina and tenacity, DC Theo Bolt and WPC Paula English. He called in Wendy and she checked the shift rosters for the four officers.

'Paula's on leave for three days, boss.'

'Get her back in, second thoughts . . .' He paused. 'No, notify her, but let her finish her leave. She can join us later. We'll manage without her. Get the others in for a briefing. Nine tomorrow morning, in my office.'

'Right, sir.'

'Brown?'

'Yes, sir?'

'This is one very strange case. First, it seems we are losing our suspects, one after the other. We will still have to prove the murders; they are crimes after all, and if we do prove them beyond all reasonable doubt, then they will be closed, with no murderer to be convicted. Second, we have to discover how our dead murderers were turned into very efficient killing machines, and who the hell did it!'

'And why, sir.'

'Yes, Wendy, and why, indeed.'

* * *

Jake dreamed he was flying. Up through the clouds, rotors whirling above him. Below, the countryside looked like one of the photographs he used to take. A patchwork, a tapestry.

When he was a bit strapped for cash, he would fly over residential areas, take aerial photos of people's houses, then walk the streets selling his pictures to the homeowners. Few said no, and he made a fair amount of money. He would use his friend's Piper for that. The little plane was easy to handle and great to take photographs from.

Now he was flying like a bird.

The rotor blades had disappeared and it was completely silent up there in the clear blue sky. Higher and higher he flew, onward into the sun. And like Icarus, he started to fall. Spiralling and plummeting towards the ground. The hard, unforgiving ground.

No! I want to fly. I have to fly! No!

* * *

As darkness fell, Alice and Ellie stood in the orchard watching the dogs check their territory for all visitors and intruders. Alice's arm rested lightly on Ellie's shoulder and she, in turn, had looped her arm around Alice's waist.

'Between the four of them, I'll bet not a single blade of grass goes un-sniffed!'

Alice grinned. 'What I like is the way they seem to communicate. Have you noticed how they look at each other if they hear a strange noise? Then they all rush off in unison.'

'Carole told me about that. They always used to look at the big, older dog, Orlando, before they acted. Now they don't seem to have a special pack leader, it's as you say, a sort of joint decision.'

'I would have thought they'd have chosen a second in command to be the big cheese now that Orlando has gone. You know, the King is dead, long live the King, sort of thing?'

Ellie tilted her head to one side. 'It's funny but I don't think they know Orlando is no longer here. Michael has seen him several times, and so has our nurse, Callum. He chased him all over the grounds at the C-M Centre. Perhaps they still see their old friend, who knows?'

Alice looked sceptical. 'The scientist in me can't quite accept that theory. I'm not denying that you believe it, and some very weird stuff has happened here before — that I can't dispute . . .'

Her voice trailed off and Ellie decided to change the subject.

'The pavilion is in much better condition than I remembered, and it's bigger too,' she said quickly.

Alice seemed happy at the change of tack. 'With a bit of work, it will be perfect. It has everything we need to be a self-contained unit. Oh yes, I spoke to Gordon Lamont today. You know, the guy who's done all the work on AZSEE for me. I told him we are expanding into a team, and he has offered his services. He would make a fantastic research man, as long as he's well enough, and won't miss his lochs and glens too much!'

'That sounds like an excellent move, Alice. His computer knowledge is really something, isn't it?'

'Second to none. Perhaps we could discuss remuneration? I have no idea what to offer him.'

Ellie shrugged. 'I'll throw that one at C-M Finances. I've already told them that the Trust needs to support you, at least one other doctor, a senior researcher and a PA. They should be back to me in a day or so with suggestions for a pay structure. The money is all there for you, it just has to be correctly arranged. That's why Michael and I set up a small financial management company, to cope with the running of the clinic and the properties, and so on.'

'Very sensible. I'm sure I wouldn't know where to start.'

'What about your new doctor? Anyone in mind yet?' asked Ellie.

'That's not quite so easy. Azimah Syndrome is very specialised. I must have exactly the right person for the job, and they must have a very good knowledge of brain chemicals. So far, and this is without advertising, I only know of two people who could fit the bill.'

'Have you spoken to them yet?'

'Not yet, but one chap was at medical school with me. A dead clever guy, but I don't know, we never really hit it off particularly well. Mind you, it's years since we worked together, and we've probably both grown up a lot, well, I sincerely like to think we have! Maybe I'll try to get acquainted with him before I mention the post, just in case.'

'Good idea. You must have someone you really get on well with, Alice, someone you can trust and respect. You'll be spending a lot of time together. Who's the other one?'

'Well, I've never actually met her. She has been following my work closely, and frequently telephones and corresponds with me from Germany. She is a highly qualified doctor, living in Heidelberg, although I don't think she is German. Her accent is more Dutch, I think.'

Ellie pulled a face and punched her on the arm. 'Excuse me! I don't think I like the sound of you taking on a beautiful Dutch woman as a partner!'

Alice smirked at her mock outrage. 'I seem to have forgotten to tell you she is well into her sixties! When I said highly qualified, I meant it. She's a retired surgeon. She gave up surgery when she developed arthritis in her wrists.'

'Ah, she's sounding better and better!' laughed Ellie.

'Joking apart, she is one heck of an interesting woman. She has something of the Carole Cavendish-Meyer about her, I think.'

'Good Lord! There couldn't be two of them, surely?'

The dogs had decided the orchard was safe until the morning and it must now be time for biscuits and bed, so Ellie and Alice walked, arm in arm, back to the house.

Alice locked doors and closed windows, while Ellie settled her charges down for the night. Alice then poured them a nightcap, and they sat for a moment before going up to bed. 'What would you consider the timescale on getting the pavilion revamped?' she asked.

'Not long,' replied Ellie. 'The company working on the pool complex are, wait for it . . . ahead of schedule! I know, it has to be a first, but I will have a word with the site foreman and see if he could pressgang a few of his workman to sort it out for you. What are we looking at? A couple of partition walls in the long room, proper work benches for the computer room, new flooring right through and a coat of paint on the whole thing. The most complicated job will be the electrics. You need good lighting, and the correct power for your AZSEE equipment. I'm assuming you will be using the hi-tec version, virtual reality and all-singing, all-dancing computers?'

'Absolutely!'

'Okay. I'll see what I can do. The manager is a nice guy, and it's all work after all, and work is money in the pay packets. I can't see too much of a problem.'

Alice smiled a warm and loving smile. 'If everyone had a Fairy Godmother like you . . .'

'Godmother sounds very old, if you don't mind.'

'Sorry, how does Fairy God-person sound?'

'Ridiculous!' scolded Ellie.

'Oh, you know what I'm trying to say!'

'Listen, if anyone had a Fairy Godmother, it was me. All I'm trying to do is spread the good fortune around a bit, okay?'

Alice looked at her thoughtfully. 'Not everyone who finds a fortune in their laps behaves like you, my darling. A lot of people would be on their third world cruise by now, and blow the rest of us.'

'Yeah, well . . .' Ellie shook the comment off and stood up. 'Right, who's for bed?'

* * *

The caravan still had that slightly musty, but not unpleasant smell that Paula always looked forward to. She hooked up the electric and the gas, ran some water through the pipes and threw open the windows. It was late, but a blast of fresh air was a necessity.

It was a small site. Carefully laid out, with no more than six vans to each grassy, tree-edged area. Her brother's plot was the farthest away from the caretaker's static and the shower block. Opposite the caravan was a gate that led into a little copse, then out onto open marshlands. It seemed that only one other van was occupied tonight. A cheery glow shone from its windows, and childish laughter could be heard on the light evening breeze. You could never tell of course, as most of the holiday makers would spend their evenings in the local hostelry, not giggling and groping their way back to their tin houses until chucking-out time.

Paula unpacked her bags, put her food away and dragged an enormous black sack, which contained her duvet and two pillows, in from the car.

Everything set up to her satisfaction, she opened a bottle of Chardonnay Semillon and lifted her glass, trying to think of a suitable toast. Her mobile ruined her train of thought, and when she looked at the green display and saw it was the police station, her salutation became a swear word!

For a moment she thought about ignoring it, but she was a professional and, with a sigh, she lifted the phone to her ear. A short while later she pushed the 'end call' button and breathed a sigh of relief. DCI Foreman could be a good old boy when he wanted. He could easily have called her in. She made a mental note that she owed him one.

She ate a pleasant supper, a selection of pasta salads and cold meats washed down with the crisp dry wine. Outside she could hear the croaking of the marsh frogs in some nearby ditch. She lay back on the couch-cum-bed and decided that life could be very sweet. She really did not ask for much, but she did seem to reap all the rewards she wanted. Paula took a few more sips from her glass and decided a short walk before turning in would be the perfect end to the day. She pulled on her jacket and locked the van door.

The moon was full and walking was easy. Last time she was here she had followed a vixen, out foraging for scraps around the site. Her perseverance had been rewarded by the sight of three fox cubs at play. Paula remembered roughly where the lair was situated, and thought she would see if the fox family was still there, or whether they had moved on.

It took her about fifteen minutes to locate the right place and, sure enough, there were fresh tracks in the soft soil. The police officer selected a concealed spot to settle in, and soon made herself as comfortable as was possible in the damp undergrowth.

She was always amazed at how noisy the night could be. She had started her nocturnal wanderings in the woods at home, when for a time, a bad back had made sleep impossible. That, and the fact that she had heard on the grapevine that some sadistic beggars were out badger-baiting. Nothing would have given her greater delight than to get her hands on the wicked sods.

Tonight, she heard all the usual rustlings, squeaks, croaks and flutterings . . . and something else.

The sound was distant. Probably coming from the Marshfields Caravan Park, she thought. But then she wasn't so sure. She had meandered away from the camp in a semi-circle around the copse. She had then skirted a flat marshy field in order to get a moonlit view of the old, deserted priory, then back towards the Park.

As the sound seemed to have stopped, she wriggled back into her hide and continued her vigil. No fox came . . . but the strange sound started again.

The breeze was distorting it and its exact location was still a mystery. A shudder coursed its way between Paula's shoulder blades. This wasn't right.

She had run a mental analysis of night noises through her computer-like brain, and the search came back — no matches found.

Her right hand went automatically to her inside pocket. Yes, she had her mobile. Sadly, no police radio this time, no cuffs or baton, and no back-up. She was very much alone out here.

She made her way in what she thought was the right direction. The noise drifted on the night wind. What the hell was it? It was somehow familiar. If only the breeze would stop. Then she could hear it clearly and recognise it. She stood still, straining her ears to make out the odd sound.

Perhaps she should go back to the Park and get some help? But help for what? She would look like a right plank, asking to be accompanied into the woods, because she had heard something funny. No, she'd find out what the dickens it was, then decide if she needed help.

The sound was drawing her back onto the path to the copse. The wind ceased, only to be followed by a feeling of dread. No, not just dread, but déjà vu.

Of course, it was a familiar sound because she had heard it all before. After all, it was she who had found the school-teacher at the Hobhole Quarry.

It was the sound of a dying child that she heard. And a repeated mantra. A nursery rhyme.

'Oranges and lemons said the bells of St Clements.'

This time it was not the gurgle from a torn throat; the gurgling and the gasping had stopped by the time she got there. It was the creaking of the rope that she heard.

Moonlight threw its silvery reflections into the tree. In a tableau in black and white, the girl swung gently back and forth, her tousled head at an unnatural angle, and her tongue sticking rudely between swollen lips.

All this was shown clearly to WPC Paula English by the cruel moon.

For a second, the sheer horror of the sight before her left her rooted as firmly as the gallows tree. Then she leapt at the child, pushed its weight upward and tried to free the rope. She succeeded in loosening it enough to get the strain off the dead weight in her arms, and crying and swearing at everything and nothing, she finally got the girl to the ground.

She knew she was too late, but she tried everything she knew to revive the child. Tried with all her might and all her heart. If sheer will power could have brought her back, the little girl would have sat up and smiled.

But she had been right the first time. She was too late.

All this had gone on without a thought for the Cockney Warbler. 'When I grow rich, said the bells of Shoreditch.'

She pulled out her mobile and dialled 999. She made a note of exactly where she was, and hurriedly retraced her footsteps back to the camp. She knew he would still be there when she got back with the police. She was sure of that because she had once met Roderick Black.

Hot tears caressed her cheek as she stumbled through the undergrowth, and she silently berated DCI Foreman for being so nice.

CHAPTER SIXTEEN

The murder room was hushed. Introductions had been made, and the joint investigation was underway.

DCI Craddock had provided the team with all the information available to them regarding the suffocation of the six young people at Elizabeth Ryder's shelter; the death of Edith Higgins, apparently at the hands of, the now also deceased, Staff Nurse Lily Frampton; and the murder of the priest, Father Dominic Hearn, allegedly by the twelve-year-old Charlie Keene.

DCI Foreman followed on with everything they knew about Roderick Black's suspected murder of five schoolchildren and intended murder of a sixth. As yet they were still collecting evidence on the death of another child, seven-year-old Tanya Jones, who had been found by one of his officers, hanging from a tree near a caravan site where her family frequently stayed. This one was in the Kent Police's area, but as it had all the hallmarks of Operation Innocents, they were sending a motorcycle rider with all the details later that day.

The men and women, both CID and uniformed, listened intently to their commanding officers. The onus to find the reason for all these terrible deaths hung heavily on them.

The meeting continued by taking each crime individually and with the officers involved filling in as much detail as they could.

A prematurely balding detective, who had been first on scene to the Edith Higgins murder, addressed his colleagues in a sombre and depressing voice that Wendy Brown felt would not have been inappropriate coming from Eeyore.

'Forensics will show, without doubt, that no one else was involved in the death. The security guard arrived only minutes after the killing. No one had entered or left the D-corridor while he was there. Video footage of the corridor also confirms that. The nurse was covered in Mrs Higgins' blood, and she was still holding the scalpel that has been proved to be the murder weapon. The scene of crime officers established that there was no other evidence of anyone else present at the scene. Pretty conclusive, I'd say.' He sat down heavily, his worried countenance remaining.

A young PC who had been researching the nurse's history then stood, and with a slight lisp, gave a glowing account of the dead woman's reputation.

'After extensive interviews with family, working colleagues, friends and ex-patients, I've only ever heard good spoken of Staff Nurse Frampton. As far as I can ascertain, she was simply a good person, kind and compassionate, with no skeletons in the cupboard that I can come up with.'

Bob Foreman stared at his notes, then asked the PC what he knew about old Edith Higgins.

'Not much to know, sir. A widow, no family to speak of. She was an Alzheimer's patient. Harmless, and often confused. Regularly wandered off, scantily dressed, and completely unaware of where, or who, she was. Lily Frampton was very good with her. Her and all the other patients with senility problems.'

'Would you think it possible that Staff Nurse Frampton had had enough of her dotty patients and just flipped when the old lady wandered off, yet again?'

'No, sir. I put that hypothesis to her ward sister, who told me she thought Lily may not have been feeling very well that day, she was very subdued apparently. She assured me, however, that Lily's attitude to the patients had been as caring and considerate as always. She showed no signs of being close to the end of her tether, sir, she just seemed tired and listless in herself, looked as if she might be coming down with something.'

'Thank you, Officer.' Len Craddock interposed. 'We have had the PM results back on our nurse and there were no abnormalities. A blood test taken on her admittance to the prison hospital showed no evidence of any drug or substance that should not have been there. She had recently taken a small dose of paracetamol, which would support the sister's theory that she was not feeling very well. Frankly, we have no idea why she acted so completely out of character, or why she went into a trance state and died.'

Bob took over at that point, explaining the situation with the schoolteacher, Roderick Black, was exactly the same.

'He was a loving husband and father, and a dedicated teacher. He had been out on a limb for abused kids more times than you or I have had hot dinners. No one had a bad thing to say about him. Interestingly, the child who survived the murders at the Hobhole Quarry still sees Mr Black as his favourite teacher. At first, we believed he had blotted out the memory of the dreadful happenings that day, but now forensics are saying that it was possible the boy, who was only injured, was the first to be attacked. He was most likely unconscious when his classmates fell foul of their master. The lad said they had been enjoying the expedition when Mr Black told the prefect, Johnny Baker, that he was not feeling very well and that perhaps the older boy should get the younger ones back to the school. He remembers nothing after that, so sadly there is no eyewitness to the murders. As with the hospital murder, the SOCOs are certain that there were no other persons involved. They went over the scene extensively and found no evidence to put anyone else at the murder site. The murder weapon was most definitely the oak club that was found in Mr Black's hand and DNA tests have found tissue from the prefect's throat under Black's fingernails. Again, there is little doubt about who killed the kids.' He exhaled with a certain amount of frustration. 'And again, the suspect went into a trance state, has died, and we don't know why.'

The meeting continued, ideas and thoughts being expounded and refuted. They broke for lunch and then continued well into the afternoon. Huge boards were set up around the room, and by three o'clock, they were covered with photos, names, times and notes of all descriptions. The reports from Kent had been held up until the following day, and at four o'clock, as the Met DCI was drawing the meeting to a conclusion, a memo was rushed into him. He hurried from the room only to return minutes later and take his counterpart to one side.

'Bob. The Keene boy has died. He slipped into unconsciousness this morning and died about fifteen minutes ago. What in heaven's name is happening here?'

'I think it has little to do with heaven, Len. As you know, I had a professor friend look that child over yesterday, and he feared for his life. I think we must assume that we are going to lose Elizabeth Ryder in the same way. Len, would you mind if I ask Amanda Gerrard to have a look at the Ryder woman? She is the best criminal psychologist I have ever worked with. Someone has to try and break through that woman's trance before she dies. We have to find out what happened to her!'

'You bring in anyone you want, Bob. You will have no argument from me, I assure you. Get on to her now and I'll tell the squad what has happened to young Charlie Keene.' He paused then turned back to Bob. 'If we do lose Ryder, we may have a bit more time with Kev Jones, the father who killed his daughter at the caravan park. He's in custody in Kent, so . . .' He shrugged and went back to the team.

Foreman left a message for the profiler to get back to him as soon as possible, and rejoined the Murder Squad. Before they closed, the two DCIs gave individual tasks to their officers, with the main priority being to find a connection between Frampton, Ryder, Black and Keene. Somehow, they had all been infected, or influenced in some way, to do that which would have been abhorrent to them in their normal frame of mind.

DI Jon Leatham was given the job of tackling medical advisors to find out exactly what kind of thing could possibly lead to a complete change of personality. All the way back to Surrey, he discussed with Wendy and Bob, the kinds of things he should be looking for. He scribbled furiously into his notebook and read out loud to his boss and his colleague. 'One . . . drugs. None were found in blood tests, but some drugs don't stay in the system for long. (Bit like Rohypnol?) Perhaps there is something that is difficult to trace? Two . . . some kind of hypnotic suggestion? Ask Ellie's hypnotist bod if that's a possibility. Three . . . an illness. Some sort of brain disease? Maybe a virus? Something really difficult to detect unless you knew what you were looking for? Or a new strain of disease? Four . . . fanaticism. Not probable, given the history of the suspects but a long shot, could a religious cult have brainwashed them?'

Wendy mumbled her agreement of his suggestions. She was quiet and Bob knew she was not particularly happy with her allotted task, which was to do a study of Roderick Black's every move over the past couple of months.

She had said she did not relish the job as she would obviously have to question his widow. It would require a depth of tact that the detective sergeant was not sure she possessed. Bob knew otherwise; she may be a bit ham-fisted but she was a good officer and would handle the situation correctly, whatever she thought.

Bob kept his mind on his driving. He focused carefully on the road, other vehicles, pedestrians, road signs, and everything and anything of interest in his peripheral vision. He wanted to clear his mind. Free it up a bit. Leave death out of his thoughts for an hour or so. It was a trick he had perfected years ago to help him focus on the really important issues, and filter out the crap. By the time he was back at his desk he would have a little more clarity to his thinking. Well, that was the plan, anyway.

* * *

Paula English declined more time off work. She also turned down the offer of counselling. She had returned home to Leatherhead as soon as she had told the Kent Constabulary all she knew, went to B&Q, purchased some wallpaper and paint, and immediately set about redecorating her flat. She remembered doing exactly the same thing after being told that her father had died. She needed a practical job, a down-to-earth job. If she had her own garden and not the communal one, she would probably have dug it from one end to the other.

As she measured paper and carefully matched the patterns, she considered what had happened. She had seen the child several times before. It had been her laughter that she heard when she had arrived at the Park. The caravan had been owned, as far as she could recall, by a London family. She had once spoken to the mother, a friendly soul with a round face and body to match. 'Smashin' 'ere init?' The woman had grinned with delight. 'Fresh air! Yer can't beat it, can yer? Blimey, where we come from yer lucky t'see across the road, what wiv all the pollution and stuff from the traffic! This is really smashin'!'

Paula was not sure if this had been the girl's mother — there seemed to be brothers, sisters, nieces, nephews, aunts, uncles, grans and grandads, coming and going at different times. She wondered how they all fitted into the four-berth van. Whatever, there was always genuine laughter coming from across the way, and Paula never recalled hearing voices raised in anger or confrontation.

She considered the similarity to the Hobhole Quarry deaths. There was no doubt in her mind that the man who killed little Tanya Jones was suffering in the same way as the teacher. She thought that it had to be some awful disease, some airborne virus, that had attacked their brains and turned them into psychos.

Cutting another length of wallpaper, she mulled over tomorrow's debriefing with the DCI. She had already spoken to him, and he had offered her the option of not joining the Murder Squad. She had deliberated long and hard, but concluded that she was a police officer, and some of the jobs were nastier than others, but this was what she did. She knew her involvement, first hand, in two of the cases would be invaluable, so she declined his offer, and promised to be in his office at seven the next morning. She wanted to report to him before joining Operation Innocents.

As she stood back to check her work, she wondered what William Hill would give as odds on the chance of her taking time off, going to a different county, and being a witness to a murder connected with her own inquiry? 'About a squillion to one, huh, cat?'

Melody danced tantalisingly close to the freshly painted skirting board and whisked her fine tail to within a millimetre of the paint tin. 'Just you dare, you little minx!'

She grabbed the cat and swung her heavy soft body up into her arms for a cuddle. For a moment, she felt the weight of the child in her arms, and for the second time since her evening promenade, Paula English cried.

CHAPTER SEVENTEEN

Alice felt as if a weight had been lifted since she decided to share the Azimah Project. Ellie had rung her at the hospital that morning and confirmed work would begin on the pavilion in the next couple of days. Then to improve things even more, she had received a fax from Heidelberg. Her Dutch doctor, Nelli Kuiper, was going to be in London for a symposium next week and wanted to meet her.

She read the memo for a second time and decided it was a perfect solution. She could take her and Ellie, and perhaps Michael too, out to dinner. Then, if they felt she was suitable, she could offer her the post.

She was just about to call Ellie and tell her, when the telephone rang. As soon as she heard Michael's tone, she knew that the tide had turned on her perfect day.

'Alice? I'm sorry to have to call you, but Maureen Shaw and I are very concerned about Jake. Maureen had to go to him twice last night, and as we have some inpatients staying at present, it was a bit difficult to calm him without disturbing the others. He had the granddaddy of all nightmares, and today he is lethargic and uncommunicative again. Any chance you could come back and see him? We really feel that he is worse than ever.'

'Of course, Michael. I was hoping to get away early anyway. I have one more round to make, and I must take a quick look at a new patient, then I'll be on my way. Just keep him as quiet as possible and get someone to sit with him. I'll do a full blood count, and I have another drug to try out, something that should help him sleep better. Poor devil, I feel so very sorry for him. Whatever we try to do for him, he just doesn't respond as he should. It's so frustrating!'

Michael thanked her, and Alice packed her papers into her old Gladstone bag and headed for the wards.

* * *

The two uniformed officers stared through the spy hole into the custody cell.

'What do you make of this, Trev?'

'Beats me. You think they would get someone in who could help the poor sod.'

'Like who? And don't forget, the poor sod, as you call him, topped his kid, didn't he?'

'Yeah, but look at him. He's away with the bloody fairies. You'd think there would be a shrink somewhere who could do something for him.'

'Like shut him up, for instance.'

'Hmm, that is creepy. Those nursery rhymes do your head in after a while, don't they?'

'Yeah, and your shift finishes at five. I've got it until ten o' bloody clock!'

'Serves you right for nicking all the overtime. You could always try singing along!'

* * *

Alice arrived minutes after Ellie had left for home, and she found her patient in her office, again logged on to the AZSEE programme.

'Jake. I'm not being difficult, but I'd rather you only use the equipment when I'm around. We're still working on it, and well, I know you wouldn't damage it in any way intentionally, but until Gordon completes the updates that he's sending me, it's a bit sensitive.'

Jake mumbled something that Alice hoped might be an apology.

She went over and put a reassuring hand on the young man's shoulder, and was quite unprepared for the rebuff.

'Get your hands off me! You're all the same! Use me as a fucking guinea pig, and look at the state of me! If you can't help me, then find me someone who can!'

'Jake! Whatever is wrong? You know we're here for you. Your well-being and quality of life are all that matters to us.'

'What fucking quality of life? I don't have any quality left! I don't have any life left!'

This time Jake did not pull away when Alice touched him. He broke down, like a child whose temper tantrum had got it nowhere, and sobbed like a baby.

Alice called Maureen Shaw and together they took Jake to his room where she administered a sedative. When he had calmed down enough to leave him for a short time, Alice spoke briefly to the nurse. 'With the kind of drug regime he is on, I really don't like to give him sedatives, but he is too distressed to leave him without some sort of medication to quieten him.'

'Dr Cross. Something, or someone, is having a terrible effect on this boy. You've seen him when he is "normal". He's a polite, well spoken, funny young man. Something is happening to him, and I'm frightened for him.'

Alice ran her hand through her hair. 'Mrs Shaw, I don't know what else to do. Apart from put him under lock and key, feed him personally, administer all his pills by hand, and watch him twenty-four hours a day, I just don't know what more we can try.'

'That's not far from what I do now, when he's here at the clinic.'

'I'm at my wits end with him, Maureen, I really am. Look, have you got a spare room upstairs, if you have, I'll stay tonight and keep an eye on him myself, give you a break. Problem is, now I've given him the sedative, I can't start him on the new relaxant I proposed. They would not mix at all. I'll postpone that until tomorrow, all being well, he can try them then.'

The night sister assured her that there was a bed for her, but would not hear of taking time off. If there was a problem with Jake she would be there for him.

Alice Cross felt a surge of relief to know that Maureen would remain on duty. Jake's earlier outburst had shocked Alice, and there was a nastiness in his manner that left her feeling very uncomfortable, and not a little vulnerable.

* * *

Far away, flying happily through a night sky, the pilot looked down on bright lights of the town below him. The lights grew fewer as he moved towards the countryside, and finally there was only blackness, as he flew out over the endless sea.

He was happy. There was no life for him without wings.

* * *

Ellie locked up and, together with her faithful Digger, went to her bedroom early. The call from Alice had disturbed her. Naturally she was sad she would not be here with her tonight, but it was the nature of the message that worried her. Prior to speaking to Alice, she had been on the telephone for about a quarter of an hour to Bob Foreman. She had explained how very upset Alice had been to hear she had been seeing murder suspects again. Bob had completely understood, and agreed to respect her wishes that she take a bit of a back seat for a while. He had told her about Charlie Keene dying, and that it seemed as if there was another murder that followed the awful pattern. He added that he had arranged for Amanda Gerrard to visit Elizabeth Ryder.

Ellie remembered Amanda Gerrard well. She reminded Ellie of a great scarlet flamingo. She wore red, red, and more red. From her crimson shoes upwards, she flamed. She commanded respect. No, she demanded respect. In fact, she terrified the daylights out of most of the Surrey Police Force with her incredible presence. Ellie had been totally in awe of the woman, and after working closely with her on one occasion, admired, maybe not her methods, or her arrogance, but certainly her strength and her determination to let justice be done. If anyone could find a way through to the real Elizabeth Ryder, it would be Amanda Gerrard.

Ellie's mind was still swimming with thoughts of the dead suspects when Alice telephoned. She relayed the events of the evening and told her of her deep concerns for Jake Kennedy. Ellie had spent some time with the young man herself that day. His aura was dreadful, tight to his body and lacking in bright colour. His physical appearance was as bad as his aura. He was dirty and unshaven; his once smart clothes were grubby and stained. Probably the worst thing of all was his behaviour. He had hardly spoken to her, and when he did it was in words of one syllable. She had been concerned enough to ask Michael if he wanted her to stay that night, although getting a dog sitter at such short notice would not have been easy. He had assured her that with Mrs Shaw to back him up, and Dr Cross on her way, she should get home to her animals. He would ring if there were an emergency, and he was sure Alice would be in touch when she had seen Jake.

She had been forced to echo Alice's anxiety, and had asked her what she honestly thought Jake's prognosis was.

'I dread to think, darling,' she had replied. 'Not a very professional opinion, I know, but I am completely mystified as to why I cannot stabilise him. I have no one to turn to on this. Azimah Siddiq had no other apostles. I was her only disciple, Ellie, and I badly need some help. I will run blood tests in the morning and get them straight off to the lab. I don't know what else to do.'

Her heart had gone out to Alice. She sounded so desolate. She had even lost her enthusiasm when she told her about the Dutch doctor's impending visit, and although she enthused over meeting the eminent lady, Ellie knew that nothing was going to lift Alice's spirits tonight.

Before she finished, Ellie made Alice promise to ring her, no matter what the hour, if she wanted to talk, or if she had another problem with her perplexing patient.

'Good night. God bless. I love you,' she said, and they had hung up.

Now, alone in her bed, except for the comforting warmth of her little dog, who had taken full advantage of the situation and snuggled in beside her, she wondered what would become of Jake Kennedy. She had not liked the sound of Maureen Shaw's words when she had suggested that someone or something was affecting the man. She had seen too many cases of nice people being affected recently.

As she sank into a restless sleep, she prayed for Jake's safety.

CHAPTER EIGHTEEN

It took Amanda Gerrard about two minutes to appreciate she was going to get nowhere with the very precise Mrs Elizabeth Ryder. However, as failure was not a word she cared to associate with, she had stayed with the unfortunate woman for over an hour. Little had been said other than the repeated requests to assist the homeless.

Gerrard had sat across the room and watched. She observed every movement and every expression that Mrs Ryder presented, and there were precious few. The psychologist had spoken quietly to the woman, using phrases and statements intended to provoke some sort of reaction, but there was nothing. Elizabeth's cultured voice had remained on the same level, and her appeal to give generously never altered. After a time, the woman had become silent, and Amanda had studied the trance-like state with deep interest.

Now, with her scarlet leather jacket thrown carelessly over the back of her office chair, she thought again about that very odd trance. She had observed physical stillness, very shallow breathing and a pale complexion.

Amanda pushed back the chair and began pacing the room. Trance was subjective and it was difficult to measure the depth. The woman had obviously directed her attention inwardly. She did not react to any external sensory stimuli, but in a 'normal' trance, if there was such a thing, she would have expected fluttering eyelids, some sort of slumping in her chair, perhaps increased lachrymation or swallowing. A trance state can increase the body temperature, but Mrs Ryder had remained bolt upright, and ice-cold to the touch.

Very odd, very odd indeed. But no odder than the fact that this woman had murdered six young people.

The tall doctor flung herself back into the chair, leaned back as far as it would go and uttered a curse. She would have gambled a month's money on the fact that Elizabeth Ryder would have found it difficult to tread on a spider, let alone kill anyone. If she had not read the forensic report and all the collected paperwork on the murders, she would have laughed in the faces of her accusers. The woman's history, gleaned from friends and working colleagues, was an endorsement to piety, altruism, compassion and sanity. She had dug deeper and found nothing in her past, or her family's history, that could have been an underlying cause for this madness. Now, all that was left was an empty shell, a husk of a human. There would be no recovery, of that she was certain. She had been told that the other victims/killers were all dead, and she was not at all surprised. If the other poor souls had been like Elizabeth Ryder, they would not have had a hope in hell of surviving.

Ah, she reined in her racing thoughts, all except one, of course. A devoted father had hung his beloved little daughter from the branch of a tree, then sat below and sung her nursery rhymes.

Her eyes narrowed and she picked absent-mindedly at a tiny loose fleck of scarlet nail varnish. This man she had to see. She would leave her call to Bob Foreman until she had arranged another visit to that strange other-world that most of her patients inhabited. A trip to Kent would not take long and, if her latest interviewee was as cooperative as the last, she would be on her way home before three o'clock. Leaving plenty of time to buttonhole DCI Foreman and ask him what the hell he was involving her in this time.

* * *

Jon Leatham sat opposite Tony Ambrose and was surprised to feel a butterfly's wing of nervousness flutter in his stomach.

It was a twofold visit. He needed to know about hypnotherapy and hypnotic techniques in order to advance his enquiries into possible causes for a change in normal behaviour. And he needed to lose the craving.

So, what if the appointment had been for him? He smiled grimly to himself. He was hardly going to let half the station know he was seeing a therapist; he'd never live it down. He didn't mind his nickname of 'Gentleman Jon', but he didn't think he would be able to handle 'Ravin' Gentleman Jon', as would probably be the case.

He had telephoned ahead and made sure that Dr Ambrose was able to give him time for both sessions, official and personal, and now he sat in the pleasant, airy consulting room, with an advanced case of the heebie-jeebies welling up inside.

'I think perhaps we should go ahead with my normal introduction, Detective Inspector. It might answer some of the questions you would be asking me anyway about this form of therapy.' Tony Ambrose smiled affably at the policeman. 'There is nothing mysterious or mystical about it. Please don't confuse me with what you might have heard about the old Victorian entertainers, or Mesmer, for that matter. I have signed a pledge, a code of ethics and professional conduct, and my only aim is to help my client achieve an attainable goal. I simply utilise a method of putting you into a state of altered consciousness, somewhere where you can access a deeper level of awareness. I only ever work with your total cooperation, and the whole procedure is done in a caring and nurturing manner. I am, first and foremost, someone who wishes to help you. I have no reason to exert my will on you for some nefarious purpose. I simply assist you to activate inner resources that are impossible to reach when in your normal day-to-day routine. I do not "put you to sleep", that's a popular misconception. I help you to relax to a point somewhere between being asleep and being awake; a place where we can look at the things in your life that bother you, and change them for the better.'

Jon found the doctor's voice easy on the ear. This guy should be on the radio, he thought. The deep melodic tone held your interest to a point where you were totally engrossed in what he was saying. He felt completely at ease with him, the nervousness of earlier having disappeared.

The detective sat back and allowed the man to continue.

'I will do a couple of little tests today, but I never use hypnosis on a first session. Today I will need a lot of history from you, and we will ascertain your receptivity to being hypnotised. I'm afraid there will be quite a few questions I have to ask. It is really important I believe you are a suitable case for this kind of treatment.'

'Can't anyone be hypnotised?' asked Jon.

'Absolutely not. I would never use hypnosis on anyone with a severe psychosis. With paranoia, or any mental illness that is typified by delusions, we would not consider hypnotherapy as a form of treatment. Also, you cannot, nor would you wish to hypnotise an unwilling subject. It is vitally important that the client and the therapist get on well. The client must have a real wish to either get better, in the case of a medical condition, or overcome the phobia, the habit, the compulsion, or whatever thought or idea is causing them unhappiness. Someone who does not trust you is not suitable, and would not allow themselves into the trance state. Simple as that.'

Jon Leatham nodded slowly. 'I can appreciate that, but you do hear of people doing really weird things while under the influence.'

The doctor sighed and shook his head. 'The lay person knows nothing about hypnosis other than all the stories and myths they see on television or read in books. There are performers who use hypnosis for entertainment, and there still may be charlatans with no medical qualifications who prey on the gullible, but think about it from my point of view. You come to me for help with a problem that you cannot deal with alone, so we have to work together on that problem. When a trust is built up between us, you, in a trance, hand over a large measure of personal control to me. Not everything, you can still perform tasks efficiently, avoid hazards and speak lucidly. I, in turn, use your altered state to help you view your problems from a better perspective. I can help you to bring about physical or mental changes by lowering your levels of tension, and by suggestion. I endeavour to make your life better. Why would I wish to hurt you? You would certainly never come back. You would tell your friends I was not to be trusted. In one move, I could destroy my entire career! Yes, in essence I suppose I could implant some unsavoury suggestion in your head, but as I said, why would I go to such lengths to build up a reputable clinic, then allow it to be brought down around my ears. More to the point, I am a medical doctor as well as a hypnotherapist. I am bound by the Hippocratic oath as well as my code of practice. I am here to practice conscientiously and to put the welfare of my patients before every other consideration.'

Jon was forced to agree with everything the doctor said, and jokingly added that the Svengali-type characters in literature had probably done his credibility no good whatsoever.

He found himself liking Tony Ambrose and decided that if he could get his head around putting himself into someone else's hands for a while, they should get on well.

He answered all the questions put to him, and then the doctor asked him to stand up straight with his feet together and his eyes closed.

'What's this for?'

'Postural Sway Test. It's the method I use to test your susceptibility. Now, I want you to recall a time as a child when you used to swing back and forth on a swing in the park. Concentrate hard and remember what it felt like.'

Jon recalled the local playground and heard his little sister calling out for him to race her to the roundabout. She spun around and around, while he swung, ever higher, on his favourite swing.

'Oh yes! No problem there. Your powers of imagination and concentration are excellent!'

Jon opened his eyes and found himself perceptibly swaying to and fro.

Tony smiled at him. 'There are lots of good ways to check, but that's my favourite. Well, Detective Inspector, I think I can help you, if you would like me to. Next visit I will put you in a light trance. Now, I'll show you how I work, then there is no mystery attached to the procedure.'

The doctor instructed Jon to lie down on the comfortable sofa, and then sat down with him at the foot end of the couch. He produced a remote control from his pocket, touched a button, and Jon saw the window blinds gently draw together. It was not dark by any means, but the bright sunlight was shut out.

'Just focus on the light source over on that bookcase.'

Jon followed the doctor's pointing finger and saw a light wheel turning silently. He had not been aware of it before, but there was soft music coming from somewhere, and as he watched the colours on the wheel, he felt an urge to shut his eyes.

'And then I just talk you down.'

Jon believed it.

'With very little difficulty, I should imagine!' Tony Ambrose laughed and said it was easy-peasy! When you knew how. He opened the shades and switched off the music.

'Now what else can I tell you to help with your enquiries?'

Jon felt cheated. He had wanted to stay in that dreamy state for a while longer. He did not want to be a policeman right now, but he knew he must, and he dragged out his notebook and put his dutiful hat back on. 'Well, you've told me a lot anyway, and I confess to be fascinated. Can I just ask, do you think someone could influence another into doing a thing that was completely opposed to his natural being?'

'I don't think so. No. I could not make you do something while in a trance that you would not think of doing while awake. You would wake up. You would come back to full awareness if I asked you to do something that was contrary to your normal beliefs.'

'What about autosuggestion? Some sort of self-hypnosis?'

'I can't see how that would work either. That is something people use for their own good, to help themselves, you know the old Couéism, "Every day, in every way, I am getting better and better." You use autosuggestion to get rid of pain, worry, or a myriad of symptoms, not to make yourself hurt people. Some hypnotists teach their clients a form of self-hypnosis to be able to continue their treatment as and when they want. In a case of insomnia for instance, the patient needs help when they are trying to go to sleep and can use the procedure accordingly. I can't see anyone being able to talk themselves into doing something evil; it just doesn't work like that.'

'Doctor, in your opinion, what could make a good person turn into a cold-blooded killer?'

The doctor rubbed his chin thoughtfully. 'Chemicals, or hate, I should think.'

Jon looked puzzled. 'Chemicals as in drugs?'

'Yes. I could give you a list of drugs, or combinations of drugs that could render you barking mad in no time.'

'And hate?'

'Hate. There is no stronger emotion. Not even love in my book, but please don't tell God, will you? If you have enough hate inside you, I think you could do anything at all.'

The police officer whistled between his teeth. 'I think I was looking for more of a . . . I don't know really . . .'

'More of a Svengali, someone having their terrible way with unsuspecting righteous souls?'

'Probably. But you've kind of convinced me that is not going to be the case. Could you give me that list of drugs?'

'No problem. I'll type something out and fax it across to you if that would help?'

'Thank you. May I ask also about illnesses? Some diseases can change a person, can't they? My uncle had a stroke and became aggressive and foul mouthed, nothing like his normal self at all.'

'Certainly, there are medical and mental disorders that can change a personality, but you generally find they present a gradual onset. It would be one hell of a powerful bastard of a disease to act so quickly, and nothing that I could put a name to right now. Perhaps you should talk to a neurologist, someone who is well acquainted with brain disease and any new encephalo-viruses. It's not really my forte . . .' Tony paused for a moment. 'In fact, how about having a word with Dr Alice Cross? She knows more about brain chemicals than anyone I know. I'm sure she would help you if she could. Hey! She's here today. Would you like me to give her a call for you, see if she's got a minute?'

Jon nodded, and then added that he would be more than grateful if the doctor had the time to see him. If not, perhaps she could give him an appointment as soon as possible.

Dr Ambrose lifted the telephone and quickly consulting a typed index of staff numbers, punched in a three-figure code. After a brief time, his call was answered. He explained the situation, and smiling at Jon, gave him the thumbs-up sign. With one hand over the mouthpiece, he gazed enquiringly at the police officer.

'Dr Cross says she will meet you in the cafe at the back of the Centre in ten minutes, if that's okay with you?'

'Brilliant! Tell her I'll be there. Oh, and thank her for me, please.'

The session over, the two men shook hands.

The doctor had a firm handshake, and Jon reaffirmed his opinion of the man. Yes, he liked him, and he almost felt confident enough to trust him with his subconscious. Almost.

On his way to the cafe, he wondered if Dr Alice Cross would remember him. His close involvement with Ellie McEwan over those dreadful murders last year had brought them into contact on a couple of occasions. He had rather liked Dr Cross, but thought she came under the heading of driven, when it came to her work. He knew about Alice's affair with Ellie, and sincerely hoped Ellie would not get set aside, while her doctor pursued her medical dream.

He sat at one of the tables and refused, as he always did, to acknowledge the fact that he had a soft spot for Miss McEwan.

Alice arrived, more than a little dishevelled, her body language exuding stress.

'DI Leatham! Good to see you. How are you doing? God! I'm sorry I'm such a mess, I've been up half the night with a patient.'

Jon thought that her movements were jerky, and her voice was a fraction too high.

'What can I do for you?'

Jon offered her a coffee and as the doctor gratefully accepted, the detective left her for a moment to order two cappuccinos. As Jon waited for the steaming cups, he quietly observed Alice Cross.

She rocked backwards and forwards on her chair, rubbed one shoe against the back of her leg, nibbled impatiently on a knuckle, puffed out her cheeks, and then drew in a huge gulp of air, and generally could not sit still.

'Don't mind me saying, Doctor, but you look about ready to blow. Is it this problem patient of yours?' He placed the cups on the table and waited for the floodgates to burst.

The doctor looked him full in the eye and sighed. No floodgates, just the sound of the air going out of the balloon.

'You'll know what I mean, Detective, when I say I'm at my wits end. You have probably been there a dozen times yourself. You know, the one case that gets you by the balls and . . .'

'Bit like the one we are on now, by the sound of it.'

'Well, as I seem to be of little or no help to myself, how can I help you?'

Jon explained as succinctly as he could and Alice bit her lip.

'To be honest, there are some very insidious diseases that can change a person beyond recognition, but Tony is right, they do not hit instantly. There is nothing I can offer you, well, nothing I know about, that could affect someone so quickly. To be honest, there is only one virus I have even considered to be a possibility. Have you ever heard of sleeping sickness?'

Jon said he had heard it mentioned, but had no idea what form it took.

'There was an outbreak, back in the nineteen hundreds, 1917, I think. It killed millions of children and adults. It is called *encephalitis lethargica.* It apparently left some survivors in a catatonic state for decades. That is the side of it that most researchers are interested in, the returning to life after forty years as a living statue. But the thing that interested me was a paper written on some of the children who survived. Kids that had previously shown no psychiatric problems suddenly became destructive and thoroughly badly behaved. I mean, to the point of severely harming animals or people. They became hyperactive and impulsive showing no empathy or morals, some even exhibited signs of sexual aggression, sadism, fetishism and voyeurism. Some self-harmed, and others became uncontrollable. The paper states that, although on some occasions the children knew their behaviour was unacceptable, they were powerless to stop and were compelled to commit all manner of atrocities.' Alice pulled a face. 'Okay, the symptoms are not exactly right, but the thing is, Jon, there is a direct link between brain dysfunction and psychopathic, or criminal behaviour. If there is a new strain of an encephalitic virus out there, it could make healthy people do some very unsavoury things, but . . .' Alice sighed and stretched. 'The problem is that I don't believe this is the case. It's too selective, one here, one there. If we were threatened by another pandemic, and some epidemiologists reckon we are overdue for something nasty, then people would be dropping by the thousands. It just does not feel right, Jon. There just has to be something else. Have you considered the fact that they may have been given some sort of hallucinogenic? That's the only thing I would suspect could affect a person in a very short space of time.'

She paused, then added that she thought maybe Ellie had discussed this with WDS Brown, as she had been enquiring about drugs just recently.

'It is certainly an idea that we have been throwing around, Alice, and to date, it is the best we have. But how five different people from totally different walks of life have inexplicably ingested the same stuff, well, it beggars belief.'

'A madman would not be particularly selective. Perhaps he just finds a way to administer the drugs, and yee-ha, who cares who comes along to partake!'

'Maybe.' Jon Leatham finished his coffee and stood. His expression was downcast. 'Thanks for your time, Dr Cross. You have certainly given me something to think about. I guess I had better press on. Give my best wishes to Ellie and I hope you have a better night. Thanks again.'

The doctor accepted the proffered hand. 'Ellie will be sorry to have missed you. She has had a constant stream of patients this morning and then the Works Manager in charge of the pool complex needed her to look at something. I will give her your regards when I see her.'

Back in his car, Jon reviewed his findings. It appeared there was little more he could do until Dr Ambrose's medication list arrived. As he pulled out his safety belt, a small smile played across his lips — at least he might have half a chance to sort himself out. If he could only manage to let go of his ingrained copper's suspicion of others, and learn to trust Tony Ambrose.

* * *

As the DI fastened his belt, Amanda Gerrard was loosening hers, and preparing herself for another traumatic visiting session. Well, it would have been for a lesser mortal. Her own feelings were so closely guarded that her new subject was little more than a laboratory specimen under her scrutiny. She was a professional, through and through. She had fought for her place of authority, and she knew what everyone thought of her, and that was fine by her. She would go along with the iron woman bit. If she terrified half the Force, well, good. Excellent, in fact.

She pulled her jacket tighter around her and locked the car. As she strode across the tarmac, the heels of her bright red shoes clicking sharply on the hard ground, she refused to respond to the nagging worry that stirred in her gut. She would never admit to anyone, least of all to herself, that she had been deeply disturbed by Elizabeth Ryder, and was now most apprehensive about her impending visit to the latest innocent murderer.

The thought had come to her, as she had sat with the woman, that she was being spoken to by a corpse, and she had not liked that one bit.

CHAPTER NINETEEN

She could hardly believe how well the workmen had done. Standing over the excavation for the main pool, hard hat firmly on her head, Ellie was completely amazed at their progress in the last month. 'Sorry, Kyle, but you chaps could totally alter my original opinion of the Great British Workman!'

'To be honest, Miss McEwan, the weather has been on our side almost since we started, and the ground here didn't give us anywhere near as many problems as we expected. It's been a bit of a charmed job, really. All the materials arrived on time and, for once, we are up to full quota with the workforce. Speaking of which, we can easily renovate the tennis pavilion for you. I have a gang down there now, clearing it out and preparing it. If you don't mind me using the same tradespeople, we can get the whole thing done fairly quickly . . . carpets, curtains, the lot. I have had their estimates back, and they seem fair. I'll get the quote up to you later today if I can. I can't believe the local firms were so speedy with their figures. This has got to be one of the smoothest jobs I've had!'

The big man shook his head in vague disbelief at their good luck so far.

'I've probably put the mockers on it now, miss.'

'No, I've got very good vibes about this construction, Kyle. It's going to help a lot of people with their health problems when it is finished, and I think we have the Divine Go-ahead to get it completed as soon as possible.'

Kyle looked doubtful, but crossed his fingers and shrugged. 'It's certainly looking good. Let's just hope we can keep it up. Now, miss, there is just one thing, the reason I've had to drag you out here.' The man produced a large architect's drawing and looked around for somewhere to lay it out. 'There seems to have been a bit of a faux pas. Look, this is the main pool, these are the therapy pools. Here' — he stabbed at the diagrams with a big beefy finger — 'is the room for the mud and seaweed treatments. Now, just to the left of that area there, we had planned a hexagonal courtyard for quiet contemplation, I understand?'

'That's right. Somewhere for the patients to sit and relax after their treatments. What's the problem?'

'Well, this was to be completed last. Stage three to be precise. All the complex stuff needed to be done first, the pools, the water drainage systems, the pumps, and purification plant, and of course, the construction of the complex itself. Anyway, we started clearing the ground yesterday to lay the foundations for the courtyard, and we came across something we hadn't bargained for.'

Ellie looked puzzled. 'Surely the surveyors did their job properly? Whatever have you found?'

'It seems to be the remains of an old icehouse. It was completely overgrown by shrubbery and is mostly below ground level. No one would have known it was there. It wasn't until the JCB driver saw the old brickwork steps under the brambles and elder that we had any idea of its existence. Come on, I'll show you.'

They made their way through the partly constructed buildings and out to the farthest part of the site. The men had carefully cleared the undergrowth away to reveal a short flight of very old steps.

'The top of the building has long since gone,' explained Kyle. 'Do you know anything about icehouses, Miss McEwan?'

Ellie admitted having heard of them, but had never seen one.

'They were very popular on large estates. Most manor houses boasted their own icehouse. I reckon this one was late eighteenth, early nineteenth century from its construction. The brickwork is first class. It has a double layer and seems to have been insulated with charcoal. They used to cut ice from the local lake or pond, and pack it down into the central cellar, sometimes with straw in between to make it easier to remove. It was used in the manor house kitchen for all sorts of things like preserving, cooling drinks and making desserts. This one is classic, it's circular, come and look, it's in a remarkably fine condition.'

Kyle was obviously very interested in their find, and his enthusiasm was infectious, even though Ellie found herself wondering what the consequences of this discovery might be.

The stairs led down some eight feet and into a large circular chamber. Kyle had put a couple of neon torches down there for her to see the house better.

'I don't think this is the original floor. It is good solid brick, but I think it might have been added later, and I would not be surprised if that bricked up area over there' — he pointed to the wall — 'was a passageway to the main house at one time. Some of the gentry preferred that the servants used tunnels and passageways rather than be seen about the grounds of the house.'

'You seem to know an awful lot about icehouses?' remarked Ellie.

'There used to be one in the grounds of my old school. I was fascinated by it, and I never forgot its history. It seemed really spooky and exciting to a nine-year-old, that and the fact it was considered too old and dangerous for the pupils to venture into, which automatically gave it more allure! This one is much better than the one at school though. I'm sure if we took the floor up, we would find a sub-dome shape base with a melt water drain.'

'Kyle. Without wishing to be a killjoy, what exactly does all this mean? Is it some sort of national treasure? Do we have to report its existence? But more to the point, where is my courtyard going to go?'

The site manager pulled a face. 'Ah! Right. This is going to be your decision, I'm afraid, Miss McEwan. It is certainly a historic find. Local antiquarians would fight to see it, and I suspect the county museum would love to come and take photographs. There is a list of known icehouses, mainly on private property, I might add. But what we do with it is really up to you, as the present lady of the manor.'

'Oh great! I'll have to get the professor's view on this. Are there any suitable alternative sites for the courtyard, just in case we decide to keep this little oddity?'

'Yes, miss. There are two areas that would be more than satisfactory. One would provide even more quiet for your patients than the original position. Let's get out of here, the cold is really chilling, and I'll show you on the plans.'

Even without the ice, Ellie was frozen, and agreed wholeheartedly with her manager to leave the subterranean cavern. As she followed him up the ancient stairs, she had an irrational thought that, heritage be damned, this was not a good place to be, and if she had her way, she would tip several tons of concrete down it.

* * *

Alice was so tired that she felt physically sick. She had only managed to snatch a few hours' sleep, mainly due to her concerns about Jake.

Jake had called out in his sleep many times throughout the long night. Each time, she and Maureen Shaw had been close by, and gone to the dreaming pilot. Once they had to calm him as he screamed out, but the words were unintelligible, and the shouts soon dulled to low moans and whimpers.

During the quieter periods, having left her patient under the vigilant watch of her night sister, Alice had returned to her computer. For hours she had searched for other cases with similar presentations, but she found nothing. Not for the first time, she considered Jake's own words. 'If you can't help me, find me someone who can.' Perhaps it was time to allow a psychiatrist to visit her patient. Maybe Jake was suffering from a mental illness brought on by the trauma he had sustained, and needed a different kind of help to support the one that she was offering.

The doctor sat in her temporary office and stared at the computer screen. She was much too tired to concentrate and decided to check her emails, then give in to a catnap on the couch. Deleting most of the messages, Alice suddenly found one from Gordon Lamont in Scotland, asking if he could come down to the Centre for a few days. The researcher told her that he had a bit of interesting software to add to the AZSEE programme, and he preferred to install it himself. 'I'm not knocking your expertise, lassie, but it developed a few glitches this end, and I'd hate to give you more problems than you already have! Plus, I can have a snoop around what could possibly be my new home!'

Alice felt nothing but relief at the news, and sent an immediate reply, telling him to fly down as soon as he could; the Trust would pay his fare, as long as it was not first class!

She lay full length along the couch, stretching her aching back until the muscles screamed at her to stop. It would be great to have some support, and Dr Nelli Kuiper would soon be with them. She closed her eyes and tried to imagine having a team to work with. Not having to shoulder all the responsibility alone. Taking a day off. She tried to remember the last time she'd done that simple thing, but too many months had passed for her to recall. She thought about the house on the salmon fishing river in Ireland. Ellie would love it. As soon as all this was over, she would take her there. They would have a holiday. A real break with nothing to do but relax and enjoy themselves. Ellie could try to trace her ancestors, and she could take time to fish in that wonderful river, something she used to enjoy so much with her late father. She had barely even seen her rods since he'd died. In her mind, Alice could almost hear the birds singing and the rushing of the foaming water over the weir. Peace and quiet. Nature surrounding them, just her and her lovely Ellie.

What she wanted most of all was to wake up one morning, her arms wrapped around her, and to know she could stay with her all day long. Thinking of this, she drifted away into a deep sleep.

CHAPTER TWENTY

Daybreak moved the night clouds gently across the sky, and replaced them with the pale milky light of dawn.

Michael, clad in casual trousers and an oatmeal sweater, made his way to the pool building site. Birds sang loudly from the trees that lined the drive to the back entrance, and the day, although still fresh and cool, promised to be a hot one.

Ellie had told him of Kyle's incredible progress with the new development, and also of their strange find. As he could boast of a good night's sleep, admittedly his first in weeks, he decided on an early stroll to view the site, and check out the icehouse. He ignored the sign that declared it to be a hard hat area. As there were no brickies to drop anything on his head, he reasoned he was probably fairly safe.

Ellie had not exaggerated, and when he saw how advanced the work was, he too was amazed. Most of the main buildings were nearing completion, and the large swimming pool had been fully excavated and partially lined. One hydrotherapy pool was almost finished, and the other was only a day or so behind.

A slender young thrush landed on a pile of bricks close to where he stood. It tilted its head this way and that, then uttered a sweet chorus just for Michael.

'And a very good morning to you too!' The professor smiled at the bird, then began to pick his way through coils of conduit, and stacks of shrink-wrapped plasterboard, to the place where the icehouse had been discovered.

It took him a few minutes, and then he found himself in the scrubby area to the rear of the newly constructed treatment rooms.

He had been a little puzzled by Ellie's reticence to return with him last evening to see this piece of their estate's history. She had pulled a face when he suggested it and told him she had a bad feeling about it. She added that although she realised the final decision about its future or its fate lay with them both, she would not care if she never saw it again.

As the green-gold morning lit up the surrounding trees, Michael peered at the old brickwork steps. There had obviously been a door, as a strong lintel and surround remained, but the door itself would have rotted many a year since. Weak light filtered down the stairwell but failed to reach the bottom.

Michael cursed himself for not thinking to bring a torch. For some reason he had imagined the cellar was only a few feet deep and he was surprised to find the steep flight of old steps leading down into the damp and dewy earth.

He started to make his way carefully down into the gloom. There had to be about thirteen steps and, sitting on the last one, Michael could just see the dark outline of a battery powered lantern. He felt a rush of relief and thanked goodness for careless workmen. The cold down there was intense, and his fingers were already finding it difficult to switch on the lamp. Finally, he managed to activate it and a strong light filled the cavern.

The chamber was completely empty.

Michael was surprised that it held none of the usual detritus left behind when such a place had lost its original purpose, and been relegated to that of a simple garden storeroom. Neither was it damp — there was no glistening moisture on the walls or dark stains on the floor. The craftsmanship used in its construction was astounding considering the only people to see the inside of the structure would have been the servants. It seemed to be insulated in some way, and the professor noted that when the old house had been in its heyday, the icehouse had had three entrances. Apart from the one he had used, there were two other sealed-up doorways, one high up in the wall, and the other at floor level.

Michael was fascinated and decided that, when he had time, he really must look back through the old deeds and conveyances to the property.

He was just about to make a more detailed inspection of the lower doorway, when the lantern flickered and lost a great deal of its power. He was not unduly worried as he could still clearly make out the square of bright morning at the top of the stairs. Just as his sensible side decided it was probably not prudent to linger too long in case the battery failed completely, he was plunged into total, inky blackness.

For one moment he felt as if the floor had fallen away under him, and he was suspended in stygian darkness. Although he would not have believed it possible, the temperature fell even further, and to his horror, he realised he was utterly confused as to his whereabouts in the awful hole. Somehow the sunlit doorway had disappeared, and he was left, shivering and blinded, paralysed by fear.

He forced himself to take deep gasping breaths, and endeavoured to control his tremors. If he could just get back to the steps, he would be safe.

After an eternity, his foot struck the rough brickwork of the bottom step. Above him he could just make out the open doorway. He started to scramble upwards, but the sigh of relief choked in his throat, as he felt something touch his leg.

The awful knowledge that he was not alone in the cellar was all too much and he lurched upwards, stumbling into the sunlight with a strangled cry.

He was too frightened to look back and ran most of the way to his apartment. He arrived at his own door, gasping like a drowning man. Once inside, he tore off his clothes and got into a scalding hot shower. He needed to wash away whatever had touched him. He stood in the cleansing, steaming water for ten minutes before towelling himself off and finding clean clothes.

His hands still shook as he made himself a cup of tea and impatiently waited for Ellie to arrive at work. He couldn't wait to give her his blessing to go ahead and fill that hell hole in.

* * *

For once in her life, Amanda Gerrard was not looking forward to telephoning the police officer with her findings. She sat at her kitchen table and stared at the half-empty cup of black coffee. It was still early and there was no hurry to reach the office yet, but she was already breakfasted, showered and dressed. All she needed was the impetus to stand up and let the day begin.

Adding more coffee to the cup, stirring it slowly and checking its sweetness, she deliberated that she always delivered her opinions and reports in the same way. With professional, plain-spoken diagnoses, and with complete and unequivocal confidence in her verdict. All right, and maybe a little grandiose flair as well, but she was always sure of her facts, and not afraid to deliver them to the waiting flat-footed brigade.

She was glad this case was under the care of DCI Bob Foreman. Of all the higher-ranking officers she worked with, he, at least, had earned her respect. The tall, slim woman gazed thoughtfully at the bright Gaugin print on her wall, and thought again about yesterday's visit to Kent. It had been the perfect end to a shitty day.

She had blasted her way through the red tape in her usual manner, and in no time, had found herself sitting opposite the child killer. Except that he wasn't a child killer.

He had stared at her. No, he had stared through her. He was singing softly and she had to strain to hear the words.

'All the King's horses and all the King's men, couldn't put Humpy together again.'

How very true, she had thought. No one will ever put you together again.

There had been one moment, one millisecond, when she thought that he may have realised she was there, but no. In a very short time, she realised this man was as dead as his daughter. The only difference was that he was still waiting to stop breathing.

She stood, brushed down her crimson skirt, and took the cup to the sink. Still unsure as to what she would present to Bob, she picked up her red leather briefcase and her car keys.

She had never seen anything like this before. Maybe she'd just tell him the truth, and ask him if he knew anything about zombies?

* * *

Callum locked his bike and strode purposefully towards the main doors. He had volunteered to get in early and help Will put up some bamboo screening in a small disused courtyard area at the back of the orangery. The yoga instructor thought it had all the attributes of a perfect outdoor location for his summer classes. It just needed a bit more seclusion. Ellie and Michael had no objections to his utilising the spot, and had offered to buy the materials if he wanted to arrange it as he saw fit.

Callum, who always loved a project, had willingly made himself available to help, and between them they had chosen some screen panels, several fan-shaped trellises and some quick-growing climbing plants. The floor was already paved in York stone and had some empty plinths along one side. Will was delighted at these, as he owned some splendid Japanese-style pots that he had never found the right home for.

The local garden centre had delivered everything they required, and on this bright sunny morning, Callum could not wait to begin.

As he approached the orangery, he could see the yoga teacher already sorting through wooden stakes and trellises.

They checked everything was there, and that their toolkit had all they needed, then decided that, if the cafe was open, a coffee and one of Sylvie's bacon sandwiches would give them a good start to their manual duties. Will continued to select nails and suchlike, while Callum loped off to get the breakfast.

There was no smell of coffee, as was usual by now, and the cafe area was deserted. Callum decided he was obviously too early, and was about to return to the courtyard, when he heard a noise coming from the kitchen.

Great, perhaps he could twist Sylvie's arm into fixing them a quick 'sarnie' and a couple of drinks. He called out softly, then a little louder, but there was no answer. The noise continued, so thinking that she must be grinding coffee and had not heard him, he stuck his head around the door.

The sight that met his eyes would have been more suited to one of his war zones. If he had come across this grisly massacre in Africa, it would have been bad enough, but in this peaceful country estate in Ripley, it was unthinkable. For a moment he was back in hostile territory. His natural instinct was to protect himself, ascertain the situation, then to help the wounded. He threw himself inside the door and down behind a long workbench. Partially hidden by a tall oven housing, he scanned the rest of the room. Sylvie lay on the floor in the centre of the kitchen. A swift glance told him there would be no wounded to rescue. She was far beyond his, or anyone else's help. The worst problem he could see at that moment was the fact that there was someone else in there with them. His brain told him that it was more likely to be the murderer than another victim. He made this deduction from the fact that the man who sat a few feet from Sylvie still had the meat cleaver in his hand.

Callum Church's brain was teetering on overload, as he noticed the size of the man's broad back. Before he thought what he was doing, he called out the man's name. 'Ed! My God! Whatever . . . ?'

The only sound was the coffee grinder, labouring away, unaware that its operator would never resume the task she had started.

It took a while for Callum to realise that Ed was in shock. He was sitting on the floor, staring unblinkingly at the blood-covered cleaver. As the nurse approached him, he was delicately running a fingernail through the fresh, red blood, tracing a pattern in the thick, scarlet liquid.

Callum spoke softly, a tremor in his voice. 'Okay, Ed. It's okay. Just sit quietly and I'll get help.' He kept his speech as even as he could, but the man was so deeply affected that there was no reaction at all. 'I won't leave you; you just stay there. I'll be back, I promise.'

He pulled his phone from his jeans pocket as he rushed from the room. Outside in the cafe's seating area, he dialled 999 and shakily asked the operator for both police and an ambulance.

Next, he punched in the number for Michael, waited a few moments, then hung up and ran back into the kitchen.

Ed sat on the floor, slowly rocking backwards and forwards. He had not moved, and was still tracing intricate patterns through his wife's blood.

As Callum moved closer to him, the cloying metallic smell that he remembered so well was overpowered by the scent of flowers. He stopped in his tracks and looked around him. The old lady stood only inches away from his right shoulder. Far from being frightened, the nurse felt an overwhelming sense of relief to see her there.

'Move away from him, my dear. You cannot help him. It's better that you leave this place.'

He felt a gentle pressure on his arm, and with one backward glance at the gentle giant, he withdrew from the room.

The woman had gone. He looked across the cafeteria and saw what he thought was a brown-and-white dog disappear around a corner. He did not chase it this time. He just let it go with its mistress, and tried once again to reach Michael.

This time he was successful, and the professor arrived at the cafe to a fanfare of sirens and blue lights.

It seemed to Callum that everything then happened at once. And everyone wanted to know what on earth had gone on but, sadly, he just had no idea.

Will took him out to the orangery and sat with him as WDS Wendy Brown asked him, as gently as possible, what he had seen. He told her honestly, but omitted to mention his elderly friend who smelled of lilacs.

He looked helplessly out of the window. Poor Ed, was all he could think. To find his beloved Sylvie like that. It must have turned his brain. Poor Ed.

CHAPTER TWENTY-ONE

A strange sense of déjà vu settled over the gathered company.

Michael, Ellie and Alice sat opposite Bob Foreman, Jon Leatham and Wendy Brown. They had all sat together once before because of murder, very different murder to this, but still murder. The shock of what had happened had yet to sink in, but everyone who had anything to do with the clinic was aghast at the apparent brutality of the attack. That, and the fact that the victim was their friend and colleague.

Bob had been horrified to get the call saying that a possible 'Operation Innocents' murder had taken place at his friends' establishment. His heart went out to Ellie and Michael. The Cavendish-Meyer Centre was their dream come true, and apart from the obvious stressful trauma to themselves, it would do their business no good whatsoever.

Ellie's face was ashen. 'Bob. There is no way Ed would have hurt Sylvie. He idolised her; she was his life. He must have found her like that, and the shock must have been all too much for the poor man to cope with. Surely, he just picked up the murder weapon without thinking?'

'I'm sorry, Ellie, but you've seen some of the other murderers. All good, kind souls who wouldn't hurt a fly. The scene of crime officers are checking out the kitchen now, but I am almost one hundred per cent sure of what their findings will be.' He leaned back in his chair and crossed his legs. 'I am so sorry this has happened here. What will you do about the clinic?'

Ellie shook her head. 'We don't know. We just don't know. We have contacted as many of our patients as we can and cancelled their appointments until further notice. Strangely, most of them have offered their condolences and are happy to resume their treatment, as and when. The ones we have not been able to get hold of are being met at the gate. We will need to send the inpatients home, as we have no means of feeding them.' She shrugged and sighed. 'How long do you think your side of things will take, Bob?'

'Hard to say, but not too long, I hope. You know we'll do all we can to be out of the way as soon as possible . . . especially if it is as clear-cut as it seems. It's the next part that is so difficult, finding out why he did it.'

The detective paused and regarded Michael. Throughout the whole conversation, the professor had not uttered a word. He appeared to be the worst affected by the death.

'Are you all right, my friend?' Bob hoped his voice held the very real compassion that he felt.

Realising the question had been directed at him, Michael Seale shifted around in his seat and hurriedly muttered that he was fine. Then he looked sheepishly up at the detective, gave a huge sigh, and spoke hesitantly.

'No. I'm not fine. Not fine at all. I had already suffered an awful fright before all this. I feel dreadful!'

Between them, his friends managed to coax the whole story out. He said he thought they might laugh at him — it seemed so petty now, in light of what had happened since, but everyone listened to his dawn adventure with the utmost seriousness.

DI Leatham then left the room to have a word with Kyle, the site manager, and to check the icehouse for himself. While he was gone, Alice offered to give Michael something to calm him, but the professor refused, saying he felt considerably better for just talking about it.

Wendy asked Ellie about the young man who had found the body. 'He is obviously very distressed, but he got control of himself enough to give me a pretty good account of times and exactly how he came to find Edmund and Sylvie Hargreaves. He mentioned working for Médecins Sans Frontières. Has he been with you long, Ellie? Do you know him well?'

'Callum has been here for several months now. He is excellent with the patients, very sensitive and caring. We, that is, Michael, myself and all the staff, like him a lot.' She glanced down at her feet. 'He came here to get away from death and suffering. I feel that we have let him down.'

'It's hardly your fault!' Alice's tone was almost accusatory. 'I'm sure you didn't orchestrate the massacre in your kitchen!'

Bob thought that Ellie looked a little hurt by Alice's comment and noticed her quick reply.

'I didn't mean it like that, Alice. I simply think that Callum has probably suffered far more than you or I know about, during his work abroad.'

'Sorry, darling.' Alice apologised and took her hand. 'It's just that it's so typical of you. Feeling sorry for everyone else when you have got a major crisis of your own. But I'm sorry, I didn't mean to snap at you.'

Ellie smiled weakly and squeezed Alice's hand.

'We've all got problems now. I suppose Michael and I should get all the staff and the practitioners together to discuss our next move, whatever that might be.'

Bob decided it was time to leave his friends to try and organise themselves. He needed to get back to the station. He hoped there would be a message from Dr Gerrard — perhaps she would like another trip to see one more kindly killer.

* * *

Jon stood at the bottom of the flight of steps. Kyle the site boss was with him.

'Bit creepy down here, I'll agree, Inspector, but I don't see how anything could have got in without the professor seeing.'

Jon thought the place was more than creepy. For some reason he felt extremely uncomfortable. 'Do you think that could have had anything to do with it?' He pointed up into the roof area where a long, motheaten rope hung down. 'Maybe a draught blew it and it brushed past him?'

Kyle looked unconvinced. 'Too short. You said that Professor Seale said something touched his leg. The rope would not even have touched the top of his head. Maybe a rat, though. Or even a bat. Bats do like old icehouses, but I haven't seen any evidence of them here.'

Jon switched the lantern on and off. It appeared to be working properly. 'Very odd. Well, whatever scared the prof did a damned good job, and I can't say that I would like to be down here alone at dawn.'

They made their way up to the sunlight.

'Is it true what they're saying about Ed Hargreaves killing Sylvie, Inspector?' Kyle looked sad and stabbed the toe of his boot at a bramble. 'My wife and Ed were schoolfriends. I know him quite well. Salt of the earth. I'm telling you, Officer, salt of the earth, that one.'

'Mrs Hargreaves is dead, yes. More than that I can't really say.'

'He couldn't have done it, sir, not Ed. No way!'

'Well, thank you for your help. I expect we will speak again later.' The young detective inspector turned as he left, and saw the man in the hard hat staring after him, still shaking his head in disbelief.

* * *

As very few of the staff of the C-M had been present at the time of the murder, the interviews had been conducted very quickly. The Hargreaves had left their precious cafe for the last time — Sylvie in a body bag and Ed in a police car, and Ellie decided it was time for a council of war. She sent Janet round to gather everyone up and tell them to be in the orangery in fifteen minutes. She felt sick at heart, but she knew they would look to her for direction, and she had to be strong. She had people's livelihoods to consider, and a responsibility to her patients. A terrible thing had happened, but she had to find a way to work around it so that the clinic and its loyal staff would not suffer too much. Her thoughts then moved from her own staff to Alice. She was about to launch her new Azimah Syndrome Clinic from here. Lord! She even had two prospective colleagues coming to see the place this week. Ellie gritted her teeth. Somehow, she had to prevent the dream turning into the nightmare. She knew that Bob and his team would do all they could to help her, but the Cavendish-Meyer had turned into a murder scene and the police had a job to do.

Then there was Michael to worry about. She felt a twinge of guilt as she remembered his excitement when she'd told him about the icehouse, and then she had refused point blank to show it to him. She cursed him for his foolhardy trip, and cursed herself for being the one who had caused it.

Janet's soft voice interrupted her reverie.

'I think I've told everyone, Miss McEwan, and I explained to Callum that you wanted him to go home, but he wouldn't hear of it. Oh yes, and Maureen Shaw wants a word with you before the meeting. It's about Jake Kennedy. She's talking to Michael in his office right now, if you could spare her a moment?'

'Of course, Janet. Thank you. I'll see you in the orangery in ten minutes.'

Ellie made her way hurriedly to the office, where she found Maureen with the professor.

'Ah, Miss McEwan. I was just explaining to Professor Seale that Jake has expressed a wish to stay here with us despite the happenings of this morning.'

'I don't think that's a very good idea, do you? He's in a pretty fragile state at present, isn't he?'

'Well, that's the point really. He is much recovered from his recent bout of depression. He has apologised to Dr Cross, and he is more his old self now. He cried like a baby when he heard that Sylvie was dead. I obviously didn't tell him all the details, but he knows she was murdered. The thing is, Miss McEwan, every time he goes home, in a matter of days his condition deteriorates. I'm more than prepared to cook for him. I have all the facilities in my apartment. I really believe he would be better off with us than on his own again.'

'He does have a family, Maureen. He could go to them.'

'I know, but he was almost as bad when he returned from a break with his father a few weeks ago. I'd feel so much happier if I could keep an eye on him myself.'

Ellie looked at Michael, and her friend nodded.

'It's fine by me. Don't forget, I am on hand here, as well. I would say that if Alice agrees, then let him stay.'

The feeling of unease did not go away, but as her partner and her night sister seemed happy with the idea, she acquiesced. 'All right, but please be sure that Alice is in complete agreement before you tell Jake Kennedy he can stay. Now, we'd better get along to the orangery for the meeting.'

Ellie was still not sure what she was going to say to everyone, but walking down the corridor, she quietly prayed for some inspiration.

* * *

The first thing she noticed, as she gazed at her assembled friends, colleagues and staff, was the strange difference in their aura lights. It was so natural for her to look at everyone's energy before anything else that she had quite a shock when she saw the colours that rose from the gathering.

For a second, she held her hand to the scar on her forehead and shut her eyes to the sight. The traumatic incident seemed to have increased the strength of some of the auras to a ferocious light show; whereas others were faded and depleted.

As much as her enquiring mind would have loved to inspect each aura individually, she knew that this was not the time, so she blocked her auric sight, and made a mental note to talk to Michael about what she had seen.

They had gathered around the open space that had once been the dance floor. Some sat on chairs, some on the low walls that surrounded the plant displays, and others on the soft floor matting.

With a heavy heart, Ellie opened her speech by telling them all what she knew about the murder. It was best that no rumours existed among these people who were so close to the Centre. She was more than aware that in no time the village and the town would be rife with suppositions and fabricated stories. At least her own staff and friends should be aware of the facts, such as they were.

There was a general murmur of disbelief, and the natural whispers from one to the other, disclaiming the very possibility that their friend had turned into a monster overnight.

'Miss McEwan? Did you know that Ed went off early yesterday?' A young man with cropped, inky black hair, who worked afternoons and some evenings at the cafe, stood and directed his words to Ellie. 'He said he felt really poorly and went home for a rest.'

'No, Paul. I didn't. Since Ed and Sylvie took over the cafe, they have organised themselves without having to report to me. I did think he looked rather pale and preoccupied when I saw him at breakfast yesterday, but he never mentioned feeling unwell. Did he say what sort of poorly he meant?'

'No, Miss McEwan. He didn't seem to want to talk, but as you said, he was a funny colour.'

'Did you tell the police when they spoke to you, Paul?'

The boy said he had, and he sat down again.

Ellie promised them all that they would be kept fully informed of developments and then went on to discuss the Centre. She stood on a small terrace, just a few steps above her flock, and spoke eloquently to them. She told them that she and the professor would do everything in their power to keep things running with the minimum of disruption. The cafe would naturally remain closed and off limits until such time as the blue-and-white cordon could come down, and the whole place be cleaned and redecorated. She voiced some thoughts she had about closing it completely and relocating it to another part of the building.

There were several noises of agreement and fervent nods in favour of that idea.

'We will never forget the Hargreaves, but we do have a lot of people who rely on us here for their well-being. We cannot let them down. I know it is going to be a struggle, but I am not prepared to lose this wonderful healing centre. If any of you feel that you want to move on, then Michael and I would understand. This is a terrible thing that has happened, and we would never ask you to stay if you were not completely happy to do so. I am going to ask you now to go home and consider what you would like to do. Those who wish to stay will receive full pay, or recompense for loss of earnings, while we are closed. As soon as the police allow, we will open again, so please, let Michael or me know how you feel, and we will take it from there. There is no rush, we will certainly not be opening our doors again until next week, so please consider your decision carefully.'

She thanked them all for their loyalty and the small crowd began to drift away.

Callum Church sat alone and stared across the small courtyard that he and Will had been about to work on. Ellie went and sat beside him, gently laying a hand on his arm.

'I'm so sorry, Callum.'

'Better me than you, Miss McEwan. At least I've seen that kind of thing before.'

'In a time of war, you expect it. You do not expect it on a summer's morning in a healing centre in Ripley. The shock would be no different for any of us. Now, would you like to talk to someone about it? A professional, I mean.'

The young man shook his tousled dark hair and gave her a rueful smile. 'I really don't need counselling. It was a nasty shock but I'm a tough kid really.' He looked at her for a while, as if there were something he wanted to say, but couldn't find the words.

'How about you come back to my office, Callum? I badly need a drink, and I haven't got a clue how to operate the new coffee maker that Michael bought me last month. If he thinks I don't use it he'll be really hurt, so perhaps you may know how it works?'

'Certainly, I'll give it a try.'

And maybe try to tell me whatever it is that is worrying you, thought Ellie as they walked slowly back to her consulting rooms.

It took the nurse about ten minutes to work out the instructions and get the first steaming cups ready.

They sat opposite each other on the sofas and enjoyed the hot coffee.

There was an amicable silence; then the young man took a deep breath and spoke slowly, using deliberately chosen words. 'Perhaps it's not the right time for this, but I think you're probably the only one who will understand. You remember I said that I was sensitive to certain things, "fey" as my dad calls it? Well, it's been happening a lot recently, and I see your friend frequently. You know, the old lady with the dog, the thin woman who wears purple. I see the other bigger lady sometimes, but not as often.' His voice became softer. 'She was with me in the kitchen this morning. She told me to get out.'

Ellie took a deep breath and held it. Michael had mentioned something about Callum being fey, but she could not remember him finishing what he was saying. She'd have to ask him what it was. And Vera? Why would she and Carole be spending such a lot of time earthbound now? Perhaps they found Callum easier to contact. She had seen their colours floating around her, especially at Snug Cottage, but other than that, and the faint contact in the orchard, nothing. She had tried meditating, then using Carole's tarot cards, and even conducting a sort of seance for one, but all to no avail. Yet Callum saw them regularly. She wondered if she could use him as a go-between.

The nurse was continuing. 'She is very kind to me, you know. I sometimes get flashbacks, and if they're really bad ones, I go into a sort of stupor. It's like I'm trapped in a moment, in a horror show. I never know what triggers them, but they are bastards to get out of when they start. Twice now, your friend has rescued me, and gently brought me back to normal. And she always seems to be around when there's a problem. A few nights ago, I was riding home when I had this weird feeling that something was not right. I was on a straight stretch of dual carriageway and there was nothing else on the road. Suddenly, I saw this cranky old car in front of me. Where it came from, I had no idea, but every time I went to overtake it, it pulled across the road and blocked me. I did not feel like taking any chances. I was tired and, frankly, I thought the driver had to be drunk. As I didn't fancy a run-in with some pissed old fart, I dropped right back. The next thing I knew, I was approaching a junction and some fool jumped the lights! If I had been riding at my normal speed, he would have had me for sure. A bit further down the road, as I was thanking my lucky stars for my deliverance, I saw the old car again. It was parked up on a grass verge, and waving from the passenger seat was the lady in purple. I'm telling you, Miss McEwan, that old lady and her friend were my guardian angels that night.'

'They were mine once, Callum. I just wonder why they're around us so much at the moment.'

'The murders, I suppose. I'm sure they won't rest while something evil is threatening us all.'

Ellie shuddered. It was not a nice thought. It had been bad enough when it had affected strangers, but now . . . she shivered again.

There was a knock at the door and Alice stuck her head around. 'Sorry to interrupt, Ellie, but I just wanted you to know that I've okayed Jake staying under Maureen's care. I have to drive up to town for a meeting, but I'll be back to Snug Cottage by this evening. Shall I get a take-away?'

'No, don't worry, I've already prepared us something for tonight. Are you sure you're happy about the Kennedy lad staying on here?'

'Yes. I think Maureen has a valid point, and if she is prepared to look after him, I'm prepared to go along with her. We'll talk later. I had better move myself, or I will be late. Bye, Callum. Bye, Ellie.'

The door closed and they heard her run down the corridor.

'But I'm not happy about Jake staying.'

The voice was soft, almost feminine in quality, and it made Ellie turn suddenly and look at Callum with surprise. 'What did you say?'

'Sorry? Say what?'

'You said you were not happy about Jake staying!'

'Well, I suppose I'm not really, but I never spoke, Miss McEwan, and when Dr Cross mentioned it just now, it was the first I've heard of it.' Callum looked as confused as she felt.

'God, I'm hearing things now! This really isn't the best of days, is it?'

'No. Not the sort you want too many of. By the way, I don't need any time to consider whether I still want to work here. I do. Perhaps you would tell the professor for me? For as long as you need me, I'm still on the team.'

'Thank you, Callum. We appreciate that. Now why don't you get off home to a hot shower and a large drink?'

'I think I'll head for the gym. A good workout is the only thing right now.' He smiled at Ellie. 'I'll have the shower and the drink afterwards. I'll be in tomorrow. I can't see why I shouldn't get on with Will's courtyard, and I expect Maureen will want a hand with Jake, if he's staying.'

'If you're sure you're up to it, that's fine by me. I'll see you then.'

Callum left, but Ellie could still hear that odd voice, one she thought she recognised, but could not quite put a name to. Or could she? Maybe she knew exactly who it was, but refused to admit it.

CHAPTER TWENTY-TWO

Ellie poured another coffee and decided to go and find Michael. There seemed to be all sorts of half answered questions floating in her head, and she desperately wanted some clarity in her mind.

As he ushered her into his room, his distress swam lazily around him like one of those long silk scarves used by far eastern dancers. The colours that surged and fell were muted and hazy; none of Professor Seale's bright spring green, his signature colour to Ellie. Whenever Michael was on good form, he was aflame with green lights. Other colours as well, but predominantly, glorious leaf green.

Ellie hated to see him like this. Apart from her concern for her friend, she was sure that no matter how much she protected herself, her own aura would be depleted by being in contact with such negativity. The term 'being brought down' by someone was very true and she witnessed it many times a day with her patients. Their sadness, misery, pain or emotional depression would affect anyone within striking distance of their unhappy aura.

Michael nibbled an uneven nail and nodded to an empty armchair. As she lowered herself into the comfortable softness of the old leather, she noticed he had already poured himself a very large scotch.

'The murder could be the finish of all this, old girl.'

'Rubbish!' Her reply held a strength that made her friend look up in astonishment. 'Sorry, Michael. I know you've had a worse day than the rest of us, but I will not let you get this low. It will affect us all, and right now, I need a tough side-kick if I'm to get us through this mess.'

Michael was completely unused to his dear friend berating him. He sat up a little straighter and opened his eyes a bit wider.

She continued in her positive tone and noticed some of his old lights slowly returning. 'Right. You started to tell me something about the origins of the word "fey". We never finished our conversation, perhaps you would fill me in on what you were going to say.'

Although looking slightly confused as to where the discussion was heading, Michael tried valiantly to remember what he had said. 'Oh yes! It was just before your dinner party; you told me Callum's father had said he was fey and I mentioned I did not like the word because of its deeper meaning.'

'That's right. So, go on.'

'Yes.' He stroked his beard thoughtfully. '*Faege*, I think, in the Old English. It meant doomed. You know, "fated to die". In fact, worse than that, many thought that someone who was considered fey, lived under the shadow of a sudden or violent death. Of course, nowadays, it has a more whimsical meaning, sort of eccentric, fairy-like or even clairvoyant. The Scots take it to mean having ESP, or being able to predict calamities and such, but you can see why I don't like the term much.'

'Absolutely. I have only ever thought of it as meaning elfin-like. I had no idea about all those darker meanings. I'm sure his dad means it in the slightly clairvoyant manner, don't you?'

'Assuredly, but sometimes, well, let's just hope there is nothing more to it. He does ride a very powerful motorcycle, and he chose to work in a war zone. I hope he doesn't have some sort of unconscious death wish.'

'What, Callum? You have to be joking! That's just his lifestyle, like thousands of other young men.'

'Well, you did ask, didn't you? I'm only telling you what I know.'

The professor's colours were considerably stronger, but Ellie battled onward, trying to put the damaged aura back together again.

'Fine, my friend, you have answered my question, but I'd rather you didn't turn into the Prophet of Doom just yet. Next is a subject you may prefer not to discuss, but I think we should, in order to do something about it. The icehouse.'

Michael stiffened at the mention of the detested place.

'I think we should ask Kyle to seal it up. Not damage it, future generations may find it interesting, but completely block it up. We will ask him to check the other entrances, just to be sure, and then close up the main staircase, at least for the whole time we own this property.'

Her friend nodded mutely, scratched his beard again and finally said, 'Whatever. I would prefer it filled in or blown up, but I understand what you're saying and the practicalities involved. Just let's get it done as soon as possible. I am probably just an old fool who let his imagination run away with him but, well, I don't even like to think about it.'

'Michael, I think something very unpleasant happened in that cellar in the past, and you, being sensitive, just picked it up. Try to forget it and I'll go and find Kyle before he leaves. He can put everything on hold until that little job is done, okay?'

'Okay. I can live with that. What is next on your list, O Great Leader?'

'The cafe.'

'Oh.'

'Did you notice how nearly everyone at the meeting seemed to think it a good idea to relocate it?'

'Yes, and it is a sound idea. No one would want to work where someone has been horribly murdered. What do you suggest we do with the present kitchen area?'

'I haven't thought that one through yet. I am more concerned as to where our new restaurant will go. I think I should telephone the architect who designed the pool complex, get him to take a look, and tell us what is feasible.' She stopped and looked intently at Michael. When she continued her words were less commanding. 'Michael. Don't think I'm being heartless, organising all this barely hours after Sylvie's death. I have to do it now, it's my way of coping, and we cannot afford to lose our dream. If I let things go, even for an hour, I will never find the strength to pick up the pieces and start again. Do you understand me, or do you think I'm a hard, uncaring bitch?'

'Definitely the cold, insensitive one! You silly woman! Don't you think I know you better than that. It is I that succumbed to the slippery path of apathy, stupid old fool that I am! Still, you have pulled me together nicely now. Don't worry, I will be your tough, gun-totin' sidekick from now on.

'Before you dash off to find Kyle,' Michael continued, 'there is something I've been wondering about. Somehow, our Edmund has become infected, or affected, by the same thing as the other murderers. As we have no idea what it is that has got at him, should we perhaps consider that it could happen to others here and keep staff to a bare minimum?'

'I asked Bob the same question earlier. He says that all the incidents are very much isolated cases. So far, they have not found any common denominator, or the means of transmitting the illness or neurosis or whatever it is.'

'Ellie? Do you think Bob would let me visit Ed?'

Ellie was shocked. 'But why? It would be terribly distressing for you to see him in such an awful state.'

Michael took a slow sip of his drink. 'Do you remember me telling you about the boy with the black aura? Well, you know how I work when I am healing, I put the missing colour back into the energy field. Not like the way you were working on me earlier. You were making me react, and in essence, I was healing my own aura. I have the ability to suffuse the patient with thoughts of coloured lights. I know

I have a spirit guide who helps me, and together we heal the damaged aura. I think I may have told you, some people believe you can see illness in an aura before it becomes noticeable in the person. If you tend to the aura immediately, you can prevent the illness from occurring. What I was wondering, and I have thought about this ever since that child in the Caribbean, would I have the power to put colour back into a black aura?'

Ellie looked at him anxiously. 'It would be a little like raising Lazarus, wouldn't it? Surely it would drain you completely. I've seen the state of you at the end of a busy day here, and that is only helping slipped discs and sinus problems.'

'I know. But I'm prepared to give it a try, for Ed's sake.'

'Michael, I'm not being funny, I know you are saying this with the very best intentions, but if you did manage a miracle and were able to save him, how could he live with the knowledge of what he has done?'

'I've thought of that as well. You see, Ellie, it's not just Ed, is it? He might be able to give us some clue as to what happened. We could possibly stop other deaths, and exonerate our friend at the same time.' He looked at her intently. 'There is a bigger picture here.'

Ellie gently rubbed her middle finger across her scar. 'I suppose I can't argue with that. But please be careful, I've lost one dear friend in a gallant fight for good, I don't want to lose another. Why not ring Bob and talk it through with him?'

Michael nodded, and without hesitation, picked up the telephone. 'I'll do it now, before I lose my nerve. You go get that hellhole sealed up. And make sure they use the very best cement!'

* * *

The police station was heaving with officers, an unusual mix of the Surrey, Met and Kent Forces. The latest incident on Bob's patch had sent the whole thing into a state of near panic. As much as they had tried to keep a low profile on the individual cases, the media had finally made the connection and were having a field day. The latest suggestion was that a foreign power was using subliminals in television soap operas. The thought of murderous messages being sent out below the threshold of the nation's consciousness in every episode of *EastEnders* had made Gentleman Jon Leatham explode with laughter.

'I know it's no laughing matter, but what are these people on, guv?'

'We have no answers for them, Jon, so they are inventing their own. Believe me, it will get far whackier than that.' Bob looked grey and grim. 'I have had a letter suggesting I check all the junk mail sent to all the suspects over the last six months. Some nutter has decided the paper has been dusted with a fine coating of a secret germ warfare chemical that only affects nice people and turns them into psychos overnight.'

'Oh dear.'

'Yes, oh dear indeed. And that's not the half of it. Even our irascible and direct Dr Gerrard is talking about the Walking Dead! What hope in hell do I have of coming up with a sensible and acceptable solution, when my hard- headed, down-to-earth doctor is throwing chicken bones in the sand and reading the runes!'

'I think the only way we are going to get on top of this, sir, is to find a connection with all our suspects. I know that all but two are now dead, but something, or more to the point, someone, must connect them. Wendy, Paula, Theo and I were wondering if we could try coming at it from a different angle, as in set the computer searches up in a slightly different way. I've been talking to a friend who employs lateral thinking when he has problems, and thought we might give it a try, with your permission, sir?'

'I don't care if you stand on your bloody heads and look at it from that angle! Just get me something to go on!'

'Thanks, sir. At least it has more intellectual challenge than the Coronation Street Killer.'

'Bugger off, Jon.'

'Right away, sir!'

Jon Leatham retreated as Bob's phone started to ring. 'Michael! What's the problem?' For ten minutes he listened intently, before slowly replacing the receiver. He thought for a moment, then picked it up again and made the necessary arrangements for Michael to see Edmund Hargreaves. He puffed out his cheeks, then sighed. This was a long shot, and he did not feel too confident that Michael was up to what he had proposed. But what else did he have?

CHAPTER TWENTY-THREE

Kyle was saddened by the professor and Miss McEwan's decision to seal up the icehouse. He had friends that would love to see it. In fact, he had a historian acquaintance who he had already mentioned it to. He was planning on motoring down from the Lake District this weekend to photograph it. Oh well, he could stall the job for a while. He had told Ellie McEwan that they would get on to it the next day and, naturally, he would go along with their wishes ultimately, but it might just slip his mind for a day or two. He was damn certain the professor would not be back in that neck of the woods, so to speak, and with everything else going on at present, he was quite sure no one would check up on him. He would just wait for his friend to take his pictures, let a few of his mates see it, then he'd brick it up . . . no sweat.

* * *

As the evening drew on, Sister Maureen Shaw and her patient sat quietly together playing Scrabble.

Jake was clean and tidy, in freshly laundered jeans and a pale-blue check shirt. Maureen had provided a substantial supper of grilled salmon, new potatoes and salad. Then, before they retired to the lounge, they had taken a long walk around the grounds. The young man had been calm and talked frequently about his days as a pilot. The sister had encouraged him to speak about his past, and asked lots of questions about flying, how his sight was now, and about his mother's stud farm in Ireland. Apart from her natural inquisitiveness, she wanted to discover what was at the root of his problem. As he talked, Maureen had watched him carefully for signs of unease or agitation, but there had been nothing.

Now as they sat, chatting affably, and considering the words on the board, Maureen was utterly confused as to how such an amenable and intelligent young man could change in an instant.

Jake sighed as he added a 'B' to her ENDING, making BENDING and giving himself very few points to his score.

'I'm not doing too well, am I?' He laughed boyishly. 'I sometimes play this with my father, but he takes it so seriously! He has one of those nasty dictionaries with two lettered words in, and he is forever looking up weird words that I've never heard of. Needless to say, he always wins!'

'I would often play a game or two with the patients in my last hospital. After hours, of course. It helped them to pass the time.' She stared at her letters and back at the board. The first three letters of BENDING stood out like a warning flag, and she thought that this was one person they had not talked about.

'Is Ben looking after your flat properly now?' She sensed him stiffen from across the table.

His voice was taut when he answered. It was clear his flatmate was not flavour of the month.

'He'd better be. Fancy having to get a bloody cleaner in after him. He's on probation. If it happens again, he's out.'

'He's not a bit like you, Jake. How did you meet him?'

Jake shifted uncomfortably. 'Long story, Mrs S . . . and very boring. Let's say he's had his uses in the past, but now I'm not so sure.'

His voice trailed off, along with his concentration, and Maureen was sure that the unpleasant Ben was somehow to blame for Jake's depression and mood swings.

Jake swung the conversation deftly to the murder, and Maureen Shaw decided to bide her time on the subject of the itinerant flatmate.

'I think I'll turn in early, Mrs S. I've got a feeling that I will sleep tonight.' He looked at her with a surprisingly tender gaze. 'I really appreciate what you've done for me. I know that it's you I have to thank for my being able to stay here. I don't think Miss McEwan would have let me, if I had asked her instead of you.'

'Nonsense, Jake. You are very welcome here. We are all delighted that you want to be with us.' *As you say,* she thought, *with the possible exception of Ellie McEwan.*

She sat for some time after he left and considered some of the things he had said. He found his sight a difficult subject to discuss. There was no great angst. He just found it hard to explain the visual disturbances that affected his eyesight. The drugs, he said, had been the saving of him. Without Dr Cross's incredible chemical cocktail, he was not sure exactly what he would have done. He knew that for some reason they were not perfectly balanced, but whatever, he was able to conduct some semblance of a normal life. He just prayed that one day his sight would improve enough to fly again.

Maureen knew the lad would never take to the skies again, but could not bring herself to dash his hopes when he seemed so much better.

He had enthused about AZSEE, the doctor's virtual Azimah programme. She had the feeling that Jake Kennedy would spend most of the hours of the day on the computer, if only Alice Cross would let him. He said, somewhat cryptically, that he could tell AZSEE what he could not tell another living soul. She thought it an odd statement to make, but she knew so little about computers and virtual reality that he could have meant anything really. He told her that, at one point in his life, he had intended to go in with a friend to launch their own computer graphics company. He liked computers and enjoyed setting up Web pages for his friends. They had talked on, but nothing else had jangled his nerves, not family, not money, not even his disability, until the mention of Ben.

The night sister tidied up the lounge, fluffed up cushions, put away the game board and turned out the lights. She would check all the rooms, all empty now, except for Jake's, then return to her apartment. She had her alarm with her, and the slightest hint of a problem with the Kennedy lad, and she would be there. She sincerely wished him a good and peaceful night's sleep, although with poor Sylvie's death hanging over them all, she rather doubted the reality of it.

* * *

Alice arrived back at Snug Cottage at eight thirty. Ellie had eaten, but her supper was ready when she finally fell through the door, and Ellie sat with her as she ate.

'The meeting finished early, so I went back to my office and phoned Nelli and Gordon. I thought I should tell them what has happened and give them the option of backing out, but good news! Both are still as enthusiastic as ever. Ellie, they both say thank you to you, they would love to stay, just until different accommodation can be arranged.'

'That's excellent. I had sort of pre-empted the outcome and I've already made up the two guest rooms. When are they arriving?'

Alice carefully cut the fatty edge from a lamb chop, divided it into four and fed it to Ellie's waiting boys. 'Ah, well actually, I have to be at Heathrow at six o'clock tomorrow to pick up Gordon. Nelli is being met by the company that is holding the conference. She should be with us in about three days if all goes according to plan.'

'Right! Early night for you! You have a good chance here to catch up on some serious sleep, so as soon as your supper has gone down, a shower and bed.'

Alice did not have the energy to argue, and in a short while was towelling herself down on one of Ellie's big fluffy bath sheets. She fell into bed, and hardly felt Ellie, as she snuggled in beside her. She just felt safe and warm, and so very, very, tired.

* * *

Michael received the call from the police station just as he was about to crawl into bed. He had permission to see Edmund Hargreaves and to try to help him. The only condition was that he must have the Force Medical Officer with him for the duration of the visit. He thanked Bob's sergeant and felt a twist of fear in his gut. It was all very well to play the courageous hero, but now, in the quiet of his room, he wondered if it was within his power to achieve what he had planned.

He pulled the duvet tight around him and prayed for guidance.

* * *

Wendy was almost too tired to follow Jonathan Leatham's explanation of how he wanted to pursue the inquiry. Lateral thinking at eleven o'clock at night was not for her. Thinking in general was becoming a problem. She glanced across at Paula and realised her colleague was having the same trouble. Theo Bolt, on the other hand, was watching Jon intently, nodding emphatically, and adding constructive comments whenever he saw fit.

The two women looked helplessly at each other and finally Paula threw up her hands and exclaimed, 'That's it! I've had enough, sir! My brain needs a break! Tomorrow I might catch on to the concept, but right now, you could be speaking Greek. I need sleep.'

'Me too,' added Wendy vehemently.

Jon laughed. He'd obviously not realised that his new and slightly complex idea may have come too late in the day for his team. 'Sorry, point taken. We'll start again tomorrow. I really think this method may give us something. Anyway, get off now, I'll see you in the morning.'

Wendy was exhausted, both mentally and physically. Driving home, she concentrated hard on the road and was very relieved when she finally drove into her own close.

As tired as she was, she did not go to bed immediately. She needed to assimilate the case in her own time and her own way. She desperately wanted to nail the bastard behind all these strange deaths. She had myriad reasons and her friend Ellie was one of them. To be involved in another murder investigation was bad enough after what she'd suffered before, but then to have one of your own employees murder his wife!

She showered and pulled on her usual night attire: an oversized T-shirt and a pair of baggy shorts. She threw herself down on the bed and lay there for a while before getting under the duvet to sleep. Just as sleep approached, she felt the gears in her brain change up a notch, and she drifted off thinking, so that's what he means! Yes, that could actually work rather well.

* * *

Callum had given the Nautilus equipment a good thrashing, swam fifty lengths of the pool, showered, and left the gym at about nine o'clock. His idea had then been to call in at his local pub for a few pints, but when he pulled into the car park, he had an uncontrollable urge to go straight home. Immediately, he turned around and accelerated off towards his family home.

He found his father sitting out on the patio under the apple trees, a frothy glass of cold beer in his hand. On the garden table in front of him sat another clean glass and two large cans of beer.

'Hoped that you'd be home soon, son. Your mother's gone to bed early, she's not feeling too hot tonight. She's been worried about you today for some reason. Funny old thing that she is!'

'Are you sure I'm adopted? She always knows when something's wrong, doesn't she?' Callum threw his gloves in his upturned helmet and picked up the cold can. The ring pull made a hissing sound as he opened the beer.

'She's always been that way with you, son. You would never get a closer bond, even if she were your natural mother.' The older man sat back and regarded his boy. 'So, what has happened today, Callum?'

Callum rubbed his eyes wearily. He was not sure if he wanted to talk about it. It was not so much the reliving of it, but the fact that he knew it would weigh heavily on his father. He compromised and gave his dad a diluted version of the facts.

'It seems that your new vocation in the peaceful realms of healing has not been everything you hoped. To be honest, son, it sounds almost as bad as your work abroad.'

Callum grinned ruefully and topped up his glass. 'Hmm, I had not expected it to be quite as hair-raising as it has turned out to be. The Cavendish-Meyer is a healing centre with a difference all right!'

'I wonder what sort of effect this will have on it,' commented his father.

'Ellie McEwan and the professor are determined to keep it going and I'll support them all the way. It would be a real shame if it went tits up. Sorry, Dad. But you know what I mean.'

His father smiled. 'I know exactly what you mean, but folk are pretty resilient to things. If it doesn't affect them directly, then more often than not they go about their daily business, and in no time the murder will be yesterday's news. That, or they bask in reflected glory, or perhaps that should be reflected notoriety! You know, "Oh, I go to the C-M Centre, the one where there was this *dreadful* murder!" I think your clinic has such a fine reputation that it will weather this storm, don't you?'

'I hope so, Dad. I really hope so. I love it there. You know, for all the dire happenings, somehow, I really feel as if I am *meant* to be there.'

'Then go with it, my boy. I'm sure you are right. Want another beer?'

Callum passed his glass to his father and they talked on into the evening.

CHAPTER TWENTY-FOUR

The Cavendish-Meyer clinic sat quietly in the early morning mist. It promised to be another hot day, and Callum thought he should get the climbers planted. Sitting around the edge of the courtyard, their roots boiling in plastic bags, would do them no good at all. Will could not get in to help him until the afternoon, but the yoga instructor had had no problem with Callum pressing on alone. They had discussed what they were going to do, and Callum needed something physical to keep himself busy. Last night, talking to his dad, he had felt easier, but this morning the horror of it all had come flooding back to him.

He had been into the house. It was deserted apart from the uniformed police officer on duty outside the kitchen area. Callum supposed it would not be long before the murder scene was declared 'clean', and then Miss McEwan would have the task of gutting it and deciding what to do with the room.

Throughout the night his thoughts had returned to that weird tableau. Then and now, it seemed unreal. He could not get rid of the picture in his head of Ed — big, smiling, lovable Ed, sitting on the blood-covered floor, next to his beloved wife. The beloved wife he had apparently just hacked to death.

As he removed a plant from its polythene covering and plunged its roots into a bucket of water, he shivered at the thought. How could it be? It wasn't just an improbable scenario; it was an impossible one.

Callum was pretty good with people. He had managed to communicate with the sick, the injured and the dying when he did not even speak their language. He had an inborn way for seeing into souls. He *knew* when he was talking to a liar. He *knew* when he was being bullshitted. He *knew* when someone had bad blood. Ed had a good heart. Callum *knew* that too.

He hammered in the metal spike that would hold the wooden stake to support the trelliswork. The ground was hard, and in a short time the sweat was pouring off him. Good, he thought, as he brought the hammer down even harder. His mind could not understand what had happened, and he needed to be distracted. There were six of these buggers to put in, and he hoped that the earth would be as solid as a bloody rock!

He swore and cursed them into the ground, then threw the hammer down and let out a whoop of relief.

'Well, that's one way to do it.' Maureen Shaw stood in the doorway to the orangery and smiled at the exhausted young man with the shaggy, dark hair and the embarrassed expression.

'Maureen! I'm sorry! I think I kind of forgot myself a bit there.'

'I saw you arrive. I thought you might like this.'

He had not noticed she was holding a steaming mug of coffee and a plate of food.

The coffee and the bacon sandwich pushed his mind back to the day before. Sylvie should have been the one to provide this. But Sylvie was lying naked somewhere, in a freezer, with an identity tag on her toe.

He smiled wanly and accepted the breakfast. Maureen was a kindly woman and he would not hurt her feelings for the world, but his appetite had disappeared.

She sat on the wall beside him, as he forced the food down. 'At least Jake had a good night. Which means we all had a good night!' She stretched and yawned. 'As soon as I know he's up and breakfasted, I'm going to get some sleep myself. I don't think he needs any special attention today, but would you just keep an eye on him for me? I'll be up again by about two o'clock, I should think.'

'No problem. I'm going to put these bamboo and trellis panels up, then have a break. I had better leave something for Will to do when he gets here!'

They chatted for a few minutes and Maureen went off to see to her patient. Callum worked for another half an hour, tentatively sniffed under an armpit, and took himself off for a shower.

* * *

Michael had a slow start to the morning. There was little to do as the Centre was temporarily closed, and he needed to prepare himself for his visit to Edmund Hargreaves. He bathed and put on fresh, clean clothes. His breakfast was minimal, just some orange juice and two small slices of toast. He spent twenty minutes in his conservatory in quiet meditation, and then telephoned the police station to tell them he was ready.

Bob had arranged a car for him, and Ellie's friend, Wendy Brown, was going to accompany him. He was glad to have a familiar face with him, as he could not admit to being totally cool, calm and collected.

The drive was uneventful, and in less time than he could have imagined, he and the detective were being escorted into the cell-like room that was Edmund's new home.

Not that Ed was aware of his surroundings. He was aware of nothing.

The Force Medical Officer joined them and proceeded to give Edmund a careful check-up. He took his blood pressure, shone lights into the man's eyes and generally went over him from top to toe. Finally, he stepped away from the prostrate man with a hopeless shrug and indicated to Michael that he could begin. 'He is in a very deep trance, Professor. I am not usually a defeatist, and I do not know exactly what procedure it is that you're planning to try, but' — he shrugged again — 'do not expect too much of yourself. I believe this man is in a cataleptic state, and may never regain normal consciousness. I have, as I believe have you, seen the other suspects, and we know what the outcome of this will probably be.'

Michael nodded, but whispered that if he could achieve anything at all, it would be better than just letting him go without a fight.

The FMO acquiesced, and stood back to give him some space.

Wendy stood alongside her medical officer and waited for a miracle.

Michael took some very deep breaths, and gently laid his hands on Edmund's forehead. He stroked the big man's hair and ran his fingers over the temples and down the cheeks. Michael moved to stand behind the man's bed, drew in more long deep breaths, and closed his eyes. His hands lay loosely on Ed's shoulders.

Beneath his palms he could feel the black aura. A terrible coldness oozed between his fingers, and for a moment, the appalling feeling made him doubt his ability to help his friend. With the greatest effort, he kept his hands in place, and let himself fall into a deep meditation.

He prayed for protection. He imagined the cell shimmering with beautiful white light. He placed a ring of gold around everyone present, and prayed for their safety. He asked for help from his spirit guide and any helpers that would come forward to assist him. After a while he felt his hands move slowly down the man's arms and rest at his elbows.

Suddenly, a soft voice, one that he recognised so well, whispered, 'Yellow. The colour of the sun, put yellow here.' He visualised the sun's warming rays flowing down his own arms, through his hands and into the unconscious man.

For the next half an hour, he moved around Edmund, gently placing his hands on, or over, different parts of the man's body. The voice spoke continually, prompting him with which colours to use.

'Now, violet; deep as the petals of the flower, and as rich as a velvet of a priestess's gown. Now indigo; the night sky, the deepest blue of evening. Now scarlet; the rose in full bloom, the drop of blood from touching the thorn, now . . .'

Michael started to shake. He prayed again, hopeful that he had done enough. He prayed and gave thanks to his guide and his helpers. He thanked the Great Spirit for love and for safety, and slowly slid to the floor.

He awoke on a couch in the FMO's consulting room, with Wendy and the FMO standing beside him. His throat was dry and his head was throbbing mercilessly.

'How is he? I must see him again!' he croaked.

The doctor helped him to sit up and gave him a glass of cool water.

'Soon, Professor. Let's just take a look at you first.' His hand gripped Michael's wrist on the pulse point, and he counted silently to himself.

'I need to check his aura, Doctor. It's important.'

'In a minute. Give yourself time to come round properly.'

Michael sipped the water and wondered what he would see when they allowed him to go back to Edmund Hargreaves.

'I don't know what on earth you did in there, Professor, but I'm going to find it very hard to describe to my guv'nor!' Wendy Brown was astounded at what had taken place.

Michael looked intently at her. 'How is he? Were there some signs of improvement? I must know, Wendy.' Michael was becoming agitated.

'Okay, if you think you can stand, I'll take you back in.'

Wendy and the FMO helped him up, and assisted him back along the corridor to the room where Edmund lay.

Michael stood over him and tuned in to his aura.

He nearly collapsed again, this time with relief, as he saw the pale, sickly lights about the man's body. The black aura had gone.

'He's sleeping, Professor. It's an odd sleep state, very, very deep. But he is no longer in that strange trance. You have pulled him out of that. We are going to move him to a room in the main hospital and see what happens when he wakes, if he wakes, of course. We are treading unknown ground here, but at least it's a bit more familiar than it was, thanks to you.'

Michael felt dizzy, and the shaking started again. 'I'm exhausted,' he said weakly. 'I need to get home and sleep.'

He felt Wendy slip her arm through his. 'It will be my pleasure to drive you home right now. Come on, hero! Let's deliver you back to your bed. I cannot wait to tell Ellie about this, it is quite incredible.'

Within an hour he was back in his apartment, thundering head on pillow, duvet pulled high up to his chin, and sleep claiming his aching body.

* * *

It was midday by the time Wendy had made sure that Michael was asleep and had arranged for someone to keep a watchful eye on him. Ellie had been fending off reporters when they got back and promised to speak to her as soon as she could get free.

Alice Cross was showing a tall, gaunt-looking man, who Wendy had never seen before, around the Centre. The detective could not help but think it was a rather strange time to pick for a conducted tour. They had only removed the body the day before, for pity's sake! She understood a little better when Alice called her across and introduced her new research assistant, Gordon Lamont.

'A bad time, by no mistake, lassie. But, well these things happen, do they not?'

She thought she rather liked this lanky Scotsman, but after a short conversation, she moved on to have a word with the officer on duty outside the kitchen.

'Hello, Sarge. Come to relieve me?'

'No such luck, Hopkins. Everything all right? No problems?'

'Everything's fairly quiet, Sarge. They are very generous with the cups of tea here. I've no complaints.'

'Well, as long as the pathologist is happy with his findings, and we'll know that later today, then we will probably be moving out tomorrow or the day after.'

'Strange case, Sarge. Everyone I've spoken to here reckons the suspect is a smashing bloke. No one has a bad word to say about him. You wonder what gets into some people's heads, don't you? What could possibly make him do a thing like that?'

'Search me, Hopkins. But we are going to have to find out somehow, aren't we?'

She left the PC and rang in to the station. She apologised for missing the morning brainstorming session, and she smiled when she noted that Jon Leatham had sounded uncertain as to whether she was being sarcastic, or whether she really meant it.

'Actually, sir, I did finally fall into what you are trying to do, and I agree with you. I should be back by half one and we can continue. Gotta go, sir.' Wendy had seen Ellie waving to her from the other end of the corridor.

They went into Ellie's office, and almost before they were both seated, the detective sergeant started to relay what had happened with Edmund.

'It could have been really spooky, Ellie, but I wasn't frightened at all. In fact, I had this wonderful feeling of peace, the whole time Michael was doing his healing.'

She told her friend what had happened, that she had witnessed one of the oddest things ever. 'I thought I saw what looked like coloured ribbons coming from Michael's hands, and passing into Edmund's body. I spoke to the FMO afterwards, and he said he believed he'd seen a sort of coloured fog drifting from Michael to Ed. Whatever, Edmund Hargreaves has left his weird trance, and is now in a deep sleep. It was awesome. But Michael is totally knackered, Ellie. I've asked your nurse, Callum, to look after him. He is sleeping like a baby at present. God, it really took everything out of him, to do whatever he did!'

'Don't worry. I will watch him like a hawk from now on. You'll keep me posted with news about Ed, won't you?'

'Of course. I'd better get back, Ellie, and I'll ring you if I hear anything.'

* * *

Ellie watched her friend leave the parking area and drive towards the gates. As she looked, a familiar car whisked past the policewoman, practically forcing her onto the grass.

'I hope she books him!' thought Ellie. 'Ben Lomax! He's a bloody idiot, driving like that. That lad is nothing but a troublemaker!'

Then thoughts of Michael pushed the incident from her mind, and she left her office for her dear friend's apartment.

* * *

Alice and Gordon had just left the tennis pavilion and were walking back to Alice's temporary office. Work had already begun on the conversion, and it was plain to see that, as there was so little to do, the job would be completed very soon.

'It'll be perfect, lassie, just perfect.'

Alice grinned. If it had not been for the terrible happenings of the day before, and Jake's highs and lows, of course, she would have felt like the cat that got the cream.

Arriving at her room, she went to unlock the door, and to her surprise, found it open. She quickly looked around, but nothing appeared to have been disturbed.

'You shoudn'a leave your monitor on, Alice. Not when you're out of the office, anyway.'

'I don't, Gordon.'

'Well, you have this time, look.'

'Ah, that explains the door, I think. We have probably had a visitor. Jake is obsessed with AZSEE. I've had to turf him out of here on more than one occasion.'

Gordon looked perturbed by that information. 'I hope he's using it properly. This programme is far from finished, and I have built in an awful lot of extra stuff that is not available to the user at present. Stuff that I can access, but should not be played around with by a novice geek.'

'As far as I know, he only knows the basic system, the way you showed me to use it.'

'I hope so. I never thought someone else would be using it without you being present. I would have hidden my little surprises a bit deeper if I thought that may be the case.' Gordon paused and looked thoughtful. 'What exactly did this Jake do for a living, before his accident?'

'He was a helicopter pilot, and an aerial photographer.'

The Scotsman whistled through his teeth and pushed a hand through his thinning hair. 'Then I bet he knows a lot more about computers than you think! Those guys have got more active brain cells than most. They need them flying those machines. Anyway, I'll take a look if you like. I will soon know if he's been investigating, or just using the basic menu.'

'Well, I need to speak to Ellie. I can leave you with your brainchild for a while, if that's okay, and I'll bring some coffees back with me?'

Gordon took off his jacket and sat down at the computer. 'Sounds good to me.'

As Alice left the room, she glanced back and smiled at her new researcher, his eyes already glued on the monitor screen, and his fingers deftly tapping out their requests to his electronic friend.

The clinic seemed like the *Marie Celeste*. It was normally so busy, and now her footsteps were the only ones to be heard along the empty corridors. Not locating Ellie, she decided to ring her mobile to discover her whereabouts. After the second ring, she answered and said she was just leaving Michael's quarters. He was sleeping at present, after his trip to see Edmund. She said she would meet her in the orangery and tell her everything that had happened.

Alice arrived first and looked around the great, deserted glass hall. It was a beautiful piece of architecture and she could understand why Ellie loved it so much. She sat by the stone pool and waited for her. She soon heard the door close, and Ellie was hurrying towards her. Alice gave her a hug and lightly kissed her hair. 'It's horrid to see the place empty, isn't it? Have the police given you any idea when you can get back into the kitchens again?'

'No, not yet, but Wendy says it shouldn't be too long. It's all down to the post-mortem. If there is no doubt that Sylvie died because of the injuries inflicted by the cleaver Ed was holding, they won't be needing to check any further.'

They sat together, holding hands, and Ellie told her what Michael had managed to achieve with Ed.

'Even the FMO was gobsmacked, to use the vernacular. He's a hard facts man like you, and he has no idea what he witnessed, but he certainly witnessed something inexplicable.'

Alice knew she was wearing her 'I-don't-really-buy-all-this-weirdy-stuff-because-I'm-a-sceptic-at-heart' look, and tried very hard to appear more open to the strange story. She was obviously failing, because Ellie gave her a withering look and declared that she could think all she liked, but the fact remained that Edmund was now in a deep, but normal, sleep.

'Is there any indication when he might wake up?'

Ellie shook her head. 'Wendy said they had no idea. There is an officer with him around the clock and they are praying he might be able to give them some clue as to what happened to him, but . . .' Her voice trailed off, and Alice finished the sentence for her.

'But, one, he might never wake up. Two, the trauma might have been too much for him. Three, he might remember nothing.'

'We can only wait.'

Alice squeezed Ellie's hand and told her that she should really be getting back to Gordon. She had promised the poor man a coffee, and that had been half an hour ago.

'You go on back to him, darling. I'll make some coffees in my office and bring them up for you. I have not even said hello to him yet.'

Alice thanked her and made her way upstairs. As she took the steps, two at a time, she wondered just how much of AZSEE young Jake had managed to access.

CHAPTER TWENTY-FIVE

DI Leatham was pleasantly surprised to find that Wendy Brown had really meant what she said about lateral thinking.

Bob had gone to London to present the details of the Hargreaves murder to the rest of the Murder Squad, so Jon had gathered his team together for an update meeting in their boss's absence.

'We have already put a few new ideas into the computer while you were out with Professor Seale this morning, Wendy. Theo has a list for you of the things we have decided to look at.'

Theo Bolt passed her a printout.

Paula English pushed back her chair and rubbed her forehead. 'I really don't think I am quite on the same wavelength as you guys on this. I find it very hard not to look at something head on. This sideways approach has me really confused.'

Theo was just about to burst forth on one of his famous diatribes on the thinking of Edward de Bono, when Wendy quietly said, 'It's all about what you don't know, rather than what you do know, and not assuming the obvious. You know the old joke . . . A man walks into a bar, but before he can utter a word, he is knocked unconscious. Why?'

Paula looked blank. 'Well, maybe . . . er, there was a raid going on? Or maybe the landlord mistook him for a villain? Oh, I don't know!'

Wendy smiled. 'It was an iron bar.'

Her colleague groaned.

'Try this.' The sergeant had a feeling that this was the way to get Paula's brain around the theory, not by giving her an academic lecture. 'A policeman is walking past a house one night, when he hears a voice cry out, "Don't shoot me! John, don't shoot me!" A shot rings out and the copper rushes inside. He finds a lawyer, an engineer and a priest standing around a body. He immediately arrests the priest. Why?'

Again, Paula raised her eyes up to the ceiling and sighed. 'Go on. Tell me. I haven't got a clue.'

'The lawyer and the engineer were women. The man had called out the name John, and the priest was the only man present.'

'Where the hell do you get these from, Wendy?'

Wendy grinned. 'The mess room. Several of my shift were sent on a course a while back. They had to do this brainstorming thing to gather new ideas and concepts. These puzzles were rife for days after, and they are, in fact, lateral thinking.'

'Give us another one. I have to get the hang of this, or I'm going to be no use to you.' Paula furrowed her brow and put on an expression of the deepest concentration.

Wendy thought for a moment. 'I've got it. A man takes his wife to a high-powered war movie. During a particularly noisy bit, he stabs her to death. How does he do it without anyone seeing him, and how does he get the body away?'

The group were silent. Even Theo did not appear to have an answer.

'Don't be led by what you are told, Paula. Think about what I have *not* told you.'

Slowly a smile crept across the WPC's face. 'Of course! It was a drive-in movie. No one saw because they were in the car, and he just drove away! Hey! Who gets a gold star?'

'Exactly.' They all laughed for a moment at Paula's delight. Then they settled down to try and apply the philosophy to the murders.

They talked for an hour, made notes and cross-checked information with each other.

After a while, Theo offered a suggestion. 'We generally try to find a connection between the victims by checking all the usual sources. You know, doctors, hospitals, same tradespeople, clubs, hobbies, sports, possible connected distant relatives, drinking buddies, et cetera. Why don't we take just one suspect, not the victims, and I think the last would probably be the easiest, and get a list of every name, of every person that man had dealings with, over a period of about a month, maybe. Let's then check the list, and see if we recognise anyone? I know it's a bit of an arse-upwards way to go, but we could give it a try, couldn't we?'

Jon thought about it carefully. 'Surely we would have most of the names from our usual enquiries?'

'Most of them certainly. But if you are asking people direct questions; for example, was your husband a member of a cricket club? Answer, yes. Can I have the names of the members? So, you get a membership list. These are direct answers. But what if the husband had got chatting to a substitute player on the opposing team? A stand in, a visitor with no name on a list. See my point?'

'That's a bit of a tall order, Theo, but worth a try. You and Wendy take the Jones murder. Get on to the Met boys who dealt with the enquiries and then approach it from your angle. Do all you can from here, but if you need to get up to town, do so. Paula, you and I will continue with what we started this morning, okay?'

The meeting broke up, and the four officers continued with their search for the link between the innocent killers.

'Sir?' Paula stood at her DI's shoulder as he punched more information into his computer.

'Constable? What's the problem?'

'I've been thinking about what Wendy said about that professor chap and his way of trying to heal Edmund Hargreaves.' She sank into the chair next to Jon and stared at him. 'What if we have been looking at this all wrong? We've been assuming that all our suspect murderers have been *given* something. A drug, a chemical, an illness or a virus. What if they've had something taken away?'

Jon looked pensively at her. 'Go on.'

'Well, the professor seems to have actually put something back into Edmund Hargreaves, to help make him better. What if the mastermind behind all the deaths did the same in reverse? What if he drained away their humanity somehow?'

'Good Lord, English! That's one hell of a hypothesis!'

'It just seems to make a twisted sort of sense. Something has happened to all those poor souls. They were, without exception, good people, until this happened.' Paula went quiet. 'It's just a thought, sir. Probably rubbish, Wendy's lateral puzzles have addled my brain!'

'I'm not putting your idea down, English. I just need to consider what you've said, and whether there is any logical way that could have happened.'

'I don't think we are dealing with logic, sir, not this time. You didn't see that father sitting under a tree and singing nursery rhymes, while his daughter swung from a branch above his head. Didn't strike me as particularly logical, sir.'

She went back to her desk and left DI Jon Leatham with an aching head.

* * *

Ellie backed into the room, balancing three mugs of coffee on a narrow tray. As she turned to greet the new member of the Azimah team, she saw instantly that Alice's good mood of a few moments ago had disappeared and was replaced by consternation.

Alice quickly introduced Gordon and told her they were very worried as Jake had apparently been using AZSEE in a most unorthodox way.

'He's a clever one all right!' Gordon Lamont was examining scrolls of data from the screen. 'It's taken me a while because he has hidden everything he's done behind a security password.' He peered over his reading glasses and gave them a cunning grin. 'Which is AVIATOR-4, if you should need it.'

'How did you work that one out?'

'Years of knowing how computer nerds think, I suppose. Knowing his vocation, it had to have something to do with flying and most people who wish to use a security password put a number in it. Four is the numerological breakdown of AVIATOR, simple, really.'

Ellie felt a little lost on this, but asked what Jake had been doing.

Alice gave her a worried grin. 'It's all a bit above my head too, but let's say that there is a lot more to AZSEE than I knew about. There are programmes Gordon was perfecting, some unfinished, others ready, but not set up for use. It appears that Jake has managed to activate some of these systems and has been using them whenever I was not around.'

'Is that a problem?'

'We're not sure yet. I don't think he can have actually damaged anything, and Gordon produced all the software himself and has back-ups for everything. It's more that he was told not to touch AZSEE, and he blatantly disobeyed me.'

'And it could take me a damned long while to sort out exactly what he's done! Every file that I open, AVIATOR-4 has been there. Sorry, Alice, this is going to take longer than I thought.'

Gordon drank his coffee and looked hard at the doctor and Ellie. 'I have one real concern. I added one accessory programme recently. It's complex and needs the new headset that I sent you to activate it. I have just tried to run it and it won't let me in . . . it keeps showing an error screen that I don't recognise. One that won't let me bypass it in the usual ways. I think your young man has locked me out of my own system, and the obvious question to ask, is why?'

Ellie felt a chill down her spine. Alice was furious. She had never seen her appear so affronted by a patient's behaviour.

'I think it's time to get our AZSEE wizard over here, and ask Wonder-boy a few serious questions, don't you?'

Alice stormed out of the office, and Ellie watched her striding across the landing to the corridor that led up to the inpatient suite.

'Now there's a sight you don't see very often, lassie!'

Ellie gave the researcher a half-hearted smile. 'I agree, but I don't think I'd want to be in Jake Kennedy's shoes right now.'

* * *

Michael awoke with a pounding head and an awful all-over aching. He felt as though he had flu. He struggled to see the clock and saw that it was five o'clock. He had slept all afternoon. He noticed that he had been checked up on as there was fresh water by his bed and two paracetamol tablets in an egg cup. He gratefully swallowed the pills and wondered what had dragged him from his healing sleep. Although he felt like shit, he also felt a tremendous feeling of relief that he had possibly averted his friend's death.

He leaned back onto his pillows and closed his eyes, contemplating the chances of Edmund waking up to something bordering on sanity. He sighed as he wondered if he had really done the man any favours.

A shout roused him. He painfully pulled himself into a sitting position and listened intently. Not just a shout. He heard running footsteps, not one set but several, and more calling out, then a scream.

He dragged himself up, pulled on a dressing gown, and groggily made his way to his conservatory.

All the furore was coming from the path to the car park on the other side of his walled garden. As quickly as he was able, he made his way to the wrought iron gate. All he could see was the back of a uniformed police officer dashing off into the bushes that flanked the drive. Looking back along the side of the big house, he saw Maureen and Ellie, holding on to each other as people do when in peril.

Without thinking about his state of dress, he ran through the gate and up to the two women.

Maureen's face was the colour of putty, and she was holding on to Ellie with a grip that would leave bruises on the younger woman's arm.

'Whatever has happened?' Michael was shaking slightly, and his legs were sending urgent messages to get off them, as soon as possible.

'God! Michael! You should not be out here. Maureen! Help me get Michael back to his room.'

The night sister visibly shook herself, and her natural instinct to help came to the fore. He felt the two women pool their strength and half carry, half drag him back, through the garden and into his room. On reaching his bed, his legs gave way completely, but still he needed to know what was going on.

'It's Jake. Something terrible happened, but we don't know what exactly. The information we have, it's dreadfully disjointed, but it seems that Ben paid Jake an unplanned visit and there was some sort of fight.'

Maureen took over from Ellie. 'I was getting dressed after my sleep. I never sleep for long, but today I didn't wake until not long ago. I heard raised voices, then a crash, it sounded like furniture breaking. I ran to Jake's room, and it was wrecked. Ben and Jake were screaming at each other, but when they saw me, Ben threw me to the floor and they both ran. I was stunned, couldn't do a thing. Then I called for help and Dr Cross came racing up the stairs.'

Michael, through his blinding headache, endeavoured to take all this on board.

'So that is who the policeman was chasing?'

'Yes. Alice, and a young PC, who was about to relieve PC Hopkins, took off after them.'

'Maureen, would you stay with Michael, I'm worried about Alice. I need to go and see if they've caught Ben and Jake.' Ellie hurried out to see what was happening.

Michael promised the sister that he was fine now he was off his feet, and begged her to go with Ellie. After some considerable cajoling he convinced her to make sure that his young friend did not get herself into trouble.

'Before you go, did anyone phone the police station?'

'Yes. PC Hopkins radioed in straight away.'

As she spoke, her words were accompanied by the sound of sirens, arriving for the second day running.

CHAPTER TWENTY-SIX

Wendy sat opposite Eeyore, or DC Gerald Burchett to the rest of the world, and scanned the never-ending list of names he had provided for her.

Theo sat across the room with an older woman detective. They were reading through a couple of undecipherable notebooks, and one detective frequently called upon the other to verify a spidery word or a sentence. It had not taken the two Surrey officers long to realise that it would save an enormous amount of time if they took themselves up to the East End and conducted their search in the place where little Tanya Jones and her father had come from. The two Met officers had met them at Mile End Police Station, where they were given a corner of an office to use as a base.

Wendy stretched backwards to relieve her aching shoulders. Eeyore continued to talk miserably on the telephone, or download more and more names for her. She was just beginning to utter curses and incantations that would rot Theo's underwear for getting her into this mire, when she was jolted back to alertness by a resounding 'Shit!' coming from the other side of the room.

'Bugger me! Look at this!' A cheap spiral-bound notepad was thrust under her nose.

'Look at that entry there. The one under Sunday!'

It took her eyes some time to fathom out the untidy scrawl. Her heart then skipped a beat. 'Jesus! How did we miss this?'

Theo looked partly aghast and partly delighted that his idea had paid off.

'Because no one knew about this franchise. DS Williams here only found out this morning that our Mr Jones had recently "bought" a cleaning company from a mate of his. It was all to do with paying off gambling debts, dead illegal, no money exchanging hands, and the parent company would have gone spare if they had known. He was working it in his mate's name, and trying to get a bit of buckshee cash stashed away for his kid.'

'Right! Get hold of Bob. Tell him what you've found. I'll get DI Leatham, we have to run Jake's name against Black, Ryder, the boy Keene, and Lily Frampton. Considering that Jake knew Hargreaves, I don't think there will be any prizes for guessing that he is our missing link! Brilliant work, Theo! All I need now is for you to tell me just how the hell he's done it?'

* * *

As Wendy listened to Jon Leatham, she felt the colour drain from her face. Placing the receiver back on its cradle, she stared at her colleagues, giving herself time to formulate her words.

'My colleagues in Surrey already know about Jake Kennedy. There has been an incident at the Centre. Jake went berserk, smashed up his room, then he and his flatmate, Ben, have driven off at speed. The problem is, PCs Hopkins and Windsor believe they are "on" something, and worse than that, they have taken one of the doctors, and possibly a male nurse, from the clinic with them, as hostages.'

A deathly silence spread through the room. Then a phone rang, and they were all plunged back into the organised mayhem that was the inquiry room.

'Roderick Black was at university with Kennedy! He visited him in hospital and at the C-M Centre.' Eeyore seemed almost animated. 'And I'd be willing to bet that Frampton nursed him in one of the hospitals he was in after his accident.'

'Okay.' Wendy was now thinking on her feet. 'We don't need to hang around to discover that the Keene boy delivered his papers or walked his dog, or that he had put a fiver in Elizabeth Ryder's collecting pot. He's dangerous . . . very dangerous. We know exactly what he can do, even if we don't know how. Someone put out an "All units, attention drawn"! We have to make sure that all officers are aware that we have a seriously sick, and potentially lethal, criminal out there! I'll find out where they were heading, and if anyone has tracked them. Go!'

Over the next hour, reports poured in from every angle.

DCI Foreman and DCI Craddock arrived at Mile End from the city, and the small station became the hub of the investigation.

Theo thought they should have been summoned back to the main murder room, but soon understood why not, when Craddock told him that Kennedy was possibly heading straight for them.

In a sombre tone, he explained that before his injury, Jake Kennedy had housed his helicopter in a private hangar, not more than five miles from where they were now. It was believed that he would try to use the chopper to get him, his friend and his hostages away.

'But, sir. He can't fly anymore!'

'Sorry, Wendy, he *should not* fly, he is banned from flying medically, but he can and probably will, if his life depends on it. We have an armed response team heading there now. If that's where he's going, he'll get a warm welcome from the Boys in Blue!'

A telephone was handed to Craddock.

'Damn it! Well keep on it, for God's sake, and let me know when you pick them up again!' He slammed down the receiver. 'They've lost them.'

Wendy noticed Theo cross himself and mutter a few words under his breath. She felt like praying herself. She wasn't sure what the likeable and handsome Jake was capable of, and she dreaded to think. She knew what he had done already, that was bad enough, but now he was completely out of control, and free as a bird. She swallowed hard, and tried not to think of how many more innocents would lose their lives before Jake was brought to justice.

* * *

'He's been heavily sedated, Detective Inspector, but I thought you should know that he is awake.'

Jon's heart lurched in his rib cage. He had never for one moment thought that Hargreaves would regain consciousness.

'I'll be there, Doctor, and thank you.'

He was by the bedside in thirty minutes. Ed was a horrible colour and his breathing was odd, sort of uneven and jerky.

The FMO regarded Jon seriously. 'The sedation is very strong. I don't know what you will get out of him. Be very careful with what you ask, DI Leatham. He does not know what he has done, and for the time being we don't want him to find out.'

'I just need to know what happened to him. It was probably the day before the murder, his staff said he felt ill. That is what I need to know more about.'

'All right. But I implore you to be careful with your words.'

Jon took Ed's hand and told the semi-conscious man who he was. 'Ed. You have been very ill. Very ill indeed. We are concerned for others who might develop this illness. Can you tell me anything? You left the cafe early, what was wrong with you?'

At first, Ed did not appear to have heard him. Suddenly, Jon felt a slight pressure on his hand.

Edmund tried to speak. The sound was whispery and hollow. 'Where's Sylvie?'

Jon prayed that he would be forgiven. He had heard the intake of breath from the doctor next to him. 'She's very poorly too, Ed. That's why we have to know about how you felt, about your illness, and what form it took.'

'My poor Sylvie.'

There was an interminable silence broken only by Ed's ragged breathing, and a small sob that escaped from his lips.

'I . . . thought I had a . . . a cold, maybe a flu virus? I felt weak . . . very weak.' He paused to get his breath. 'All night I was frozen. Not to touch. Inside, I was frozen. By morning I was numb . . . but I had to go to work . . . numb.'

The sedative took him and he slept again.

'I think that's enough, Detective Inspector.'

More than enough, thought Jon.

On his way back to the station he rang the Cavendish-Meyer Centre, but got no answer. He tried the mobile number for Ellie, but her voicemail cut in. A slight shiver of concern crept between his shoulder blades. He hoped she was okay. She did have Hopkins and Windsor with her, but he would call them up as soon as he got back. Just to make sure.

* * *

The doctor had never really been frightened before. He might have thought he had, but until this actual moment, he had not truly known fear. There was a terrible energy coming from Jake, and even though the pain was almost intolerable, he had a flash of insight into what had been affecting the staff at the Centre, what had made his sensitive friends aggressive and vile tempered.

It was Jake Kennedy. His disturbed mind had contaminated them with its torment and bitterness, like an insidious toxin that crept into their minds, sapped their strength, and poisoned them.

As he tried to ease the broken rib into some form of comfortable position, he decided that he was not frightened, he was terrified.

His slight movement provoked another vicious kick that sent pain arrowing through his ribcage, making him choke against the makeshift gag that had been forced into his mouth.

Even through his agony, he realised that whatever the young brute in the flying jacket had taken, it had given him enhanced strength. He remembered the force with which he had been grabbed and thrown to the ground. With no effort at all, he had been tossed like a bag of rags, into the back footwell of the car, and a shiny boot had crashed down into his chest snapping one, or maybe two ribs, like matchwood.

Trying to keep still, he begged God that the bone would not pierce the lung. He was a doctor and knew that if that happened he would receive no quarter from his captors. He would die. Plain and simple.

CHAPTER TWENTY-SEVEN

Jake Kennedy had disappeared.

After eleven hours in the East End, Bob Foreman returned through deserted streets to his Surrey base. He arrived back at around five in the morning and rang Rosie to say that he would not be home. Sadly, he could not answer her tentative enquiry as to when she might see him again, because he didn't know. As soon as is humanly possible was all he could tell her. God! How he loved her, and how he hated these cases that kept them apart. She was one in a million, his bright star that shone through all his darkest days. His only truly honest constant, in a world inhabited by murderers, thieves, liars, and the scum of the earth in general. Rosie, and their kids. He made sure he sent a message to each child, even his feisty teenage daughter, Frances. They were all aware that their father had a dangerous job, and he believed that keeping in contact, no matter how, was critical to their peace of mind.

'Love you, babe. Keep safe.'

He sat back, and in the comparative quiet of his office, tried to get the occurrences of the previous day and night into some sort of perspective.

He had called a briefing for eight o'clock, but prayed that before his officers gathered around him, some sighting would have been made of Kennedy and his bastard friend. And their hostage, poor sod!

Bob dragged his weight from the chair and left his office in search of black coffee and several bars of chocolate. He found Paula English still grafting away at her desk and offered her a hot drink. She looked up gratefully, but volunteered to go to the machine for him.

'You keep up the good work, Officer. Milk and sugar?'

'Yes please, sir. One spoonful. Oh, sir. I've just spoken to the hospital. They have released Callum Church into Miss McEwan's care. Apparently, he has no serious injuries, just cuts and bruises, and a bump on the head.'

Bob lumbered off to the coffee machine and returned with two polystyrene cups of hot, dark liquid.

He placed one of the coffees and a chocolate bar beside the WPC and returned to his office.

Well, at least Callum Church had not been another victim of this lunatic murderfest, as had first been thought. For the second time, he read the report that had come in from the Cavendish-Meyer. In short, it appeared that the male nurse had been walking in the grounds, when he discovered a visitor, Ben Lomax, surreptitiously sharing some form of drug with Jake Kennedy. Callum, knowing the disastrous effect that any chemical substance would have on his patient, challenged Jake and insisted he return with him to find Dr Cross. The two men ran from him and he followed. They ran quite some distance, finishing up near the deserted building construction site. At this point, Church was brutally attacked and pushed down a flight of exposed steps into a sort of well, or cellar. Bob thought they probably meant the recently discovered icehouse. It seemed that his two assailants had then returned to Kennedy's room, where an altercation took place between them. The noise drew the attention of the night sister, Maureen Shaw, who was pushed to the ground and stunned. She was found a few minutes later by Dr Alice Cross, who enlisted the aid of PC Windsor, and the two gave chase after the escaping men. A little too much time had elapsed for them to catch Kennedy and Lomax. On running into the visitor's car park, they witnessed one of the Centre's doctors, Tony Ambrose, locking his car and walking towards the house. Unfortunately, he got in the way of the two desperate young men and was viciously attacked and bundled into Ben Lomax's RAV4. PC Windsor reached the vehicle as it accelerated away, and although he threw his baton at the window, it failed to break. In the frenzy of the chase after the car, the policeman thought he saw what could have been another person, huddled in the back of the four-wheel drive. When Callum Church could not be found, it was wrongly assumed that he had been abducted as well as Dr Ambrose. Hopkins had radioed in the situation and Windsor added his observations. Hotel 01, the police helicopter, was sent up, and finally located the vehicle as it approached the outskirts of London. A heat-seeking device had shown only three occupants, and a search had begun for the missing nurse. Extra officers were drafted into the hunt and the whole mansion house and grounds were thoroughly searched. Church was heard calling out from the underground room and was soon rescued. He thought he must have hit his head on the brick steps and become disoriented, as he did not seem able to find his way out. An ambulance had been called and he was taken to the Royal Surrey County Hospital for examination.

Foreman closed the report.

He was still gutted by the fact that the criminals had managed to evade their pursuers. The police helicopter had locked on to the vehicle, frantically sending their location to the units on the scene in the ground chase. It was their bad luck that it was the rush hour. The sheer volume of traffic and solid jams had made a successful pursuit impossible. Then the RAV4 had disappeared.

Bob heard his own teeth grind together as he relived the anguish of Kennedy's next move. The driver had entered a massive underground car park. Deep below the London streets, the two half-crazed men had abandoned the four-wheel drive and stolen another car to make good their escape.

Nothing had been seen or heard of them, or their hostage, since.

Bob leafed through more paperwork. The armed response unit were still guarding the pilot's helicopter that sat in its private hangar not far from Docklands. Kennedy's flat was under surveillance, although no one expected him to show up there. His father and his mother had been alerted and their homes were also being closely watched. Every known haunt of Ben Lomax was covered by plain clothes bobbies.

He threw the papers onto the cluttered desktop and swore softly. What else could they do?

A sobering thought crossed his mind: more to the point was what else could Jake Kennedy do? He was the connection between all their 'innocent' murder suspects. That fact had been swiftly confirmed by the Met and themselves, as soon as Theo had provided them with a name to work on. So, what the hell kind of power did this young man wield?

He finished his drink and glanced at the clock. Six fifteen and he was tired out. He pulled up another chair to rest his feet on, leaned back and closed his eyes. Just an hour. It was all he could afford, but hopefully it would charge him up enough to get something constructive going at the briefing.

They had to stop this madman, and they had to find the hostage, before Jake unleashed his deadly weapon on the good Dr Ambrose, and only God knew how many other innocents.

* * *

Gordon Lamont had worked all night too. Unpicking his precious work. Unravelling the tangled skein woven by Jake Kennedy to conceal what he'd added to the AZSEE programme.

'Cunning little sod!' he muttered, for the tenth time. 'If he wasn't barking bloody mad, I'd employ him!' Another tiny piece of the puzzle had slotted into place.

He ran a hand over a stubbly chin, and wondered what he had expected of his trip to England. It most certainly hadn't included arriving, sitting in front of a monitor, and staying there for nearly twelve hours. He had not even unpacked! Damn it! He had not even really arrived. He was going to stay at Snug Cottage in Compton, and he had not even seen the place yet.

He stretched and yawned. Then he smiled. He was nearly there. He had found Jake's secret file and waded his way through enough encrypted garbage to scramble his grey cells; but he was nearly there all right. He looked at his watch. Another half an hour and he should see what the lad had been up to.

Alice and Ellie had stayed the night in the inpatient rooms. Alice had wandered down, off and on, throughout the small wee hours, bringing drinks and sandwiches for him. Ellie had come down at one point, and just sat with him for over an hour. Just giving him her support, she had said. At four in the morning, she had driven to the hospital to collect the nurse she called Callum, and his colleague Maureen, who had gone with him in the ambulance.

He realised they were both worried sick about Jake, but Gordon knew that he needed to be following the only clue he could to helpfully assist the inquiry. He was good with computers, very good. He already knew more about J. Kennedy, Esq. than any of them, and he had not reached his goal yet.

He was about to return to his work when the door opened and Alice came in with a plate of toast and a giant mug of tea. 'Sorry, it's not the full English. Cooking is not my forte, I'm afraid. When the world is up and about, I'll send out for a proper breakfast. How's it going?'

'Another thirty minutes, I should say.'

'Gordon? What do you think you will find?'

The Scotsman pushed back his chair and focused fully on Alice. 'From what you've told me, and what went on yesterday, something very nasty, I should think. From the particular bits of the software he has accessed, or in some cases, modified, would you believe, I suspect we'll know Mr Kennedy's deepest, darkest secrets . . . so if you would just allow me to continue?'

Alice gulped, and said sorry, she'd leave the man in peace.

As the door closed, Gordon took a deep breath and decided that 'peace' was probably not on the menu.

* * *

The dawn crept slowly over the wall surrounding Michael's garden. Ellie stood alone in his conservatory, the sound of gentle snoring issuing from her friend's bedroom. She watched the dark sky recede, and a pale light illuminate the dewy grass with a misty lustre.

She felt helpless. They had all known their patient had problems. Serious problems, at that. But who could have thought that Jake, handsome, intelligent Jake, could have caused such devastation? She still thought of him as a sick, confused young man, not a ruthless killer.

Perhaps it wasn't him — maybe it was Ben.

A silly thought, but she decided she could be forgiven for trying to shift the blame from him. But it was him; in her heart she knew it. She just had no idea how he'd achieved such havoc. And what of Tony Ambrose? PC Windsor said that he had been severely kicked before being pushed into their vehicle.

She considered the even-tempered therapist. He had a calmness about him, a serenity that helped enormously with his work. The thought of him injured, with his life in jeopardy, sickened her. She rubbed her eyes, which felt as if sand had been ground into them. They were painful to touch.

Looking over the waking garden, she tried to decide what her priorities were now. She would have to leave the saving of the life of Tony Ambrose to the police. There was nothing she could do there. She had Michael and Callum to worry about. At least the Scrubbs had valiantly moved into Snug Cottage to look after her dogs, so she had no concerns about home, and Gordon was apparently hot on the trail of whatever clues Jake had left them on AZSEE. She decided to leave him under Alice's wing for now.

Jon Leatham had phoned with the news that Ed was conscious, and had offered some sort of information, giving them an idea of how he felt the day before he committed the murder. The murder he did not yet know about.

The sun burst over the red brick wall in a glare of orange light. Unprepared, it hurt her tired eyes, and she turned back to her two wards.

Callum slept in Michael's guest room. It was easier for her and Maureen to take care of them if they were close together, so knowing that Michael would not mind, they had made up his spare bed for Callum. The young nurse's parents had been notified about his accident, and seemed most appreciative that Ellie had offered to look after him. They had thanked her profusely and promised to visit him in the morning.

She sat with Michael for a while, but he slept on, in what appeared to be a deep and dreamless sleep. In the next room, the tousled head of Callum showed like a dark brown mop between the duvet and the pillow.

She had the urge to gently stroke the soft, wild curls. She felt, once again, responsible for him. He lay in some semblance of tranquillity, but the purplish bruise that stained his forehead told a different story.

Ellie cursed Kyle for not having attended to her wishes immediately. He had had the whole day to brick up the damn door, and now Callum was hurt because of his laziness. When she considered what could have happened to her nurse, she shuddered and made a mental note to have a very strong word with Kyle when he arrived for work.

She returned to the sunroom and sat in one of the rattan chairs. All she could do now was help to build up Michael's strength. His mammoth effort had drained him to the point of complete physical breakdown. That and keep a watch over Callum until they were sure his bump on the head was no worse than just that.

She felt a drowsiness creep over her and her gritty eyes began to shut. It would not hurt to close them for a while.

Her charges were safe and she would hear them if they stirred. Her last thought as she slipped into sleep was of Jake, laughing with Callum in the orangery, a story of flying, no doubt.

* * *

Wendy had stayed in London. That was the last place Kennedy and Lomax had been seen, and Bob had felt they should have at least one of the Surrey officers in that area.

She had accompanied several of the Met boys in a raid on Jake's Docklands flat. They hoped that they might find something to tell them where to look for him. They had bagged up the contents of a flap-fronted desk, and after grabbing a catnap in one of the cells for a couple of hours, Wendy was now wading through letters, receipts and junk mail to try and find something helpful.

As the shift change was taking place, she decided to get herself some breakfast. As soon as it was reasonable, she would ring Ellie and see how Michael and Callum were doing. What a shitty mess the Cavendish-Meyer Centre was in. It really wasn't fair. It was bad enough to have a murder take place there, but to discover that all the recent deaths might be directly down to one of your patients! She was not sure how the clinic was going to come out of this. Not smelling of roses, that was for sure.

Her phone rang and disrupted her thoughts.

'WDS Brown.'

'DCI Craddock here. I think we have something you should see. We have a body, Sergeant, apparently thrown from a car, according to a couple of winos who witnessed it. Down at the Beaver and Dunstable warehouse on Cygnet Street. Rambling old place, mostly derelict, but a few small units still working. We think the dead man is connected to our investigation. Meet me there if you would, pronto.'

He hung up and she rushed off to grab an available officer with a car to spare.

It was going from bad to worse for Ellie. If they were right about it being connected to their case, then it had to be the hostage, Dr Ambrose.

Ten minutes later her driver pulled in next to Craddock's car. Flanked by tall, dirty buildings, the dead man lay in a pathetic heap in the gutter. The cluster of officers obscured her view until she was practically standing over the lifeless body of Ben Lomax.

'Bloody hell! I thought it was going to be Ambrose!'

'As did we, Sergeant. But sadly, if he can do this to his best friend, I don't hold out much of a chance for the good doctor, do you?'

'What's he playing at, sir?'

They stared down at the empty expression on the young man's face. He was wearing an old flying jacket and a white silk scarf. The pure white fabric had draped itself elegantly across a torn black plastic sack that spewed out mould-covered fast-food containers, and what was either a motheaten broom head, or an unidentifiable dead animal. Its pristine cleanliness against such detritus, left an indelible picture on Wendy's retina.

'It's not confirmed, but it looks like a broken neck. We have not touched him and forensics are on their way now. Our reliable witnesses, over there' — he indicated a scruffy gaggle of bearded men who had gathered together a few yards away — 'tell us that it happened about an hour ago, and swear they haven't nicked anything off him. I believe them about the time, but who knows as to whether they've rifled his pockets or not. We are going to do a sweep of this entire warehouse area. I don't think he is here, and he could have got a hell of a long way from here in an hour, but we'll search it anyway.'

'I'll inform DCI Foreman, sir.'

Wendy left them and rang Bob, just as he was getting ready for his briefing. He instructed her to stay with the Met team, and to let him know what the pathologist said about Ben's cause of death.

She found her driver and hitched a lift back to the station. As they left the site, police cars and vans were pouring in from every angle to search the austere and decaying buildings.

She could not get her thoughts away from the vision of the pure white scarf, and at the same time, deep down somewhere in her mind, something was niggling away at her. As she had stared down at the man in the World War Two flying jacket, a flash of perception had hit her, and annoyingly left her equally quickly. What the hell was it that she had thought of? *Oh, bugger it,* she thought, *I suppose it will come back to me.*

* * *

Halfway through Bob's meeting, he was handed a telephone. It was an extremely worried Dr Alice Cross, begging the DCI to come immediately to the Centre, and could he bring his criminal psychologist with him. She had some very disturbing information for them, about Jake Kennedy.

CHAPTER TWENTY-EIGHT

'Okay. Run that past me again. And this time as to a nitwit, please, as that is obviously what I am!' Amanda Gerrard was buying herself some time. She was very aware she was no nitwit, but needed to consider what she and Bob Foreman had just been told.

Alice looked apologetic. They were all sitting in the orangery, in preparation for their lesson in computer wizardry in Alice's office. 'I know this sounds so weird, but when you see the computer programme, you'll understand. Gordon here produced AZSEE to help patients show their doctors exactly how Azimah Syndrome had affected their vision. You know from Ellie that A.S. sufferers see bright lights around living things, they see their auras. Well, Gordon's latest update, when used with a special headset, can as near as damn it replicate exactly what the patient is seeing, as they see it. Now, without my consent or knowledge, Jake Kennedy, who has a deep interest in technology, has been hacking into this programme, and he has modified it. He hid it from us very carefully. He even locked Gordon out of his own system to prevent him knowing what he had used it for. What we are going to show you is a virtual reality trip, inside the mind of a very sick young man. He has created a visual diary of what he sees, what he feels, and worst of all, what he seems to have done. I have to warn you that it doesn't make very nice entertainment. Gordon and I only saw a little, then decided to call you.'

Bob shifted his weight around on the folding chair, causing a creaking of wood. There was a look of concern from Gordon.

'There's something I would like to know before we are party to Kennedy's Tales from the Crypt.' Despite the sarcasm, the detective's expression was solemn. 'Alice, you only saw a small portion of this. Did it give you the impression that Jake Kennedy is responsible for influencing several people to commit murder?'

'Absolutely. No question.'

'Then it's Freak Show time, everybody!'

As she followed him up the stairs, the psychologist had the feeling that it would not be long before Bob Foreman gave up making caustic jokes. She had hated everything to do with this case from its outset. She had run a personal analysis on her uncommonly negative reaction to these murders, and had concluded that she could not handle being out of control. To her there was nothing worse than being unable to understand and command a situation.

So, it was with a certain amount of discomfort that she sat with the others and waited for Gordon Lamont to begin running the programme.

Despite her discomfort, Amanda Gerrard soon came to understand that Jake Kennedy's computer skills were impressive. He had created, within AZSEE, a multilevel game. A game that was his life. He portrayed himself as a blond, winged angel that had to accept challenges and battle with devils and demons. Initially it seemed much like any heroes and villains' computer game, until you realised that his challenges were real. His day-to-day battle with recovery, with depression, and with his damaged sight were all manifested in monsters of one kind or another. To make things more difficult to follow, he had interspersed his fight scenes with the explosive-coloured bursts of glaring light that he had seen when he first began to suffer from Azimah Syndrome.

She watched intently as an element of unease began to slither into his story. In a very short time, everyone in the room realised that the 'beautiful angel' was harbouring some extremely unpleasant emotions. Then some of the beasts, his enemies, started taking on uncomfortably recognisable features.

Amanda was transfixed by what she saw.

Hate and bitterness swam from the 'hero' in sickening waves. His inability to accept his disablement was eating into him like acid through flesh. Until this point, Amanda had noticed that the 'angel' rarely won his challenges, hardly ever overcame his oppressors. He was sick with resentment, but powerless to overcome. Then another character entered the game, a handsome young imp, complete with horns and forked tail, a smart caricature of Ben Lomax. There was an amusing little cameo of the angel being tempted by the devil. The angel, naturally rejecting all temptation. Then he faltered and the imp increased his allurement. Finally, he coaxed and seduced the angel, his persuasiveness becoming more than the angel could bear. He accepted the forbidden fruit, and the screen blasted into an unthinkably brilliant visual cacophony of colour.

'Jesus!'

The whole assembly lurched away from the monitor. Gordon toned down the brilliance and paused the programme.

Alice spoke softly. 'The drug regime I use to correct the sight aberrations caused by A.S. leaves no room for *any* other chemicals. By that I mean that one aspirin could tip the balance. We even disallow tea and coffee, because of the caffeine content, it is that delicate.' Alice inhaled deeply, and shook her head slowly as if she were weighed down with more responsibility than she could bear. 'His delightful flatmate started visiting him while he was still in hospital. I suspect he started in a small way, just slipping his friend a little something to lift his spirits. I am not defending Lomax in any way, but Jake was bordering on suicide, and I think the original drugs were Ben's attempt at saving him with happy pills.'

'So what was that last blast all about?' asked Bob.

'Cocaine, I should think,' whispered Amanda.

'Cocaine. It should have shown up in the blood tests, and would have done if he were a regular user, but he took it very rarely. Possibly only five or six times, until now, of course. What the hell he is up to now, God alone knows. The tests I did were always too late to pick anything up, and let's face it, he was loaded with drugs anyway — the ones that I was administering! I never dreamed . . . I mean, I trusted him implicitly. Several times I noticed that his central nervous system was stimulated, but I thought he was reacting to something I had given him, I never . . .' Alice's voice faded into oblivion.

'Are you ready to proceed?' Gordon regarded his audience. 'Although I have a wee suspicion that it might get worse.'

Amanda silently agreed with that assumption, but nodded mutely.

The next twenty minutes were horrible. Horrible, but enlightening, as they gave Amanda one of her first flashes of total understanding of this lethal young man. Her brain slipped into a higher gear and she considered the main possibilities. If one were to assume that the time of mixing his medical drugs with his designer ones coincided with his meetings with Lily Frampton, Rod Black et al, then the lethal cocktail gave him some, as yet unexplained, ability to damage them. Mortally, it seemed.

She asked Gordon to hold the programme again. She knew only a little about computers, and cross-examined the expert as to whether there was a log of dates and times when Jake had used AZSEE illicitly.

He assured her that there was, and he would print her off an access history as soon as they were through.

It would not be conclusive as Jake may not have been able to get to the computer to fill in his 'diary' regularly, but it would certainly add to the evidence being built up by Kennedy himself.

They braced themselves for the final viewing and Gordon resumed.

Jake's hate and anger, his frustration and his hurt flooded out of the screen in a series of scenes, designed to be like a child's cartoon strip. In the first, a matchstick angel lay in a hospital bed. A matchstick nurse came up to him, patted his hand, put a tender hand on his head, fluffed his pillows and brought him a cup of tea. The angel flew into a rage, beat the bed with both hands, smashed the cup, and put his matchstick fingers around her throat and choked her. She staggered away from him, crawled along the floor and into another room, where she produced a knife and chopped her little 'matchstick' self into pieces. Unsurprisingly, there were five of these.

The last, however, was in a different format, similar to his earlier 'Tomb Raider' style. Amanda had a strange feeling as it started, a nasty wriggly worm of a suspicion, that this was going to impart something she did not want to know.

The cyber-angel paced his cyber-home. His shoulders were hunched and his wings hung pathetically at his sides. The house was a mess. The angel flopped onto a cyber-sofa and cried. Then another character entered with a step ladder and a mop and bucket, and a wonderful aura. He positively glowed. This cheerful cyber-chap moved around the room, tidying and cleaning. Soon it was spotless, and the dazzlingly energetic cleaner went over to the gloomy angel and patted his back encouragingly. The angel leapt from the sofa and hit the man with his mop, his bucket, and his fists. The more he was injured, the dimmer his aura became. Then he, like the nurse, the teacher, the charity worker and the choirboy, crept away into another room. The crushed man, with only a fuzzy black aura around him, took a rope and hung himself.

The finale, although Gordon said that he thought the mad graphics designer had been totally unaware that it would be the finale, was simple. In blazing colour, the angel confronted each of his victims.

The angel, a sad parody of Jake, had no aura, and clipped, ragged wings. He stood in front of his five 'good' friends, and drained them of every atom of their energy force. But he remained the same, and they were left like empty shells. Like dead men walking.

Like Jake.

* * *

Tony Ambrose had passed from painful consciousness to blissful nothingness so many times that he had no idea of the time or the day. His whole world had gone from being ordered, pleasant and untroubled, to a mishmash of agony and confusion.

At least he had returned from his last bout of insensibility with a semblance of normality about him. He was no longer frightened about the broken ribs. After being manhandled into a second vehicle, he felt confident that if it had been going to puncture a lung, it would have done it then. The broken wrist, however, did give him cause for concern. The longer it remained unset, the more likelihood of problems in the future.

Tony choked back a giggle. He was not too sure if he actually had a future, so why worry about a fractured wrist. Confused as he may be, he knew that his life was in the hands of a psychopath. Whereas this was probably not the kind of person he would have selected, he really didn't have a choice, so he scoured his brain for some tiny piece of information that could help him.

They were in some kind of a storeroom. The walls were hung with hoses, old clothes and a strange assortment of tools. There was an oily smell about the place, and every so often there was a deafening roaring noise that he recognised but could not put a name to. His feet were tied, but Jake had left his hands free. He had simply wrapped some thick sticky packing tape around the fingers and thumb of his good hand, which rendered him virtually useless. It passed through his mind that there was still some kind of humanity lurking somewhere in Jake's heart, or he would have callously bound his broken wrist as well.

The once handsome man sat opposite him on a pile of dirty blankets.

The eyes were empty, and he stared at nothing.

Tony had been fed a chocolate bar at some stage of his incarceration, and there was a grimy mug full of water next to him. He was obviously not expected to die just yet.

He gently lifted his injured arm with the bound hand, and winced with pain. If only he had some analgesics. He lowered the arm back into a slightly easier position and saw that Jake Kennedy's empty eyes were focused on him. He experienced a thrill of alarm as he watched the young man get to his feet and rummage around in the drawers of an old, battered office desk that looked as if it doubled up as a chopping block.

He heard a faint crackly rustle, and Jake was approaching him again. The man lifted the mug of water, pushed two white chalky tablets in his mouth, and with surprising gentleness, held the mug to his lips. Tony glanced across to the desk and recognised the blue-and-white paracetamol packet.

He swallowed the tablets greedily and gave his captor a grateful half smile. He wanted to talk to Jake, but knew it could be fatal. Any conversation needed to begin at Jake's bidding, not his. He leaned back and closed his eyes.

'We have to wait.'

The voice literally made him jump, then squeal with the spasm in his chest.

'We'll go when it's dark. It will be safe then.'

'Go where?' He chanced the question.

'It will be wonderful. A fabulous flight, through the night, and on until dawn.'

'That sounds good,' lied the doctor with a painful gasp, 'but where to?'

Jake paused and put his head on one side. 'I don't know what you would call the opposite to a maiden voyage, do you?'

Tony shivered. He did not like the sort of words he was coming up with. Words like concluding, final and terminal. 'No, not really. Ultimate, maybe?'

'That's a nice word. That will do. We are taking our ultimate voyage, Doctor Ambrose. You and I.'

So, he knew who he was — that was interesting. A few hours ago, he would have put money on the fact that he was totally off the wall and wouldn't have known him from Margaret Thatcher. Which led him to believe that whatever he had taken was wearing off. So, would he become more lucid, perhaps even open to suggestion? Or would he take another hit and start murdering people again? He suspected that Jake had killed the other sadistic young beast — the one in the flying jacket — although he could not be sure. He had been half conscious at the time, and only vaguely remembered a struggle taking place and the car driving away. He must have blacked out then, because his next memory was of Jake returning in the car, alone.

'Flying is my life.'

'I know, Jake.'

'When I was a boy, my bedroom was full of model planes. They hung from the ceiling, sat on shelves and covered the floor. I wanted wings more than anything in the world. I envied the birds, butterflies, bats, anything that could fly.' He looked sadly at the doctor's deformed wrist. 'I broke my arm once. I jumped off a stable roof. It was worth all the pain of landing, just to fly for a second or two.'

Tony felt strangely vulnerable and bewildered. Jake Kennedy was directly responsible for some twenty deaths over the last few months — in other words, he was a mass murderer. So why was the eminent Dr Ambrose listening to this killer's reminiscences with something like empathy? Because he remembered another little boy, one who could not swim. His sister always taunted him about this deficiency. He remembered how it had been worth jumping into the swollen river, worth the icy water roaring into his ears, and worth being dragged ashore, more dead than alive, just to see the look of disbelief on her face. Yes, he understood why the young Jake had leapt from the roof, for a moment of freedom — a moment of bliss.

'I am sorry. I have no food for you. Are you hungry?'

His mind raced. Could he get the man to leave him for a while? Send him for something to eat, then try to escape? One look at the rapt expression on young Kennedy's face told him to forget it.

'It doesn't matter.'

The expression changed. 'But it does matter! We are going on the trip of a lifetime. We must have some nourishing food before we go.' He looked wistful. 'We should have champagne really, but I don't have enough money on me.' His expression was vague. 'I seem to have lost my wallet.'

'There's a ten-pound note in my jacket. Not enough for champagne, I know, but take it. Perhaps we could make do with a sparkling wine?' God, listen to yourself. Tony felt sick. He was not sure who was the mad one at present.

He felt Jake reach into his inside pocket and remove the note. 'Thank you. I'll go later, when it's quiet, when the workers have gone home. Thank you.'

He slipped back into silence, and Tony frantically tried to formulate some sort of plan of escape. He was not sure how much time he had left, but somehow he had to get away before they set sail on the trip of a lifetime, their final journey.

CHAPTER TWENTY-NINE

Ellie and Maureen remained with their patients constantly. They took it in turns to prepare food, run errands and watch over the two men.

Michael was brighter, but 'limp as a lettuce' as he put it, and utterly 'good for nothing'.

Callum had woken up feeling as if he had been 'hit by a bus', and made no protest when he was told to stay in bed for the day.

Alice called in, wearing her professional hat, and gave both men a thorough examination. Michael, she thought, would be fine with a few days of complete bed rest to regain his strength, and although Callum's injuries seemed quite minor, Alice felt that he was either suffering from shock, or perhaps he was coming down with something. She recommended that, in the event of the C-M Centre being closed anyway, Ellie and Maureen continue with their nursing duties, and keep her up to date with their progress.

Alice had decided not to burden Ellie with the whole truth about Jake. She would tell her when she was not so concerned about Michael and Callum. She told her that there was some damning evidence on the computer, and Bob was taking it away for police analysis. Gordon was going too, as he was the original programme's inventor. Poor shell-shocked Gordon had shaved, showered and changed his clothes in an inpatient's room, and had been whisked off in a fast car to DCI Foreman's enclave. And Alice left it at that. There would be plenty of time for the truth later.

* * *

Paula English had finally verified the whole list of connections between Kennedy and the five suspects. The nurse had been easy to check. She had been on his ward when he was first brought over from Ireland, and she'd seen him in an outpatient clinic, just prior to murdering Edith Higgins.

The teacher had been easy too. He had heard of his old university friend's accident and visited him twice, once in hospital and once at the C-M Centre, two days before he took his class on a most unusual field trip.

Elizabeth Ryder, it appeared, made frequent sorties around different areas of London, rattling her collecting box as she went. She called in at cafes, public houses, shops, anywhere she thought she could raise some money for her shelter. Her diary told of a trip to Docklands, a trip that had been most successful according to her entry for that day, and an uncashed cheque had been found in a paying-in book, one signed by J. Kennedy.

Kev Jones, her clandestine nursery rhyme singer and pseudo-cleaner, had been already proven, which left the most difficult one to place. Charlie Keene. It had taken some while to discover that the little lad had just been in the wrong place at the wrong time. Charlie and a couple of friends had been on their way home from choir practice. Ahead of them, a man had dropped a sheaf of papers and seemed to be having trouble collecting them up. He told the boys that he was partially blind. His friends, anxious to get home and watch a video that one of them had rented, left Charlie with, as it seems, Jake Kennedy. The two boys recognised the police photos of the man and recalled that not only had Charlie picked up all the sheets, he had walked off with the guy, carrying his paperwork and another bag. Good old Charlie, they had thought. Father Dominic would be proud of him, doing his good deed for the day. What a plonker!

Yeah, thought Paula, some good deed! It killed him, and his friend the priest. She finished her report, placed it in a manila envelope and marked it up for the boss's attention. She was about to take it to his office when she noticed she had an email. Opening it, she found a request from Sergeant Wendy Brown asking her to do a bit of ferreting around for her.

'It's manic here at present, Paula. Do us a favour and check a few addresses out for me, see if these businesses are still operating, or if they've moved, find 'em for me. Ring me on my mobile as soon as you can. It's urgent. I could be barking up the wrong tree but I've got a funny feeling about this and I don't want to look daft in front of the Met, now do I? I owe you one. Brown.'

There were two addresses, but only one had a telephone number, and every time she tried it, she got the engaged signal. After a few minutes she had managed to discover that Rotor Man Inc. had moved to Hampshire, but was not fully operational until the end of the month. In answer to her question, they told her they were civilian helicopter repair specialists. She asked them if they knew of the other company on Wendy's list. The man she was speaking to gave a derisory laugh and commented that, yes, he knew of them, but for 'Flying High Repairs', please read, 'Wyatt Earp and his Cowboy Brother'. He gave her two numbers for them and an address in Essex, then added. 'To be honest, they are not that bad at their work, good engineers, ex-forces and all that, but they don't have a clue about business. They double book people, forget to pay their bills and their rent, that's why they've moved again. They've had three addresses in the last five years because of eviction for defaulting on the rent.'

Paula thanked him and rang Wendy. A disembodied voice told her that the phone she was ringing was unobtainable. No signal, damn and blast. She rang the station and was told that Sergeant Brown had left some while ago to check up on an address. They could not contact her as she had used her own car, there being nothing free in the way of police vehicles.

Once again, she rang Wendy's mobile. This time she got through, although the line was poor. Wendy explained, between interspersed crackles and silences, that needing to do something constructive while waiting for Paula's call, she had gone to look for Flying High Repairs. Paula filled her in on the company's slightly dodgy history, and gave her the new address. She also told her about the conversation with Rotor Man Inc., and their new location. Wendy decided that the Hampshire company was now based too far away to be of help, but she might take a ride out of town and have a word with the Wyatt Earp Brothers. Paula felt uncomfortable at the thought of her friend, capable as she was, running a solo investigation and made her promise to keep in touch. Wendy assured her she would regularly check in with Surrey, especially to be kept updated regarding any sightings of Jake and Dr Ambrose.

Through a blare of atmospherics, Paula heard the sergeant promise to call for back-up if she discovered anything at all suspicious. She then shouted that the signal was getting impossible, and the line went dead.

Paula felt a moment of panic as she hung up the phone. She had not been able to ask Wendy what exactly she was looking for. The mere fact that it concerned helicopters meant it was directly to do with Jake, but what was she chasing? Just background information, or something more? The WPC made a careful note of the time that they had spoken, and the address in Essex where Wendy was heading, then resumed her trek to her boss's office with his overdue report.

* * *

Maureen and Ellie stood in the guest bedroom and both cast worried glances at the huddled form of Callum Church. He had complained of feeling freezing cold and now, although covered by an extra duvet, the two women could visibly see his body shaking under the heavy quilt.

'It's shock, I'm sure,' said Maureen.

'Undoubtedly. It often comes out late, and not only was he attacked, which was bad enough, he was pushed down a steep flight of stairs, knocked out, then the lad woke up in the pitch dark. He must have been terrified. Michael was frightened stiff, down in that hole, and he went there voluntarily.' Ellie shuddered at the thought.

'Plus, there is his history of working in extreme conditions, so there is a stress factor to consider . . . and only the day before he had wandered in on a murder scene, complete with still-warm victim and blood-soaked murderer! Is it any wonder that he's in shock, poor little devil?' Maureen shook her head.

'His aura is terrible, but I would expect that after everything he has suffered over the last few days. I think sleep will do him more good than anything else at present, don't you?'

'That and lots of tender loving care.' Maureen paused, smiling down at the young man she was so fond of. 'I must say I liked his parents. They were most concerned for him, and so grateful for you keeping him here. Really nice people.'

Ellie agreed and they made their way back to Michael's room. 'Well, this patient is looking a better colour, I must say!'

'In more ways than one. His aura is slowly getting back some of its energy. Not much, but a sure improvement. If he keeps up the recovery at this rate, he will be his old self in two or three days.'

Michael opened his eyes and smiled weakly at his two friends. 'Any chance of a snack?'

'Definitely on the mend! What would sir like? A little smoked salmon and scrambled egg, perhaps?'

The tired eyes lit up for a moment, then clouded over again. 'How is Callum? And Edmund? Is there any news about him?'

Maureen was the first to speak. 'Callum is suffering from shock, Michael. He's sleeping now, and we are keeping a close watch on him. Alice is around too, if we need her. The poor lad has been through an awful lot in the last forty-eight hours.'

Ellie sat on Michael's bed and looked at her old friend. 'And Ed has woken up. Not for long, but I hear from our two resident police officers that Jon Leatham spoke to him for a short while. He has no idea about Sylvie, Michael. He believes that he has an illness, and that Sylvie has it too. He thinks she is seriously ill. He is under very heavy sedation at present, but you saved his life, Michael. He is very poorly, but he is speaking quite coherently, and from what I gather, you must have healed his aura enough for him to start regenerating it himself. You did it, Professor Seale.'

'Now I feel responsible for him, and God knows what will happen to him when he finds out what he has done. It does not bear thinking about.' Michael looked haggard and both women felt for him. He had brought the man back from certain death to a living hell, and no one was too sure which was the best option for Edmund Hargreaves.

'The main thing is the original reason why you attempted to save him. He could tell the police something that could stop others dying. You have to hold on to that, Michael. As you said yourself, there is a far bigger picture to consider than just the one man.'

Ellie sat holding Michael's hand in hers. She felt deeply sorry for him. She knew his decision had been the right one, but grasping the double-edged sword was always painful, and Michael was cut and bleeding. 'PC Hopkins tells me that Jon is coming down this evening to talk to Alice about his meeting with Ed. I'll see if he has time to call in and see us. Perhaps he can tell you a little more. Meanwhile, I suggest you take up the good sister here on her offer of nourishment . . . it sounded pretty good to me, and we need you fit and well, to get this clinic back on its feet again, as soon as possible!'

* * *

The small office was jammed with computer equipment and bodies. Bob had pulled in one of the station's civilian IT men to assist Gordon extract every bit of information that they could from AVIATOR-4.

Amanda Gerrard was given her printout log of times and dates, and at her request, Gordon copied to disc, the 'cartoon' and the animated sections for her to go over and see what she could discover about the mind of Jake Kennedy.

The one thing that stood out to everyone who had witnessed the programme was the fact that each of Jake's victims had proceeded to kill themselves. Not just kill themselves, but use the very method that they, in real life, had inflicted on others.

Amanda went over and over the graphics, trying to follow the emotions of the 'angel'. Each time it seemed that his anger and hatred had been vented on the one person who showed him kindness. It didn't take Einstein to fathom out where his bitterness came from, but nowhere could she pick up any further intentions to hurt or maim. It seemed that on several occasions, one kind act had sent him into a rage that culminated in the Good Samaritan being drained of their life's energy, and simply committing suicide. No hint existed in the programme of Jake turning them into murdering monsters, sent out into the world to destroy others at his bequest. He did not appear to be a fiendish mastermind, manipulating others into doing his bidding; in fact, the more she looked at the angel's adventures, the more she believed him to be a bitter and hurt young man who had lost his life's dream. A young man, who foolishly messed with his complicated drug regime and turned himself into a modern-day Jekyll and Hyde. So, what had gone wrong?

The more she studied the blond angel, the more she thought that if his intention had been to have his teacher friend kill his pupils, then he would have shown it in AZSEE. It would have made gripping animation, and shown exactly what was on his mind. No, there was some kind of glitch, of this, she was sure. He had made a balls-up of his drugs and when someone was really nice to him, he could not hack it, could not accept their kindness. He sent himself off into a crazed fury, and in some way, though God knows how, sapped them of their will to live.

The picture of the battered angel with the torn wings, desperately trying to absorb his victim's energy, came back to her. He needed their life force to make him whole again. All he wanted was to fly again.

This thought made her shiver, and she pulled her mobile from her scuffed red handbag.

'Bob? Amanda. Look, can you check on something for me? Do the Met still have his helicopter under surveillance? I feel they should immobilise it in some way if they can. I have a hunch he is going to try to fly it, one way or another. I had thought he might try to steal one, or maybe take a light aircraft from somewhere, but now I don't think so. All his computer stories show him with his own helicopter; it seems somehow very special to him. I think he needs to fly, but I don't think his madness will allow him to take anything but his own whirly bird.'

After the call she felt a little relieved to know that there was no way Kennedy would get past the armed officers that would be his welcome wagon, should he choose to show up. The chopper was guarded day and night, and the police sharp shooters were well concealed. He would be unaware of their presence until it was too late. Bob had assured her she could rest easy on that one. Jake Kennedy would not take to the skies on that particular bird's wings.

She went back to the computer, put on her glasses and endeavoured to learn a little more about the aviator.

CHAPTER THIRTY

As Wendy Brown drew up outside the ramshackle building, she was transported back to the moment of seeing Ben Lomax lying dead on the filthy East End pavement.

That odd feeling of recognising something came flooding back to her as she gazed at the badly painted sign on the gate. 'Flying High' used a World War Two flying helmet, goggles and streaming white scarf as their logo. She had seen the printed version, considerably more professionally drawn, on a letter head that came from Jake Kennedy's flat. The address had been different, but the name and the picture were the same.

Lomax, in death, with his silk scarf flying over the collar of his jacket and onto that dirty black sack, had somehow reminded her of this.

Across the yard was a dilapidated door with a hand painted 'Reception' over it. The dark red paint had run, giving the notice a distinct 'Hammer House of Horrors' effect.

The door stuck, but finally gave to her hearty push.

'Yeah! Sorry, luv. Gotta fix that. Along wiv all the rest! Bloody heap of a place this is, by no mistake. Well, 'ow can I 'elp you?'

The man did not look like a regular cowboy. He looked far more like a regular outlaw. He had long, greasy hair and a moustache to match. His clothes were of indiscriminate colour, predominantly oil based, and he wore a huge pair of CAT workmen's boots. In his favour, he was not wearing a leather holster, or packing a Colt 45, and he did have an enormous tooth-filled grin. He was totally unimpressed by being confronted by an officer of the law, and offered her a seat, rickety and grubby as it was, just as if she had been his visiting auntie.

She declined the chair and, passing him a photograph, asked him if he knew Jake Kennedy.

'Oh yes, miss, eh, Sergeant. One of Mark's customers. Good bloke, I'm told. Mark's dun loads a stuff for 'im. Not recently though. We rung 'im when we were movin' and 'e told Mark 'e'd got eye trouble or sumick?'

'When did you see him last?'

The man puffed out his cheeks. ''ard to say. Must have been six months back. As I said, my bruvver deals wiv 'im, but I fink he fitted him a new cyclic control friction adjuster.'

Wendy decided she would not ask any silly questions about that — she had enough trouble trying to locate the oil reservoir in a Ford Fiesta.

'And you've not heard from him since?'

'To be 'onest, me bro, Mark, usually deals wiv Mr Kennedy. His particular bird is a favourite of 'is, so 'e likes to work on it 'imself. You've just missed 'im, Sarge. I was just knockin' off meself.' The man looked longingly at a big yellow plastic wall clock with a cracked face.

'Don't worry, sir. I'll not be keeping you. I'll give you my card, if you or your brother, or any of your staff for that matter, see Mr Kennedy, please stay away from him, and ring 999 immediately. If you hear from him, ring me straightaway, failing that, 999. It is most important that you don't approach him.'

'Jesus! Wot's 'e dun?'

'He's sick, Mr? Sorry, your name again, sir?'

'Jeff, Sarge. Jeff Rowe. Owja mean, sick?'

'Just don't approach him, Mr Rowe. He's dangerous, okay?'

'Phew, and Mark reckoned 'e was a really nice bloke too. Yer never can tell, can yer?'

Wendy made to leave, then turned back.

'What's your security like here? Do you have any helicopters in that are flightworthy?'

'Me cousin Ted, and his German Shepherd, Flossie, walk the perimeters off an' on durin' the night. When 'e ain't ratted, that is. There's not much here though, miss, most of what we 'ave in at the minute is in bits! There's quite a few old birds in the big hangar but all of them need attention, and 'onestly, there ain't too many folk can fly these machines. They're pretty safe here.'

'Thanks for your help, Mr Rowe. We will probably be back tomorrow, take a look around, and have a word with your brother if he's in, okay?'

'Fine, Sarge. 'E'll be 'ere. Yankie guy is bringing him in an old Huey. 'E'd get in if he 'ad two broken legs! Luvs those birds!'

'Huey?'

'Bell HU-1 Iroquois, Sarge. Yanks used them in Vietnam. Mark loves old military stuff, he can't wait to get 'is 'ands on it, so 'e'll be 'ere, all right.'

Outlaw Jeff locked the door behind her, and walked with her as far as a big Chevrolet Jeep.

'See ya t'morra.'

The engine gunned throatily, and the man roared off towards the main road into Rainham.

Wendy sat for a while, then tested her mobile phone for signal. It showed low but she managed to get hold of Paula back in Surrey to tell her that she was okay, but no further forward. The WPC told her there was no news of Jake or his hostage, so she signed off rather than waste her battery.

She drove slowly along Jeff's perimeter fence. It was a joke really. The wire was rusty and had great gaping holes in places. His hangars looked to be in the same condition. She stopped for a moment and looked across the torn and cracked tarmac, where grass grew in clusters like lush green islands on a black asphalt sea. The old hangars looked ready only for demolition. The whole place was scattered with outbuildings and storerooms. Wendy viewed its dereliction and decided they would need to be very good mechanics and engineers to get any business at all. If it were down to image, they would be well on their uppers by now.

She put her car into gear and was about to pull away when she saw a movement near one of the hangars.

She moved the car into the shelter of a cluster of trees and parked it out of sight of the buildings. Probably Ted and Flossie, she thought. Yes, most likely, but it would not hurt to check. She did not want to come upon a German Shepherd unannounced. She had seen some of the police dogs' behaviour when surprised, and she didn't need to test out her tetanus jab for effectiveness, so she walked openly in the main gate and round onto the concrete test area.

There was no sight nor sound of a dog. She was tempted to call out, but another movement someway to her left caused her to stiffen, then slowly move back into the shelter of a disused shed.

She should phone for help. She reached into her pocket for her phone but, after a moment's hesitation, she put it back. It would be bad enough if it were her own mates and she dragged them out for a stray cat or an urban fox, but the Met! No way. She'd find out what was messing around in the hangars; then she'd decide who to call, the Met or the RSPCA.

She moved as quietly as she could, no mean feat for her — she was not renowned for her fleet of foot, and she eased herself between some discarded polystyrene packaging and a pile of rotting timber.

There was a definite sound coming from the next building along. It was a store of some kind, with one grimy window to the back. As she inched her way around the wooden shack, she heard the click of a door catch, then feet moving quickly away.

This was not Ted, or Flossie for that matter. She moved to the rear of the building and peered through the window.

On the floor was a man. He was obviously injured and partially tied with rope and what looked like packing tape. She instantly realised this was no job for the RSPCA, or for her. Well, not alone. She pulled out her mobile and began to punch in 999.

Before she hit the last nine, she was spun round and flung with bone-jarring strength to the ground. Her mobile shattered into plastic debris as a foot crushed it into the concrete.

She fought for breath and tried to recall everything she had ever been taught about self-defence and overpowering an assailant. Sadly, she had only got to page one of the manual, when a blow to the side of her head rendered her incapable of calculating her next move. The last thing she saw, as oblivion closed in, were the empty eyes of Jake Kennedy.

* * *

That evening Jeff Rowe caught up with his brother in the bar of the Red Lion. He talked him into buying him a pint and told him about the visit from the Old Bill.

'Blimey! Poor guy! I really took to 'im, too. Didn't seem the type to go root-toot, did he?'

'You knew 'im better 'n me, bro.'

Mark took a long swallow of beer and stared into the froth-covered glass. 'Yeah, s'pose so. Do you fink 'e'll come looking for his bird?'

Jeff looked puzzled. 'But 'e keeps it up in that private Docklands heliport, doesn't he?'

'Oh, that's the new Sikorsky S-76, the posh one. I'm talkin' about his baby, the Robinson R44.'

'Sorry, bro, you've lost me!'

'Jeff, my son! We still have his original helicopter in the hangar. He left it with me a year or so ago, just to play with when I had the time. He's had several ships since that one, but it was his first helicopter — a present from Mummy when he got his wings. He couldn't bear to part with it, but it had taken a bit of a bashin' over the years. He asked me to do it up, no rush, no sweat, and loads of akkers, bro, off the books.'

'That was bloody ages ago!'

'Yeah well, I never got to finish it. She's still in the hangar.'

'Jesus, Mark! Will it fly?'

'Nah . . . well, yes, it will fly . . . sort of. I mean, I flew her over to Essex when we moved, but I've still got some stuff to do on it.' The man looked at his brother. He was slowly catching on to what he was thinking. 'Oh shit! He could fly it, but if he attempts autorotation for any reason, he'll fall out of the sky like a granite bullet!'

'I gotta tell that lady cop! I bet the fuzz don't know he's got two helicopters! And where is Ted? Is he going out to the unit tonight?'

'Flossie's got kennel cough. He ain't going, as far as I know.'

Jeff ran a hand through greasy locks. 'Great! Just great. Now where is that bloody rozzer's card?'

After two attempts to get hold of Sergeant Brown, Jeff Rowe dialled 999.

* * *

Callum had never felt so ill. Except maybe when he had malaria. This felt similar, but without the sweats. Perhaps he should tell Ellie and Maureen that he had been struck by the infection while in Africa? Perhaps he needed anti-malarial drugs? It had been a particularly nasty parasite that had got him. It had given him a seventy-two-hour cycle of fever, shaking, headache, and severe general aches and pains. He had been told that if the infection didn't completely leave the liver, he might develop future attacks. Perhaps . . .

He seemed to be in a half sleeping, half waking state, where concentration was impossible and speech difficult. When he slept he had awful dreams. Not nightmares, just uncomfortable feelings of heaviness and exhaustion. At one point he was being chased by some vaguely frightening being, but his legs were like great, bloated sandbags, and he was wading through thick, glutinous mud. Next, he felt a threatening of some kind around him. Nothing specific, he simply had the notion that he was sharing the room, and the inside of his head, with something menacing. There was something sinister here, and he was too tired to even open his eyes.

Then there was the cold. He lay in the foetal position and pushed his frozen hands between his legs for warmth and comfort. As the malaria had burned him up, then whatever this was, was freezing him to death. He had felt another duvet placed gently over him and he welcomed it, but wished they would stop their fussing. For some unexplained reason he could not cope with the nurturing right now.

As he slipped back into his uneasy dormancy, a lucid moment made him remember a young African soldier he'd tried to help. He had been traumatised by seeing his friend ripped to pieces by sniper fire as they shared a stolen cigarette. His eyes were wide with fear and he had shaken with a paralysing cold that seemed to come from deep inside.

Ah, shock, thought Callum, as he drifted away to confront more nameless bogeymen.

* * *

'Ellie? Will you be all right here if I go into town? We need some fresh food, and I have to go to the bank.'

Maureen Shaw did not really like leaving her boss with both patients, but she was running out of cash, and they all needed good, nutritious meals at the moment.

'These guys are no problem, Maureen. And if you are worried about me, forget it . . . we have two healthy young coppers around the house, and Alice is working in her office. I only have to call her if I'm concerned about anything. You get away. Oh, and if you're going to the supermarket, could you get lots of fruit? Michael's bowl is down to a black banana and a wizened orange the size of a golf ball!' Ellie handed Maureen a signed, open company cheque. 'Go to the supermarket at Cobham, we use that one for all the major shopping for the Centre. They know us and will accept this with one of our business cards.'

Maureen took the cheque, picked up her room keys and left. A second later she stuck her head back around the door.

'Er, Ellie, I have my mobile. If you should get any news about Jake and Dr Ambrose . . . ?'

The younger woman smiled sadly. 'Of course, I'll ring you, and I know how worried you are about Jake. Even after all that's happened, I cannot believe it either.'

'I am absolutely certain that he never wanted to hurt, let alone kill anyone.' Maureen sighed, and closed the door softly behind her.

But he has, thought Ellie. Too many people are hurt or dead to make excuses for him, and she wasn't sure if he had finished yet. Where was Tony Ambrose? Was he fighting for his life, or had he already lost the battle?

* * *

The noise was horrendous. It was a vibrating clamour that sent her injured head into paroxysms of pain. It took her several minutes to realise, from the pitching and swaying, she was airborne.

Apart from not daring to move her head for fear of sending more flashes of agony through it, she surmised, foggily, that it would be better if her captor did not know of her return to consciousness.

To her surprise, she found that she was wearing big, padded ear protectors. God alive! What on earth would the noise be like if she did not have these?

She tried to understand where she was in relation to the pilot. The roar of the engine and the spinning of the rotor blades above seemed to rob her of her already abused senses. She was laid full length on some slightly smelly blankets, with empty seats above her. She turned, very slowly, calculating that there was no way she would be heard even if she screamed out like a banshee. It would be movement that would be detected, and she fervently hoped the pilot, who was, unquestionably, Jake Kennedy, would be putting all his concentration into flying this contraption.

She was in a footwell behind the pilot's seat. In front of her she could make out the shape of Jake's flying helmet above the back of his seat, and strapped in next to him was another man.

Dr Ambrose! Thank God, he was still alive! She wished her brain would function properly, but the discomfort was making logical thinking almost impossible. She took some deep breaths and felt an excruciating pain slice between her shoulder blades, making her recall the force with which she had hit the ground when Jake had first discovered her. She reduced her breathing to shallow gasps, easing the spasms somewhat. At least they were both alive — the doctor and herself. Jake's plans obviously did not require them dead . . . yet.

Her inability to think straight was becoming more of a problem, and being in such a cramped and uncomfortable position on the floor was not helping either.

Lifting the ear protectors, she could vaguely hear voices, melting in and out of the din. A gentle voice was speaking continuously, although it was hard to make out the content of the message. Slowly realisation sank in. It was the doctor, the hypnotherapist, as she recalled, talking very slowly and carefully to Jake. His words were interspersed by a higher, more agitated voice. No, she corrected herself, not agitated. It was excited, almost joyous.

She strained to hear him, but it was impossible. She could not make out whole sentences. However, Jake seemed euphoric. He was where he wanted to be, up in the clouds and flying.

The doctor seemed to be encouraging him, something that she did not quite understand. Tony Ambrose continued to talk, and finally she fell into what he was trying to do. She wondered if she could attract the doctor's attention without alerting Jake to the fact that she was awake. She moved her neck a little more, but another sliver of intolerable pain coursed its way through her head, and she felt herself slip away and become part of the terrible thundering noise that filled her world.

* * *

The Murder Squad, along with the armed response unit, had arrived at Flying High Repairs too late.

Jake had brought his beloved bird out from the darkened hangar into the early evening air, packed on board his precious cargo and taken off into the big cloudless sky over Essex.

One of Bob's men had found the broken pieces of Wendy Brown's mobile phone, and on checking her empty car, the correct deduction had been made, that Jake Kennedy now had two hostages.

Every kind of warning was put out. With the help of Air Traffic Control and the RAF, it would not be long before he was tracked.

Bob felt sick. They had him in their sights, at last. But he in turn had Wendy Brown and Dr Ambrose.

How on earth were they going to get the hostages away from him? Apart from that, the lunatic had flown off into the sunset in a defective machine. Mark Rowe, ex-Royal Navy helicopter pilot and engineer, was ghostly white when he explained to the detective how easy it would be for Kennedy to crash the helicopter.

'If as you say, guv, this geezer just can't wait to get up there again, he's gonna wanna do some fancy stuff, fer sure! Sheer joy of gettin' back in the air. I'm willing to bet, at some point, he will attempt autorotation, then 'e's a gonna! 'Im and everyone wiv 'im!'

'What the hell is this autorotation, anyway?' barked Bob.

'It's a simulated forced landing, guv. Mr Kennedy is a bloody good pilot, and 'e would have loved these. Basically, you are taught to fly as if the engine would quit at any moment. That's what yer do, yer cut the power. If your bird is in flight, then yer 'ave to push the collective fully down to neutralise the pitch angle, then . . .'

'Enough. Just tell me why, if he is so good, will he not be able to pull out.'

'From five hundred feet he will 'ave twenty-five seconds to react to the power failure, then 'e 'as to go through a fast series of manoeuvres to bottom the pitch, turn into the wind . . .'

'Please, Mr Rowe! Spare me the aerodynamics lesson! If he does decide to play silly buggers with my sergeant and an injured doctor on board, is there any chance that they will come out of it alive?'

'No. I was working on the antitorque rotor, the tail rotor . . . I ran out of time . . .' His voice trailed off. 'He *could* land it, if he's careful, but if 'e pushes her too hard, she'll just go, 'e won't be able to correct it and they'll fall out of the sky, fast.'

Bob left the man gnawing on a half-devoured nail and staring up into the evening sky.

The light was fading now. Night clouds were gathering in a dark and ominous ridge on the horizon. Not many more minutes before nightfall. DCI Foreman also looked skyward, and prayed. It wasn't something he did regularly; in fact, it was such a long while since he had done it that he did not know where to start. He stumbled through some apologies for not praying regularly. It wasn't because he wasn't grateful for his lot in life . . . he loved his wife and kids . . . *Oh, damn it! Just help them! Get them down! Wendy, the poor soul, does not deserve this, nor Ambrose! They are good people God, so help them . . . please!*

He waited for a while, watching the sky deepen into indigo. A warm wind blew around him, and there was a catch in his throat as he heard himself softly repeat the word, please.

'Sir! Detective Chief Inspector Foreman!' The urgency in the tone was unmistakable, and the big policeman hurried back in the direction of the reception office.

'Sir.' The young officer looked ashen. 'We've just had a call from Derbyshire. An unidentified helicopter has crashed on the Dark Peak.'

CHAPTER THIRTY-ONE

Alice sat on Michael's bed and thankfully accepted the mug of tea from Ellie. 'So, they are sending a car for me. I say, that Dr Gerrard is a bit frightening, isn't she? It wasn't so much a request that I go to the station to talk with her, it was more an ultimatum!'

'Strange lady, I agree,' said Ellie, 'but she is good at her job.'

'Well, do you think you guys will be okay without me for an hour or two? I tried to cry off, but she was rather insistent.'

'You must go, darling. If she was that emphatic, then she really needs your input with her inquiry. Go get it over with. She doesn't actually eat people!'

'That's not what I've heard.' Michael gave her a lopsided grin. 'Terrifying woman, so rather you than me.'

'Oh, thank you so much, Professor!' groaned Alice. Then the doctor's smile turned to one of consternation. 'Where is Sister Shaw?

'Don't worry, Alice. She's only gone to Cobham. We need provisions and she's gone to the supermarket.'

'Oh Lord! They've just told PC Hopkins and PC Windsor they can report back to the station. The forensics team are satisfied with the findings. No one else is suspected and the crime scene is officially clean now. But that leaves you three alone, and I don't like that one bit!' She paced the room, her nerves jangling. 'I know! I'll ask Hopkins to radio in and see if he can hang on, just until I'm back.'

'If it will make you feel happier, but honestly, Jake will not be coming back here, I know it. And don't forget, Maureen will be back in a couple of hours, as well.'

'I'm sure you're right, Ellie, but I really would feel better to know that there is someone else around for you.' She placed the half-empty mug on a coaster and left to find the constable.

Ellie was filling the kettle when she returned. 'It's okay. Our lad Hopkins has to get back, but PC Windsor has volunteered to hang on here. He is officially off duty, but said he's happy to help out for a while.' She hugged Ellie and looked deep into her eyes. 'I wish this were all over. I want to get my clinic up and running, then spend some time with you. Some quality time together, that's what I want, and I know that it's long overdue.' She kissed Ellie tenderly. 'The car will be here any minute. I'll be as quick as I can. Callum is sleeping, but if you're at all concerned about his condition, ring me. My mobile is switched on, okay?' She gave Ellie a final hug and left for the meeting with the Red Queen.

* * *

Michael sat in front of the television. His mind was everywhere but on the screen. Mainly he thought about Edmund. He was sad that Jon Leatham would not be coming to see them. As Alice had been called into the police station, he had decided to speak to her there rather than at the clinic.

He rubbed his beard thoughtfully. He needed to talk, and the detective inspector would have fitted the bill perfectly.

He tried once again to get back into the TV programme, but his attention span could not cope with the varied and incomprehensible characters of the soap.

Out in the hall, he could hear Ellie talking with Police Constable Windsor. Callum was snoring softly in the guest room, and he was so tired he thought he may have to return to bed himself. He walked back into his room and pulled his curtains. Even that simple action seemed to drain him. He sank onto the edge of the bed and hardly noticed Ellie when she came into the room.

He felt, rather than saw, that something was terribly wrong. Without thinking he got up and put his arm around her.

She stood, unmoving, her face like a mask.

He led her to the bed and they sat together in silence. He wanted to question her, but knew she would tell him everything, as and when she could.

He felt a great sobbing sigh wrack her body. 'He took Wendy, Michael. Wendy and Tony.' Another sob. 'Jake had two helicopters. The police were watching the wrong one. He kidnapped Wendy as well as the doctor, and flew off with them. Now they hear that a helicopter has crashed in the Peak District.'

Michael stiffened with horror. 'Are they sure it's them?'

'Nothing is confirmed yet, but the flying time tallies. Windsor has gone back to the station to see what is happening. He will ring us later, when he knows more. Oh Michael! Poor Wendy, and Tony!'

'Come on, old girl. Hang on in there until we know something for certain. Terrible coincidences do happen. Let's make sure of our facts before we give up on them.' Michael sincerely hoped he sounded more confident than he felt.

'I won't ring Alice. I'm sure she will hear about all this when she reaches the station. Dr Gerrard might not even need her now.' She brushed away a tear.

Michael looked at her with compassion and considered that the two years before had been bad for her, but this one was turning out equally as horrible. All he could see was Ellie's friend, Wendy. Big, clumsy Wendy, with a heart to match her size. Ellie, whose face was still mask-like, must have been fighting not to picture the detective lying somewhere, dead or dreadfully injured. His heart went out to her.

They remained sitting together, his arm still around her, while vague chatter filtered in from the television that he had forgotten to switch off. The sound of deep breathing still issued from Callum's room.

Maureen would be back soon. That would help.

* * *

The police station was stunned by the news. Bob had driven directly back to Surrey and was now ensconced in his office with Jon, Alice and Amanda.

News was trickling in, but as yet no definite identification of the helicopter or its occupants. All they could do was wait.

'Does Ellie know what has happened? She will be devastated if Wendy is . . .' Alice left the sentence unfinished.

'Yes, she knows. Windsor told her for me.'

Alice thought that Bob's iron-grey hair seemed a shade whiter, and the furrows on his face were deep and craggy.

'I'll stay just until we know something positive, if that's okay? Then I will get straight back to the Centre. She'll be needing me.'

'Of course. Perhaps you could just answer a couple of questions for Dr Gerrard first? They are about Azimah Syndrome, and we need something to occupy our minds right now.'

Without waiting for an answer, Amanda Gerrard said, 'Dr Cross. I have been speaking to Mr Lamont, as a sufferer himself he has given me a great deal of help. There are, however, one or two things he suggested that I speak to you about.'

'Fire away.' Alice felt that she was apparently losing her earlier fear of the psychologist.

'Everything ties in, timewise. When Jake abused your carefully balanced drugs programme, it set up some sort of awful synergy that caused him to "injure" the first person that showed him sympathy or kindness. It started with the nurse. He infected her after she saw him in the outpatient clinic.

She recognised him and went over to see him. This much we know from other hospital staff. I have also discovered that Ben had given him a "little something"' the day before his trip to the London hospital. I do not know if he took it that night, or maybe during his hospital trip with Callum, his nurse.'

'Hmm, Jake was so up and down that Callum would probably not have put any importance on a mood swing.'

'Exactly. All the others fit in, too. His friend, the teacher, the charity worker, the choirboy and the contract cleaner. Each one saw him around the same time Lomax provided him with one of his deadly gifts.

'Now, on a deeper investigation of his computerised diaries, I discover that we were right in our assumptions. Jake could see auras, and he coveted these good people's clear, bright life lights. He was damaged. Dreadfully mutilated in his own eyes. He wanted to steal their life force to enhance his own, to make him better. But it didn't work, and he hated them for the fact that they had not healed him. He discarded them. Cast them out and left them to wither and die. Their concern and their fawning over him had come to nothing and he hated them enough to wish them dead. I believe he drew away their auras and left them with one last thought . . . to kill themselves.'

Alice felt somewhat taken aback, and a glance told her that Bob and Jon felt the same.

Alice knew from Ellie and Bob that Amanda Gerrard thrived on facts and proven psychological theory. She had probably met every kind of psychosis and psychotic. The unstable mind was her playground, and although some of her profiles would make you sick with distaste, she always made sense. This time she was embracing the surreal, and that was something that, clearly, no one present had expected.

'Consider this. Disease can deplete the energy field, can it not, Doctor Cross?'

She nodded emphatically under the penetrating gaze. 'Yes, that is proven.'

'Certain chemicals can do the same?'

'Yes.'

'Bad surroundings? Some kind of radioactivity for instance?'

'Definitely,' Alice assured her. 'You can pick that up with special cameras.'

'And the Force Medical Officer will confirm that Professor Michael Seale healed what appeared to be a black aura. He replaced the life lights of a dying patient. A patient who was one of Jake Kennedy's victims. I put it to you that the professor returned that which Jake had stolen. Possible?'

'Put like that . . .'

Bob looked lost, fighting his way through what Alice thought he would consider mumbo jumbo, but like it or not, there was a certain logic there.

'I suppose if the professor's goodness is capable of sending the life's energy in one direction, it stands to reason that an evil heart could drain it away, then . . .'

Jon finished his sentence for him. '. . . put in a hypnotic suggestion. The victim is so depleted and weak, they do not have the energy to fight it.'

A murmur of compliance.

'Brainwashing the subject when it is at its lowest ebb.'

Amanda spun around to gaze at her. 'Exactly! Now, Doctor Cross? What went wrong? Why did they not comply? They were totally in his control, were they not?'

Alice felt herself wriggle under that eagle eye. A little of her original nervousness returned, and she was stuck for words.

'No. Actually they weren't completely under his control.'

All heads turned to Jon Leatham.

'I spent quite a lot of time with Tony Ambrose.' There was a painful silence as they all considered the man's probable demise. 'He assured me that there were times when hypnotism was not appropriate, or possible. I think, Dr Gerrard, that you are correct with your analysis, but the glitch is simply human nature. Jake gave them all his terrible command, but omitted to consider the power of the human being to survive. The hold on to life. We all know fantastic stories of endurance, surviving beyond the bounds of belief. What if he infected them with just a little of his own corruption? Their own survival became uppermost, but the hypno-suggestion was still there eating away at them . . .'

Alice found her tongue. 'So, instead of killing themselves, they turned on others . . .'

Amanda took up the final line. 'But being essentially good at heart, and totally burned out by their actions, they receded into a trance and died.'

Bob gave a loud groan, pulled a face and rubbed his eyes. 'Get that to stand up in court, if you will! There is more sodding fact in *The X-Files*!'

'It will never go to court, you know that.' Amanda's eyes burned into his.

'I sincerely . . .'

'Excuse me, sir.' A white-faced Paula English handed him a computer printout. 'This has just come in, and DCI Craddock is on the line for you.'

She retreated to the outer office.

The room crackled with tension. Then, placing the receiver back in its cradle, he stared hard at them.

'A search and rescue team were already up on the Peak looking for a bunch of ramblers who were overdue at their meeting point. They were a long way away, but they saw a helicopter come down and burst into flames. They passed on the possible crash site location to the air ambulance, who located the wreckage near a place called Tintwistle Knarr. It's an abandoned quarry apparently.' He paused, not for effect, just to formulate his words.

'Jake Kennedy is dead. It was confirmed that it was his helicopter, and although the body is in a bad way, the description is pretty conclusive. Same height, build, colouring. His clothes are identical and he was wearing a family ring. I think the formal identification is just that, a formality. Now, the thing is . . . they are searching the area now, but so far, they only have the one body.'

Jon looked puzzled. 'How do you interpret that, sir?'

'Three answers to that in my book, DI Leatham.' Amanda adopted her fierce creature look. 'One, he never took them. Two, he ferried them somewhere else, or three, he jettisoned them, dead or alive, I know not which.'

'The Met have taken the helicopter repair place to bits,' said Bob. 'There are signs that both Sergeant Brown and Dr Ambrose were there. Now they aren't. I'm certain he took them with him. Wendy phoned WPC English when the place was closing at five. She disappeared a short time after that, along with the helicopter. He may have ejected them, but how could he manhandle them out of the machine, and still keep it flying. They are notoriously difficult to fly. I am going with the theory that he dropped them off somewhere. Hopefully unharmed.' He turned to Jon. 'Let's get a major search underway. Get on to the Derbyshire and Staffordshire Police. We have to start somewhere. It might as well be there.'

The thought that their colleagues could still be alive galvanised the entire station into action, and Alice found herself alone with a strangely subdued Dr Gerrard.

'You look pensive.'

She turned her piercing stare on to the young doctor. 'I have a very unpleasant feeling in my stomach. As I never eat in the canteen, I suspect it is of a nervous origin. I am worried, Dr Cross. Very worried, indeed.'

'Surely this latest development could be good news?'

'It's not about the hostages.' She was abrupt, almost spitting the words at her. 'It's about the late Mr Kennedy's "victims".'

Alice shook her head. 'I'm not surprised. It is one heck of a lot to take on board, and an awful lot of supposition, too. I . . .'

'Listen!' The word hissed into her ears. 'Shut up and listen. DI Leatham visited Edmund Hargreaves again. Did he tell you?'

Alice swallowed hard. 'Eh, yes, but he was interrupted by the other news about Kennedy. I don't think he finished.'

'Hargreaves gave him a very good account of what happened the day before he topped his wife. It appears, with a little bit of artistic licence, and filling in a few gaps, that two days before he was "taken ill", he found Kennedy very early that morning, wandering around in the orangery, high as a kite! He went to try and help him, and Jake turned on him, and upset him with his language and his vehemence. Not long after, Hargreaves complained of feeling very poorly and very cold. That continued for all of the next day. He even went home early as he thought he had picked up a bug. He remembers getting up early on the day he killed Sylvie, thinking he was very ill indeed. He described feeling dead. Numb and dead. But although he has no recollection, we know he made it to work. Unfortunately for his wife.'

Alice still looked confused.

'The point I am making, Dr Cross, the rather nasty theory that has just crossed my mind is this, and please correct me if I am wrong . . .'

She stood up and strode restlessly about the office. 'Jake had a visit from Ben. Ben gave him some cocaine, or similar. Callum discovered them, chased them, fought with them, but is not killed by them. How *is* Callum, Dr Cross?'

Her voice was like iced water trickling down Alice's spine. She stuttered, 'H-he is sick, shock, I think. Oh my God! You don't think . . . ?'

Her face told Alice that she did.

'Ellie! Michael!'

She dropped her phone in her hurry to get it out of her pocket. She fumbled with the buttons; her hands shook uncontrollably. Any second, she would hear her voice . . . any second now . . . come on, come on! Oh sweet Jesus, where are you?

They ran from the office to find Bob Foreman.

* * *

Their agitation told him everything, and after swiftly telling him of their fears, he responded by throwing the search organisation at Jonathan, grabbing WPC English as a driver and the four of them ran to the car park.

Ripley had never seemed so far away.

Bob radioed the Guildford police station to get a unit out to the Centre. He was adamant that they do nothing to frighten Ellie, Michael or Maureen. He asked them, if they got there first, to get some officers covertly into the house and see what they could find out. What he hoped to do was get young Church to a hospital to be kept under close observation by the medics and police.

His mind raced. It could be a wild goose chase. He prayed it was. The lad could well be suffering from shock, as Alice had originally thought. There was absolutely nothing to really suggest he had been in some way infected by Kennedy, but Bob knew that he was deluding himself.

His stomach writhed like a sack of snakes.

* * *

Alice thought of nothing but Ellie, Michael and Maureen. Why had she not connected Callum's flu like symptoms to Edmund Hargreaves' 'bug'?

She thought of Callum, a good man, a kind and brave man who wanted only to help the suffering of others.

A good man like Jake's other victims.

A good person who massacred the people closest to them, like Ellie, Michael and Maureen.

* * *

Amanda did not want to visit Callum Church in a cell. Did not want to sit opposite dead eyes. Did not want to listen to hymns, nursery rhymes or country proverbs. She perversely wondered what Callum might chant? An *Ohm*, maybe? Or perhaps an African tribal song?

There was no doubt in her mind that Callum had been infected by Jake. The pilot would have bitterly resented

Callum's strength and health, plus his interference would have been intolerable.

At this stage in the game, Jake Kennedy was probably more than aware of what the drugs were doing to him, the carnage and the heartbreak he was causing. Although he might not be your textbook psychopath — strangely he still seemed to be able to embrace some feelings for others — she was sure that his psychosis had pushed him over the edge.

Amanda shivered. She could almost imagine Jake's mental process, his delight at killing two birds with one stone. Because who would Callum turn on? Almost certainly Ellie McEwan. Ellie, who had overcome Azimah Syndrome, when he was disabled by it. God, how he must have hated her!

For once in her life, just this once, Dr Amanda Gerrard FBPS, BA, PhD wanted to be wrong.

* * *

Paula just drove. With every ounce of skill that she could muster. She pushed away the thoughts about her friend Wendy, and the consternation about what they might find at the C-M Centre, and drove.

CHAPTER THIRTY-TWO

They huddled together in the dark. The thought that they would probably die if it were winter kept skipping through Wendy's befuddled mind. The fact that the doctor thought he knew where they were did not make her feel relieved. What good was it to know where you were, when you had no way of letting anyone else know. Rescuers, for instance.

The doctor was quite badly injured, she knew that much, and she had endeavoured to make him as comfortable as possible with the old blankets that had been tossed out with her. They might as well try to get through the night. Then, in the daylight, they could re-evaluate the situation. He was injured, but she was having awful trouble thinking properly. All sorts of stupid things kept roving around in her mind and every now and again she would giggle inanely — at what, she had no idea. She huddled closer to him, trying to keep warm, but without hurting his broken ribs or arm.

It was so difficult to stay awake and there he was waffling on about Damn Busters. She attempted to sing the famous theme tune but it got all mixed up with *Greensleeves* somehow and she started to laugh again.

The grass smelled sweet and fresh under the oily cover. Oh dear, she thought, where did I leave the car? I hope the cowboys don't steal it.

* * *

God, he was never going to keep her awake now. He felt so useless. The policewoman clearly had concussion, but he was not one hundred per cent sure that she did not have a fractured skull.

When they had finally fallen out of the helicopter onto solid ground, he thought they were saved. He even knew where they were. He had spent more holidays on the White Peak than he cared to mention. He had also carefully watched the mileage and scanned the darkening sky for giveaway landmarks. He never dreamed that he would be able to talk their Machiavellian pilot into letting them go. He had not actually hypnotised Jake, but somehow, he had convinced him that he should make his wonderful final voyage alone. He told him that he should share the moment with his one true friend, the helicopter he had originally begun his flying dream with. Whatever he had said, it had worked. One minute they were flying low over the Ladybower Reservoir towards Kinder Scout, the next Jake was circling back on himself, heading for the gentler heather lands of the Dales.

Tony thanked every god he could think of that he had not left them on the inhospitable slopes of the Dark Peak. Certainly, the tors and the ridges held a breathtaking beauty, but for two injured ex-hostages, there was a high chance of not leaving the rugged and treacherous terrain alive. He suspected, although he was by no means certain in the dark, that they were in the Manifold Valley. He thought he had made out the distinctive shape of Thor's Cave as the helicopter had dropped gently down to land. If this were the case, then they stood a good chance of being found.

He sighed and allowed the sick woman to press a little closer to him. His mind returned to the sudden change of heart that Jake had experienced. He had been dragged out of the side door, not exactly roughly, more with impatience. He stayed exactly where he had fallen, fighting the excruciating pain that flooded his body. He could still see the demented young man pulling the police officer from the helicopter, throwing the blankets that she had been lying on after her, leaping back into his machine and soaring skywards.

He wondered where he would go. The man had never said as much; his brain was by now on a different planet, but it seemed from his animated dialogue that he would just fly on . . . until the fuel ran out. He guessed there was no other way for his ultimate journey to end.

He was just eternally grateful that they were not sharing the experience.

* * *

She could not believe it. Her trolley loaded with shopping, darkness falling . . . and a flat tyre. Not just a flat tyre, she sighed with exasperation, her spare was in the garage, having a slow puncture repaired.

Patience had never been her strong point, and when the polite young man in the yellow jumpsuit told her that it would be a forty-five-minute wait, she had left the tyre with him and said she would call back for it the next day. Then they had the trouble at the Centre and, now, here she was in a supermarket car park, heavy bags of shopping and no car!

Pushing the squeaking trolley back to the bright lights of the shop, she cursed herself for not sitting stoically in the garage waiting room, reading an out-of-date copy of *AutoCar*, and leaving an hour later with a safe tyre.

She searched through local cab company adverts next to the payphone.

'Sorry, madam. All our cars are committed at present. I'm afraid we can't help you for at least another hour and a half.'

'What? Immediately? You have to be joking, we're rushed off our feet. You could give Cheetah Cars a buzz, they have more cabs than us.'

Five companies later, she settled for a one-hour wait for a cab from Salts & Co., which she later found stood for Strictly All Ladies Taxi Service.

After organising that, she rang Ellie and told her of her problem. Ellie sounded dreadful, although she assured her that Michael and Callum were fine. She finally coaxed it out of Ellie that her friend Wendy had been abducted by Jake, and now there was a report of a helicopter crash. Wendy, Tony and Jake may all be dead . . . she was just waiting for news.

Maureen had never felt so powerless.

As she sat on the white plastic seat at the back of the checkouts, she swore to try and cultivate that old virtue of patience in the future . . . but right now it was proving very difficult indeed.

* * *

Ellie had put on a CD for Michael. He was obviously tired and worried sick, but he was struggling against sleep until they had received more information about the hostages.

She did not want his recovery held up and hoped that the gentle music might lull him into, at least, a catnap. It was certainly having that effect on her. The waiting was a physical pain, and she felt as drained as Michael looked.

When the telephone had rung a few minutes ago, she jumped up as if shot, but it had been Maureen, marooned at the supermarket for an hour or more. Sadly, there was nothing she could do to help. The three of them were isolated in the clinic, until Alice got back.

She closed her eyes. She wanted to ring her, share her grief, but she knew that Alice would get home just as quickly as she could anyway. Best she get her duties over first. Then she would use her shoulder to cry on.

With waves of melodic strings and an evocative strain from the piano, she drifted into a light slumber and thought about Wendy.

* * *

There was something he had to do. He felt sick and cold, but he must . . . what? It was just out of reach. He shivered and hugged himself tightly under the covers.

The urge was so strong that he painfully dragged himself from the bed. At first, he thought he were back in one of the horrible dreams. His legs were still heavy and slow to move, and he felt as if his life blood had been replaced with thick, sticky mud.

He stood silently in the half light and regarded his reflection in the mirrored door of the wardrobe. Dark bruising stained his face and torso, but other than that, he looked the same as always. So why did he feel so different inside. He felt an odd numbness, an emptiness. But he had to do something, didn't he?

He laboriously pulled on his jeans and T-shirt. Every move had to be carefully considered, nothing worked normally or automatically. Finally dressed, he dragged his heavy legs from the bedroom and into the hallway. Music floated from Michael's room.

Michael? The urge to find the missing memory was stronger. Was it something to do with Michael, or maybe Ellie?

A dark thought oozed across his brain, then evaporated into nothingness.

No, it was about him. It was about Michael. Callum needed to do something to Michael. That was it, he was sure.

He stood, swaying slightly, holding on to the door frame for support, and regarded his two sleeping employers, or were they his friends? He wasn't sure. He was not sure about anything.

Slowly he made his way to the kitchen. He blinked myopically in the bright light and wondered why he was there. Yes. He was thirsty. Thirsty and frozen.

He could do something about the thirst, but he knew he would never be warm again.

He quietly lifted the clear plastic water filter and drained the jug. Now, wasn't there something else? He thought he needed something else, but what? He looked around, then silently slid open the cutlery drawer and scanned the contents. There was a good selection, which was a problem to him. His bewildered brain was telling him only half the story. Why did he need a knife?

He looked at a big, bladed chef's knife, then the small meat cleaver. Puzzled, he settled for a slim, steely fish filleter. Its long, narrow blade glinted dangerously under the neon strip.

Standing in the pristine and sparkly kitchen, he was suddenly overwhelmed by the urge to drag the clinical steel across his soft, pliable skin. He laid its coldness on the creamy soft flesh on the inside of his wrist. He felt his wrist tilt back, offering the veins, the arteries, the delicate bones and wafer-thin tissues to the tempered steel.

A fine dark line appeared.

There was no pain and his eyes were fixed, like a rabbit in a headlight, to the gossamer thread of blood that was slowly, very slowly, drawing its way over the fragile membrane of his arm.

If he pressed a little harder . . . but his right hand seemed to have no pressure. He gripped the knife harder, but the damned hand refused to obey him. So maybe it wasn't him that had to die? Maybe there were others more deserving of death than him.

That was it. This knife should certainly bite into flesh, but not his. A tiny drop of scarlet blood dripped onto the freshly washed floor. He stared at it, and in his mind, it grew larger, and larger. It became a pool, a lake, an ocean.

Sounds were creeping insidiously into his head, and he recognised them immediately. The screams, the shouts, terrified cries. They always accompanied the blood.

Then, through the confusion came a thought. Wasn't there someone who helped him now? Wasn't this the moment when he was handed a bouquet of lilacs?

He looked down, but there were no flowers in his hands, just the single metal stem that was capable of producing a billowy crimson blossom.

With the cacophony of suffering in his ears, he left the kitchen.

He waited in the dimly lit hallway. He could see their sleeping figures. He on the bed. She in the chair. He took a step forward. They slept on. Another step. A flicker of light took his attention to the doorway. A faint hazy glow crept across his sanguine river.

What was she doing here? She should not see this! Not her! Not his mother! It was between him and them. This was not for her eyes.

He faltered, and the light became stronger. Maybe it was not his mother? The noises out of Bedlam were receding and he could hear a soft voice talking to him.

It took all his failing strength, both physically and mentally, but he finally did as she bade him, and followed her from the apartment and out into the night.

* * *

The closing door woke Ellie. Her mind felt fuzzy, trying to catch up with everything that had happened.

Michael also opened his eyes, and glanced at the clock. 'Sorry, old girl. I think I dozed. Any news?'

'No. Just Maureen, stuck at the supermarket with a flat tyre and no spare.' She stretched and looked around wondering what had disturbed her. 'I'll make a cup of tea, Michael. Want one?'

'Love one, please. How's Callum?'

She walked to the door. 'I'll check. He's been in the land of nod for hours, maybe I should wake him and get him to try and eat something.'

In the guest room, she tiptoed across to his bed and gently went to rearrange his tangled duvets, but soon realised he wasn't there.

Her shock at finding the bed empty was nothing to finding droplets of fresh blood on the kitchen floor, and in the hall. She ran to the door, but the outer hall was empty. The French windows out of the conservatory were still locked, so he seemed to have left through the main building.

Where the hell was he going?

She ran back to Michael, who realising something was wrong had hurriedly pulled a big sweater over his nightwear, and was struggling to get a pyjama-ed leg into his slacks. 'He's gone, hasn't he?'

'Yes. I'll ring Alice.'

'No time. Let's find him and get him back to safety. Shock affects people in funny ways. We'll make sure he's okay, then call the doctor. We don't want him wandering around in the shrubbery and falling down those bloody steps again. There are two torches in the broom cupboard, Ellie.'

He pushed his feet roughly into his loafers and lurched after her.

Ellie pushed the door open and they hurried down the corridor to the Centre's entrance hall. A smudge of reddish-brown on the big front doors showed his route out of the building.

In the foyer's soft light, Ellie saw her friend's washed out and greying skin colour. 'Michael. Stay here. Ring Alice. I'll go look for Callum. He could be anywhere, and you're just not up to this.'

After a moment of hesitation, when he must have realised his energy level was lower than he had thought, he caught her arm, and looked at her intently. 'I'm not up to it, I know that, but neither am I leaving you, do you hear? We go together.'

The intensity of his voice left her no room for argument, and they descended the steps, stopping at the bottom to decide which way he might have gone. Then, having no clue to his whereabouts, they chose to check the tennis pavilion first.

Plasterboard and cans of paint littered the floor, but the partially renovated building showed no sign of Callum.

They went back to the drive and called loudly for him.

A gentle wind rustling through the leaves was the only sound that returned to their ears.

'What's that?' asked Ellie. 'There was a movement over there!'

Michael stood perfectly still and looked in the direction of Ellie's pointing finger.

Further along the curving avenue, now clearly lit by one of the drive marker lights, was a large brown-and-white dog, with one snow-white ear.

'Orlando!' His voice was hushed in amazement.

'And I see him, too!' Ellie was transfixed.

There was one bark, and the animal dashed off down the path to the new complex. Without discussion, the two of them followed him.

There were no lights along this road to the construction site, and the beams from their torches bobbed and jumped as they ran. Through the trees they could see the glare of the halogen security lights on the high walls of the pool complex.

'He's heading for the pool area!'

Ellie hoped Michael was right, but she had an awful feeling that he may not be going there at all. And all that was beyond, apart from the road to the back entrance, was the icehouse.

They stood for a moment, near the great cavity that would be the main pool, to give Michael a chance to catch his breath. Then, under one of the flood lights, they saw Callum. He was working his way across the area very slowly, as if he were wearing lead boots, or trying to walk under water.

Ellie felt Michael's fingers grip her arm, but neither of them spoke.

There was something about his posture, about the way he moved. He reminded Ellie of one of those ghastly old black-and-white films, where the monster trudged, in zombie-like fashion, after the shrieking heroine.

Except that instead of a scantily dressed woman, the man was following a soft glowing light. It preceded him, avoiding pitfalls and obstacles, and was leading him away from the building site, and as Ellie had dreaded, towards the icehouse.

Michael's grip became tighter, and she knew he'd realised where Callum was heading.

'What's happening here, Michael?' she whispered. Her fear was matched by her need to help Callum. Even Wendy had left her thoughts for the moment. There was an ill-defined anxiety chewing at her. 'This isn't shock, is it?'

Michael sank down onto a pile of bricks, and leaned forward drawing great gasping breaths. She thought he was about to have a heart attack, but as he looked up, she realised he was just trying to pull himself together, in order to give her an answer.

'Sit, for a minute, Ellie. He is going nowhere, other than where the light leads him, and from the gentle amethyst colour of that glow, I assume he is in Vera's care.'

She sank down beside him.

'Can you see auras in the dark?'

The question surprised her. It was not normally possible, she knew, but the Azimah Syndrome had made her able to view auras in any conditions.

'Yes, can you?'

'Not in the dark, no. But under artificial lighting as strong as that' — he pointed to the arc lights — 'yes, I can. What did you see when you saw Callum?'

'Nothing. I didn't tune into him.'

'I did, Ellie. He has no aura.' His eyes were sad. 'Correction, he probably does, but it will be black. Jake Kennedy, if he should now be dead, has left us a legacy, or should I say he has left Callum a legacy.'

The nagging ghost of alarm flickered into light, and sitting on a pile of bricks, on a summer's eve, in the beautiful old manor house garden, Ellie saw that once again her life was turning into a twisted nightmare.

'I must think!' Michael put his head in his hands and rocked backwards and forwards on his makeshift seat.

Ellie thought of a hundred ideas, each one relegated as soon as it was formulated. They had to help Callum, but how? If he followed the pattern of all the others, all Jake's other victim-killers, then he was both lethal, and destined for death. A good man, bent on murder. They should get the police. But if they left him, he might kill himself.

Michael sat up, with a look of determination on his face. He took Ellie's hand in his. 'I think you will agree that we cannot allow this to happen, but if we follow the path that I believe is the only way to save him . . . well, let's just say that we *have* to succeed. To fail would mean death, of that I have no doubt. I believe that from the very start of all this, Carole and Vera have been trying to involve us, in order to save Callum. They hassled you into helping Bob Foreman, then visiting the "Killer-Victims". You told me about their auras, or lack of auras, which led in turn, to saving Ed. It all follows a pattern, Ellie, and the one thing that stands out is that Vera has shown herself to Callum on many occasions. She and Carole even intervened on the night he was driving home late. He could have died, would certainly have been injured, when that car pulled out on him. They want him alive. He is important to them for some reason.'

Ellie bit hard on her thumbnail. 'They, Vera especially, have been protecting him from his flashbacks, too. Michael, do you think she led him away from your flat to stop him hurting us?'

'I do, and by doing that she has stopped him hurting himself. She has taken him somewhere where she can hold him until we endeavour to save him. Ellie, I think that ultimately Callum has some very important role to play. Not now maybe, but our spirit friends are desperate to keep him here on earth for a time. They cannot do it alone; they need us to help them. Are you game for this?'

Ellie thought of Edmund Hargreaves. 'You are going to try to heal his aura, *before* he goes on a killing spree!'

'Not me, Ellie. My energies are too depleted. I have little left to give, certainly not enough strength to save that boy's life.'

There was a silence as they both considered what the professor had *not* said.

'Michael! I can't heal like you! I only diagnose. I would not know where to begin!'

'You would not be alone, Ellie. I would guide you, tell you everything to do. You have the power, I know that. You've just never used it, that's all.'

'Not exactly the best time to start practising, I should have thought!'

'Ellie. We have to stop him. If we don't, there will be deaths anyway. His, yours, mine, Alice's, Sister Shaw's, who knows? Vera is holding him in some way, but she won't be able to do that forever. We have to heal his aura, and give him back his life! Look, if I am willing to go back into that hell hole, will you come with me? Please, Ellie?'

She shivered and stared at the ground. Little piles of sand and cement stood out in relief on the flattened grass. She exhaled. 'So, what exactly do I have to do?'

CHAPTER THIRTY-THREE

An eerie glow issued from the cavernous mouth of the ice-house, and as her foot stepped down onto the first brick stair, a wave of terror shot through her. It was the realisation that Michael's earlier fright here had not been from the past at all. It had been a clairvoyant vision of the future. Of right now.

Michael's hand clasped her shoulder, and together they inched down into the well. Michael was praying out loud, a steady incantation, asking for protection and for help. Finally, they felt the solid floor beneath their feet. Even though they carried their torches, clutched to their chests like a talisman to ward off the creatures of the night, they were unnecessary, as the circular room pulsated with light.

There was only one dark place. The tiny bit of the floor where Callum sat. His back was to the wall and he sat with the gleaming blade clasped in both hands. His head was bowed and the knife point was inches from his throat.

Ellie looked at him with a mixture of fear and pity in her expression. As Michael had said, he had no aura.

In this deep, dark, cold place, she heard a noise. Michael's prayer had stopped, and she heard singing.

It came from Callum.

She did not know the music. It had a rhythmic chant. An African quality. Never looking up and never moving, he continued, over and over, to sing the wordless song.

The black area he occupied was surrounded by the amethyst light. A giant halo that encapsulated the man and the darkness surrounding him. Around that there was another layer of colour. This time, a vivid Aegean blue.

Ellie's heart leapt to know that Carole was with her as well as Vera.

Michael whispered to her urgently. 'We must begin. We don't have that long.'

She slowly approached Callum.

'That's close enough.'

Michael was with her. 'Now, you cannot touch him as we normally would, and you cannot break that circle of light. Our healing colours will travel through it to the boy. I will give you the colours, and tell you where to apply them, then with our dear friends' help, it will be up to you. Project the colours into him with all your might, okay?'

Ellie took a deep breath, prayed vehemently for protection and nodded to Michael.

As she could not lay her hands on Callum, Michael had told her to imagine that she were a tremendous powerhouse of energy, something like a massive pylon. She was to hold her hands out to the young man, and send the colours on a current down her arms, in a surge of electric-like energy. 'Start with his heart area. Send him green, Ellie. The colour of fir trees. Deep, lush, rich green, think of a pine forest.'

She imagined the colour, and willed it down her outstretched arms, and into Callum's chest. She felt the energy, but the colour was weak.

'That's fine, fine. Keep your mind on the colour. Try to blot everything else out, other than the colour green. Now, same area, but a lighter green. Send him fresh young beech leaves, green grass, think of a sprinkler in the sunlight, the colour of the lawn beneath it, send him the colour of limes, of green apples.'

Her mind concentrated hard on the words that Michael was giving her. This time the energy was accompanied by a burst of rich green that filtered through the violet shield, and showered Callum with light. Her sudden feeling of delight at accomplishing the transferral of colour was obliterated when Callum's head snapped up, and two baleful yellow eyes regarded her.

A cry flew from her, but Michael's hand was on her arm.

'Steady, steady. He can't hurt you. There is more here than I thought, something else is trying to take him from us. Thank God we have our friends helping us. He can't leave that ring of light, and you have obviously made contact, so keep it up, even if he fights it, keep it up, Ellie! Now, go! His solar plexus, send yellow. The sun! The hot rays of the sun. Send him fresh lemons, citrus yellow, canary yellow, sulphur yellow, daffodils, Ellie! A field of golden daffodils.'

He continued to give her key words that she endeavoured to bring to life with streams of colour. Her fright had weakened the energy, but as Michael's voice bombarded her with descriptive words, the power increased and had the desired effect.

Callum started to writhe on the floor, clutching his stomach.

Oh God, she was hurting him! Her energy stopped, and she caught a sly look, a slit-eyed glimmer of contempt from the contorted face.

'Ellie! Don't allow the power to stop flowing! He is manipulating you! Keep going!' Blue to his throat . . . Greek seas, cloudless blue sky, lapis lazuli, sapphires . . .'

The Callum-thing continued to fight her. He found a voice and implored her to stop. He begged and grovelled on the brick floor. He threw back his head and howled like a wolf. The awful sound echoing and vibrating around the cellar. His vulpine face melted into a disgusting parody of Alice. Then it swirled into a poor reflection of her dear mother, then Carole, then Vera.

But Ellie now understood what was happening, and it was down to her to fight on. Now, instead of weakening her, it made her all the stronger.

Somehow, encouraged by Michael's words, a litany chanting scarlet roses, pink carnations, lilacs, lavender and marigolds, Ellie kept up the steady stream of light and colour. Finally, she saw Callum's features regain the human, gypsy-like quality she recognised.

Callum went quiet, and Michael touched her arm again. 'Not much longer. He's tiring!'

But so was she. She stared at the man in the circle of light. An almost imperceptible glow was slowly forming around him. Her heart leapt. An aura!

Michael's grasp became tighter. 'A few minutes more, old girl. Can you do it?'

Her head was starting to pound and the blood was thumping through her veins. The answer, if she had had the strength to reply, would probably have been 'no', but she looked at the shattered, tousle-haired young man who lay shivering on the floor in front of her, and she heard herself tell Michael to give her more colours, more help.

She forced colours into the faded halo that was steadily growing around Callum. She was going to win; she would not lose him.

She dropped her eyes for a moment, needing to gather what little energy she had left . . . and heard a low, throaty growl.

Very slowly, Ellie raised her head. His aura was gone. So was the protective shield of violet light.

He advanced towards her. It was not Callum. She could barely recognise anything human in it at all.

The knife still glistened in his hand. A horrible remembrance coursed through her aching body. A sick re-enactment was taking place.'

Blood was thundering in her ears, and suddenly an anger burst from her. This would not end the same way!

A blue haze was swirling around the cavern, getting stronger with every step that the Callum-thing took towards her.

The blue mist touched her forehead, and a picture leapt into her mind. 'Michael! You have to help me! Send him a rainbow. Now!'

With every last atom of strength that she possessed, she hurled every colour in the spectrum at him, in one beautiful ribbon of light. She felt a blast of air whistle past her with the force of a tornado, and Michael's surge of colour cascaded into hers in a kaleidoscopic explosion. The light blinded her with its intensity.

Before she sank to the floor, she heard a long, whispery sigh and felt the whole cellar fill up with a dazzling blue radiance. Then the brilliant glow dimmed and paled into nothingness.

* * *

The police car screamed up to the front doors of the Cavendish-Meyer Centre, just as Maureen was paying the woman taxi driver. She stood, surrounded by white plastic carrier bags, a picture of disbelief, as Alice blurted out a hurried precis of the story. Bob watched as she dropped the shopping on the steps, and ran along with the others to Michael's apartment.

The flat was empty. Bob put out a call for back-up and spoke hurriedly to Jon Leatham to let him know the situation first hand. Jon swiftly gave his boss one piece of good news, and got off the line.

Bob and Amanda started checking the main house while Alice, Maureen and Paula took the grounds.

'Stick together, no heroics! Keep in touch! Anything at all, okay!'

Paula would have needed no telling; she had seen enough deaths on this particular case to last her a lifetime.

Bob ran, with the criminal psychologist beside him, through every room in the big house. There was nothing, just a few drops of blood in the professor's kitchen, and a smudge on the front door.

'They have to be in the grounds! Come on! No!'

Bob stopped and grabbed Amanda's scarlet sleeve. 'Jesus! Here we are running round like headless chickens! I've just thought of something.' He spoke quickly into his radio to Paula English.

Her reply was definite. 'Not yet, boss. We've covered most of the drive and the gardens, and the tennis pavilion. We are heading that way now. Okay, we'll wait for you on the building site. There are lights up there.'

Bob and Amanda arrived, breathing hard. 'Alice, do you know where that place is that Michael had such a scare in, the same place where Callum was thrown? The icehouse?'

'No, not directly. I never saw it myself, but from what Ellie said, it must be somewhere to the back of the new treatment rooms.'

'And they would be where?'

'Ah . . .' Alice tried to get her bearings. She turned and scanned the half-built walls and new brickwork. 'Yes, over there!'

Together they ran, jumped and tripped over discarded ladders, acro-posts, and assorted builders' debris. They fell into the bushes like a pack of hounds after a fox. No thought for subtlety, they all seemed to know it was speed that counted, not caution.

'Bob! Over here!' Amanda was peering down into a tunnel of steps. A meagre luminescence showed feebly at the bottom of the stairs.

They gathered, listening. An owl broke the stillness with an unearthly screech, and Alice dashed past them, down into the cellar beneath.

Bob swore softly and followed her. In fact, he cannoned into her on the last step.

Bob had never been to Madame Tussauds, but he had heard of the Chamber of Horrors, and this place would give the punters a right chill. The icehouse had an eerie feel to it that made the hairs on the back of his neck ripple.

And that was to say nothing of the three entwined bodies that had captured Alice's horrified gaze.

'Jesus Christ! Don't just stand there, you two cretins!' Amanda Gerrard's command ricocheted around the walls and jolted Bob and Alice into action.

Alice ran to Ellie, who had her back to the wall and was cradling Callum's head on her lap. Michael was draped around her shoulder, with a hand on Callum's head.

She went from one to the other checking vital signs. 'They're alive! But only just. We have to get them to hospital, and fast.'

Bob sent Paula up top to call an ambulance, then helped Amanda and Alice get the three casualties into the recovery position.

'What in heaven's name happened here?' He heard his own voice, gruff and accusatory. They knew no more than he did, but it helped to disguise the enormous relief he felt at not discovering the one thing he had dreaded.

'Bloody hell! It's cold down here. English!'

Paula ran back down the steps. 'Ambulance is on the way, boss!'

'Run back to the house and find some blankets, will you? If whatever tried to kill them fails, hypothermia will get them anyway.'

Alice pulled Ellie gently from the floor and cradled her in her arms. She held her close, as if trying to warm her cold body with her own.

Maureen Shaw pulled off her coat and wrapped it around the unconscious woman.

A tear glistened in the torchlight and there was a catch in Alice's voice. 'I don't know how much longer they will hold on in this temperature.'

'What are our chances of getting them all up the stairs, without injuring them?' he asked.

'I think we need the professionals, Bob. The paramedics will have the right kind of stretcher to get them out safely.'

'Do you need help down there, sir?' Windsor's familiar voice shouted down the stairwell.

'How many of you up there, Constable?'

'Eh, three of us, sir.'

'Then all three of you get your jackets off, and bring them here, fast!' If Windsor had been puzzled, he did not show it.

Bob took his grey suit jacket off as well and they draped the clothes around the lifeless bodies.

Although it seemed an eternity to the detective, Paula was soon back with an armful of blankets from one of the treatment rooms. As gently as they could, they cocooned the three unconscious friends in as much warmth as they could provide in that cold and gloomy sepulchre of a room.

Bob went to Michael and lifted a cold hand in his. He chafed it gently, as he would have done one of his children. 'Hang on in there, old friend. You'll soon be safe and warm.' To the professor he spoke gently and with real compassion, but inside he screamed . . . *Where's that sodding ambulance!*

CHAPTER THIRTY-FOUR

'Five minutes! No more, understood?'

'Perfectly, sister.' Bob looked suitably chastised, then pushed past through the door into Ellie's room.

She was as white as the hospital bedlinen. A drip snaked its way from her wrist to a clear plastic sack that hung from a stand beside her bed.

Alice sat at her side, holding her hand.

'Is she conscious? he asked softly.

'Yes, more or less. She is suffering from total exhaustion. She hasn't actually spoken yet, but she knows I'm here. I did get a feeble smile a few minutes ago.'

'Thank God.' As Bob drew up a chair, Ellie opened her eyes.

The lids looked as if they weighed a kilo each. She finally focused on the big detective and smiled. 'Wendy?' The whisper was almost inaudible.

'Better than you, my friend! Safely ensconced in a soft bed and having oodles of attention lavished upon her.' Bob stood up and tenderly brushed a wisp of blonde hair from her eyes. 'She is going to be fine, Ellie. A slight concussion and a nasty back strain. She was so lucky, and Dr Ambrose, too. He will make a full recovery. Broken ribs and a busted wrist. But not life threatening. They didn't even have to spend all night out on the Peak. A local heard the helicopter land, reported it to the police, and half the village of Grindon turned out to search for them.'

She squeezed Alice's hand and smiled weakly. 'Thank heavens, I thought I would never see her again. But Jake is dead?'

Alice and Bob nodded in unison.

'Michael? And . . .' The effort was too much for her.

Alice gently stroked her hand. 'Don't try to talk. Michael is doing well, sweetheart. He is in much the same condition as he was after healing Ed. All he needs is lots of rest and relaxation, and he will be fighting fit again.'

'And Callum? Oh, Callum! Did we do enough? Is he . . . ?'

Bob spun round, as another voice joined in the conversation.

'Callum is just fine.' A bandage circled his wrist, and his eyes were sunken and tired, but the pale young man with the wild, dark hair, smiled down at Ellie with undisguised admiration and affection.

'But if I'm to stay on at the clinic, I really have to talk to you about the job description.'

THE END

THE JOFFE BOOKS STORY

We began in 2014 when Jasper agreed to publish his mum's much-rejected romance novel and it became a bestseller.

Since then we've grown into the largest independent publisher in the UK. We're extremely proud to publish some of the very best writers in the world, including Joy Ellis, Faith Martin, Caro Ramsay, Helen Forrester, Simon Brett and Robert Goddard. Everyone at Joffe Books loves reading and we never forget that it all begins with the magic of an author telling a story.

We are proud to publish talented first-time authors, as well as established writers whose books we love introducing to a new generation of readers.

We won Trade Publisher of the Year at the Independent Publishing Awards in 2023. We have been shortlisted for Independent Publisher of the Year at the British Book Awards for the last four years, and were shortlisted for the Diversity and Inclusivity Award at the 2022 Independent Publishing Awards. In 2023 we were shortlisted for Publisher of the Year at the RNA Industry Awards.

We built this company with your help, and we love to hear from you, so please email us about absolutely anything bookish at feedback@joffebooks.com

If you want to receive free books every Friday and hear about all our new releases, join our mailing list: www.joffebooks.com/contact

And when you tell your friends about us, just remember: it's pronounced Joffe as in coffee or toffee!

ALSO BY JOY ELLIS

ELLIE MCEWAN SERIES
Book 1: AN AURA OF MYSTERY
Book 2: THE COLOUR OF MYSTERY

JACKMAN & EVANS SERIES
Book 1: THE MURDERER'S SON
Book 2: THEIR LOST DAUGHTER
Book 3: THE FOURTH FRIEND
Book 4: THE GUILTY ONES
Book 5: THE STOLEN BOYS
Book 6: THE PATIENT MAN
Book 7: THEY DISAPPEARED
Book 8: THE NIGHT THIEF
Book 9: SOLACE HOUSE
Book 10: THE RIVER'S EDGE

THE NIKKI GALENA SERIES
Book 1: CRIME ON THE FENS
Book 2: SHADOW OVER THE FENS
Book 3: HUNTED ON THE FENS
Book 4: KILLER ON THE FENS
Book 5: STALKER ON THE FENS
Book 6: CAPTIVE ON THE FENS
Book 7: BURIED ON THE FENS
Book 8: THIEVES ON THE FENS
Book 9: FIRE ON THE FENS
Book 10: DARKNESS ON THE FENS
Book 11: HIDDEN ON THE FENS
Book 12: SECRETS ON THE FENS
Book 13: FEAR ON THE FENS
Book 14: GRAVES ON THE FENS

DETECTIVE MATT BALLARD
Book 1: BEWARE THE PAST
Book 2: FIVE BLOODY HEARTS
Book 3: THE DYING LIGHT
Book 4: MARSHLIGHT
Book 5: TRICK OF THE NIGHT
Book 6: THE BAG OF SECRETS

Made in United States
Orlando, FL
02 June 2024

47457372R00203